NABOKOV, RU
TRANSNATIONAL

Nabokov, Rushdie, and the Transnational Imagination

Novels of Exile and Alternate Worlds

Rachel Trousdale

NABOKOV, RUSHDIE, AND THE TRANSNATIONAL IMAGINATION

Copyright © Rachel Trousdale, 2010.

All rights reserved.

First published in hardcover in 2010 by PALGRAVE MACMILLAN® in the United States—a division of St. Martin's Press LLC, 175 Fifth Avenue, New York, NY 10010.

Where this book is distributed in the UK, Europe and the rest of the world, this is by Palgrave Macmillan, a division of Macmillan Publishers Limited, registered in England, company number 785998, of Houndmills, Basingstoke, Hampshire RG21 6XS.

Palgrave Macmillan is the global academic imprint of the above companies and has companies and representatives throughout the world.

Palgrave® and Macmillan® are registered trademarks in the United States, the United Kingdom, Europe and other countries.

ISBN: 978-1-137-34674-2

The Library of Congress has cataloged the hardcover edition as follows:

Trousdale, Rachel.
  Nabokov, Rushdie, and the transnational imagination : novels of exile and alternate worlds / Rachel Trousdale.
    p. cm.
  Includes bibliographical references and index.
  ISBN 978-0-230-10261-3 (alk. paper)
    1. Cosmopolitanism in literature. 2. Transnationalism in literature. 3. Nabokov, Vladimir Vladimirovich, 1899 –1977—Criticism and interpretation. 4. Rushdie, Salman—Criticism and interpretation. 5. National characteristics in literature. 6. Imagination in literature. I. Title.

PN56.C683T76 2010
809'.933552—dc22   2009039245

A catalogue record of the book is available from the British Library.

Design by Scribe Inc.

First PALGRAVE MACMILLAN paperback edition: August 2013

10 9 8 7 6 5 4 3 2 1

Mum, Dad, Nick

CONTENTS

Acknowledgments		ix
Introduction: Hybridity and Transnational Fiction		1
1	Alternate Worlds	15
2	Vladimir Nabokov's Invented Americas	37
3	Realism, Relativity, and Frames of Reference in *Ada* and *Pale Fire*	71
4	Cosmopolitanism and the Shiv Sena in *Midnight's Children* and *The Moor's Last Sigh*	91
5	Authority, Self, and Community in *The Satanic Verses*	119
6	What Actually Happens: Degrees of Reality in *The Ground Beneath Her Feet*	141
Conclusion: Incest, Monsters, and the "International Fraternity"		163
Notes		197
Bibliography		219
Index		231

Acknowledgments

This book would not exist without the help of many friends and colleagues.

The project began as my PhD dissertation at Yale University. I am grateful to my advisor, Vera Kutzinski, for her help and patience. I am also deeply indebted to Leslie Brisman for his unfailing kindness. My research at Yale was supported by the John F. Enders Grant, the John Perry Miller Fellowship, and the Yale University Dissertation Fellowship.

I would like to thank the librarians at Agnes Scott College, Mumbai University, and the New York Public Library's Berg Collection. The Agnes Scott College Professional Development Fund helped me conduct research in Mumbai, London, and New York. Thanks to my students, particularly those in my Postmodern Fiction class, for their energy and insight; to my delightful colleagues Peggy Thompson, Charlotte Artese (who told me where Estotiland was), Brian Artese, Christine Cozzens, Amber Dermont, Steve Guthrie, Willie Tolliver, and Waqas Khwaja; and to Susan Doughtery and Drew Homa for their constant help. Thanks to Sujata Patel for discussing the history of Bombay with me, and to Nitya Jacob, Grace Jacob, and Evelyn Farbman for making that discussion possible. All errors are very much my own.

Many friends have read and discussed stages of the manuscript. Particular thanks to Catherine Rockwood Scott, who lived with it, Stephen Burt, who honed it, and to Michael Wenthe, Rebecca Boggs, Isaac Cates, Joel Slotkin, and Margaret Litvin for their insight and patience. To Christy Palmer, Jenn Cunningham, Gregg Favolora, Amy Lovell, David Smith, Eron Smith, Allen Smith, Dana Goldman, Jonah McDonald, Nealin Parker, Coby Janesen, Luba Ostashevsky, Megan Drinkwater, Gabriele Ottone, Laura Palucki Blake, Katherine Smith, Jim Wiseman, and the Caloric Intake Seminar, I owe more than I can say here, although Amy and Gregg get particular thanks for their help with relativity.

Thanks to David Brown for introducing me to India; Susanne Fusso and Howard Stern for giving me *Seven Gothic Tales* for Christmas in 1988; Eleanor Wolff for her temper; Herbert Meyer for his "good for you!"; Krista, Ilona, Ben, and John Trousdale; Chris Meyer, Mary Rivet, and Miranda Meyer; John Meyer; Fay Beauchamp, Gary Beauchamp, Ray Beauchamp, and Quiara Hudes.

Thanks to my father, Bill Trousdale, for teaching me to love physics, history, and adventurous speculations, and for his essential aid on relativity. Thanks to my mother, Priscilla Meyer, for showing me what it means to be a scholar not only through her own work but also through her constant intensity and precision. Her help with every stage of the manuscript has been incalculable.

Finally, thanks to my husband, Nick Beauchamp, without whom this would be an entirely different and less interesting book, for a thousand long arguments on a thousand long walks.

Introduction

Hybridity and Transnational Fiction

In Stone Town, on the island of Zanzibar, is a little restaurant with a dark wooden facade with a small sign reading "Mercury's." Through the window you can see the red-and-white checked tablecloths associated in America with Italian restaurants. The interior does not match the view from the street—in fact, it is hardly an interior at all: the restaurant lacks a back wall, and it is difficult to say where the main room stops and the terrace over the beach begins. True to its name, the restaurant leads its patrons between worlds—not the worlds of heaven and hell, in the style of the Roman god Mercury, but the worlds of east and west, play and seriousness, normality and intoxication, in the style of its namesake, the Zanzibar-born lead singer of the rock band Queen, Freddy Mercury. It is one of the few bars in Zanzibar that will attempt a margarita.

This book examines the literary equivalents of Mercury's: novels in which apparently quite separate and incommensurable countries, cultures, and identity categories begin to interpenetrate. These novels provide public spaces, accessible places in which—as in a bar on a beach—passers-by can congregate, meet, and begin to form a community. And sometimes, late at night, a fist fight breaks out.

* * *

How do migrants and exiles find communities? Can the shared experience of displacement be transformed into a satisfactory substitute for a centuries-old culture? Can migrants write for international readers without ignoring or exoticizing their homes? And how can novels help create a new form of national identity? They cannot do so without imagination. This book will argue that transnational writers use imaginary worlds to address practical and theoretical problems of migrancy.

Transnational literature is full of fictional countries, alternate histories, and science-fictional worlds because fantastic locations create communities that replace national cultures. Novels set in imaginary worlds use the rhetoric and epistemology of nationalism to enlist readers and writers into a new kind of group identity. Alternate worlds begin as refuges from exile but become kernels of a real home.

These alternate worlds reveal their real power when scrutinized from two apparently separate theoretical standpoints: the postcolonial and the postmodern. Theories of postcolonialism and cosmopolitanism account for the real-world political stakes in fiction written by migrant and multilingual writers by highlighting hybridity, the fusion of disparate cultural elements. Scholars of postmodernism give a history of the evolution of fictional spaces; the impossible places Brian McHale describes as "the zone" become urgently meaningful when they are understood as means by which national and communal identity can be rescued from exclusionary nationalism.[1] Transnational novels continually renegotiate the balance between the physical and the abstract, the historical and the fantastic, and the real and the speculative.

Critics who treat hybridity primarily as a response to power imbalances in colonial societies miss hybridity's potential to redefine identity in imaginative, rather than reactive, terms. Fiction is uniquely able to create new approaches to self-definition because it can operate on both the personal and the national scales. Using the paradigmatic examples of Vladimir Nabokov and Salman Rushdie, two of the most important practitioners of transnational world-fashioning, this book shows how supernatural, science-fictional, and alternate-historical settings provide the bases for forming new communal identities. The fictional nations staged in fantastic novels render common identities portable and accessible. Imaginary worlds let writers reshape the notion of national identity into an intellectual and emotional, rather than geographical, affiliation.

The result of this world-fashioning extends beyond the writer and the novel. By inviting readers to share in the creation of these imaginary worlds, transnational writers help create a community of migrants whose shared culture is one of displacement and self-invention. In these novels, the markers of communal identity are no longer in cultural references (familiar places, foods, or jokes) but in a shared intellectual standpoint. Fictional worlds solve the central problem faced by transnational writers: they help create an audience of readers who understand descriptions of a writer's old homeland, of his new homeland, and of how the two overlap. The novels' critiques of traditional nationhood lead to a new way of conceiving of and creating an intentional community, one that makes explicit use of its fictionality. Transnational writers examine the origins of power, community, and loyalty to reveal identity as a participatory process in which there is no passive audience.

Most criticism of transnational fiction categorizes writers by political circumstance: writers are called colonial, postcolonial, exiled, or cosmopolitan and are compared to other writers from the same category. Others are labeled by their place of origin, and a writer who has lived on three continents may be simply "African" or "South Asian." These categorizations are misleading because writers in very different political positions use imaginary worlds in remarkably similar ways. Postcolonial theorists such as Edward Said, Homi Bhabha, or Robert Young, who define hybridity as a phenomenon specific to the colony and colonial subject, stop short of showing how cultural hybridity has redefined identity throughout twentieth- and twenty-first-century literature. Hybrid alternate-world fiction, no matter what the biography of its author, demands that all its readers see themselves as migrants and exiles.

This introduction provides a brief overview of the problems inherent in applying the major theories of hybridity and cosmopolitanism to the work of transnational writers. Some of these problems will find solutions in the discussion of fictional worlds and readerly responsibility in Chapter 1, but many will reappear throughout the book.

Hybridity, Binaries, and Interpretation

Homi Bhabha uses the term "hybridity" to discuss colonial or postcolonial appropriations of cultural artifacts from the colonizer. For Bhabha, hybridity is explicitly political: local people who incorporate elements of the colonists' culture into their practices implicitly assert equality (although not equivalence) between the two cultures. Colonial hybridity diminishes the distinction between the colonizer and the colonized, and this erosion of difference undermines the colonizer's claim to superiority.

Bhabha's paradigmatic example of hybridity in "Signs Taken for Wonders: Questions of Ambivalence and Authority Under a Tree Outside Delhi, May 1817" is a group of Indians who have read a Hindi translation of the Bible and converted to Christianity. They refuse to believe that their new sacred text is also the sacred text of the "European Sahibs": the British, the Indian Christians argue, cannot possibly be practitioners of this newly revealed religion because they are so unenlightened that they "eat flesh."[2]

To Bhabha, the Indians' Christianity exemplifies how hybridity is "the sign of the productivity of colonial power."[3] The colonists import a cultural artifact (the Bible) and make a gesture toward adapting it to local needs (translating it into Hindi). The colonists do not intend to change the text's meaning; the translation is purely a means of rendering it accessible to the colonized population, thus saving souls and facilitating colonial rule. The text is received by the Indians, however, not as an imported Western artifact but as a new, local production—an indigenous revealed religion. The Indian Christians do not consciously decide to adapt the imported text to local needs any more than the British do; they simply interpret it using their preexisting moral and religious systems.

While both the Christian missionaries who have translated the Bible into Hindi and the Indian readers who have converted to the religion it describes find the text compelling and believe its contents to be true, the truths that they perceive in the text vary so greatly that neither party considers itself kin to the other. Each group of readers perceives the other as having failed to understand the text. The British missionaries will note that the Indian readers have misunderstood the text's provenance; the Indian readers will claim that the British missionaries have misunderstood its meaning.

The ambiguity of hybridity, then, comes in part from the ambiguity of texts, which always require interpretation. Thus, writes Bhabha, "Resistance is not necessarily an oppositional act of political intention, nor is it the simple negation or exclusion of the 'content' of another culture, as a difference once perceived. It is the effect of an ambivalence produced within the rules of recognition of dominating discourses as they articulate the signs of cultural difference and reimplicate them within the deferential relations of colonial power."[4] For Bhabha, the Bible's ambiguity stems from its displacement: "the presence of the book [is] wondrous to the extent to which it is repeated, translated, misread, displaced."[5] Bhabha's hybridity is at once a process and a product of displacement, and its primary attribute is ambiguity. This ambiguity comes from decontextualization: the hybrid text is no longer cocooned in the familiar systems that have helped create its meaning.

In Bhabha's account, the hybrid is by definition inauthentic and is seen constantly in double exposure. Displacement renders a text ambiguous to the point of illegibility: for Bhabha, reading is almost entirely dependent on context. Hybridity is a "mimicry" or "mockery" of recognition, not true understanding, and thus provides the false appearance that the colonized acknowledge the power of the colonizer.[6] Hybridity undercuts colonial authority not for the participants but for the onlookers: since the Indian Christians do not acknowledge the British as the source of their sacred texts, it is only the observer—the missionary, historian, or reader—who is forced to reconsider the sources of colonial power.

Bhabha's insight that reading is an act almost entirely defined by context establishes one of the fundamental problems faced by writers who, unlike the Indian Christians in "Signs Taken for Wonders," consciously seek to combine several cultures in their own work. These writers cannot assume that their readership will know more than one culture. An English-language writer who wishes to write about India and publish in America, for example, is faced with a difficult choice: either she must explain the nuances of Indian culture for the American reader (implicitly treating India as "foreign"), or she must risk misinterpretation by readers who lack the context that defines the text's meaning. Readers of such texts, in turn, must begin by admitting their own ignorance and questioning their own interpretations.

Bhabha's hybrids are brought into existence through an act of misreading and thus are awkwardly joined, prone to rupture, and, as in the case of the Indian Christians, easy for "authentic" members of either the colonized or the colonizing populations to identify and debunk. While Bhabha may celebrate the Indian Christians' refusal to believe that the Bible was imported by the British, the fact remains that Bhabha's prototypical example of hybridity depends on a fundamental misunderstanding—rather than a conscious redefinition—of the hybridized text. For all Bhabha's insistence that colonial space is double—both/and rather than either/or—his argument retains a framework in which one interpretation of the text at hand, the Bible, is factually correct and the other incorrect. While the Indians may have understood the spirit of the text, their account of its history is wrong.

SEX AND THE SINGLE CULTURE

Since the publication of "Signs Taken for Wonders" in 1985, critics of postcolonial literature have moved away from implicitly Manichean (right vs. wrong, history vs. interpretation, England vs. India) readings of hybridity. In *The Rhetoric of English India* (1992), Sara Suleri argues for reading "against the grain of the rhetoric of binarism,"[7] and a new generation of critics has followed her, treating hybridity as much more than a form of resistance. Many of these critics see hybridity and creolization as the way, in Rushdie's much-quoted phrase, "newness enters the world."[8] This broader-ranging and often celebratory treatment of hybridity has generated debate about the political import and aesthetic value of cultural synthesis, both among migrants and as a product of globalization.

The recent debate has called the term "hybridity" itself into question. As Robert Young argues in *Colonial Desire* (1995), the notion of hybridity is inescapably a biological one and has a long history in which the fertility of hybrids has been questioned.[9] Race theorists of the nineteenth century argued that mixed-race people would, like mules, turn out to be sterile. While the claim that the products of miscegenation cannot produce offspring is obviously nonsense, the anxiety that hybrid unions will be intellectually sterile remains throughout the twentieth and into the twenty-first century. By privileging metaphors of sexual reproduction, theorists of hybridity—and novelists—limit and direct the ways in which cultural hybridity can be understood. The reproductive model suggests at once the urgency and the danger of cultural fusion, implying that mixture stems from a deep biological drive but that its offspring will be outcasts and, since sterile, unable to form their own sustainable community.

The sexual model of hybridity does not only offer a means to condemn miscegenation: it can also recast single-culture transactions as masturbatory, incestuous, or homosexual, and thus also incapable of producing offspring. While the most conservative colonial literature may privilege heterosexual, single-culture relations as the sanctioned means of reproduction, transnational writers frequently treat homosexuals—Emmanuelson in Dinesen's *Out of Africa* (1937) and Alan in Naipaul's *The Enigma of Arrival* (1987), for example—as models of monoculturalism. (We will see in the Conclusion how incest complicates sexual descriptions of cultural solipsism.) The metaphor of sexually reproductive hybridity, then, is problematic not only because it suggests a binary and innately heterosexual origin for cultural fusion but also because it leaves almost no viable alternatives: the products of cross-cultural unions risk sterility, but monocultural unions produce no offspring at all.

The problem with the word "hybridity" is that it provides a biological model for a nonbiological process. The metaphor of sexual reproduction implicit in the term reduces the number of possible variables that go into the hybrid to two (one male, often dominant, white, European; one female, often submissive, brown, colonized). This dynamic recalls the sexual exploitation of native and enslaved women by male European colonists, and the child of such a union almost inevitably experiences ambivalence about its own existence.[10] The term "hybrid" is thus deeply problematic, carrying dualistic, heteronormative implications. The biological model of hybridity emphasizes transnational writers' anxieties about building self-sustaining, productive communities and elucidates the necessity of creating a shared space for scattered, migrant cosmopolitans to inhabit, replacing the soil of a home country with the body of the hybrid individual. This is not, however, the only model for literary or cultural production, and cross-cultural writers are increasingly rejecting it in favor of more pluralist, less-prescribed ways of describing the combination and recombination of cultures.

Bhabha's discussion of hybridity, which focuses on unconscious responses to strict hierarchies, does not satisfactorily describe the possible range of transnational texts by twentieth-century writers such as Nabokov, Rushdie, Dinesen, Ondaatje, and Kingston, but it does explain some of the novels' central concerns. As we shall see, transnational fiction's alternate worlds provide a different kind of physicality for experimental fusions into which the individual may sink his roots. Bhabha's account of the source of hybridity, however—the power of the reader to interpret and sometimes distort a text's meaning—is essential: while contemporary writers may seek to escape the biological overtones of "hybridity" that constrain our readings of transnational texts, Bhabha's emphasis on interpretation suggests the multifarious and participatory role of transnational readership.

COSMOPOLITANISM AND ITS ORIGINS

In part because of the limitations inherent in the notion of hybridity, critical attention has increasingly turned to the figure of the cosmopolitan, a type Revathi Krishnaswamy describes as the "itinerant intellectual," an "international figure who at once feels at home nowhere and everywhere."[11] Theorists of cosmopolitanism, who often come from the social sciences, trace their intellectual genealogy back to Kant's "Idea for a Universal History with a Cosmopolitan Purpose," which argues that cosmopolitanism provides "a perfect civil union of mankind."[12] This union provides a pathway to world peace: Kant argues that rational human beings share the same moral principles, which take precedence over the national allegiances that cause wars. This lineage is what Martha Nussbaum invokes when she discusses the "very old ideal of the cosmopolitan . . . the person whose allegiance is to the worldwide community of human beings."[13]

What would such an allegiance mean? Jonathan Rée suggests that early interpretations of Kant's cosmopolitanism are impractically idealistic or even "ingenuous."[14] It is impossible, cosmopolitanism's critics argue, to feel the same loyalty toward the abstract notion of humanity that one feels toward one's family, tribe, or nation. We may be loyal to humanity by extension from our feelings toward our kin, but it cannot be an *equal* loyalty. Cosmopolitanism, according to this argument, is a shallow commitment that cannot compete with the deep commitment we feel toward our local ties. While this position may be flawed in its conflation of emotional attachment with moral imperative, most people do seem to feel more loyalty toward their nation than toward an abstract concept of mankind.

A related and more pointed critique of cosmopolitanism appears in Stanley Fish's "Boutique Multiculturalism or, Why Liberals are Incapable of Thinking About Hate Speech" (1997). Fish claims that "boutique multiculturalism"—which, he argues, differs from the "strong" multiculturalism of the cosmopolitan only in the extent of its pretended tolerance—"is characterized by its superficial or cosmetic relationship to the objects of its affection."[15] Fish argues that the cosmopolitan's humanity-wide allegiance is meaningless because "a boutique multiculturalist does not and cannot take seriously the core values of the culture he tolerates. The reason he cannot is that he does not see those values as truly 'core' but as overlays on a substratum of essential humanity."[16] For Fish, a Kantian commitment to the "civil union of mankind" is merely a dodge to avoid the often-unsavory reality of alien cultural practices. Cosmopolitanism, by this account, is a condescending insistence that the Other is really like us somewhere underneath the trappings of culture, even if the poor soul doesn't know it himself.

While Fish demolishes the pretensions of cultural tourists, however, he does little to address better-informed and better-theorized attempts to bridge cultures. Recent approaches to cosmopolitanism respond both to Fish and to the critics who deny the possibility of privileging "humanity" over one's kin by writing about what Kwame Anthony Appiah calls "rooted cosmopolitanism"[17]: a cosmopolitanism grounded not in a general appreciation of humankind but in a simultaneous commitment to local particularities and to a global conception of humanity. (Homi Bhabha, too, discusses this phenomenon when he talks about "vernacular cosmopolitanism."[18]) For Appiah, cosmopolitanism is a "dialogical universalism"[19] that posits a commitment both to a particular (local) position and to dialogue with multifarious other (equally local) positions. The results of this dialogue will not be hybridity in Bhabha's sense, since Appiah describes a dialogue between rooted equals; it may not even be hybridity in the looser sense of cultural mixture, as dialogue between cultures does not necessitate borrowing cultural artifacts or practices. Instead, rooted cosmopolitanism facilitates a conscious and voluntary cultural interchange, which may lead, at various moments, either to what Fish describes as a "cosmetic" use of other cultures (when a white American puts Indian slipcovers on the sofa cushions) or to a substantive exchange of ideas in which both parties in the dialogue reach new conclusions.

Appiah's notion of rooted cosmopolitanism also helps address another major problem of cosmopolitan discourses: their paradoxical limitation of scope. Cosmopolitanism tends to concentrate on the urban, largely because cities—especially "global cities" such as New York, London, or Bombay—are frequently loci of cross-cultural encounters. By taking the examples cities offer, however, theorists neglect exurban cultural encounters and fail to address the process by which migrants, many of whom come from rural communities, arrive at cities to begin with. This failure is problematic in part because it makes no effort to distinguish between the idiosyncratic cosmopolitanism of individual cross-cultural encounters, on the one hand, and corporate globalism, on the other—the difference between fusion cuisine and a New Delhi McDonald's.[20] The notion of rooted cosmopolitanism partially solves this problem by reminding us that cosmopolitans still come from specific locations.

Appiah describes a prosperous community of individuals with pleasant homes and well-stamped passports—people with ties to a particular locality who are also comfortable crossing borders and encountering unfamiliar ideas. His account of cosmopolitanism has inevitably been attacked for its neglect of impoverished Third World migrants. But Appiah's model of cosmopolitanism closely resembles the community that transnational writers seek. The problem with his model, for their purposes, is that it does not contain an account of its own origins. In *Cosmopolitanism: Ethics in a World of Strangers* (2006), Appiah treats cosmopolitanism as a heritable cultural affiliation like any other, passed down from parent to child. How can an individual who has been separated from his roots achieve such a state? This process is one of the central concerns of transnational fiction. Appiah's rooted cosmopolitanism is the end state that these writers hope to achieve; the difficulty lies in getting there.

Appiah comes close to describing how to gain access to rooted cosmopolitanism when he discusses fiction. He argues that reading novels gives us a model for how cross-cultural dialogues take place. For Appiah, the novel is "always a message in a bottle from some other position, even if it was written and published last week in your hometown," and its meaning derives "from an invitation to respond in imagination to narratively constructed situations."[21] For Appiah, fiction is an exercise in communication from which we learn to respond to the worldviews of others. This may seem like a partial account of communication: in true dialogues, each party has the opportunity to respond. While the reader of fiction may be educated in the viewpoint of the novel's characters, she does not get to answer them. However, we shall see that, for some transnational writers, the power of fiction to educate readers in sympathy becomes both the central purpose of the novel and a way to make fiction-based communication, rather than culture or proximity, the catalyst of community formation.

Arjun Appadurai takes Appiah's version of cosmopolitan interchange to an extreme. In his account, the borders crossed by Appiah's rooted cosmopolitans have functionally ceased to exist. Appadurai argues that, between the increasing cosmopolitanism of both the elite and the labor force and the increased globalization of corporations, we are living in a "postnational" era in which national borders present bureaucratic technicalities rather than real demarcations of linguistic, cultural, or economic difference.[22] This suggestion has come under fire from theorists of transnationalism like Nina Glick Schiller, who points out that "while borders may be cultural constructions, they are constructions that are backed by force of law."[23] Yet Appadurai's claim that the imagination has been recentered by globalization provides a useful starting point not only for a discussion of the identity of the migrant intellectual but also for understanding transnational literature.

Reframing hybridity as dialogue—Bakhtin's model rather than Bhabha's—removes some of the anxieties surrounding the products of cross-cultural encounters. The dialogue metaphor for cross-cultural communication lacks most of the limitations of the biological metaphor. While the word "dialogue" suggests a discussion between two speakers, cosmopolitan discourse can easily be broadened into a multiparty conversation. Participation is not limited by race, gender, or degree of kinship to one's interlocutors, since it depends on nothing but shared language. Most importantly, the outcome of a dialogue need not be a single, fixed conclusion, in the way that a single hybrid body is the outcome of a miscegenized union, but can continue to change and evolve. Defining cosmopolitanism in terms of dialogue also suggests the possibility that interlocutors may achieve communication despite some mutual incomprehension: while Bhabha's hybridity describes a misreading of a received text, Appiah suggests ongoing responses and reactions on both sides.

While Appiah's rooted cosmopolitanism may appeal to the boundary-crossing writer, its omissions make it more a challenge than a solution. How can a migrant begin a lineage of rooted cosmopolitanism? How can a writer make sure his "message in a bottle" meets with a response?

Nations, Transnationalism, and Imaginary Worlds

Appadurai's claim that we are living in a postnational world rests on his argument that "imagination has become a collective, social fact. This development, in turn, is the basis of the plurality of imagined worlds."[24] Imagination, "especially when collective, can become the fuel for action."[25] Appadurai describes culture in the same wave-or-particle terms that Bhabha uses to define hybridity: "culture is not usefully regarded as a substance but is better regarded as a dimension of phenomena, a dimension that attends to situated and embodied difference,"[26] an interpretive process rather than a set of facts.

Appadurai draws explicitly on Benedict Anderson's discussion of the nation in *Imagined Communities* (1991). Anderson defines a community as a group of people who share major cultural characteristics such as language and religion and who consciously distinguish themselves from other such communities. Anderson's definition of community is part of his larger definition of the nation, "an imagined political community—and imagined as both inherently limited and sovereign."[27] Communities of shared language or culture are large enough that the members cannot all meet each other, so the sense of shared identity is gained not by personal knowledge but by belief. These communities, and the nations they form, are brought into existence only through a collective act of imagination. For Appadurai, this imagined commonality can extend in several directions, so collective imagination can produce simultaneous, noncompeting allegiances—flexible conceptions that, if they become the markers of identity, would render exclusive national allegiances obsolete.

Anderson's notion of the imagined community and Appadurai's of the imagined world are particularly useful in a discussion of fiction because of their implied decoupling of cultural identity from physical location. This separation of concepts suggests how members of diasporic communities retain "national" (rather than "cultural") identities.[28] Such a separation helps explain, for example, the intensity of V. S. Naipaul's disappointment on his first trip to India after a lifetime of identifying as "Indian." But while location—whether place of birth or place of residence—may not be the determining factor in an individual's identity, the concepts obviously cannot be separated entirely.

By suggesting that the imagination defines not only the borders of the group but also the borders of the "real," Appadurai suggests how groups can form communities defined by attributes besides traditional ones like geography, language, or religion. While Anderson rightly notes that nations are qualitatively different from other ideological commitments, pointing out the "absurdity" of the idea of "a Tomb of the Unknown

Marxist," Appadurai's notion of the imagined world nonetheless implicitly expands the boundaries of the nation-like commitment.[29] Appadurai's formulation validates the experience of Bhabha's Indian Christians not as an act of accidental rebellion but as an authentic discourse of faith; it suggests a means of taking their Christianity at face value while retaining the outsider's understanding of the source material. Just as importantly, it indirectly suggests a framework, based at once in anthropological and literary theory, for understanding the work of writers who engage in far-more-conscious hybrid reformulations of Western texts. The objections to Appadurai's notion of the postnational contain their own response: his "imagined world" can make real-world sense if we reframe it in terms of the *trans*national rather than the *post*national.

Transnationalist discourse, in Michael Peter Smith's formulation, "insists on the continuing significance of borders, state policies, and national identities even as these are often transgressed by transnational communication circuits and social practices."[30] As Brenda Yeoh, Karen Lai, Michael Charney, and Tong Chee Kiong put it, "transnationalism draws attention to what it negates—that is, the continued significance of the national."[31] Transnationalism, in other words, tries to have it both ways: to cross borders and to acknowledge them, to fuse separate places and to recognize their separation. James Clifford anticipates the essence of the current transnational position: "The world is increasingly connected, though not unified, economically and culturally. Local particularism offers no escape from these involvements. Indeed, modern ethnographic histories are perhaps condemned to oscillate between two metanarratives: one of homogenization, the other of emergence; one of loss, the other of invention. In most specific conjunctures both narratives are relevant, each undermining the other's claim to tell 'the whole story,' each denying to the other a privileged, Hegelian vision."[32] The local nation and the global transnational maintain an ongoing dialogue. Transnationalism, despite its potential for inclusivity, is also a means of preserving national difference. While Pheng Cheah condemns "hybrid cosmopolitanisms" that "ignore the necessity of the nation-state precisely because they regard cultural agency as unmoored from . . . the field of material forces that engenders culture," the transnational imagination sees ties between culture and the geopolitical world in the same way that the rooted cosmopolitan sees ties between himself and his location: as both present and negotiable.[33]

Like Bhabha's "hybridity" or Appadurai's "culture," transnationalism can be regarded as a process: Lina Basch, Nina Glick Schiller, and Cristina Szaton Blanc define it as "the process by which immigrants forge and *transnationalism as process...?*

sustain multi-stranded social relations that link together their societies of origin and settlement."³⁴ Basch, Schiller, and Blanc emphasize the temporary nature of the transnational: once the transnational community has been created, a stable identity category in its own right, it ceases to appear transgressive, and the active role of the transnational who must "forge and sustain" a set of relationships may give way to a comparatively passive identification with a group. While, as Gayatri Spivak argues, "culture alive is always on the run, always changeful," transnational culture is still more fleeting, as it synthesizes its hitherto separate components.³⁵ Transnationality is the process by which new identity categories are created and not the means by which they are maintained—the missing piece in Appiah's rooted cosmopolitanism.

* * *

Transnational writers, who claim active participation in more than one nation, provide a rooted approach to the problems posed by cultural synthesis. Rather than "negating" nationalism, their transnationalism co-opts and redefines it, drawing on the identity-building techniques of nationalist movements to provide alternative identities not simply for members of diasporas or migrants from a single location but for what Rushdie calls a "community of displaced persons,"³⁶ each one of whom is simultaneously rooted in a place of origin and in the imagined world of transnationality. Unlike the naïve readers we see in Bhabha or the "boutique multiculturals" of Fish, transnational writers are consciously committed to more than one national identity, as when Derek Walcott, "divided to the vein," insists on his simultaneous, incompatible histories as both black and white.³⁷ In the process of negotiating their multifarious identities, transnational writers renegotiate their allegiances, forsaking the possibility of absolute belonging in a single real-world location. If we are to understand any given work of transnational literature, we must understand not only the local allegiances of the writer but the broader framework of transnational fiction as a whole. Like the writers, readers of transnational fiction must become rooted cosmopolitans, aware of both local customs and idioms and the global literary conversation.

* * *

This book will show how transnational fiction provides cosmopolitans with community-defining physical spaces that answer the concerns of both theorists of postcolonial hybridization and theorists of national and postnational identity. These spaces vary in scale from the personal (the hybrid and sometimes monstrous bodies of fictional characters) to the global (the alternate worlds that those characters inhabit). In either case, novels provide the kind of spaces Mary Louise Pratt calls "contact zones": "social spaces where disparate cultures meet, clash, and grapple with each other."[38] While Pratt emphasizes real-world encounters, transnational writers negotiate between imaginative and realist approaches to physical space: their work emphasizes the simultaneous possibility and impossibility of separating the self from location and location from history.

In the next chapter, Joseph Conrad, V. S. Naipaul, Isak Dinesen, and Maxine Hong Kingston will demonstrate the range of ways in which the imaginary worlds of fiction can provide loci for real-world identity, moving from the temporary balancing act of the transnational to a rooted cultural synthesis. The rest of the book will discuss Vladimir Nabokov and Salman Rushdie, showing how, over the course of twentieth-century transnational fiction, fantastic hybrid worlds become the imaginative home of ever-expanding cosmopolitan communities.

CHAPTER 1

ALTERNATE WORLDS

JAMES CLIFFORD ENDS HIS CRITIQUE OF EDWARD SAID'S *ORIENTALISM* (1978) by asking, "Must the intellectual . . . construct a native land by writing like Césaire the notebook of a return?"[1] While Clifford implies that such a construction cannot satisfy, exiled and migrant novelists of the twentieth century have increasingly contested the boundaries between fiction and national identity. Novels have become the sites of experiments in cultural fusion, hybridity, and alternative identity categories. Both novels and nations teach us to read the people around us as either like or unlike ourselves and provide a logic for the demarcation of national and cultural boundaries. For that reason, novels can also redefine the motives and materials of such demarcations, showing how voluntary commitment to a community can trump even the familiar narratives of history. The fictions of transnational writers can bring readers a nation-like consciousness of shared identity, replacing traditional markers such as language and geography with the less tangible common grounds of exile, bilingualism, or outsider status. Such texts draw on an established tradition of nationalist novels. At the same time, they also subvert the fundamental premises of nationalist movements by suggesting that communities are not formed by a shared culture but by shared attitudes toward culture.

Novelists and nationalists both ask their interlocutors to share and cocreate a vision of a world. Novelists usually acknowledge that the resulting world is a fictional construct, whereas nationalists claim to describe an objective truth. Novels and nations are both brought into being by the collaboration between an author or leader and a participatory audience whom that leader guides through the act of creation. According to Wolfgang Iser, the writer assumes a reader who will join him in the world in which the fiction takes place, and who will, at least for the duration of the novel, believe in that fiction's existence.[2] Iser observes that texts guide their readers through the process of assembling a world out of the partial and sometimes incorrect observations of characters and a narrator.[3]

This claim resembles Anderson's description of the origins of the modern nation in print culture: there, too, each participant must have "complete confidence" in his conationals' "steady . . . simultaneous activity."[4] In both cases, the shared fiction is unequally constructed: while novelists and nationalists depend on their audiences' belief to create their fictional worlds, neither writers nor nationalist leaders are, as a rule, willing to surrender creative control.

In transnational novels, however, readers are given unusually high degrees of agency. Traditional novels and nations require collaboration and obedience: members of a nation and readers of a novel enter into a collective fiction on the terms of the author or leader. Antiauthoritarian novelists face a difficult problem, then, if they wish their novels to lead us into a pluralist, egalitarian community. *Uncle Tom's Cabin* (1852) teaches us to agree on a particular point—that slavery is evil, a claim based in the authority of Harriet Beecher Stowe, channeling the higher authority of the Christian God. The antiauthoritarian, pluralist novel faces a more complex task: it must teach readers not only that diversity is good but also how to participate in a contentious dialogue. Such novels must reject the totalizing power of the author, instead granting narrative power to readers. Rushdie's solution to this problem in *Midnight's Children* (1981) is Saleem's dissolution into the throngs of India, which cedes narrative power to the collective; Zadie Smith, Vikram Chandra, and Michael Ondaatje also end novels with a dissolution of authority. Novelists who are interested in creating intentional, participatory communities also demand conscious decision making by the readers: embedded puzzles, contradictory or ambiguous endings, and other postmodern devices give readers an unusually active role in constructing the plot. In solving these puzzles, readers remain subordinate to the author, but they have agency within the world of the book because they are required to determine its outcome.

The pluralist commonality of the transnational novel stems primarily from shared displacement: readers are asked to join a geographical and cultural migrancy that, the novels suggest, is the lot of the twentieth- and twenty-first century intellectual. The nation, for these communities, is not located in the mythologized "homeland" but in the alternate world of the novel itself. The world of fiction provides a locus for "transnational space," a term Peter Jackson, Philip Crang, and Claire Dwyer use to discuss "not just the *material geographies* of labour migration or the trading in transnational goods and services but also the *symbolic and imaginary geographies* through which we attempt to make sense of our increasingly transnational world."[5] Presenting "symbolic and imaginary geographies," the novel offers not simply a means of reading and understanding migrancy but an alternative homeland, a fictional nation. Novelistic worlds provide migrants with proof that they are not alone and an external referent with which to explain themselves to others. Fictional communities become participatory and meaningful by straddling lines between home and exile, reality and invention, consensus truth and objective fact. In the process, they teach readers to take control both of the text and of their real-world surroundings.

This chapter demonstrates how the alterity of a fictional world can create community through displacement, and how four writers—Conrad, Naipaul, Kingston, and Dinesen—confront the attractions and pitfalls of creating hybrid communities through reading and writing. In order to understand how the text produces worlds so complex that they can actually gain a reader's allegiance, however, we must begin with textual epistemologies and with some of the possible relationships between reality and fiction.

Typologies of Fictional Worlds

All fiction, no matter how realistic, is to some extent located in an alternate world: events happen within the world of the novel but not within the world of the reader. Realist novels claim nonetheless to represent the world as it is. They remind us of knowledge we already have or tell us things we do not know but could: the barbarism of slavery or degradation of the London poor. Fantastic novels, on the other hand, often claim to represent a world as it could be rather than the world as it is (although Ursula K. LeGuin, in an influential essay, argues the reverse: "I am not predicting, or prescribing. I am describing.")[6] As a result, they make different imaginative demands upon their readers: we are responsible for creating, rather than recognizing, the fantastic fictional world.

The settings of traditional fiction tend to acquire a kind of objective textual reality, recognizable to the reader, beyond that accorded by any character. Two characters may disagree over a physical fact (is Anne's hair red or auburn?), but most texts, whether realist or fantastic, contain a "right" answer to the disagreement (it's red). Postmodern novels like Thomas Pynchon's *The Crying of Lot 49* (1966), by contrast, contain destabilizing points of disagreement (the presence or absence of the Tristero conspiracy), in which the physical reality of the fictional world is undercut by the extreme variance among characters' points of view and the inadequate evidence provided by the text as a whole. These novels can be unsettling, and Bakhtin's account of the dialogic novel helps us explain why: the dialogic novel, which resists the "degrading *reification* of a person's soul," recognizing instead the soul's "freedom and its unfinalizability,"[7] is taken to an extreme in postmodern fiction, in which the subjectively described world itself appears to be in the same flux as the individual characters. Transnational fiction draws on these devices: it negotiates between personal and global unfinalizability. In it the instability of the individual consciousness reflects and affects the changing physical world.

Foucault argues that fantastic worlds actually change the meanings of the words used to describe them: "*Heterotopias* . . . secretly undermine language, because they make it impossible to name this *and* that."[8] Fantastic worlds add to the possible meanings of words by increasing the number of referents to which they can apply. Descriptions of fantastic worlds and places contain real-world references that implicitly modify our understanding of the real world and its places, too.

Brian McHale uses Foucault's heterotopia to account for the impossibility of the world of Pynchon's *Gravity's Rainbow* (1973): "Here . . . a large number of fragmentary possible worlds coexist in an impossible space . . . associated with occupied Germany, but . . . located nowhere but in the written text itself."[9] McHale treats Pynchon's impossible world, along with Italo Calvino's *Invisible Cities* (1972) and other logically contradictory locations, as prototypically postmodern: for McHale, the hallmark of postmodernism is the coexistence within the text of mutually incompatible physical spaces. He cites Guy Davenport's "The Invention of Photography in Toledo," in which Toledo, Spain and Toledo, Ohio are fused into a single heterotopia, and Davenport's "The Haile Selassie Funeral Train," in which a train "passes through Barcelona, along the Dalmatian coast of present-day Yugoslavia, to Genoa, Madrid, Odessa, Atlanta (in the State of Georgia, USA!), and back to Deauville again."[10] McHale argues that such absurd geographies differ qualitatively from the fictional geography of the fairy tale. (He finds no ontological problem in the purely fantastic, which, lacking real-world referents, is not self-contradictory.) Real-world referents establish the fictionality and impossibility of the postmodern "zone," which, unlike the nation, cannot be mapped onto a preexisting geography.

If impossible fictional geographies are the hallmark of postmodernism, then transnational writers, whatever their era, appear inescapably postmodern, for their fictions constantly address the overlap of geographically and ontologically incompatible worlds. These writers are particularly dependent upon their audience's cooperation, as they frequently acknowledge: "Believe me, believe me," begs Boori Ma at the end of Jhumpa Lahiri's "A Real Durwan" (2000). Nabokov's Humbert tells readers of *Lolita* (1955), "I shall not exist if you do not imagine me."[11] McHale cites Nabokov's Antiterra as an example of the "zone." But many of the incompatible worlds of transnational writers blur the line between postmodern impossibility and fairy tale coherence. The disruptive geographies of their impossible combinations produce a sense of instability and displacement. Davenport's Spanish–American Toledo and his transatlantic train produce a "zone" because their travels are impossible and their geographies self-contradictory. When transnational fiction presents its new geographies, however, whether in fairy-tale spaces or on our own world, the travels that the texts document are possible. While transnational writers invent distinctive physical geographies, they do so not only to disrupt the reader's sense of the "real" but also to convey the compatibility of apparently disparate locations, which are linked by the author's real-world experience as well as by fictional juxtapositions. Apparent postmodern disjunction gives way to coherence by the end of the text.

McHale argues that postmodern texts demand that readers recognize the impossibility of their fictional worlds; transnational fiction, by contrast, teaches us to recognize that the boundaries and cultural demarcations in our mental geographies are subjective and can be redrawn. Transnational fiction instigates dialogue between a series of real and possible worlds: the home country and the adopted country, both of which exist in the real world but are understood through competing epistemologies; the world of the book, which juxtaposes and synthesizes the home and adopted countries; and an implied fourth world brought into being by that synthesis. This fourth world, produced by the text, also exists by implication outside the text in the minds of participating readers. It thus becomes the product of the novels' pedagogical and community-forming projects.

Lubomír Doležel argues that fictional worlds are "composite . . . constituted by symbiosis, hierarchies, and tensions of many domains. They have to be semantically heterogeneous in order to provide the stage for many and diverse acting persons, stories, and settings."[12] Despite their heterogeneity, however, Doležel emphasizes that fictional worlds are stable loci in which a given set of facts ("Emma Bovary committed suicide" or "Emma Bovary died of tuberculosis") are either true or false.[13] The Emma Bovary test of intratextual accuracy indicates that, for Doležel, individual claims about truth and falsehood are subject to verification by the overall world of the text, which may be partially conveyed by individual characters' accounts but is a creation of the cooperating elements of the text as a whole. Events outside the text (the life of a hypothetical real-world woman named Emma Bovary, for example) do not affect the text's internal truth.

The Emma Bovary test provides a useful metric for the complexity of a text's truth claims and thus of the degree to which the reader is being asked to recognize his own acts of cocreation. Within *Madame Bovary* (1856), there is one right answer to the Emma Bovary test (she swallows arsenic). On the other hand, when the character Emma Bovary appears in Woody Allen's short story "The Kugelmass Episode" (1977), we are given a set of alternative "facts" in which, following Kugelmass's magical intrusion into Flaubert's novel, readers everywhere are shocked to find that "a bald Jew is kissing Madame Bovary."[14] In "The Kugelmass Episode," the truth of *Madame Bovary* develops contradictory layers: while *once* it was true that Emma Bovary had two lovers, it is *now* true that she has three. "The Kugelmass Episode" asks us to believe in three competing realities simultaneously: the one in which Emma Bovary has two lovers, the one in which she has a third, and the one in which she does not exist. The story's world is constructed not out of a single truth but out of the contradicting truths in the different versions of the novel. Allen's text creates a narrative equivalent of McHale's "zone," in which incompatible events (rather than geographies) are superimposed upon each other to create a vivid sense of impossible possibility.

"The Kugelmass Episode," by illustrating how fictional events can have the same kind of unfinalizable instability as postmodern geographies, also illustrates the reader's role in recognizing the cues that distinguish contradictory layers of truth and falsehood. "The Kugelmass Episode" takes place in a doubly fictional world: one in which real people can magically gain entry into books and one in which Flaubert's character Emma Bovary has a third lover. The story's fun comes from the way it draws its fictional difference from two worlds at once: the real world of the reader and the real world of Flaubert's novel. "The Kugelmass Episode" thus becomes *more fictional* than *Madame Bovary*, since its fictionality is created in opposition to *Madame Bovary*'s truth. But this trick can only work if the reader recognizes the source; otherwise, the story collapses into an ordinary fantasy.

The Emma Bovary test, then, suggests that some fictional worlds are more fictional than others, not by virtue of their realism (Tolkien's Middle-earth is not more *fictional* than Flaubert's France, though it is less *real*) but by virtue of their metafictionality. Metafictional worlds in dialogue with the real world and the previous worlds of fiction emphasize both their own contingent, constructed nature and, paradoxically, their power to undermine and destabilize the reality and the texts upon which they depend. Lighthearted as "The Kugelmass Episode" is, it illustrates the stakes of postmodern and transnational fiction: intense emotional involvement with a fictional text may allow us to shape not only that text but our understanding of the real world.

The reader's responsibility for recognizing real-world and metafictional references explains why transnational texts appear to oscillate between a plausible fantastic world and the surreality of McHale's "zone." These texts have more contexts than most readers can recognize and evaluate, with the result that readers must miss some of the information about how and where the text is anchored to the actual world. While plot can generally be understood without this information, truth claims about settings cannot. Readers who do not recognize real-world references must also fail to understand the degree to which they are being asked to construct and believe in alternate realities. McHale's "zone" depends on a reader's knowledge that Deauville and Atlanta cannot be connected by train tracks; a reader who lacks this knowledge may mistake it for realism. Without such real-world references, a text's acknowledgement of its own fictionality disappears, as do any larger effects that rest upon that acknowledgement.

Any writer faces the possibility that her references may not be familiar to her readers, but transnational writers confront more such possibilities than others; and not only because they may refer to real places. Nabokov's trilingual puns, for example, escape most readers of any background. If works containing such references are to be read and understood outside a coterie, the texts must provide some internal alternative to source recognition as a means of producing the novel's world. Transnational writers frequently address the problems of missed references and of "zone"-like juxtapositions by setting their texts in overtly alternate worlds. These may be alternate historical (Nabokov's *Ada, or Ardor* [1969], Rushdie's *The Ground Beneath Her Feet* [2000], and some of Isak Dinesen's *Tales* [1934]); fantastic (Maxine Hong Kingston's *The Woman Warrior: Memoir of a Girlhood Among Ghosts* [1975], Rushdie's *Midnight's Children*, or Vikram Chandra's *Red Earth and Pouring Rain* [1995]); or more subtle in their alterity, as in the mystery-novel world of Kazuo Ishiguro's *When We Were Orphans* (2000), the fantasy-novel references of Junot Díaz's *The Brief, Wondrous Life of Oscar Wao* (2007), or the plausible fictional country of Joseph Conrad's *Nostromo* (1904). However we categorize these fictional worlds, they all enter into unstable dialogues with the real world.

These books often trace the creation of a transnational community based on experiences shared by the characters, as in Dinesen's *Out of Africa* or Ondaatje's *The English Patient* (1992). In each case, however, the fictional worlds of the novels (or for Dinesen, the fictionalized world of the memoir) do not only tell stories of cross-cultural encounters but also create spaces in which those encounters become the norm. In these texts, the plot can become an example of the larger project of community creation; the novels' juxtapositions become test cases in hybridity. Transnational writers only appear to relish impossibility; instead, they seek to transform an apparently surreal or fantastic juxtaposition of incompatible cultural and textual elements into a plausible reality. Their textual transformation of the impossible into the ordinary models and mimics their transformation of cultural synthesis into an identity category.

FAILED SYNTHESES: CONRAD AND NAIPAUL

Transnational writers may make their novels the scenes of productive, carnivalesque fusions—as Nabokov, Rushdie, Ondaatje, and Dinesen do. They may instead argue that meaningful cultural combinations are impossible. In the latter case, attempts at cultural fusion will devolve into chaos or sterile mimicry. Novels of failed fusion tend to follow Bhabha's model of hybridity as an unconscious response to colonial oppression; frequently, hybrid characters in these novels become merely shallow copies of the dominant power from which they seek to free themselves. Rather than erasing boundaries between cultures and between layers of fictionality, these novels seem to warn against the boundary crossing they describe.

Joseph Conrad and V. S. Naipaul take such views. Conrad's position on the compatibility of cultures is encapsulated by Jim's leap from the *Patna* in *Lord Jim* (1900): for Conrad, there is an unbridgeable gap between the familiar and the unfamiliar. A character in a Conrad novel who chooses a new culture must abandon his old one entirely. The apparent absence of Polish from Conrad's texts suggests that the competition is not simply between the colonist and the colonized: while individuals may move from one culture to another, they cannot, in Conrad's novels, bring much with them—or when they do, they do so in the patched-together manner of the harlequin in *Heart of Darkness* (1899). It is instructive, however, to begin the discussion of transnational world-fashioning with Conrad and Naipaul, who help us understand the risks and goals of transnational fiction. They provide a clear warning against linking personal identity to an imaginary world, arguing that such self-fashioning is sterile and solipsistic. These emphases on the risk of solipsism, however, arise in part because Conrad and Naipaul are, in the end, more interested in the individual than the group. For these writers, the imagined community of the nation is too fragile—and too suspect—to replicate in fiction.

While Conrad's novels contain dramatically failed cultural fusions (Kurtz's semiassimilation into the African "heart of darkness," for example), these failures present arguments not against fusion itself but, more importantly, against the notion of stable group identities. Conrad is deeply suspicious of anything that lets individuals escape introspection. In *Nostromo*, the citizens of a South American province achieve independence and a national identity but at the price of individuality and authenticity. The survivors of the revolution are revealed (to the reader, though not to each other) as frauds. In the end, Conrad suggests that national identity or a sense of community is a delusion, and that individuals (Marlow, Jim, Nostromo, Decoud) can only understand themselves when separated from the crowd. Attempts at cultural fusion are misguided not because cultures are incompatible, but because individuals should not think of themselves as representatives of a group. Colonial settings in Conrad's novels provide contact zones between the individual and the group rather than between cultures; his interest in colonies comes from their destabilization of group identity, which frees individuals (often alone, in the dark, on the deck of a moving ship, cut off from buttressing cultural identifications) to understand themselves separately from their surroundings.

V. S. Naipaul, on the other hand, is deeply concerned with the possibility of cultural synthesis for its own sake, but he finds few examples successful. Writing of India during the Emergency, he identifies not successful synthesis but a synthetic pose: "Indians say that their gift is for cultural synthesis. When they say this, they are referring to the pre-British past, to the time of Moslem dominance. And though the idea is too much part of received wisdom, too much a substitute for thought and inquiry, there is proof of that capacity for synthesis in Indian painting . . . In the nineteenth century, with the coming of the British, this great tradition died."[15]

Naipaul sees the death of the "capacity for synthesis" as the cause of the "sterility of contemporary Indian political life,"[16] a claim whose bitterness suggests how much Naipaul hoped, on his first visit to India, to find such synthesis still vital. He blames Gandhi for this stasis. To account for the sterility he sees in Gandhian nationalism, Naipaul writes of Gandhi's radicalizing encounter with racism on a South African train as a failure of racial consciousness: "If Gandhi had resolved his difficulties in another way, if (like the imaginative novelist) he hadn't so successfully transmuted his original hurt (which with him must have been in large part racial), if he had projected on to India another code of survival, he might have left independent India with an ideology, and perhaps even with what in India would have been truly revolutionary, the continental racial sense, the sense of belonging to a people specifically of India."[17]

For Naipaul, Gandhi's idea of India, a confederation of unlike groups, does not produce a "continental racial sense" because it involves a conscious embrace of pluralism. The Indian secular nationalist movement's devolution into self-congratulatory stasis stems, according to Naipaul, from its failure to create a national identity: Indians will not learn from each other, nor from the rest of the world, until they think of themselves as "Indians," not as members of castes and subgroups.

What is striking here is not only Naipaul's endorsement of racialized nationalism but his description of the pluralist Gandhi as being "like the imaginative novelist." For Naipaul, imaginative novelists do not have the solution to national problems because they "transmute" experience rather than dealing with it (and its ideological import) directly. Novelists, in other words, are not political thinkers because they sublimate trauma into art. But Naipaul's novels nonetheless repeatedly address problems of national identity and conclude that his transcultural protagonists are doomed to alienation.

Cross-cultural encounters are not Naipaul's primary interest, however, any more than they are Conrad's. While his characters' alienation may appear to spring from their displaced lives in postcolonial societies, it turns out, in such texts as *The Enigma of Arrival*, to derive from the universal fact of time and change, so that English farmers, shepherds, and aristocrats are in the same position as the Trinidadian Indians of *A House for Mr. Biswas* (1961): each group watches the world they have taken for granted decay. While imperialism has done its part to bring about this decay, the main villain is time, which will ultimately leave us all in exile. Naipaul appears to believe that the work of the imaginative novelist is not to resolve this alienation but to document it, together with the temporary solutions found in the fragile "sacred world" constructed by "every generation."[18] Naipaul's novels present individuals who attempt, and largely fail, to move from one cultural context to another in search of impossible permanence. Cultural synthesis is not Naipaul's goal; rather, attempts at cultural synthesis are part of a larger project of documentation, reclamation, and repair, in which the novelist at once chronicles and performs an attempt to salvage something valuable from inevitable decay.

While Conrad and Naipaul discuss cultural combinations, then, neither writer is particularly interested in synthesis for its own sake, and both treat world-fashioning with suspicion. For Conrad, cross-cultural encounters and attempts at synthesis reveal the frailty of the individual; Naipaul uses them to show the instability of the world in time. The cultural syntheses in their novels fail because they are means by which characters delude themselves. Both writers suggest that the work of the imaginative novelist is to "transmute" an individual's pain into an illusory world: to provide, in other words, a false sense of universality. But why must universality be false?

The rest of this book will examine writers who seek more substantive transmutations of individual experience. For these writers, cultural combinations become not simply the topic but the goal of the text. Vladimir Nabokov, Salman Rushdie, Michael Ondaatje, Kazuo Ishiguro, Zadie Smith, Jhumpa Lahiri, Isak Dinesen, Michael Chabon, and Maxine Hong Kingston all share not simply a subject—the interactions of cultures—but an approach: each writer stages those interactions in an alternate world designed to promote cultural synthesis over cultural competition. These worlds provide the means to form a new community of readers and writers that supersedes the nation; in this new community all readers may become members.

ALTERNATE-WORLD MEMOIRS: KINGSTON AND DINESEN

Like the novels McHale cites in his discussion of the "zone," Maxine Hong Kingston's *The Woman Warrior: Memoirs of a Girlhood Among Ghosts* is set in two contradictory worlds: the America Kingston grew up in and the ghost-haunted China of her mother's "talk-story."[19] Kingston's ghost stories convey her childhood sense of displacement in America, demonstrate the incompatibility of the countries she discusses, describe her mother's cultural norms, and show how racism and xenophobia make people view each other as inhuman. Kingston's mother's China and her own America appear to belong to different worlds rather than simply to different continents because they operate under entirely different epistemological rules: China is literally full of supernatural ghosts, whereas the "ghosts" in America are merely non-Chinese Americans, whom the young Kingston comes to identify as real people. Her mother's China's alterity—its distance from the "real" world—is marked by the fact that Kingston can communicate with the Chinese people she encounters in America only in English. The dialect of "our village" is incomprehensible to them: Kingston's mother comes from a place unrecognizable even to other Chinese-Americans.

Incompatible as these worlds may appear, however, readers know that they really coexist and that the difference between them is a product of human understanding and representation. The memoir's ghost stories slowly shift from literal truths, as received by the young Kingston, to metaphorical truths. Far from indicating that the narrator is unreliable, the memoir's multiple worlds are the hallmark of sanity: "The difference between mad people and sane people . . . is that sane people have variety when they talk-story. Mad people have only one story that they talk over and over."[20] If the reader experiences the book as set in the "zone," it is not because the geographies *The Woman Warrior* depicts are impossible but because the reader is asked to duplicate the experience of the young Kingston as she seeks to understand the worlds within and without her family's house. The resolution of Kingston's memoir suggests that these two worlds ultimately do coexist within a single space—the space both of California and of the book itself.

In *Out of Africa*, Isak Dinesen, too, makes the worlds that meet on her African farm appear ontologically separate, as when she thinks about accusations of witchcraft against one of the women on the farm:

> I had by now become used to the idea of witchcraft, it seemed a reasonable thing, so many things are about, at night, in Africa.
>
> "This old woman is mean," I thought in Swaheli [sic], "she uses her arts in making Kaninu's cows blind, and she leaves it to me to keep her grandchild alive, on a bottle of milk a day, from my own cows."
>
> I thought: "This accident . . . [is] getting into the blood of the farm, and it is my fault. I must call in fresh forces, or the farm will run into a bad dream, a nightmare. I know what I will do. I will send for Kinanjui."[21]

By switching from a European language to Swahili, Dinesen also switches epistemological systems, entering a world in which magic is plausible and risking entry into the world of dreams.[22] Dinesen's switch from European languages to Swahili also changes the farm's hierarchies: when Dinesen confronts a problem that requires Swahili understanding, she ceases to be the farm's supreme authority (as she has been in matters of Western medicine and cooking) and must "send for Kinanjui," the local chief.

Dinesen's switch to Swahili is not simply a naïve claim to have moved from a "European" to an "African" understanding of magic, however. Despite the apparent divide between them, the worlds of English and Swahili turn out to be compatible. Kinanjui's authority comes not from tribal but colonial appointment: he has been made a chief by the British and thus provides an overlapping space for local and colonial power systems. Kinanjui gains his power from the colonists but uses it to deal with indigenous problems like witchcraft. Thinking in Swahili does not place Dinesen in an authentically African mindset, then, but in a colonial framework that mediates (however imperfectly) between the African and the European.

The possibility of a middle ground between European and African is emphasized by the fact that Dinesen thinks about witchcraft in Swahili, the East African lingua franca, rather than in Kikuyu, the local tribe's language. Swahili, a creole of Bantu and Arabic, suggests the long history of precolonial cultural fusion in East Africa, in which Dinesen places herself and her farm. She argues that cosmopolitanism is commonplace there: every herdboy on the plains knows "Englishmen, Jews, Boers, Arabs, Somali Indians, Swaheli, Masai and Kawirondo. As far as receptivity of ideas goes, the Native is more of a man of the world than the suburban or provincial settler or missionary, who has grown up in a uniform community and with a set of stable ideas."[23] By thinking in Swahili, Dinesen does not become "local" in the sense of becoming Kikuyu; rather, she enters a longstanding tradition of East African cultural fusion, in which rationality and magic, too, meet and communicate. By invoking the African history of cross-cultural communication, Dinesen stages her farm as a meeting ground of worlds only apparently divided: in fact, the "African" and the "European," like the magical and the rational, meet easily and quickly become inseparable.

It is important to note that these examples of invented worlds are not novels but memoirs. Kingston and Dinesen straddle the line between reality and fiction not only in their subject matter but also in the imaginative demands they make on their readers. *The Woman Warrior* and *Out of Africa* present the double vision of incompatible worlds and their resolution into a single, three-dimensional space not as fictional construct but as biographically verifiable truth. The novelistic structure of the memoirs, however, continually demands that readers engage in the same kind of world-creation as readers of novels. This double demand, both for belief and for imaginative participation, also appears in much of the fiction of transnational writers: the novels, while overtly fictional, contain pedagogical or testimonial elements. Readers are asked to believe and to learn from these elements even while they help create fictional worlds.

For Dinesen and Kingston, contact between cultures is like contact between the rational and the supernatural. Naipaul and Conrad, on the other hand, treat cross-cultural world-fashioning as self-indulgent delusion. Dinesen, Kingston, Conrad, and Naipaul between them establish the main problem and the main attraction of hybrid world-fashioning: it may allow union between cultures and with the novel's readers, but it also risks delusional self-involvement. In the rest of this book, we shall see how a balance between solipsism and inclusivity informs the self-conscious world-fashioning of transnational fiction.

ALTERNATE COMMUNITIES AND PHYSICAL SPACES

The alternate worlds of many transnational novelists are as clearly invented as the "talk-story" China of *The Woman Warrior*. Writers adopt elements of the supernatural or the alternate historical in order to stage conflict or communication between cultures. These alternate worlds frequently collapse by the end of the novels that describe them, but in their collapse they suggest how their cultural mixtures can be achieved in the real world.

Once again, memoir gives us a starting point. Dinesen blurs the distinction between "African" and "European" to make her farm, rather than their countries or cultures of origin, the primary object of its inhabitants' allegiance. Dinesen describes the community on the farm as a single entity, forged by adversity when "the long rains failed": "we were all merged together into a unity, so that on another planet we shall recognize one another, and the things cry to each other, the cuckoo clock and my books to the lean-fleshed cows on the lawn and the sorrowful old Kikuyus: 'You also were there. You also were part of the Ngong farm.' That bad time blessed us and went away."[24] Divisions among "Swaheli, Masai and Kawirondo" have been superseded by the farm itself, in which people, animals, and inanimate objects become inextricably fused. Dinesen's memoir is a story of the creation of a new, nation-like community, whose members speak a distinctive common language, and who by the end wish for self-governance: when Dinesen leaves Africa, the people on the farm wish to stay together, and Dinesen spends her last few months there working to arrange it.

Dinesen's memoir suggests the degree to which the worlds of transnational texts are verifiably not our own. Her memoir differs dramatically from the verifiable facts of her life.[25] It is neither a simple autobiography (we learn that she was married, for example, but not her husband's name) nor fiction. Instead, Dinesen presents a version of her story that has been explicitly modified in the service of her vision of unity with the workers on her farm.[26] Her account of the farm and the unity of European, Somali, and Kikuyu that it brings about requires a suspension of disbelief—which Dinesen deliberately makes difficult when she includes accounts of the torture and murder of a Kikuyu servant by British colonists in Nairobi.

Dinesen's idealized account contains its own negative. The memoir provides grounds for a searing criticism of colonialism through its account of the brutality of British colonists and Dinesen's feudal relationship with the "squatters" on her land. The farm is revealed, within and beyond the text, as a fictional construct, one doomed by the cruelty of British rule. But the fiction of idyllic unity is not simply Dinesen's, or so she would have us believe; it is also a fiction in which her servants and farm laborers participate, and readers are invited to join. Like the workers united by drought, we are to experience the blessing of the "bad time" and enter the community that rejects the abuses of colonial rule.

Dinesen's memoir shows how important shared places are for the creation of alternate identities. John Clement Ball, Robert Alter, and others have shown how cities provide space for such fusions.[27] But transnational writers emphasize the ways smaller physical spaces contain and determine culture by turning individual houses into models for cultural synthesis: the ruined villa of Ondaatje's *The English Patient* (1992), for example, enables the trans-Commonwealth characters (an Englishman who turns out to be Hungarian, two Canadians, and a Sikh) to build a microcosm of renewal from the rubble of World War II. The villa, like Dinesen's farm, creates a locus for community in which the "bad time" can "bless us." Similar sited communities appear throughout transnational literature: the monkey's room and the courtyard in Chandra's *Red Earth and Pouring Rain* and the San Tomé mine in *Nostromo* are also specifically designed to enable the creation of new shared identities among the people who inhabit them. Many houses in transnational novels, like Rosa Diamond's in *The Satanic Verses* (1988) or the Belsey house in Smith's *On Beauty* (2005), suggest that hybridity can be owned and determined by the hybridizer. In each case, shared experience in the communal space supersedes prior identities, transforming separate individuals into a community.

Identities grounded in real places must, however, be temporary in a community of migrants. Transnational novels also chronicle the relocation of identity-defining places into fictional, rather than physical, space. *On Beauty*, which is modeled on E. M. Forster's *Howards End* (1910), provides a particularly good example. In Forster's novel, an old house in the English countryside helps fuse the "inner" intellectual life of the Schlegel family with the "outer" business life of the Wilcoxes; the novel ends with the families joined in a happy community among the English hay fields, with the suburbs of London slowly encroaching. Smith begins her own novel with a similar house in suburban Boston, belonging to the interracial Belsey family. But the Belsey household is in chaos following the husband's infidelity, and the house turns out to be inadequate to the task of forging a united identity. Instead, the defining object in *On Beauty* is a Haitian painting of the Voodoo goddess Maitresse Erzulie. Smith replaces the house with a painting both for immediate symbolic reasons—a painting is portable—and to indicate the shift in the basis of identity for the novel's characters: by the end of *On Beauty*, affiliations with *places* are superseded by the characters' aesthetic allegiances to artistic *traditions*. For Smith, the most important marker of identity is not where we live but what we want to look at. Like the painting of Maitresse Erzulie, transnational novels offer a focal point for identity: for writers like Smith, our allegiances are both created and identified by what we read.

Readers can only come to such an allegiance through repeated readings, however. First-time readers of a text that draws on several cultures must learn to understand the references backward, using the novel as a key to the culture rather than the other way around. By the end of a transnational text, readers have received a covert education in the text's cultures. The process and result of this education turns readers into the text's best audience: both their initial incomprehension and their eventual understanding are necessary for the shared experience of displacement and unity. Rereaders can laugh at jokes they missed the first time through. This is true not only of a text's internal references (foreshadowing, etc.), which no first-time reader can pick up but also of the external references that readers learn to recognize.

Transnational texts educate readers not only in a culture but also in the experience of living with multiple cultures. While some address this education in biculturalism directly (Julia Alvarez's *How the Garcia Girls Lost Their Accents* [1991], for example), most alternate-world fiction teaches readers about the experience of biculturalism through the act of reading: in these texts, all readers are outsiders who must become familiar with unfamiliar surroundings. Just as Dinesen brings her readers through an experience of loss that duplicates the experience of the community on the farm, transnational writers bring their readers through the experience of displacement, repeating the transnational acculturation that the author has undergone. Readers who assimilate the lessons of the text come to see the fictional worlds of the novels as places where their own references, as well as those of the writer, are understood.

Nabokov and Rushdie

The next five chapters of this book show how Vladimir Nabokov and Salman Rushdie, two of the most controversial and uncategorizable writers of the twentieth century, use real-world references and metafictional games to create a series of possible communities. Nabokov and Rushdie provide a catalogue of approaches to world-fashioning and community building, ranging from the intimate groups of family memories to magical-realist claims of national unity. They are exemplary of twentieth and twenty-first-century transnational writers both for what they share—a common sense of humor and love of transgression—and for how they differ, in their countries of origin, for example, and in their politics.

Nabokov and Rushdie's attraction to and distrust of imaginary worlds as the meeting ground of disparate cultures makes them an ideal case study in transnational literature. John Burt Foster, arguing for Nabokov's place among the European modernists, suggests Nabokov's power to reconfigure national literary traditions around his own work, and the next two chapters will show how those reconfigurations provide the bases for shared communities arising from the readership of his novels.[28] For Rushdie, Nabokov presents both a model for cultural synthesis and a means of access to two international literary traditions at once: Nabokov belongs in the twentieth-century modernist-postmodernist canon of difficult and allusive English-language writers like Joyce and Pynchon and at the same time in the equally difficult and allusive community of exiled and migrant writers (to which Joyce also belongs). By building on Nabokov's models of cultural fusion, Rushdie challenges readers to enter a state of displacement in which all loyalties and purities are suspect and in which the world must be constantly made anew.

Nabokov was born in 1899 in St. Petersburg, Russia, to a progressive aristocratic family and was a "perfectly normal trilingual child" until the Russian Revolution forced the family to flee in 1919.[29] The parents settled in Berlin, and Nabokov attended Cambridge, graduating in 1922. Then Nabokov moved to Berlin, and married Véra Slonim in 1925. The Nabokovs stayed in Berlin until 1937, moving first to Paris and then, in 1940, to America. Nabokov published nine novels in Russian from 1926 to 1938. His first novel in English, *The Real Life of Sebastian Knight*, was published in 1941, but he did not become famous in the English-speaking world until the scandal following the 1955 publication of *Lolita*. Nabokov lived and worked in America until 1961, when he and Véra moved to Montreux, Switzerland, where they remained until his death in 1977.

Nabokov disdained politics. While *Invitation to a Beheading* (*Priglashenie na kazn'*, 1938) and *Bend Sinister* (1947) are set in imaginary dictatorships and read like critiques of the Soviet and Nazi regimes, Nabokov denied that such a reading was appropriate: "The story in *Bend Sinister* is not really about life and death in a grotesque police state."[30] "Nothing bores me more than political novels and the literature of social intent," he wrote.[31] Nabokov's novels are frequently stories of individual quests: Fyodor of *The Gift* wants to become a writer; Krug of *Bend Sinister* tries to save his son from the state's torturers; Humbert to recapture his lost love Annabel in *Lolita;* Kinbote to recreate his lost Zembla while John Shade looks for evidence of life after death in *Pale Fire* (1962). In each case, the quest, sometimes unbeknownst to the protagonist, has a supernatural component, often in the form of ghostly help from a dead relative or lover. Nabokov's novels are deeply concerned with life after death, and each contains intimations of guiding supernatural forces.

Apart from the central facts of privilege, migration, and notoriety, Salman Rushdie's biography looks very different from Nabokov's. Rushdie was born to a well-to-do Muslim family in Bombay, India, on June 19, 1947, fifty-six days before India achieved independence from Britain. Rushdie attended primary school in Bombay, followed by Rugby in England. Like Nabokov, Rushdie attended Cambridge (Nabokov was at Trinity, Rushdie at King's). In 1964 his family moved to Pakistan; after graduation, Rushdie joined them there. He returned to England soon thereafter, in part because of censorship in Pakistan. (A production of Edward Albee's *Zoo Story* had to have the word "pork" excised: "'Pork,' a TV executive told me solemnly, 'is a four-letter word.'")[32] His first novel, *Grimus*, was published in 1975 to minimal notice; his second, *Midnight's Children* (1981), met international acclaim, eventually receiving the Booker of Bookers in 1993 and the fortieth anniversary Best of the Booker prize in 2008. *Midnight's Children* generated scandal—Indira Gandhi sued Rushdie to have a sentence removed from *Midnight's Children*—but Rushdie really became famous with the publication of *The Satanic Verses* in 1988. The book's depiction of a brothel containing prostitutes named after the wives of the Prophet Muhammed caused riots and book burnings and led to an Iranian *fatwa*, issued on February 14, 1989, calling for Rushdie's death. Rushdie spent the next ten years in hiding. As the danger from the fatwa receded, he began to make more public appearances and settled in New York City.

Unlike Nabokov, Rushdie writes avowedly political fiction. *Shame* (1983) and *Haroun and the Sea of Stories* (1990) critique Pakistani leaders. *Midnight's Children* centers around the Emergency, that is, the suspension of Indian constitutional rights between 1975 and 1977. The book's political critique is so central that as he was writing it, Rushdie worried that it might eventually appear dated: "One day, I knew, the subject of Mrs Gandhi and the Emergency would cease to be current . . . and at that point, I told myself, my novel would either get worse—because it would lose the power of topicality—or else it would get better—because once the topical had faded, the novel's literary architecture would stand alone, and even, perhaps, be better appreciated."[33]

* * *

To the extent that Nabokov's politics can be ascertained, they differ significantly from Rushdie's. In his early work, as Patrick Colm Hogan argues,

Rushdie demonstrates a strong sympathy with communism,[34] whereas Nabokov, driven from his home by the Soviets, was strongly opposed to it. Rushdie's approach to the supernatural also differs from Nabokov's. The supernatural pervades Nabokov's novels, but it appears covertly, frequently taking a form that could be dismissed as coincidental. Rushdie's novels contain characters who are psychic, or can fly, or become animals. Unlike Nabokov, too, Rushdie is interested in (and critical of) organized religion: Hindu iconography informs many of his novels,[35] and Islam plays a double role, providing important philosophical subtexts in some and appearing as a repressive political power in others.[36] Despite Rushdie's supernatural plot elements, however, his novels deal with decidedly earthly problems (political repression, national identity, the postcolonial condition), while the less-visibly supernatural Nabokov is concerned with proving the existence of a transcendent realm.

Nabokov's novels tend to be tightly focused, tracing the development of one or two characters. Rushdie's sprawl, drawing on vast casts and dozens of locations. Nabokov often writes about death, generally of a beloved individual; Rushdie tends to write about migration. Critics of Nabokov's work often classify him as a modernist; Rushdie is one of the major postmodernists. Berad-Peter Lange, in an article comparing Nabokov and Rushdie's narrative techniques, spends more time pointing out their differences than explaining why we should see the two writers together.[37]

Despite their very different lives and oeuvres, however, Nabokov and Rushdie have a great deal in common. The central fact of both men's lives is migration. Both come from privileged backgrounds; both left their childhood homes for good, involuntarily, at an early age; both attended Cambridge; both have lived in Europe and America, rarely seeming permanently settled in either; both have caused scandals. The novels, too, share key stylistic elements. It is equally true to say of either writer that his work is densely referential, drawing both on the Anglophone literary tradition and on elements likely to be unfamiliar to Western English-speaking readers; that his work is full of linguistic play and puns, many of them informed by multiple languages; and that his frequently unreliable narrators attempt to enlist their readers in sometimes outrageous allegiances to political or aesthetic positions.

These similarities stem from much more important common attitudes. Both writers connect high and low culture and make references ranging from medieval texts to popular music. Both frequently appear to explain their references, as when Rushdie explains that "buddha" is Urdu for "Old Man" or Nabokov, in the anagrammatic guise of Vivian Darkbloom, translates a Russian phrase in the notes to *Ada*; these explanations, however, are often partial, creating complex overtones available only to privileged readers who share the full reference. Nabokov and Rushdie both use these references and puns to construct multilayered texts, which reveal changing stories, puzzles with multiple solutions, and deepening insights depending upon a reader's level of attention or knowledge.

Rushdie's appropriations of Nabokov reveal the extent of their common interests. We will see in Chapter 5 how Nabokov informs *The Ground Beneath Her Feet* (1999); but Nabokov first appears in Rushdie's work in two passages of *The Satanic Verses*. On the first occasion, a British woman named Allie Cone tries to talk to her Indian lover Gibreel Farishta about "Nabokov's doomed chess-player Luzhin, who came to feel that in life as in chess there were certain combinations that would inevitably arise to defeat him, as a way of explaining by analogy her own (in fact somewhat different) sense of impending catastrophe (which had to do not with recurring patterns but with the inescapability of the unforeseeable), but he fixed her with a hurt stare that told her he'd never heard of the writer, let alone *The Defense*."[38] Nabokov's first cameo in *The Satanic Verses* is as a test of Western cultural literacy. Gibreel is the least Europeanized of the main characters in *The Satanic Verses*, and, not coincidentally, the least formally educated. But Gibreel is not the only one to miss a reference here. The narrator explains that Allie's allusion is misguided, since her "sense of impending catastrophe" is "in fact somewhat different" from Luzhin's. Unbeknownst to Allie, however, the reference to Luzhin is appropriate, for Gibreel is about to embark on a series of schizophrenic hallucinations echoing Luzhin's, and both men will eventually commit suicide: Luzhin by leaping out of a window, Gibreel by gunshot after throwing Allie from the roof of a skyscraper. Allie's reference to *The Defense* to explain her sense of "impending catastrophe" appears to be "somewhat different" but is actually entirely relevant. Luzhin, the mad émigré chess player, warns us that individuals who cannot move between different frames of reference risk missing warnings about their own fates: Allie cannot see that her "sense of impending catastrophe" is tied to the "recurring patterns" of fiction because she is inside the novel, and Luzhin cannot escape the "combinations that . . . arise to defeat him" because he is inside a fictional chess game. For both Nabokov and Rushdie, as for Kingston, the possibility of moving between cultures mirrors the possibility of moving between different layers of fictionality and reality.

Allie's reference to Luzhin sets up Gibreel's impatient response when his nemesis, Saladin Chamcha, quotes from Nabokov's *Pale Fire*. Chamcha responds to an encounter with a racist drunk by quoting a line in imaginary language:

"'Minnamin, Gut mag alkan, Pern dirstan,'" Chamcha replied. 'It means, "My darling, God makes hungry, the Devil thirsty." Nabokov.'
'Him again,' Gibreel complained. 'What bloody language?'
'He made it up. It's what Kinbote's Zemblan nurse tells him as a child. In *Pale Fire*.'
'*Perndirstan*,' Farishta repeated. 'Sounds like a country: Hell, maybe. I give up, anyway. How are you supposed to read a man who writes in a made-up lingo of his own?'[39]

Gibreel's criticism—"How are you supposed to read a man who writes in a made-up lingo of his own?"—is reasonable. It is a criticism frequently aimed at both Rushdie and Nabokov by first-time readers. Each writes from heights of cultural familiarities impossible to expect of a general English-speaking audience, and each appears potentially critical of readers who do not understand him. Of course, *Pale Fire* is not written in Zemblan any more than *The Satanic Verses* is written in Urdu. But both novels are dependent on made-up lingos: *Pale Fire* is full of Zemblan proverbs; the names of the major characters in both novels have meanings in several languages; and Gibreel himself speaks in Bombay *filmi* English, peppered with interjections of "yaar" (man) and "baba" (father).

By quoting Kinbote's Zemblan proverb, Rushdie suggests both the appeal and the futility of writing in made-up languages while emphasizing that it is not, in fact, what either he or Nabokov is doing. To what extent, *The Satanic Verses* asks, is writing in a made-up language the result of attempting to combine dissimilar cultures? Made-up languages avert Foucault's objection that fantastic worlds undermine linguistic meaning, but without real-world referents, the text becomes incomprehensible. How, as Gibreel asks, are we supposed to read it? The paired references to *The Defense* and *Pale Fire* suggest that "made-up lingos" are penetrable, but only from the extratextual perspective; Saladin, Gibreel, and Allie cannot know the nature of the world they inhabit. The fate of the transnational writer, Rushdie suggests, is to write in a made-up language, understood only by readers who are not too deeply involved in one of the cultures that provides its components.

The next five chapters show how Nabokov and Rushdie have it both ways in their fiction, creating "made-up lingos" that still contain compelling and comprehensible real-world referents. The first of these will be the national rhetoric of America, a country that prides itself on its own self-invention. Nabokov's rewriting of American national myths demonstrates that heterotopias really do destabilize reality: his alternate Americas reveal the constructed nature of the real-world country and suggest how it could be rebuilt by active readers.

CHAPTER 2

VLADIMIR NABOKOV'S INVENTED AMERICAS

TRANSNATIONAL FICTION BUILDS ITS HOME IN THE NO MAN'S land between fact and interpretation. It asks us to recognize that cultural demarcations, like historical narratives and national boundaries, gain their status as "true" from group consensus. The fantastic literary worlds of transnational fiction lead readers through a trial-and-error process, teaching us what materials are most amenable to reinterpretation and recombination. Like transnationality itself, hybrid world-fashioning can produce durable changes in our understanding of group identity. Readers are asked to use the imaginative underpinnings of identity categories to render cultural affiliations and national histories portable between languages and continents.

Vladimir Nabokov's novels ask readers to distinguish between objective and interpretive truths as they sift through evidence provided by the narrators. *Lolita*'s Humbert, *Pale Fire*'s Kinbote, and *Ada*'s Van create unreliable hybrids that are implicitly contrasted with Nabokov's own unification of his cultural worlds. Humbert, Kinbote, and Van's failed hybridizations teach us the power as well as the limits of interpretive truths: their self-serving readings of their surroundings are an education in the (limited) flexibility of the physical world and imply the possibility of a transcendent synthesis of the personal and the national.

Nabokov's novels use the interplay between constructed and objective truths to renegotiate the relationship between geography and culture. In *Lolita*, landscape participates in the narrative, first contradicting Humbert's romantic claim to unite Europe and America and then providing glimpses of better hybrid worlds beyond the scope of Humbert's imagination. In *Pale Fire*, the American landscape turns out—despite Kinbote's alienation from it—to be where art and fact meet. Using Renaissance travelers' tales as a model, Nabokov makes his fictional landscape a contact zone not only between cultures but also between a host of apparently incompatible things: Russia, Europe, and America; the past and the present; life and death; art and science; objective truth and individual interpretation; romantic utopianism and hard fact.

Nabokov's Americas—which he had to "invent" to write *Lolita*—show the degree to which fiction can affect our understanding of real places and demonstrate how historical and cultural narratives are amenable to reconstruction and reinterpretation.[1] While the natural world does not respond to the impositions of the world-fashioning narrator, America is already a real-world locus of cultural synthesis as well as the subject of a panoply of utopian visions and national discourses.

Each synthesis in Nabokov's fiction models and enables others. As we will see in *Lolita* and *Pale Fire*, attempts to achieve only a single kind of synthesis, such as the simple juxtaposition of two distant countries, invariably fail.[2] As *Pale Fire* and *Ada* show, however, complex and ambitious syntheses that juxtapose elements from multiple levels—space, time, culture, metaphysics—are more likely to work. This chapter examines how America becomes the site of Nabokov's syntheses in *Lolita*, *Pale Fire*, and *Ada* in order to establish—and begin to solve—a fundamental problem facing transnational writers: how to bring their physical surroundings and their imaginary worlds into dialogue. This sited union of the physical and the imaginary is both an end in itself and a step toward Nabokov's more unusual rejection of linear time, which we will examine in Chapter 3.

Don Barton Johnson argues that Nabokov's memoir *Speak, Memory* (1967) treats America as the "synthetic" arc in the spiral of Nabokov's life, combining the "thesis" of Russia and "antithesis" of Europe. Susan Elizabeth Sweeney describes how Nabokov's novels "compensate for his exile 'by some sleight of *land*'—that is, by transposing one country onto another."[3] For Nabokov, America, more than any other country, provides a meeting point for old and new worlds. Nabokov's Americas provide philosophical models not only for other fictional worlds within his own novels but also for writers like Rushdie and Chabon. These worlds draw readers into allegiances not to particular places or times but to memory, to the process of pattern-recognition, and to cultural fusion itself.

For the last two decades, critics have followed Véra Nabokov's lead in treating a supernatural "otherworld" as the "main theme" of Nabokov's work. (Johnson and Vladimir Alexandrov brought this theme to broad critical attention.[4]) But while the supernatural is indisputably important, the novels also suggest the possibility of remaking the real world: Nabokov urges his readers to make "curiosity, tenderness, kindness, ecstasy . . . the norm" in their real lives.⁵ Just as Nabokov requires readers to puzzle out the novels' plots—who killed John Shade in *Pale Fire;* the location to the keys of Fyodor's apartment at the end of *The Gift* —so too does he require readers to cocreate an implied ideal country, one that combines the best of exile and of a lost homeland. Through his puzzles, Nabokov invites readers to participate in the reinvention both of America and of our metaphysical understanding of boundaries.

LOLITA AND THE RESISTANCE OF THE PHYSICAL WORLD

Lolita is a complicated book, but it lays out the problem of cultural and geographic synthesis more simply than many of Nabokov's works, because Humbert's world-fashioning fails more spectacularly than that of any of Nabokov's other narrators. The synthesis of Europe and America Humbert tries to achieve is impossible because it is too local, too superficial, and, most importantly, too purely physical.

Humbert describes himself as a cosmopolitan product of Europe: his father is "a Swiss citizen, of mixed French and Austrian descent, with a dash of the Danube in his veins" and his mother "an English girl."⁶ His first love, Annabel Leigh, is "half-English, half-Dutch."⁷ Humbert grows up in the "private universe" of his father's hotel on the French Riviera, attends an English school, and is read to out of *Don Quixote* and *Les Misérables*.⁸ Humbert refers to his "solid Swiss citizenship"⁹ but does not seem to consider himself to have any particular national identity; if he has an allegiance, it is to the nymphets' "intangible island of entranced time," to which he and his fellow "nympholepts" are drawn.¹⁰ We will see in the Conclusion how this "European" persona underlies both his monstrous self-conception and the incestuous nature of his love for Lolita. For now, the important point is Humbert's independence from physical locations: his discussions of the Swiss, English, and French are largely cultural, defined by texts rather than descriptions of places. His childhood takes place in a "bright world of illustrated books, clean sand, orange trees, friendly dogs, sea vistas and smiling faces."¹¹ The exception to this lack of physical places in Humbert's childhood is the rocky cove in which he attempts to make love with Annabel: "a desolate stretch of sand . . . in the violet shadow of some red rocks forming a kind of cave."¹² Otherwise, Humbert's Europe seems less a continent than a multilingual, literate population, among whom he and his beloved find no privacy: even in the "desolate . . . cave," they are interrupted by "bearded bathers." Humbert's Europe is made almost entirely of people; when he and Annabel try to find a private "Kingdom by the Sea," they are crowded out.

Humbert's description of Annabel hints at the Euro-American fusion he will seek. Her pseudonym, taken from Poe's "Annabel Lee," suggests that his account is deeply influenced by subsequent American events: Humbert remembers Europe through an American filter. His visual images of Annabel are overlaid with Lo, and his memory of his first love has become an embodiment not just of his own sexual desires but of a hybrid of Europe and America. At the same time, hidden in his description of Europe are hints that such broad-reaching hybridity is the logical outcome of the pan-European fusion Humbert grows up with. Like all "intelligent European preadolescents," Humbert and Annabel share an "interest in the plurality of inhabited worlds"[13]; for Humbert, imaginative exploration is fundamental to European identity.

Like Europe, America appears in *Lolita* as the scene of cultural fusion, although to different effect. The Haze house appears to be a patchwork of American and European, old and new, pretense and honesty: "The front hall was graced with door chimes, a white-eyed wooden thingamabob of commercial Mexican origin, and that banal darling of the arty middle class, van Gogh's 'Arlésienne.' A door ajar to the right afforded a glimpse of a living room, with some more Mexican trash in a corner cabinet and a striped sofa along the wall . . . an old gray tennis ball that lay on an oak chest.[14] Charlotte's Mexican knick-knacks suggest, albeit in a "commercial," bastardized version, a pan-American culture independent of both Humbert's European imports and Lo's crooners and soda fountains.[15] Their placement with the quickly dismissed van Gogh reproduction make Charlotte's house a parody of European-American fusion. Nonetheless, the artifacts hint at the presence of fertile artistic production, as well as its kitschy knock-offs, on both continents. The aged tennis ball and the unopened oak chest further suggest a history and an interiority to which Humbert has no access.

Charlotte's first words—"Is that Monsieur Humbert?"[16]—mark her attempt and her failure to mimic European elegance. The house as a whole, however, turns out to be the scene of a broader fusion beyond the range of Charlotte's ambition. It contains many juxtapositions and hybridities, which disturb Humbert: "I could not be happy in that type of household with bedraggled magazines on every chair and a kind of horrible hybridization between the comedy of so-called 'functional modern furniture' and the tragedy of decrepit rockers and rickety lamp tables with dead lamps. I was led upstairs, and to the left—into 'my' room. I inspected it through the mist of my utter rejection of it; but I did discern above 'my' bed René Prinet's 'Kreutzer Sonata.' And she called that servant maid's room a 'semi-studio'![17] Old and new furniture, Mexican knick-knacks and French painters (one of whom depicts a Russian story of infidelity), comedy and tragedy: the "horrible hybridization" in Charlotte's house is a parodic miniature of the hybridization at work in the novel. Charlotte herself seems to aim, at best, for a low-level version of Fish's "boutique multiculturalism." But the variety and complexity of the accidental juxtapositions in the house also suggest the potential for a more thorough synthesis, in which not merely artifacts but times and ages meet.

Charlotte's house sets the stage for Humbert's vision of European-American synthesis: his first meeting with Lolita on the "piazza." When Humbert first sees Lo sunbathing in the backyard, "a blue sea-wave swelled under my heart and, from a mat in a pool of sun, half-naked, kneeling, turning about on her knees, there was my Riviera love peering at me over dark glasses."[18] Humbert's perceived synthesis here is not in juxtaposed cultural artifacts but in Lolita's body and is achieved not through importation (the origin of the van Gogh and the Mexican objects) but through repetition or rediscovery. Humbert's emphasis on Lolita's body as a duplicate of Annabel's reminds us that true hybridity requires physical fusion rather than mere spatial juxtaposition: Lolita-as-Annabel provides the synthesis of Europe and America that Charlotte's house merely parodies.

The problem with Humbert's vision of synthesis is, as he admits later, its solipsism. His fusion of Annabel and Lolita is just as artificial as the synthesis between Europe and America in Charlotte's house. The superficiality of his interest in Lo is marked by the same thing that made it convincing: its intense physicality. This physicality consists not only of Humbert's sexual response to Lolita but also of his emphasis on imagined or recollected landscape: she is "my Riviera love," and Humbert himself becomes a part of the Riviera when "a blue sea-wave swelled under my heart." His first glimpse of Lolita places her in the European landscape—even though Charlotte's pretentious description of the garden as the "piazza" warns against just that.

As this "European" description suggests, Humbert's gestures toward adapting to America are not really adaptations at all. Even when he claims he is becoming American, he does so in ways the authentically American Lo cannot recognize: "In former times, when I was still your dream male [the reader will notice what pains I took to speak Lo's tongue], you swooned to records of the number one throb-and-sob idol of your coevals [Lo: 'Of my what? Speak English']."[19] While Humbert claims that Lolita is his "Riviera love," however, Lo turns out to be intimately associated not with French but with American landscape, which interferes with Humbert's attempts at mastery. Humbert never recreates the scene at the red rocks.[20] He claims that the initial moment of recognition made recreation unnecessary: seeing Lo on "that shoddy veranda, in a kind of fictitious, dishonest, but eminently satisfactory seaside arrangement (although there was nothing but a second-rate lake in the neighborhood)" has "liberat[ed]" him from his obsession. But real American beaches prove intractable: "foul weather" and "muddy waves" on one and "hurricane winds" on another prevent attempts at sex. On a third, Lolita is "all gooseflesh and grit," like the "gritty and clammy" sand. Instead, Humbert prefers to site Lolita in the metaphorical seascape of his "Kingdom by the Sea," a phrase borrowed from Poe's "Annabel Lee" (the source of Annabel's pseudonym) to indicate the European-American fusion Humbert thinks he has achieved. As Michael Wood notes, Humbert's explanation of his failure to replicate the seaside encounter shows that while "psychiatric explanations of behaviour are often idiotic . . . certain psychological realities are undeniable"[21]; at the same time, Humbert shows the incompatibility of his internal and external realities. The "island of entranced time" inhabited by nymphets is, like Charlotte's house, another parodic version of synthetic art, which competes with its surroundings rather than transforming them.

The whole American landscape turns out to be similarly uncooperative. Unlike the "public parks in Europe" where he could encounter schoolgirls, the American outdoors thwarts him. This, he says, is not the place's fault:

> The disappointment I must now register . . . should in no wise reflect on the lyrical, epic, tragic but never Arcadian American wilds. They are beautiful . . . those wilds, with a quality of wide-eyed, unsung, innocent surrender that my lacquered, toy-bright Swiss villages and exhaustively lauded Alps no longer possess. Innumerable lovers have clipped and kissed on the trim turf of old-world mountainsides, on the innerspring moss, by a handy, hygienic rill, on rustic benches under the initialed oaks, and in so many *cabanes* in so many beech forests. But in the Wilds of America the open-air lover will not find it easy to indulge in the most ancient of all crimes and pastimes. Poisonous plants burn his sweetheart's buttocks, nameless insects sting his; sharp items of the forest floor prick his knees, insects hers; and all around there abides a sustained rustle of potential snakes—*que dis-je*, of semi-extinct dragons! while the crablike seeds of ferocious flowers cling, in a hideous green crust, to gartered black sock and sloppy white sock alike.[22]

Humbert's attempts at outdoor sex convince him that the American landscape is hostile, in contrast to the "Arcadian" habitable and humanized outdoors of Europe. The "innerspring moss" becomes a mattress, and the "initialed oaks" blur distinctions not only between wild and tame but also between landscape and text. The European outdoors with its furniture is

"Arcadian"—not just hospitable but idealized, adapted to human needs. In that setting, the "crime" of outdoor sex is sanitized, and with it crime in general: the lovers who "have clipped and kissed" come from "The Maunder's Praise Of His Strowling Mort" (1673), a love poem spoken in thieves' cant.

The European landscape is a convenient setting for human affairs. The American landscape's "wide-eyed . . . innocent surrender" suggests instead the landscape itself as an object of desire. Humbert finds America's appearance, like Lolita's, alluring, but he discovers in it a resistance so strong as to prevent him from taking advantage of it. "Innocent" America, with its unnamed creatures and "potential snakes," resembles a prelapsarian Eden, in which Humbert does not belong; his invocation of mythology to describe the American landscape undercuts itself.

Humbert tries to disguise America's resistance to his mythologization by describing the landscape in terms taken from the European literary tradition, either as counterexample ("never Arcadian") or parodically, as when he mentions the "Chateaubriandesque trees" shading the motels he and Lolita stay in[23]; as Priscilla Meyer notes, those trees are part of a long tradition of European writers who imagine a romanticized America without much reference to real geography or indigenous culture.[24] The impossibility of Chateaubriand's utopian version of America is suggested by the way Humbert describes what those trees shade: "the stone cottages . . . the brick unit, the adobe unit, the stucco court, on what the Tour Book of the Automobile Association describes as 'shaded' or 'spacious' or 'landscaped' grounds."[25] The European romantic version of America in his self-described "Flaubertian intonation" proves no more accurate than the advertisements in the Tour Book.

Humbert's attempt to deceive himself about America's resistance to his European overlays fails, however, just as he finally admits that his treatment of Lo has been abuse. The two truths appear simultaneously, during his visit to Coalmont, where he finds that the grown-up, pregnant Lolita is "only the faint violet whiff and dead leaf echo of the nymphet I had rolled myself upon with such cries in the past; an echo on the brink of a russet ravine, with a far wood under a white sky, and brown leaves choking the brook, and one last cricket in the crisp weeds."[26] As Humbert's love for Lolita becomes less solipsistic, the imaginary country he builds around her becomes more three dimensional. Lolita is no longer, for Humbert, a creature of the island of the nymphets but an inhabitant of a larger, more complex natural world. The "russet" of the ravine and the "white" of the sky echo the colors Humbert repeatedly ascribes to her body. Ominously, the "dead leaf" and the "brown leaves choking the brook" suggest both her aging and her unexpected but imminent death. In this passage, Lo's body itself has become the landscape of a wild America, subject both to uncontrolled growth and to the decay to which such growth leads.

The country with which Humbert associates Lolita remains imaginary, however. Humbert's description of the adult Lo comes during the portion of the narrative that, if we accept Christina Tekiner's hypothesis, is entirely the work of Humbert's imagination.[27] Humbert claims he last sees Lo on September 23, 1952, but he also tells us that he has written his memoir during his fifty-six days in prison. We know from John Ray's introduction that Humbert dies on November 16. This chronology suggests that Humbert is arrested on September 21, and everything taking place after that date is Humbert's invention. Lolita, then, appears in a doubly invented landscape: it is an imaginary encounter in which Humbert compares her to an imaginary place. The visit to Lolita, like Quilty's murder, is part of Humbert's attempt to atone for his sins, but his technique—the near-hallucinatory superposition of his desires onto reality—remains the same as it has been throughout. In his remorse for solipsizing Lolita, Humbert solipsizes his own life—projecting his desires onto the truth until he cannot tell them apart.

While Humbert retreats into fiction at the end of his memoir, embedded in that fiction is a moment of complete honesty. His final understanding of both Lolita and America comes as he looks at another mountain view, not of the Alps but of an unnamed mining town. Humbert is in a classic European traveler's pose, describing the landscape in what Mary Louise Pratt calls the "Monarch of All I Survey" scene.[28] But unlike accounts by Pratt's travelers, Humbert's description cedes local authority to the dwellers in the landscape and moral authority to his reader. This memory is the climax of the novel, the realization toward which the invented passages in Coalmont and Quilty's mansion are directed:

> One could make out the geometry of the streets between blocks of red and gray roofs, and green puffs of trees, and a serpentine stream, and the rich, ore-like glitter of the city dump, and beyond the town, roads crisscrossing the crazy quilt of dark and pale fields, and behind it all, great timbered mountains. But even brighter than those quietly rejoicing colors . . . was that vapory vibration of accumulated sounds that never ceased for a moment . . . Reader! What I heard was but the melody of children at play, nothing but that . . . an almost articulate spurt of vivid laughter, or the crack of a bat, or the clatter of a toy wagon, but it was all really too far for the eye to distinguish any movement in the lightly etched streets. I stood listening to that musical vibration from my lofty slope, to those flashes of separate cries with a kind of demure murmur for background, and then I

knew that the hopelessly poignant thing was not Lolita's absence from my side, but the absence of her voice from that concord.[29]

Humbert's view of the mining town combines the idealized natural America of Chateaubriand ("great timbered mountains," "a serpentine stream") with the real America ("city dump"). The "geometry of the streets" suggests the order of the human intellect, the "great timbered mountains" the enormity of nature; the two worlds meet in the "crazy quilt" of the farm land. This moment of real memory embedded in the false memories of Quilty's murder stands out both for its admission of guilt and for its recognition of the complex interpenetration of nature and civilization, work and play that characterizes ordinary American life. This vision is neither of the "toy-bright Swiss villages" nor of the impenetrable wilds but of a coexistence between real humans and real mountains. Humbert's view of the town provides the novel's one moment of unity, in which the European's idealized vistas of America can be combined with gritty reality. That combination is necessary for Humbert to realize the falsity of his view of Lolita and thus to convict Quilty (and himself) of wrongdoing: the vision of the mining town provides a synthesis of idealism and realism, "quietly rejoicing" and "almost articulate" in its balance between nature and human life.

Humbert depends on the reader for his very existence: "Imagine me," he begs us, "I shall not exist if you do not imagine me."[30] Sweeney, pointing to Humbert's appeals to the "winged gentlemen of the jury,"[31] argues that "Nabokov makes his readers acknowledge . . . responsibility [for sentencing Humbert], in *Lolita*, by prompting them to find a verdict and pronounce a sentence even though no sentence can be carried out."[32] Similarly, the reader must find the boundary between Humbert's real and imaginary memories and must identify the edges of the novel's constructed and natural worlds. It is up to us to produce the "crazy quilt" map that diagrams the novel's negotiation between the real and the imaginary. The stakes of this responsibility are high: if we draw the line in the wrong place, we become complicit in Humbert's crime of solipsism.

Humbert's relationship with the American landscape has important implications for world-fashioning transnational writers. The physical world does not respond directly to imaginative reinterpretation: insects will sting Humbert however he describes the woods. Nonetheless, some interpretation of the natural world is necessary if the migrant is to put down (psychological) roots in the (physical) soil. While Humbert's vision of Europeanized America fails, his description of the mining town demonstrates that it is possible to understand and interact with new landscapes: the miners, unlike Humbert, are able both literally to enter the soil of the new country and to establish a liminal space between human rationality and the natural world. For world-fashioning to work, then, it must remain within limits of physical plausibility, negotiating the human-nature divide as the "crazy quilt" fields do. Deviating too far from the truth of physical fact will result either in a zone-like disorientation or in self-delusion.

PALE FIRE AND COLLABORATION WITH THE PHYSICAL WORLD

Kinbote, another of Nabokov's mad émigrés, almost succeeds where Humbert fails. Like Humbert, he invents an imaginary world to suit himself. Unlike Humbert, however, Kinbote attempts to work with the natural world, both that of the Europe he has left behind and the America he now inhabits. His success is equivocal, of course, because his lost homeland, Zembla, does not exist even within the fictional world of *Pale Fire*. But Kinbote's Zembla provides him with an identity and a sense of self. And unbeknownst to Kinbote, the overlaps between nonexistent Zembla and the real America suggest the possibility of a productive and sustainable fusion of the two—not only Europe and America but also the imaginary and the real. Through Kinbote's Zemblan fantasies and John Shade's poetic world-fashioning, the text of *Pale Fire* as a whole demonstrates and critiques a range of approaches to how literary texts can mediate between objective physical reality and pure imagination.

Pale Fire consists of a poem, "Pale Fire," by the fictional poet John Shade and a critical apparatus (preface, notes, and index) by Charles Kinbote.[33] Shade's poem tells the story of his daughter Hazel's suicide and his own search for evidence of life after death. Kinbote's notes, on the other hand, chronicle the life of the exiled King Charles the Beloved of Zembla. Toward the end of the book, Kinbote reveals what readers may have already guessed: that he himself is the exiled king. Embedded in the text, however, are clues that poor Kinbote is really a mad Russian named Botkin. Shade's death at the end of the novel, then, has two explanations: according to Kinbote, he has been shot by a Zemblan assassin named Gradus, who was really gunning for Charles the Beloved; according to everyone else, Shade is shot by a man named Jack Grey, who has mistaken Shade for the judge who sentenced him to prison.[34] But as Wood says, in *Pale Fire* "the real is not an explanation, it is a (disputed) territory," and Zembla's reality in the text waxes and wanes depending on how closely we examine the evidence.[35]

Zembla is a bravura piece of creative and scholarly hybridity. The country's language fuses English, Danish, Swedish, Russian, German, and

Latin.³⁶ Kinbote gives Zembla a history, myths based on the Norse *Eddas*, folklore, and a theatrical tradition. Zembla's mixture of northern European languages and cultures is quite unlike the "horrible hybridization" of the Haze household in its literacy and its conscious construction of a world. The country can also adapt cultural imports: Zembla has access to Shakespeare's plays in (bad) translation; its king admires the American educational system; its cosmopolitan aristocracy summers in the south of France. Zembla's intradiagetic nonexistence, in contrast with the "real" existence of the fictional town of New Wye in the state of Appalachia, is established only by the reactions of secondary characters and by Kinbote's attempts connect Zembla to his American surroundings.

Kinbote's difficulty in connecting Zembla to America is not that he is unwilling to adapt to a foreign culture but that he cannot turn illusion into truth. His dependence on Shade reveals his odd double bind. To convince anyone of the country's existence, Kinbote must first admit that Zembla is fictional, because only through the medium of fiction will the nonexistent country gain credence from nondelusional readers. Much as Humbert asks his readers to pass judgment on his actions, implicating us in his fantasy America, Kinbote wants Shade to chronicle his journey from Zembla in order to make it "true." When Shade asks how Kinbote knows that "all this intimate stuff about your rather appalling king is true," Kinbote replies that its truth lies in Shade's hands:

> "My dear John," I replied gently and urgently, "do not worry about trifles. Once transmuted by you into poetry, the stuff *will* be true, and the people *will* come alive. A poet's purified truth can cause no pain, no offense. True art is above false honor."
>
> "Sure, sure," said Shade. "One can harness words like performing fleas and make them drive other fleas. Oh, sure."³⁷

Kinbote tacitly admits that Zembla is his construct: the people have yet to "come alive" and poetry is needed to make the "stuff" true.

Shade's answer is even more revealing than Kinbote's admission: it shows that Shade understands poetry to have a very limited power to convince or compel its readers. This limitation is implied in his defense of Kinbote to Mrs. H. (overheard though unacknowledged by Kinbote himself):

> "That is the wrong word," he said. "One should not apply it to a person who deliberately peels off a drab and unhappy past and replaces it with a brilliant invention. That's merely turning a new leaf with the left hand."
>
> I patted my friend on the head and bowed slightly to Eberthella H. The poet looked at me with glazed eyes. She said:

"You must help us, Mr. Kinbote: I maintain that what's his name, old—the old man, you know, at the Exton railway station, who thought he was God and began redirecting the trains, was technically a loony, but John calls him a fellow poet."[38]

While Shade defends Kinbote's madness as "brilliant invention," he also implies that such inventions are ineffective: his inability to rescue himself when he discovers he has been overheard, and Mrs. H.'s replacement of Kinbote with old Mr. What's-his-name, both suggest that poetic invention lacks real-world consequences. (The "loony" cannot have had much success directing trains.) Kinbote, on the other hand, remains hopeful on the subject. When he steals the manuscript of "Pale Fire" after Shade's death, he exults, "I was holding all Zembla pressed to my heart"[39]—not realizing that Shade has not taken Zembla for his subject. Kinbote's madness, then, includes a form of optimism: he insists that poetry can replace, recreate, and validate one's own experience and, more unusually, stand in for a three-dimensional physical space.

What exactly such a replacement would mean is a difficult question. Clearly Kinbote cannot literally inhabit a poem any more than Humbert can inhabit the kingdom of Poe's "Annabel Lee." The problem of how and for what purposes poetry (or text) and physical places can be treated as interchangeable is central to *Pale Fire*. It is also the subject of some of the book's most systematic internal misreadings, including Shade's discovery of "Life Everlasting—based on a misprint!"[40]

The novel's treatment of mountains provides an important model of the dialogue Nabokov establishes between imaginative text and physical geography. The two appear at first quite separate. When Kinbote refers to Zembla's central mountain range, his descriptions smack of the guide or the textbook—nonfictional texts intended to inform readers about objective truths:

> The two coasts are connected by two asphalted highways: the older one shirks difficulties by running first along the eastern slopes northward to Odevalla, Yeslove and Embla, and only then turning west at the northmost point of the peninsula; the newer one, an elaborate, twisting, marvelously graded road, traverses the range westward from just north of Onhava to Bregberg, and is termed in tourist booklets a "scenic drive." Several trails cross the mountains at various points and lead to passes none of which exceeds an altitude of five thousand feet; a few peaks rise some two thousand feet higher and retain their snow in midsummer; and from one of them, the highest and hardest, Mt. Glitterntin, one can distinguish on clear days, far out to the east, beyond the Gulf of Surprise, a dim iridescence which some say is Russia.[41]

The asphalt, the praise of the grading of the road, the "scenic drive," and the measurements of altitude emphasize the physical solidity of the place, and even the evocative "dim iridescence" of Russia is a glimpse of a verifiably existing physical location. Despite the king's "shiver of *alfear*" as he crosses them,[42] the Zemblan mountains have a strong physical presence in the book: their "dim valleys" require "intercalcated cotton-wool bits of cloud that seemed placed between the receding sets of ridges to prevent their flanks from scraping against one another"; Mt. Glitterntin has "a serrated edge of bright foil"; and "granite and gravity" must be "overcome" to ascend the pass.[43] On reading Shade's poem, Kinbote laments their absence from it more than his own: "Where were the battlements of my sunset castle? Where was Zembla the Fair? Where her spine of mountains?"[44]

Kinbote's insertion of the mountains into his notes to "Pale Fire" is based on a flimsy pretext. The line that prompts the geography lesson above is Shade's phrase "one foot on the mountaintop," a description of Shade's sensation of disintegration during a childhood fainting fit. While both the king's escape from Zembla and Shade's fit are explained in terms of geography, they are opposite in import: Kinbote describes a geographical displacement using a few supernatural terms, whereas Shade experiences spiritual displacement in geographical terms. While Kinbote makes his Zemblan landscape implausible by infusing it with fantastic experiences, Shade makes his spiritual experience oddly earthly by describing it as part of a map of Europe.

Shade's use of mountains to describe a spiritual experience does not mean that he treats the spirit as physical. Where Kinbote's mountains are literal chunks of rock, Shade's mountains are much more nebulous. While he says, "I love great mountains,"[45] the mountains in Shade's poems tend to be distant, metaphorical constructs, unlike the "granite and gravity" the king overcomes. Shade's mountains not only render spiritual experience earthly, they also render physical reality insubstantial. In Shade's poem "Mountain View," the mountain's most important feature is the opportunity it gives a viewer to perceive the intervening haze:

> Between the mountain and the eye
> The spirit of the distance draws
> A veil of blue amorous gauze,
> The very texture of the sky.
> A breeze reaches the pines, and I
> Join in the general applause.

* * *

> But we all know it cannot last,
> The mountain is too weak to wait—
> Even if reproduced and glassed
> In me as in a paperweight.⁴⁶

Far from being a permanent object, the mountain is "too weak to wait"— for the arrival of the breeze or to appreciate distance and sky. The permanence in the poem is all the speaker's, and the poem itself, reproducing the mountain as the paperweight or the memory does, becomes the long-lasting object. The mountain is no more real than the metaphorical paperweight, and Shade's interest in it is only as a pretext for the discussion of the "veil" that lies between them.

In "Pale Fire," Shade suggests that real mountains actually interfere with readers' understanding of poetic mountains. Normally charitable to the people he writes about, Shade is merciless to Mrs. Z, who tries to compliment him on one of his poems:

> I loved your poem in the *Blue Review*.
> That one about *Mon Blon*. I have a niece
> Who's climbed the Matterhorn. The other piece
> I could not understand. I mean the sense.
> Because, of course, the sound—But I'm so dense!⁴⁷

Mrs. Z's low level of literary sophistication is signaled not only by her attempt to pronounce "Mont Blanc" but also by her suggestion that climbing the Matterhorn is relevant to reading about it. Shade's poem, which Kinbote does not reproduce, is evidently sufficiently unlike the real mountain that the niece's trek is irrelevant.

Both "Mountain View," with its "veil" between the speaker and the mountain, and the untitled poem on "*Mon Blon*" contain echoes of Percy Bysshe Shelley (a poet Shade, who admires Pope, might not list as an influence). The allusion to Shelley's "Mont Blanc" emphasizes the poet's physical distance from his subject matter and suggests what insight that distance might grant. Shelley's poem opens in the "everlasting universe of things" that "flows through the mind," allowing entrance to "gleams of a remoter world."⁴⁸ The mountain in Shelley's poem is part of the "universe of things," the realm of real objects, but communion with the mountain brings both the speaker's thoughts and the Ravine of Arve itself together "In the still cave of the witch Poesy." The "cave of Poesy" is an intermediate realm, neither the "universe of things" nor the "remoter world" glimpsed in dreams and beyond death. In the vision Poesy gives Shelley, Mont Blanc "pierc[es] the infinite sky," becoming a physical link between the realm of "things" and the realm of the infinite, and the surrounding Alps appear "unearthly." Despite the distance between nature and the observer, the mountains "Teach the adverting mind": Mont Blanc, for Shelley, mediates between the human mind and the infinite. In exchange, Shelley provides the mountain with meaning:

> And what were thou, and earth, and stars, and sea,
> If to the human mind's imaginings
> Silence and solitude were vacancy?

The distance between the observer and the mountain in Shelley's "Mont Blanc" is essential for the mystical union, and the "cave of the witch Poesy" must remain an equivocally physical place for the mountain and the observer to meet there.

Like Shelley, Shade sees poetry as a means of making distant objects accessible to the poet. But comparison with Shelley's "Mont Blanc" also indicates a lack of ambition in Shade's "Mountain View": where for Shelley, the mountain must remain "infinite" in order to do its work, Shade's mountain can be miniaturized. Distance between viewer and viewed becomes a trick of the eye, not a space to be bridged. In contrast to Shelley, who makes Poesy a semiphysical intermediate realm between real and ideal, Shade treats poetry as a means of encapsulation or miniaturization. No one can live inside, or on, it. Kinbote, then, has come to the wrong shop for a poetic corporealization of his imaginary country: rather than making imaginary worlds real, Shade prefers to render the real world imaginary. Shade's versions render the sublime mundane, reducing the mountain to the artificial view in a paperweight. Kinbote wants Shade's help because he wants access to the borderline reality of Shelley's "cave of the witch Poesy"—a literary space that is both physical and metaphorical. Shelley, who writes in the "Defence of Poetry" that "poets are the unacknowledged legislators of the world," would have made a more cooperative accomplice than Shade.[49]

Lacking help from Shade's verse, Kinbote tries another borderline reality, one founded on Renaissance travelers' tales. Zembla contains two Baron Mandevils: Kinbote's page Baron Radomir Mandevil, and Radomir's cousin, the extremist Baron Mirador Mandevil, "who had lost a leg in trying to make anti-matter."[50] There is also a Mandevil forest. The name Mandevil suggests a supernatural fusion between man and devil (with the divine conspicuously absent), but it also, as Monica Manolescu points out, invokes the fourteenth-century travel narrative of Sir John Mandeville, "a remarkable case of literary forgery" that was "paradoxically . . . more successful in popularizing the geographical and encyclopedic knowledge of medieval explorers than all his sources put together."[51] Mandeville's presence in *Pale Fire* reflects Kinbote's pastiche of northern European cultures and traditions (like Mandeville, Kinbote has assembled his components far and wide) and acknowledges Zembla's implausibility (like Kinbote, Mandeville "visits" a series of fantastic destinations). It is also a hint at Kinbote's ambition: Mandeville's *Travels* were the most popular travel literature of their day, and despite their implausibility (they contain accounts of lands inhabited by monsters like cyclopes and "folk that be both man and woman")[52] were taken seriously by medieval and early Renaissance readers.

Shelley's cave, like Plato's, makes no claims to literal existence: it is a metaphorical location dramatizing a metaphysical interaction. Mandeville, on the other hand, makes direct truth claims. Kinbote's inclusion of Mandeville in the country he wishes to see immortalized in poetry suggests either that he cannot distinguish between these metaphorical and physical spaces or, more interestingly, that he is ambivalent about the kind of reality he wants for Zembla. If Mandeville is Kinbote's fallback position after his failed attempt at Shelleyan metaphysical reality, then Kinbote may be a better reader than his critics think: he is aware that Zembla is a forgery and is seeking a more legitimate way to bring his imagined country into existence. Just as Humbert lets his awareness of his guilt slip into the text through the details he includes (Lo cries "every night, every night"[53]), Kinbote reveals his inventions through his sources.

While Zembla remains imaginary, failing to enlist readers either into Shelleyan metaphysics or Mandevillian plausibility, America comes to resemble Shelley's Mont Blanc, bridging apparently incompatible worlds. Kinbote refuses to see even superficial resemblances to Europe in the American natural world, resenting the American robin as a "suburban impostor."[54] But despite Kinbote's skepticism, Appalachia and New Wye are the scene of biological, if not cultural, fusion, as Shade points out:

> my friend had a rather coquettish way of pointing out with the tip of his cane various curious natural objects. He never tired of illustrating by means of these examples the extraordinary blend of Canadian Zone and Austral Zone that "obtained," as he put it, in that particular spot of Appalachia where at our altitude of about 1,500 feet northern species of birds, insects and plants commingled with southern representatives . . . Shade did not seem to realize that a humble admirer who has cornered at last and has at last to himself the inaccessible man of genius, is considerably more interested in discussing with him literature and life than in being told that the "diana" (presumably a flower) occurs in New Wye together with the "atlantis" (presumably another flower), and things of that sort.[55]

As in Shelley's poem, mountains facilitate the communication between realms: the altitude of the lower slopes of the Appalachian mountains brings the north and the south into the same place. The landscape provides exactly the fusion Kinbote is looking for (Zembla is a "distant northern land"[56])—but Kinbote misses it, just as he does not recognize that the "flowers" are butterflies. Kinbote, for all his attention to detail in Zembla, turns out to be a poor observer of the natural world: he sees the differences between places all too clearly, but is blind to their similarities—a mirror image of his wildly inventive notes to "Pale Fire," where he manufactures similarities between his own story and Shade's.

The American landscape provides the grounds for many hybridizations within *Pale Fire*. These hybridizations are not only between north and south but between art and nature, real and ideal, even Kinbote's Zemblan hallucinations and immediate physical reality. The most important of these is the transposition of Kinbote's crown jewels into the landscape. The jewels, which Kinbote says he hid in Zembla, are rescued by the American natural world: "my gemmed scepter, ruby necklace, and diamond-studded crown [hidden] in—no matter, where"[57] are transformed into the "empty emerald case" of a shed cicada carapace in Shade's poem.[58] The translation of the jewels from their fastness in Kobaltana[59] into the metaphorical jewels of nature shows that, as Meyer argues, "the 'nationalized' jewels found in the descriptions of nature in John Shade's poem do grow on trees"; in Shade's depiction of the natural world the jewels are "accessible to us all."[60] Unlike the mountain Shade makes into a paperweight, the jewels gain in their transformation: their American versions are alive and self-renewing. The cicada that abandons the "emerald case" on the day of Hazel's suicide sings again on Shade's sixty-first birthday.

America not only offers a way to import Kinbote's private, aristocratic imaginings into a democratically accessible landscape, it also provides a literal space for literary realms. America bridges the real and the textual in the alley of Shakespeare's trees on the Wordsmith campus:

> that admirable colonnade of trees which visitors from England have photographed from end to end. I can enumerate here only a few kinds of those trees: Jove's stout oak and two others: the thunder-cloven from Britain, the knotty-entrailed from a Mediterranean island; a weather-fending line (now lime), a phoenix (now date palm), a pine and a cedar (*Cedrus*), all insular; a Venetian sycamore tree (*Acer*); two willows, the green, likewise from Venice, the hoar-leaved from Denmark; a midsummer elm, its barky fingers enringed with ivy; a midsummer mulberry, its shade inviting to tarry; and a clown's sad cypress from Illyria.[61]

The Shakespeare alley mediates between continents and realities. To begin with, many of the trees are not native to Appalachia. Some are not even native to the settings in which Shakespeare imagines them and have thus been doubly imported, first into the fictional country of the play and then into the "real" country of Appalachia. More importantly, the trees in Wordsmith's colonnade have been translated from the literary to the physical. Kinbote's description emphasizes the geographical aspect of importation; the trees are "from Britain" or "a Mediterranean island" rather than from *King Lear* or *The Tempest*. By eliding fictional sources in favor of geographical origins, Kinbote suggests that Shakespeare's settings have achieved the kind of extratextual reality that Kinbote wants for his own creation. But the trees' attraction comes from their explicitly textual origins: they are both literally rooted in the American soil and epistemologically rooted in Shakespeare.

The source text renders the interaction between Europe and America more complex, however. Most of the trees Kinbote remembers are from *The Tempest*. While technically set in the Mediterranean, *The Tempest* is based on the account the 1609 shipwreck of the *Sea Venture* in Bermuda. European self-conceptions and conceptions of America meet in the real trees of the Shakespeare alley. Even though the island of *The Tempest* does not exist, it has enough physical and historical reality to cause a palm tree—foreign to both England and Appalachia—to be planted on the Wordsmith campus.

In fact, like the trees, Kinbote himself is made real by his importation into America. Kinbote's first-person narrative fuses with his narrative of Charles the Beloved's escape at the moment that the king first touches American soil, arriving by parachute in a field. While the king is described in third person as he wrestles free of his parachute, Kinbote switches pronouns in midparagraph as soon as the king has disentangled himself: "I relaxed on a shooting stick."[62] Kinbote *qua* Kinbote only exists on the continent of America itself, brought into being by exile; like Shakespeare's trees, America is where he leaves the textual for the physical realm.

While Nabokov's American landscape is incompatible with Humbert's fantasies, then, it is not hostile to all importations. America can welcome foreign and imaginary elements, whether the Shakespearean trees or the fusion of the Canadian and Austral zones. The difficulty for would-be transnationals comes in how those adaptations are to occur. Simple transposition of Europe to America or fantastic to real is impossible, resulting in the "impostor" American robin or in Kinbote's misannotation of Shade's text. The transnational must find a compromise: either a metaphysical meeting ground, like Shelley's cave, or a fusion he cannot control, like the landscape of Appalachia.

Kinbote dislikes the available forms of synthesis between geographical and metaphysical zones—Appalachian wildlife, the Shakespeare alley—because they are insufficiently personal. Kinbote's real tragedy is not his inability to recreate Zembla but his inability to find love: he has two ping-pong tables in his basement, but no one will play with him twice. He wants a poetic medium for his imaginary country because he needs companionship. Shade's poem would have provided not just verification of Zembla's existence but an act of friendship by Shade himself; it would invite readers both to accept Zembla's "reality" (treating the poem as Renaissance readers treated Mandeville's *Travels*) and to become friendly with the text's authors. James F. English notes that Nabokov's humor "turns on the social categories of in-group and out-group; but its distinctive movement is an attempted overturning of these categories, a reordering of the participants" in order to "transcend . . . the contingent social realities on which lines of division and exclusion are based and experience . . . perfectly open communication, tolerant and noncoercive social practice."[63] Kinbote's artistic project—or the project he designs for Shade—is to turn his American readers into Zemblan insiders, making exile into a community.

By the end of the novel, Kinbote has confronted and been confounded by the primary obstacles faced by world-fashioning transnational novelists. He makes up Zembla, which he prefers to his country of origin (Russia) and his country of residence (America). He tries to make Zembla more compelling by asking Shade to join him in its creation, not only because Shade's poetry will make the place more "real," but also because Shade himself is one of Kinbote's ideal inhabitants for Zembla. Shade's refusal of Kinbote's invitation—his refusal to write the poem Kinbote requests—places Kinbote's country in the realm of madness rather than that of poetry: if Kinbote is Zembla's only inhabitant, he is not a "fellow poet" but a "loony."

Nonetheless, Kinbote ends his commentary by suggesting how he might find the happiness he seeks. His last vision of an alternate future constitutes the final shift in the novel's epistemological ground. While within the world of the book, Kinbote commits suicide,[64] some aspect of Kinbote and of Zembla itself migrates into the reality not only of Nabokov but also of the reader—the "audience" Kinbote imagines himself and his author to lack:

"And you, what will *you* be doing with yourself, poor King, poor Kinbote?" a gentle young voice may inquire.

God will help me, I trust, to rid myself of any desire to follow the example of two other characters in this work. I shall continue to exist. I may assume other disguises, other forms, but I shall try to exist. I may turn up yet, on another campus, as an old, happy, healthy, heterosexual Russian, a writer in exile, sans fame, sans future, sans audience, sans anything but his art.[65]

Kinbote hopes to undergo the transformation he has not achieved for Zembla: to become assimilated into another person—who appears to be Nabokov himself. As Wood points out, Kinbote is unique here: "When previous characters in Nabokov discover they are characters in a novel, they think of themselves as authored, their lives scripted, written from elsewhere. Kinbote sees himself not only as a character in a novel but as the potential author of other works of fiction."[66] The list of things he will lack in his exile reveals exactly what this potential authorship means: the phrasing is borrowed from the exiled Jaques' description of old men in Shakespeare's *As You Like It*: "Sans teeth, sans eyes, sans taste, sans everything."[67] Kinbote's final borrowing from Shakespeare reframes the textual transformation he seeks. Kinbote hopes to be transformed as the trees are, finding a new body and identity outside the text. *Pale Fire*'s final suggested fusion is its most daring and its most possible: the text achieves solid, literal reality by inhabiting its author. At the same time, Kinbote's description of this movement from the imaginary to the real is also a description of loss: the "writer in exile," without a readership, is as deprived as Jaques's old man, who has lost his physical senses. The audience, in this rewriting, embodies the text, providing it with teeth, eyes, and taste. While Kinbote imagines himself ceasing to be fictional, he also describes Nabokov as abandoning the world of the senses in favor of the world of art.

Nabokov's cameo at the end of *Pale Fire* seems to tell us that the final fusion of the book takes place between a supposedly isolated, and certainly exiled, Nabokov and Nabokov's own creation. At the same time, however, Nabokov does not lack an audience: *Pale Fire*, coming after the scandalous *Lolita*, can expect readers. Instead, then, Kinbote's last fusion is with a fictional rather than a realistic version of Nabokov. The real Nabokov stands outside the text, along with the reader. *Pale Fire* teaches readers to take part both in Kinbote's search for an embodiment of Zembla and in Nabokov's superior fusion of Russia and America: Nabokov, unlike Botkin, makes up satisfying imaginary countries (New Wye, Zembla, and a possible world that contains both) without losing his mind.

By asking readers to join him in constructing his own persona, Nabokov shares with us his privileged position as the maker of the text.

Nabokov's enlistment of his readers has generated an avid fan base. Readers can become so invested in the text that they argue for their own position as the "right" reader: Russian speakers, for example, point out puns inaccessible to non-Russophones and argue that without these references Nabokov's texts become illegible. At the same time, such readers miss obscure references in English and French. French, English, American, and Russian readers of Nabokov's work each have privileged information, and each gains ownership over the text based on and determined by that point of entry. Nabokov makes Kinbotes of us all. The peculiarity of his texts is not simply their range of linguistic, literary, and scientific reference but their ability to transform readers into a community of rival partisans.

Despite his madness, then, Kinbote provides a model for transnational authors not only in his lyrical, preposterous evocations of Zembla but also in the fluid approach he teaches us to authorial power and textual reality. Kinbote's devices—placing his imaginary worlds in the realm of poetic truth, basing more literal truth claims in fantastic but nonfictional texts like early travel narratives, relocating the fictional setting into the person of the author and the readers—are deployed again by Nabokov in *Ada*, and by Rushdie in *Midnight's Children* and *The Ground Beneath Her Feet*. Transnational fiction as a whole performs the same series of approaches to world-fashioning, treating the fictional world alternately as reportage, romantic utopia, and intermediate space where epistemological, cultural, and textual opposites can meet.

GEOGRAPHY AND HISTORY IN ADA

Lolita and *Pale Fire*'s depictions of America center on the country's physical landscape—the mountains and beaches that resist or cooperate with the narrators' interpretations and inventions. In *Ada*, America's defining features lie in the more malleable realm of history. While the young Ada's interest in botany provides the pretext for descriptions of the natural world, in those scenes the narrative microscope is focused on individual orchids or caterpillars. The woods around Ardis in Van's descriptions shift and blur in the service of his memory and his narrative; unlike Humbert and Kinbote, Van does not even accidentally give us access to the physical truth of his surroundings. The text of *Ada*, unlike that of *Pale Fire*, does not contain answers to the physical contradictions in the novel. When, for example, Van's mode of transportation mysteriously changes from car to carriage to horse, we have no way to know what he was "really" riding when he left Ardis in 1884. Nabokov's rendering of *Ada* as a narrative without a physical "right" answer is particularly interesting because the text is supposedly the product of multiple points of view: it has been composed by Van, transcribed by his secretary Violet, edited by Ada, and prepared for publication by Ronald Oranger. But *Ada* remains Van's memoir, and the truth it reports is the "truth" of his memory rather than that of a real physical world. The truths that creep into the narrative despite Van's intentions are not physical but social and historical, revealing both Van's misdeeds and the structure of the world he lives in. Van's slips and Ada's interruptions construct Antiterra's alternate history rather than its physical attributes.

Ada is set in an alternate-historical America constructed not through literal description or the metaphysical realm of poetry but through a return to the contested truth claims of Renaissance travelers' tales. *Ada* expands *Pale Fire*'s use of Mandeville's travels through allusions to the sixteenth-century narrative of the Brothers Zeno. In the process, the novel carves out an intermediate space between fiction and truth in which literary and historical texts can shape and inform each other.

Antiterra's backstory becomes one of the puzzles the reader must work out, and its coherence helps determine the success or failure of Van's text: he intends *Ada* to be not only a memoir but an alternate afterlife, and Van and Ada are to die "*into* the finished book." [68] Van wants to manufacture a world so compelling as to provide a space between this life and the next, one far more accessible than Shelley's cave. Van's goal is a literal variation on Humbert's hope in the closing lines of Lolita: "I am thinking of aurochs and angels, the secret of durable pigments, prophetic sonnets, the refuge of art. And this is the only immortality you and I may share, my Lolita."[69] Humbert's treatment of art as a form of immortality is ultimately metaphorical—"the only immortality you and I may share" suggests the existence of other immortalities as well, making the text a surrogate for the Lolita-less afterlife he expects to enter. Van, on the other hand, hopes to make text and afterlife synonymous.

Nabokov undermines Van's attempt at world-fashioning through the text's many odd moments of extranarrative intrusion, which call the reader's attention to the circumstances of Van's composition. In these moments Nabokov points at the fundamental problem with Van's approach to fictional world-building: like Kinbote's, Van's attempt at immortality is too local, too private. Effective world-construction demands not only commitment from the author but also participation by the audience. If Van's memoir is to have only two readers, it will go unread after those readers die. While Van's intentions for *Ada* are local, however, Nabokov's intentions for the text are far more wide ranging: the "real" payoffs of *Ada* are the reclamation of Nabokov's lost past and an invitation to readers to join him in a world that is both personally responsive and broadly welcoming. *Ada* is "a family chronicle" not only because it centers on the Veens but also because it makes possible the creation of a new family of shared experience consisting of Nabokov and his readers. *Ada* renders the private world Nabokov chronicles in *Speak, Memory* publicly accessible.

This redrawing of the boundaries of the family to include Nabokov's fractious, multilingual readership necessitates a new understanding of nations and historical origins. The rest of this chapter shows how *Ada* treats historical accounts of community and the nation as constructed and thus malleable. The travel narratives in *Ada* show how collectively determined truths can shape our reactions to and understandings of the physical world. While physical geography is objectively real (a mountain is either there or not), history is continually subject to reinterpretation and reorganization. Historical truth provides a nonfictional middle ground between the objective and the abstract: unlike Shelley's cave of Poesy, which foregrounds its own allegorical nature, historical narratives span interpretation and fact. In *Ada*, reinterpretatations of history redraw the political map of North America in favor of a pluralist, multilingual "paradise"—albeit one ultimately exposed as false.

Ada, the story of the love affair between Van and his sister Ada, takes place on a world called Antiterra. Antiterra and our world (almost certainly the mysterious "Terra" that appears throughout the text) have similar but not identical histories. The physical geography—the locations of oceans and mountains—on the two planets is alike, but the political geography varies, Van explains: "Ved' ('it is, isn't it') sidesplitting to imagine that 'Russia,' instead of being a quaint synonym of Estoty, the American province extending from the Arctic no-longer-vicious Circle to the United States proper, was on Terra the name of a country, transferred as if by some sleight of *land* across the ha-ha of a doubled ocean to the opposite hemisphere where it sprawled over all of today's Tartary, from Kurland to the Kuriles!"[70] In Antiterra, the words "America" and "Russia" are synonymous, indicating the area we know as Canada. (That name also exists on Antiterra, modified to "Canady," as Brian Boyd points out, "to avoid a superfluous 'ada'").[71] "Tartary," which spans northern Eurasia, replaces our twentieth-century Soviet Union in both its location and its "Golden Veil,"[72] a romanticized Iron Curtain.

"Russia" and "Tartary" embody two versions of our world's Russia. The "Russia" synonymous with "Estoty" belongs to "Russian peasants and poets [who were] transported to Estotiland, and the Barren Grounds, ages ago,"[73] who occupy places like "Gamlet, a half-Russian hamlet."[74] This prerevolutionary Russia contains the peasant and aristocratic cultures of Nabokov's youth. Gamlet suggests contact between English- and Russian speakers in Estoty not only geographically but also literarily, in the Russianized Shakespearean name. "Tartary," on the other hand, is a dictatorship whose name implies primitive barbarism, the Russia of both postrevolutionary communism and the Golden Horde. As Van's dismissive "sidesplitting" suggests, something has been split in half.

The imaginary world of *Ada*, then, contains both a new fusion and a new division: the best of America and Russia combined in Amerussia, the worst of Russia left behind in Tartary. Splitting our world's Russia in two means there is no question of exile in the novel—or rather, that Van's narrative of exile and reclamation is the quest for a lost childhood rather than a lost homeland. It is perhaps because of this absence that critics like Robert Alter or Douglas Fowler take the book to be romantic or celebratory.[75] Van's idyllic account of his childhood appears also to be an account of Nabokov's ideal, multicultural world, a world that is, as Fowler puts it, "simply the happily ever-after portion of Nabokov's lifelong attempt to create out of his art a fairy-tale, and the only villain that survives is time itself."[76]

Even after Van explains it, however, the history of Antiterra's "Russia" remains puzzling. The explanation that "Russia" has always been a synonym of "Estoty" includes an admission that the Russians were "transported" to America from somewhere else "ages ago"; their origin is never specified. Moreover, the word "ved'" in Van's description of Terran geography suggests that Antiterran hybridity is incomplete: Van has to translate the Russian words he uses for his readers. Departing Ardis in 1888, Van mourns his estrangement from Ada in untranslated English-French puns followed by a translated Russian dialogue with his chauffeur:

> *N'est vert, n'est vert, n'est vert. L'arbre aux quarante écus d'or*, at least in the fall. Never, never shall I hear again her "botanical" voice fall at *biloba*, "sorry, my Latin is showing." *Ginkgo*, gingko, ink, inkog. Known also as Salisbury's adiantofolia, Ada's infolio, poor *Salisburia*: sunk; poor Stream of Consciousness, *marée noire* by now. Who wants Ardis Hall!
>
> "*Barin, a barin,*" said Trofim, turning his blond-bearded face to his passenger.
>
> "*Da?*"
>
> "*Dazhe skvoz' kozhaniy fartuk ne stal-bï ya trogat' etu frantsuzskuyu devku.*"
>
> *Bárin*: master. *Dázhe skvoz' kózhaniy fártuk*: even through a leathern apron. *Ne stal-bï ya trógat'*: I would not think of touching. *Étu*: this (that). *Frantsúzskuyu*: French (adj., accus.). *Dévku*: wench. *Úzhas, otcháyanie*: horror, despair. *Zhálost'*: pity. *Kóncheno, zagázheno, rastérzano*: finished, fouled, torn to shreds.[77]

Van does not tell us that "*n'est vert*" (pronounced almost like "never") means "is not green," that "*l'arbre aux quarante écus d'or*," "the forty-gold-pieces tree," is a French name for the gingko, or that "biloba" means "two-lobed." The transliterated Russian, on the other hand, merits grammatical explanation designating *Frantsuzskuyu* as an adjective in the accusative case and marking, in the explanation, the stresses on polysyllabic words—the kind of trot found in a language textbook. French and Russian in Estoty are separated not only by Trofim's leathern apron but also by linguistic accessibility; while Van takes our knowledge of French for granted, Russian, which interrupts Van's thoughts, requires formal explanation. This pattern continues throughout the text, as both Van himself and the notes provided by "Vivian Darkbloom" (whose location in Van's world or ours is never clear) offer basic explanations of the Russian, while most of the French puns and subtexts are unglossed. Far from teaching us to see the separation between Anglo America and Russia as "ludicrous,"[78] the novel reframes the distinction between them as linguistic rather than geographical. Instead of displaying the fusion of America and Russia as natural, Van's insistence that these two distinct linguistic cultures belong together raises the question of how his bilobed Amerussia fits together at all.

A clue to the origins of Estoty comes at the end of the book, in Demon's description of Ada's husband, Andrey Vinelander, who is descended from "one of those great Varangians who conquered the Copper Mongols or Red Tartars—or whoever they were—who had conquered some earlier Bronze riders—before *we* introduced our Russian roulette and Irish loo at a lucky moment in the history of Western casinos."[79] Demon's account of Andrey's ancestry tells us that the original inhabitants of North America were displaced not by the British and French, but by the Varangians—the Vikings. Vinelander's name indicates the point of contact between America and Europe: Estotiland goes back to the Vinland settlement, the Viking colony founded about the year 1000 somewhere in North America.[80] In Van's world, apparently, the settlement survived, and the New World was colonized by Europe five hundred years earlier than in our world, followed by a pan-European colonization resulting in Demon's Russian-Irish-American "we." This earlier colonization can account for some major differences between the Americas on Antiterra and Earth: the Native Americans, whose name Demon cannot remember, were killed or driven out even earlier and more thoroughly than in our world, and Russians crossed the "ha-ha" of the Arctic Ocean sooner and in larger numbers to take their place.

The Viking settlement of Estoty also appears in the blurb at the end of the novel: "Ardis Hall—the Ardors and Arbors of Ardis—this is the leitmotiv rippling through *Ada*, an ample and delightful chronicle, whose principal part is staged in a dream-bright America—for are not our childhood memories comparable to Vineland-borne caravelles, indolently encircled by the white birds of dreams?"[81] The blurb's anachronistic picture of "caravelles" (large ships used in the sixteenth century) arriving at Vineland (which in our world was settled and abandoned in longships in the tenth and eleventh centuries) offers a romantic but transparently false history. But the blurb's peculiarity does not lie in its nautical inaccuracy. America is both the setting of the book and the destination of "our childhood memories," which resemble not America but the ships that take us there. America, here, ceases to be the setting of the narrative and becomes instead its goal: memory, like a ship, becomes a mobile, physical space moving between present and past. America is both the pretext of the narrative and the impetus that causes the voyage. It is not, however, the voyage's true object because for Van, as we shall see in the next chapter, memory (rather than accuracy) becomes an end in itself.

Nabokov designs Van's memoir not around reconstructing Van's childhood but around the process of memoir writing. Nabokov's real subject in *Ada* is not Van's memories but the means by which memories can be used to make a free-standing textual world. The worlds of memory occupy a position between literal and imaginative truth: like travel narratives, they claim to be based on objective facts, and, like Shelley's cave, they place narrator and reader at a distance from their subject.

* * *

A clue to the relationship between memoir and travel writing, and thus to the nature of Van's world-fashioning, is embedded in the name Estoty. Boyd traces "Estoty" to two sources. In *Paradise Lost*, "cold Estotiland" marks one extreme of terrestrial weather faced by Adam and Eve after their expulsion from Eden. This reference links Estoty, Van's home, with exile in the hostile postlapsarian world. As Boyd notes, however, Estotiland first appears in the account of the Venetian Zeno brothers, published in 1558.[82] The Zeno brothers provide Nabokov not only with the name of his alternate-world Russia but also with a textual model of precisely the kind of world-fashioning and reconstruction practiced by Van. The Zeno document also models the kind of editorial misunderstanding inserted into the text by Ronald and Violet Oranger.

The following argument for the Zeno document's importance in *Ada* is partly speculative, as *Ada*'s references to it are comparatively few. As Manolescu notes in her discussion of Marco Polo's *Travels* in *The Gift*, Nabokov's use of medieval and Renaissance travel literature can be both tantalizingly present and frustratingly difficult to substantiate.[83] The Zeno brothers certainly provide the name of Van's home country, however, and their text suggests that, along with the name, Nabokov gives Van an authorial and editorial approach to history that places *Ada* in the lineage of dubiously reliable medieval and Renaissance travels. The Zeno subtext in *Ada* shows how Antiterra's components simultaneously provide it with a coherent, millennium-long narrative and reveal its impossibility.

Van is associated with Renaissance explorers through his "Mascodagama" act, a performance in which he walks on his hands, whose name combines the Renaissance explorer Vasco da Gama with a mask (and exploration with inversion). Bobbie Ann Mason argues that "Van's mixture of art and science reflects his inability to maintain clear control over either art or life, and his Mascodagama act is symptomatic of his tendency."[84] If we follow Mason's lead, the travel narratives in *Ada* may be linked to the novel's interpenetrating layers of fiction and reality. The Zeno brothers provide a model for the in-between reality of Antiterra: the planet is both an absurd invention and a possible alternate vision of the real world. The Zeno document shows how *Ada* is built of contradictory narratives, in which historical events both really did and did not happen.

Most of the Zeno account deals with the brothers' military campaigns on behalf of the Count of Frislanda (possibly the Faroe Islands). Embedded in the brothers' travel narrative, however, are the adventures of a fisherman from Frislanda, who is blown west by a storm and finds himself in Estotiland, where he finds "a fair and populous city," whose king has a library of European books.[85] The text's authors take the library as evidence of sustained contact between Estotiland and Europe because only continual Europeanization can account for the natives' literacy. The fisherman journeys further south to Drogio, a land inhabited by cannibals who suffer from the cold but lack "the sense to clothe themselves with the skins of the animals which they take in hunting."[86] The fisherman continues southwest, reaching a land where "they have cities and temples dedicated to their idols, in which they sacrifice men and afterwards eat them. In those parts they have some knowledge and use of gold and silver."[87] Finally he returns to Frislanda and tells his story to one of the Zeno brothers.

Editors agree that if Estotiland and Drogio exist, they are somewhere in North America. Estotiland is generally taken to be Newfoundland, and the point of contact with Europe to be the Viking colony at L'Anse aux Meadows. The southern civilization is evidently based on Spanish accounts of the Incas and Aztecs in Mexico. The Zeno account of Estotiland was accepted by some early twentieth-century American historians: Ida Sedgwick Proper, for example, identifies the "barbarous tribe" to the south of Estotiland as the Native American inhabitants of Maine, and the "civilized nations" further south as "those dwellers in Central America, whose temples and villages Lindbergh has been flying over and exploring during the past year."[88] This description of North America, however, with cannibal savages wandering naked through the woods of Maine, is sufficiently implausible that most contemporary historians treat the American portion of the Zeno document as forgery.

The appearance of the Zeno document in *Ada* suggests a change in Nabokov's use of the Vikings after his adaptation of the *Eddas* for *Pale Fire*. For while there may be questions regarding the date and authorship of the *Eddas*, or slight inaccuracies in their accounts of geography, they are not forgeries. The Zeno document, on the other hand, is much more likely to be forged, and its presence in *Ada* calls into question the reliability not simply of Van's narration but of the text of *Ada* as a whole, locating the alternate-historical world not in the realm of might-have-been but the realm of make-believe.[89]

The key to Antiterra's simultaneous reality and unreality lies both in the Zeno document's description of Estotiland and in the textual history of the document itself. Van's discussions of Antiterran history are never contradicted or mocked by his interlocutors, and the name Estoty is widely used, suggesting that unlike Kinbote, Van does not "have hallucinations real bad."[90] But while within the novel Antiterra "really" exists, the Zeno document provides a catalogue of the ways Van's narrative may be unreliable, both subject to and the result of interpretation, redaction, and misconstrual.[91]

The Zeno document has a remarkably Nabokovian backstory, told by a series of unreliable narrators. The voyage of the Zeno brothers, Nicolò and Antonio, supposedly happened around 1390, but the account was not published until 1558. The published version is based on letters sent from Nicolò to Antonio and later from Antonio to a third brother, who remained in Venice. These letters are assembled and edited by a descendent of Antonio's, also named Nicolò Zeno, born 1515. Nicolò Junior is responsible not only for the letters' preservation but also for their destruction: at the end of the text, he explains,

> All these letters were written by Messire Antonio to Messire Carlo his brother, and I am grieved that the book and many other writings on these subjects have, I don't know how, come sadly to ruin; for, being but a child when they fell into my hands, I, not knowing what they were, tore them in

pieces, as children will do, and sent them all to ruin: a circumstance which I cannot now recall without the greatest sorrow. Nevertheless, in order that such an important memorial should not be lost, I have put the whole in order, as well as I could, in the above narrative; so that the present age may, more than its predecessors have done, in some measure derive pleasure from the great discoveries made in those parts where they were least expected; for it is an age that takes a great interest in new narratives and in the discoveries which have been made in countries hitherto unknown, by the high courage and great energy of our ancestors.[92]

The Zeno document, in other words, is a text after Nabokov's heart: the biography of one man (Nicolò Senior), written by another (Antonio), and torn up by a third (Nicolò Junior) who seeks to atone for the destruction by reconstructing the original. (Such catastrophes befall texts throughout Nabokov's work, with similar results for the authorship of the reconstructed texts; Charlotte's letter to Humbert, for example.[93]) The document itself is full of accidental ambiguities, particularly in the last few pages of the text when the pronoun "I" appears, used first by Antonio in a letter to Carlo and then immediately following by Nicolò Junior in the apology to the reader quoted above. (Manolescu argues that similar shifts in the referent of "I" in *The Gift* stem from the fluid referents in Marco Polo's *Description of the World*.[94])

The Zeno document is most readily available in the 1873 Hakluyt Society edition, edited and with an introduction by Richard Henry Major. (The Harvard and Cornell libraries owned copies of this edition during Nabokov's years at each university.) Major's edition adds another Kinbotian layer: a 102-page introduction arguing for the accuracy of the 15-page manuscript. Major's argument rests on the hypothesis that inaccuracies in the text and the map appended to it were introduced by Nicolò Junior in his attempt to clarify and expand his ancestors' materials. Major makes sweeping editorial changes, arguing that a place called Islanda is sometimes Iceland and sometimes Shetland, and even "correcting" the names in the text to reflect his reading. Major insists on the importance of the Zeno family, citing family exploits as proof of Nicolò Junior's veracity;[95] at the same time, he explains wilder elements as "bombast" typical of "Venetian exaggeration."[96] In Major's account, Nicolò Junior emerges as a tragic figure: the scion of a great line, descended from a doge, whose contribution to the family greatness is first the destruction and then the boastful, inaccurate reconstruction of a vital piece of family history.

Major's edition of the Zeno document bears striking parallels in form and content to *Ada*. Nicolò Junior reconstructs his ancestors' voyages based on found letters; so do Van and Ada, who first appear in the novel working out their parentage from old letters and journals. The resulting reconstruction is narrated in both texts by a speaker whose pronoun "I" shifts in reference between the "I" of the past (Antonio, young Van, young Ada) and the "I" of the present (Nicolò Junior, old Van, old Ada). This shifty document is then edited, with dubious textual emendations, by an unrelated Anglophone editor (Major, Oranger).

Major's spelling changes, "corrections," and indications of when the speaker is the unreliable Nicolò, resemble Oranger and Violet's intrusions into the text through editorial notes and their accidental inclusions of Van's extratextual asides. These asides, generally addressed to Violet as she takes dictation, occur at emotionally important moments in the novel, as with the interruptions "tentaclinging hair—t,a,c,l" and "Now I've lost my next note" during Lucette's suicide.[97] We also hear Van spelling to Violet when he reports Demon's speech about Andrey Vinelander: "the scion, s, c, i, o, n, of one of those great Varangians."[98] Violet's transcription of Van's instruction associates *Ada*'s theme of faulty editing with the Zeno brothers' material on pre-Columbian settlements. While Major's intrusiveness into his text is by no means the sole model for the Orangers, the similarity between the two suggests that Van may be accused of forgery in his memoir: like Nicolò Junior, Van attempts to recreate a past he himself has destroyed, and in the process he introduces absurd falsehoods.

Nabokov uses the Zeno subtext in *Ada* to rewrite the European conquest of America as benevolent. The king of Estotiland's library, the first library in America, is a forerunner of *Ada* itself: a multilingual importation of European literature into an American landscape, rescuing the inhabitants from barbarism. The origins of Estotiland in forgery, however, undercut Van's claims for Antiterra's superiority, even while arguing for the civilizing and hybridizing power of literature. The Renaissance travel narrative skirts the boundary between fact and fiction, making truth claims at once stronger and less compelling than those of a novel. Read as a source for Van's description of his home, it becomes a warning against both literalism and excessive skepticism: the story's overt claims about America may be false, but its kernels of truth give us insight into the mechanisms by which "America" has been construed and appropriated. While Van's propagandistic accounts of Antiterra obscure moral flaws and dangers in the world they describe, his history of Antiterra also suggests that literature teaches us to see—to seek—"curiosity, tenderness, kindness, ecstasy" everywhere.

Like Terra, Antiterra "cheats": Van gives us—or tries to—the sanitized version of his world.[99] But Van's self-serving version of Antiterra is closer to "truth" than Humbert's account of his "island of entranced time" or Kinbote's importation of Zembla into Shade's poem. Van is unreliable, but he describes his "real" world, substantiated by other characters around him. While Van often accidentally reveals his own cruelty (toward Kim Beauharnais, or toward prostitutes in the floramor brothels), the distortions and omissions in his narrative undercut Antiterra's alterity only to the same degree that propaganda undercuts the reality of real-world history.[100]

Antiterran propaganda makes us distrust both Van and the pronouncements made by authoritative narrators in general, but it does not require that we doubt the physical reality of the world. Antiterra's peculiar chronology and technology are implausible, but we lack a strong textual basis to doubt their internal reality, just as the Antiterrans who receive sanitized accounts of Terran history might doubt that the German leader "Athaulf the Future" is quite as heroic as he seems, without going so far as to doubt his existence.[101] Indeed, as Ellen Pifer points out, such "romantic idealization of 'Terra the Fair' serves to jolt Nabokov's readers, inhabitants of Terra, into sudden recognition that there are worse forms of hell [than Antiterra] in this, our very own world."[102] Antiterra's unreliability turns out to be no greater than Earth's.

At the same time, Antiterra as collectively described in the text undermines Van's accounts of his world's virtue and its history. The most notable alternative version of Antiterran history, which blends Van's world with our own, is Vitry's film adaptation of Van's novel, *Letters from Terra*. Boyd argues that Vitry reveals that "the novel's world, hitherto accepted as Antiterra, as comically distant, proves to have been our own world, with its Roosevelt (Old Felt) and Stalin (Uncle Joe), its Nazi Germany and Soviet Russia, even its de Gaulle. This disturbing collapse of the book's world insists on the fact of evil and suffering in the world we know."[103] While Vitry's film "insists on the fact of evil," however, his exposure of Terra's violence does not necessarily mean that Terra and Antiterra are the same place; instead, each world contains a revealing vision of the other. The imaginary world of the novel provides a standpoint from which to critique our own, allowing us both to plant our feet and to shovel the ground out from under them.

In *Lolita* and in the Zeno brothers' material in *Ada*, we see Nabokov playing with European versions of America: in *Lolita*, America is the scene of Romantic idylls, and in *Ada*, it is a savage place civilized by European contacts. Both of these Americas provide visions of a pan-European culture imported to new shores, and both Humbert and Van (misleadingly) dismiss the non-European elements—Lolita's crooners, Charlotte's Mexican souvenirs, Demon's "Copper Mongols." While the hybrid elements the narrators describe may be present in the "real" America, the narrators' claims for synthesis are partial and self-serving. The implicit America behind the narrators' claims remains full of potential, however. The natural world of *Lolita* and *Pale Fire* resists solipsization as no character can, and the worlds of the books achieve an independent existence beyond the perceptions or control of any individual character.

As Sir John Mandeville and the Zeno brothers suggest, however, the text itself can shape our understanding of the real world and teach us to recognize our constructed and sometimes false interpretations of physical facts. Nabokov's ideal America heightens its citizen-readers' awareness of nature—butterflies, plants, grains of sand—while retaining the pan-European literary consciousness that young Humbert and Annabel or Van and Ada share. The implied ideal American is a scholar and a careful observer of the natural world who avoids erroneously Edenic European visions of America, instead gaining some authorial control over historical and cultural identity. Nabokov intends these Americans—who are indistinguishable from the ideal readers of the novels—to edit the world, revising history in favor of beauty and inclusivity and extending the scope of artistic reference and personal sympathy.

* * *

Nabokov's novels create several possible Americas out of varied raw materials: mythologized pasts, outsiders' romanticizations, the physical attributes of the actual place, and the possible cultures the place may someday contain. These Americas are utopian societies, natural parks, and visions of hell, depending on the angle of the light. In this array of Americas, Nabokov sets out some of the alternatives available to world-fashioning writers: the imagined country can be treated as a hallucination or a misperception, or it can establish a dialogue between fact and interpretation, acknowledging its own constructed nature while drawing strength and physicality from its "real" components and the reader's commitment. The next four chapters expand on this key theme, that is, how multiple identity categories and intellectual commitments accrete around the name of a country, a locus that turns out to exist on multiple geographical, fictional, and metaphysical planes simultaneously. Despite its many flaws, Antiterra provides a model for world-fashioning writers through its translation of the private world of Van's childhood into a public world with history, geography, and a literary tradition in which the reader can participate. And as we shall see in the next chapter, the real world's natural landscape contains patterns that, once we have learned to separate interpretive from objective fact, can be used to mediate between distant places. *Speak, Memory* renders the physical landscape of America malleable, juxtaposing Arizona with northern Russia through Nabokov's passion for butterflies—a juxtaposition based on love, knowledge, and the temporally synthetic power of memory, rather than on self-deception.

CHAPTER 3

REALISM, RELATIVITY, AND FRAMES OF REFERENCE IN *ADA* AND *PALE FIRE*

As we saw in Chapter 2, Nabokov's novels contain and imply at least three layers of fictional truth: the reality of the narrator; an implied literary reality that, like Shelley's "cave of Poesy," provides a space from which the narrator's claims can be examined; and the synthetic reality of the book as a whole, constructed by the author and the reader. These fictional realities are in dialogue with the real world, contesting the boundaries between countries, time periods, and metaphysical states. The previous chapter showed how those layers of reality are strategically separated in the texts of *Lolita*, *Pale Fire*, and *Ada*, each layer suggesting a different approach to world-creation. This chapter examines how those texts recombine the elements they have separated. In a surprisingly realist move, this recombination is made possible through the texts' use of science to delineate their worlds' alterity. Twentieth-century physics teaches us that even physical reality is subject to interpretation and debate and makes it possible to treat real-world facts as malleable.

We have seen how *Lolita* and *Pale Fire* suggest an ideal America fusing the best of European civilization and the natural world. But this ideal America is only a preliminary (and largely uninhabited) model of the ideal community. *Ada* treats the natural world more thoroughly to demonstrate fundamental principles that, Nabokov believes, underlie our experience of both the physical world and the alternate reality of novels. In *Ada*, Nabokov adapts special relativity to show how a novel can collapse time and space and to bring his readers into a unifying frame of reference outside both the novel and the "real" world of common experience.

Postmodern writers such as Thomas Pynchon and Tom Stoppard frequently use scientific metaphors to explain human experience. For

Pynchon in *The Crying of Lot 49*, Maxwell's Demon acts as a metaphor for the diffusion of information; for Stoppard in *Arcadia* (1993), fractal geometry mirrors the recurring patterns in the human search for knowledge. Pynchon and Stoppard look for ways to reverse entropy, that is, prevent death. But a novel's scientific content may also constitute an argument for the possibility of the fictional world, and the novel's treatment of its scientific underpinnings can provide instructions for how that world may be brought into existence.

Like hard science fiction, transnational novels emphasize the real underpinnings of their alternate creations. Fictions based on science make radical claims about their possibility: as Carl Freedman puts it, science fiction takes the reader "far beyond the boundaries of his or her own mundane environment, into strange, awe-inspiring realms thought to be in fact unknown, or at least largely unknown, but not in principle unknowable."[1] Many of these novels draw on physicists' theories of chance and causation, especially the many-worlds interpretation of quantum mechanics, which suggests that all possible events *do* happen in multiple simultaneous universes. Quantum mechanics does for the real world what Lubomír Doležel's theory of possible worlds does for fiction: it suggests that any reality we see is only one of many interconnected and mutually constitutive layers of possible and probable events. Scientific alternate-world fiction suggests that we should understand human life as part of a larger context of possible experience, emphasizing not only the contingent elements of history and chance but also the fundamental possibility of the world of the novel.

More even than hard science fiction, transnational fiction demands that readers recognize its worlds' possibility. Nabokov's adaptations of electromagnetism and special relativity show how science provides not just a framework but a motive for transnational fiction.[2] As I argue elsewhere, Nabokov uses electricity in *Pale Fire* and *Ada* to provide a metaphor for how the spirit world can occupy the same space as the physical world.[3] In the same texts, Nabokov rewrites relativity to argue that novels can create physical spaces combining elements from multiple places and times. These spaces are literary, multilingual, and, as we have seen, antiutopian. But they are also impossible to dismiss as purely "imaginary." In the liminal space of Antiterra, balanced between realism and fantasy as well as among France, Russia, and America, scientific accuracy becomes essential: it provides the structure of the book, the physical processes by which Van understands his world and an instruction to the readers in reinterpreting the real world to produce better cultural and temporal fusions than Van's.

The scientific undercurrents of Nabokov's work help explain why so many transnational novels are set in alternate worlds: indeed, for later writers like Zadie Smith, Michael Chabon, and Salman Rushdie, part of Nabokov's appeal comes from his combination of solidity and mystical eternity. The fantastic elements of these novels are not mere wishful thinking or postmodern indeterminacy. Instead, they are serious arguments in favor of a programmatic reinterpretation of the world we inhabit. Controversies in science demonstrate that even apparently stable physical truths are subject to interpretation and reconstruction. Transnational novels draw on the subjective aspect of physical truth to suggest the possibility of their own cultural constructions. Nabokov's use of physics—especially special relativity—is an extreme version of the transnational project of world-creation: it is a recipe for a disciplined and rational recombination of space, time, culture, and language, showing how apparently separate objects coexist in the same space. Finally, it blurs the distinction between writers and readers.

This chapter examines Nabokov's treatment of special relativity as a model both for the reader's relationship with the novel and for the transnational writer's relationship with his multiple countries. This treatment of science as fluid metaphor and hard truth explains the transnational novel's liminal position between realism and fantasy. World-fashioning novels use hard science to create hitherto impossible locations—and to render them habitable.

COMPRESSING TIME AND SPACE IN *SPEAK, MEMORY*

Antiterra is peculiar for its combination of wild, carnivalesque cultural fusions with a very narrow focus on the obsessions of its narrator. The text unites all three of Nabokov's French, Russian, and English literary histories: Don Barton Johnson demonstrates that Byron, Chateaubriand, and Pushkin provide subtexts containing parallel incest plots as a metaphor for artistic creation, for example, and Annapaola Cancogni shows Nabokov's debt to French literature in the Ardis sections.[4] Sidney, Austen, Marvell, and de Maupassant all put in appearances.[5] While the text uses a multitude of literary sources, however, the story is an incest narrative, and nearly all the characters are blood relatives. But the incestuous "family chronicle" does not limit the novel's scope: while, as Ellen Pifer argues, "the act of incest embodies that creative principle of inbreeding which nurtures both nature and art," the incestuously artistic family spans three continents, languages, and centuries.[6] How, then, does a novel of such scope also turn out to be the story of one of Nabokov's most solipsistic narrators? The answer, which lies in *Ada*'s blending of science and art, provides parallel insights into the sterility of solipsism and the necessity of placing both writers and readers in a frame of reference outside the work of art. For Nabokov, fiction teaches readers to merge countries, languages, and eras into a single, unified whole. In his discussion of the physics of Antiterra, Nabokov suggests that the problems of transnational fiction are illusions stemming from writers' failure to distance themselves and their readers sufficiently from their subject matter.

Brian Boyd argues that reading a Nabokov novel has "much in common with the process of scientific discovery."[7] Nabokov was a serious scientist,[8] and the ways his work in lepidoptery informs his fiction are well documented.[9] In an essay on Nabokov's "poetics of science," Stephen Blackwell argues that butterfly mimicry and the repetition of patterns in nature reveal, in Nabokov's novels, "the hidden truth of 'life itself.'"[10] Nabokov's butterflies—and his other scientific references—often imply the existence of a scientifically unproven spirit world, the world of life after death. His treatment of communications between this world and the next resembles his treatment of communications between his old and new countries: *The Real Life of Sebastian Knight*, for example, treats death and exile as continuous. His scientific metaphors follow this pattern both by blending the physical with the spiritual and by their parallel use of sources from Russia and the West.

If science is the meeting ground between the worlds of the living and the dead, Nabokov also suggests that separate spaces within the real world meet and merge under the influence of art. This geographical synthesis is one of Nabokov's major artistic goals and is inextricably intertwined with his melding of different levels of "reality"—the "truth" within the novel, the real-world truths reflected in the novel, and the supernatural realm possibly reflected in both.

A story about butterfly hunting in *Speak, Memory* shows how juxtaposing apparently separate elements of real life can synthesize separate times and locations. As several critics note, a description of "a July day—around 1910, I suppose"[11] in which the young Nabokov "felt the urge to explore the vast marshland beyond the Oredezh" gives way to a description of America three decades later: "Mariposa lilies bloomed under Ponderosa pines. In the distance, fleeting cloud shadows dappled the dull green of slopes above timber line, and the gray and white of Longs Peak."[12] We have been warned that such a transformation might occur when Nabokov recalls his childhood desire to discover a new species of butterfly, which he follows by the fragmentary sentence, "And then, thirty years later, that blessed black night in the Wasatch Range"—the mountains in Utah where Nabokov finally caught and identified a new species.[13] In retrospect, the desire to catch a new butterfly and the accomplishment of that desire become interchangeable, and, as they do, the locations of dream and reality interpenetrate: Russia opens a window onto America, and the flora of the two continents, "the fragrant bog orchid (the *nochnaya fialka* of Russian poets)" and the "Ponderosa pines," grow in the same place.[14] Nabokov's juxtaposition of orchids and pines is both ostentatiously improbable and easy for an inexpert reader to miss: readers must pay scrupulous attention to the plants in order to understand the text.

The attentive reader might initially treat this impossible geography as an example of McHale's postmodern "zone," but its placement in Nabokov's memoir rather than in fiction asserts the "truth" of the connection between places. Nabokov implies that when memory seizes on a particularly important pair of moments, the physical and temporal separation of those moments becomes irrelevant to the memoirist. Nabokov follows his reminiscence of the view of Longs Peak with a discussion of time that will mystify a reader who has not spotted the geographical switch:

> I confess I do not believe in time. I like to fold my magic carpet, after use, in such a way as to superimpose one part of the pattern upon another. Let visitors trip. And the highest enjoyment of timelessness—in a landscape selected at random—is when I stand among rare butterflies and their food plants. This is ecstasy, and behind the ecstasy is something else, which is hard to explain. It is like a momentary vacuum into which rushes all that I love. A sense of oneness with sun and stone. A thrill of gratitude to whom it may concern—to the contrapuntal genius of human fate or to tender ghosts humoring a lucky mortal.[15]

Nabokov exposes his own authorial device, admitting where he has folded his magic carpet to make distant points in space and time to overlap. Readers may share Nabokov's position on the magic carpet if we can; we are invited to join him and the "tender ghosts" in the ecstatic role of outside observers.

Nabokov's characters frequently try to combine times and spaces as Nabokov does in *Speak, Memory*. But while the compression in Nabokov's memoir is fluid and almost invisible, his characters' juxtapositions tend to be more awkward. Part of the difference lies in Nabokov's examination in his fiction of the pitfalls of making distant times and spaces meet. Dependence on memory can result in the kind of meaningful overlaps found in Nabokov's memoir, but it can also lead to the kind of solipsism Conrad and Naipaul warn against and to which Humbert falls prey. This tension between celebrating space-time compression and warning readers away from it is encapsulated in Nabokov's use of special relativity as a metaphor for artistic creation.

"Special Reality" in *Pale Fire*

If Nabokov models a "right" way to synthesize separate times and places in his memoir, he also gives shows the "wrong" way to combine fiction and reality in *Pale Fire* with the Zemblan artist Eystein:

> Eystein showed himself to be a prodigious master of the trompe l'oeil in the depiction of various objects surrounding his dignified dead models and making them look even deader by contrast to the fallen petal or the polished panel that he rendered with such love and skill. But in some of those portraits Eystein had also resorted to a weird form of trickery: among his decorations of wood or wool, gold or velvet, he would insert one which was really made of the material elsewhere imitated by paint. This device which was apparently meant to enhance the effect of his tactile and tonal values had, however, something ignoble about it and disclosed not only an essential flaw in Eystein's talent, but the basic fact that "reality" is neither the subject nor the object of true art which creates its own special reality having nothing to do with the average "reality" perceived by the communal eye.[16]

Eystein's revelation of the "special reality" of art comes from his inability to achieve it: Eystein's talent is flawed by his dependence on the "communal eye." "Special reality" is outside such considerations as whether the materials of a painting are "really" wood, velvet, or canvas; art transcends the binary of truth or falsehood. This is a familiar aesthetic stance, for which Nabokov is sometimes attacked as elitist or amoral. But it is important that in this description, part of art's purpose is to communicate the noncommunal "special reality" to its viewers and to teach them to share the artist's privileged position. Real art, according to Kinbote, leads to a new reality in which art's component parts are synthesized. Shade and Kinbote both seek such results in *Pale Fire*: for Kinbote, a synthesis of Shade's American poem and his own fantasies of Zembla, and for Shade, a synthetic vision of this world and the afterlife.

The "flaw" in Eystein's talent comes from his failure to synthesize "real" and "artistic" elements, and his name and the term "special reality" connect his failed synthesis to Einstein's special relativity. In *Pale Fire* and *Ada*, Nabokov takes Einstein as an equivocal model for his own world-fashioning, both in the physics of his fictional world and in his claims about how real and fictional worlds interpenetrate each other.

Stephen Blackwell finds Einstein's relativity in *The Gift*, and suggests that the theory is both a source of "the novel's playful relation to temporal flow" and an indication that established theories can be overthrown: Nabokov, Blackwell argues, hopes for a theory that will change our understanding of evolution just as relativity changed our understanding of Newtonian mechanics.[17] But Nabokov also uses modern physics both as a metaphor for artistic creation and as an underpinning for his science-fictional alternate worlds. In *Pale Fire* and *Ada*, Nabokov uses relativity to suggest that time becomes fluid when observed from a distance and that this fluidity can be correctly understood only by an observer who retains both inside and outside perspectives on the time under consideration. The final responsibility for the creation and success of fiction in this system lies not with the writer but with the reader, who can synthesize all the perspectives of the novel. The reader must complete the fictional world, gaining an authorial ownership over the novel's layers of cultural references and linguistic play.

RELATIVITY AND FICTION

Since its first publication in 1905, special relativity has been a touchstone for writers and critics seeking a metaphor for subjectivity and unreliability. As Julie M. Johnson writes, "the great gift of relativity theory to modern literature, and to the arts as such, has been to lend the imprimatur of 'fact' to the wholesale relativism which had already seized the fancy."[18] As Johnson's quotation marks suggest, relativity's use by philosophers and literary critics is often based on inexact understanding of the theory. In *Higher Superstition: The Academic Left and its Quarrels with Science*, Paul Gross and Norman Levitt accuse scholars in the humanities of taking Einstein's work as permission to indulge in reckless relativism that, based only on a coincidence of vocabulary and "the conscription of science as metaphor," rejects any form of absolute value.[19] Gross and Levitt make the academy sound as though it were peopled with Kinbotes. Their catalogue of literary misunderstandings provides at best a partial account of how modern physics changed the humanities. But even critics' most accurate uses of special relativity often remain metaphorical. Wai Chee Dimock, for example, argues that relativity and literature share a central concern: determining whether time is unidirectional, or two way and thus retrievable.[20] For Julie M. Johnson and for Teri Reynolds, who treats physics as a "cognitive metaphor,"[21] special relativity remains an intellectual starting point for literary exploration.

Einstein argues that events will be described in different ways depending on the relative motion of the observer and the observed. He certainly never argued that there is no such thing as truth. If naïve interpretations of relativity are set aside, however, novelists—especially postmodern and transnational novelists—can make legitimate use of Einstein's discussion of how distance from observed events alters our understanding of those events. Even treated as a "cognitive metaphor," relativity can elucidate the difference between lived and remembered or reported experience. More importantly, it can also provide a model for a real-world purpose of the novel: to set readers at a distance from the content of the text, helping them determine both inside and outside interpretations of the novel's events.

For transnational fiction, relativity implies not that time and space can be casually modified but that movement away from remembered spaces can cause them to blend. Special relativity lets us combine disparate geographical and temporal elements—at the price of removal, since the observer must be outside them. The spaces of transnational fiction provide frames of reference outside the real world, and, like all places in a relativistic thought experiment, they serve double duty: we can observe them from our standpoint in the real world, or they can be the place from which we view the real world, allowing us to see how separate spaces in our own world overlap.

Memory also blends times and places when Nabokov folds his magic carpet, but Einstein's relativity changes the juxtaposition in several important ways. It provides a clear scientific framework for an otherwise subjective phenomenon. It reminds us of the physicality of remembered places and times and suggests that the combination of those places may also have a solid physical and temporal reality. Relativity separates the novel's chronotope from the reader and writer who produce it, thus making it independent and, unlike memory, capable of providing shared direct experience. Most importantly, relativity emphasizes the distance between the observer and the blended times and spaces: relativistic space-time compression depends on motion, and the observer must always be in a frame of reference outside the compressions he observes.

Far from providing a pretext for reckless indeterminacy, relativity makes textual compressions of time and space more concrete. For Nabokov, time and space overlap measurably and comprehensibly. With a proper understanding of the physics underpinning Nabokov's treatment of time, we find that Nabokov's novels are constructed so that no measurement in any frame of reference need be lost.

TIME AND SPACE COMPRESSION IN RELATIVITY

From his preliminary notes for *Ada*, Nabokov retained ninety-eight index cards on topics relating to the physics and philosophy of time. Of these cards, ten are labeled "Relativity" and another seven "Simultaneous Events"; the rest, while more philosophical than scientific in subject matter, refer to problems of duration and simultaneity raised in response to Einstein. Debunking relativity seems to have been one of Nabokov's first aims as he began writing "The Texture of Time," the novella that was the original seed of *Ada* and that constitutes part 5 of the final text. In an index card dated January 8, 1958, five years earlier than the bulk of the notes, Nabokov wrestles with the difficulty of discussing time without space: "the present is merely our awareness of the building up of the past, its rising level [Alas, I'm using using [*sic*] spatial terms!]."[22] Nabokov finds special relativity counterintuitive: when asked how he saw time, he responded, "I've drawn my scalpel through spacetime, space being the tumor, which I assign to the slops. While not having much physics, I reject Einstein's slick formulae; but then one need not know theology to be an atheist."[23] But while Nabokov lists the concept of the space-time continuum as the origin of his objection to special relativity, space-time reasserts itself in "The Texture of Time" as a model of the same physical and temporal unification enacted in the butterfly hunting episode in *Speak, Memory*.

Special relativity asserts that all measurements are dependent on frame of reference and that communications between frames of reference are limited by the speed of light. An observer in one frame of reference, measuring either the passage of time between two events or the physical size, speed, or location of an object, may get a different result than an observer in another frame of reference if the two frames of reference are in motion relative to each other.[24] The speed of light and the overall space-time coordinates are the only constants. Time, speed, distance, acceleration, and so forth—the traditional units of measure of Newtonian mechanics—vary, depending on the relative motion between the observer and the observed. Space and time, the axes on the space-time diagram, may appear to grow or diminish proportionately to each other.

The fact that the speed of light is constant across frames of reference causes time and space to behave in very strange ways when we observe something traveling close to light speed. If we watch a spaceship traveling away from us at light speed, we will observe two bizarre phenomena: first, time on the ship will appear to slow down, and second, the ship will appear to shrink until it becomes a single point. An astronaut looking out the window of the spaceship as it leaves will observe the same phenomena happening to us.

As a result of the way fast-moving objects shrink, events that seem physically separate within one frame of reference may appear adjacent from another, and two events that take place sequentially within one frame of reference can appear from another to take place at the same moment. As we have seen, this is also, for Nabokov, the function of art:

special relativity describes a process resembling the "cosmic synchronization" Nabokov describes in *Speak, Memory*. Nabokov draws a tenuous connection between the two concepts in that text when he quotes his "philosophical friend," "Vivian Bloodmark": "while the scientist sees everything that happens in one point of space, the poet feels everything that happens in one point of time."[25].

Cause and effect are preserved under special relativity: events cannot be synchronized if one is necessary to cause another. (We can never see a fire burning before we see the lighting of the match used to start it, for example.) Nabokov draws on this basic premise of special relativity to reveal the cause and effect of a larger pattern in his own life and the lives of his characters: the "organism of events"[26] created by an outside consciousness, the authorial God hinted at in Nabokov's work. Compressed events reveal the causes of that pattern. The "magic carpet" of memory allows not only a retrospective reorganization of life, but an insight into unsuspected causal forces.[27] Such reorganizations of life through memory are common—and commonly made explicit—in transnational fiction, from Dinesen's temporal patchwork in *Out of Africa* to Rushdie's discussion of "memory's truth" in *Midnight's Children*, but Nabokov's treatment of mnemonic chronology stands alone in providing a physical mechanism whereby we can understand and regulate the process of temporal fusion.[28]

Van's Objections

Van "reject[s] without qualms the artificial concept of space-tainted, space-parasited time, the space-time of relativist literature,"[29] and gives lectures on time at "Counterstone Hall."[30] Nabokov's notes for *Ada* suggest that on Antiterra, special relativity was to have been debunked: one card includes the passage, marked as used but absent from the final text, "We need not bother with the 'relative theory' It has been disposed of by the recent discovery of velocities easily encompassing the speed of light. [do not bother to specify but 'drop' elsewhere a hint] . . . or, in other words by the discovering of 'slow light' and 'dying' electromagnetic ripples!"[31] The dropped hint has so far eluded critics. Instead, debunking relativity becomes one of Van's tasks in "The Texture of Time," and it is a task at which he fails—even within the context of Nabokov's own critique of Einstein.

Nabokov's adaptation of relativity is also an argument about the necessity of collaboration between writer and reader: as we shall see, the reader is asked to mimic the kind of measurement taken in relativistic thought experiments, placing herself alongside the writer outside both the novel and the "real" world. According to Nabokov, this removal reframes real-world events, synchronizing disparate past times and places and making the past both accessible to the memoirist and communicable to the reader. For Nabokov, Einstein's relativity is flawed by its suggestion that it is impossible to stand outside the pattern.

Nabokov's treatment of relativity is drawn in part from Henri Bergson's *Duration and Simultaneity* (1922), in which Bergson seeks to reconcile relativity's mathematical definition of time with his own definition of perceptual time. (Leona Toker and John Burt Foster both demonstrate Nabokov's debt to Bergson.[32]) For Bergson, relativists' claims that time dilates under special relativity are a kind of scientifically sanctioned solipsism: the relativist "is free to rule whatever he pleases; his system will be motionless, by very definition, if he makes it his 'system of reference' and there installs his observatory"[33]; "he has the absolute right (ill assured in the old physics) to adhere to his personal point of view and to refer everything to his own system of reference."[34] Bergson argues that time as we know it is a product of human perceptions but that these perceptions represent a universal time frame of the sort rejected by relativity. Bergson sees the relativist belief in variable times as internally inconsistent, since "the doing away with the privileged system is the very core of the theory of relativity. Hence, this theory, far from ruling out the hypothesis of a single time, calls for it and gives it a greater intelligibility."[35]

Van, whose treatise "The Texture of Time" is also written in 1922, adopts Bergson's premises about the perceptual nature of time. His conclusions about the relationship between time and space differ from Bergson's, however: for Van, "perceptual time" remains strictly the time of his *own* perceptions, whereas for Bergson, time "is not personal memory."[36] Nabokov contrasts Van and Bergson in order not only to demonstrate the flaws he sees in relativity but also to imply the difference between Van's understanding of time and his own. "The Texture of Time" contains two rejections of relativity: Van's, which is based on solipsistic grounds, and Nabokov's, which is based on a humanistic definition of time. For Van, time is made arbitrarily flexible by memory, which allows him to make all times into simulacra of his own childhood; for Nabokov, time is made flexible by distance, which allows the artist and the audience to see a life or a work of art as a whole.

Van argues that time is created by individual perception, and that therefore, "nothing prevents mankind as such from having no future at all—if for example our genus evolves by imperceptible (this is the ramp of my argument) degrees a *novo-sapiens* species or another subgenus altogether, which will enjoy other varieties of being and dreaming, beyond man's notion of Time."[37] According to Van, who makes what Julie M. Johnson calls a "leap . . . from physics to solipsism," time only exists when perceived by human consciousness.[38] Should all of "mankind" vanish, "time" itself will cease to exist, as the word "time" is merely a description of human cognition—a position that, as Toker points out, is drawn from Bergson. But while Bergson's account of time depends on human consciousness as a measurement of duration, Van's account differs from Bergson's in its insistence on *individual* consciousness; for Van, time is the creation of the individual experiencing it, rather than of human consciousness as a whole. Van thinks there is no time for any given individual before that individual's first memory, and there will be no time for that individual after his death. The idea that "time" begins with one's first conscious memory explains the flashback-based structure of the novel: the history of the Veen family is given in the order Van discovers it because, for Van, events take place only in the order that he learns of them. Van makes an error Nabokov describes on an index card relating to the speed of light: "If the light from a star takes then [*sic*] years to reach me and I see it as it was in the past, this does not mean that I am actually seeing the past. It only means that I see its lingering light, just as I can see the ten-thousand yearold pictures of animals still lingering on the wall of the cave."[39] Van's time differs from Bergson's in the narrowness of its conception of consciousness: while Bergson's time depends on the perceptions of humanity as a whole, Van's version depends only on himself.

Van's real derision, however, is aimed at Einstein's elimination of "the simultaneity of distant events" and the twin paradox, a thought experiment that suggests that if one of a pair of identical twins were to board a space craft and travel away from Earth at the speed of light and then return to Earth, he would, as a result of the variable times in the two frames of reference, return younger than his brother who remained on Earth. Van refers to the twin paradox in a long disquisition on relativity:

> At this point, I suspect, I should say something about my attitude to "Relativity." It is not sympathetic. What many cosmogonists tend to accept as an objective truth is really the flaw inherent in mathematics which parades as truth. The body of the astonished person moving in Space is shortened in the direction of motion and shrinks catastrophically as the velocity nears the speed beyond which, by the fiat of a fishy formula, no speed can be. That is his bad luck, not mine—but I sweep away the business of his clock's slowing down. Time, which requires the utmost purity of consciousness to be properly apprehended, is the most rational element of life, and my reason feels insulted by those flights of Technology Fiction. One especially grotesque inference, drawn (I think by Engelwein)

from Relativity Theory—and destroying it, if drawn correctly—is that the galactonaut and his domestic animals, after touring the speed spas of Space, would return younger than if they had stayed at home all the time. Imagine them filing out of their airark—rather like those "Lions," juvenilified by romp suits, exuding from one of those huge chartered buses that stop, horribly blinking, in front of a man's impatient sedan just where the highway wizens to squeeze through the narrows of a mountain village.

Perceived events can be regarded as simultaneous when they belong to the same span of attention; in the same way (insidious simile, unremovable obstacle!) as one can visually possess a unit of space—say, a vermilion ring with a frontal view of a toy car within its white kernel, forbidding the lane into which, however, I turned with a furious *coup de volant*. I know relativists, hampered by their "light signals" and "traveling clocks," try to demolish the idea of simultaneity on a cosmic scale, but let us imagine a gigantic hand with its thumb on one star and its minimus on another—will it not be touching both at the same time—or are tactile coincidences even more misleading than visual ones? I think I had better back out of this passage.[40]

Van's rejection of the twin paradox seems reasonable, in part because the paradox presents a sticking point for students of relativity.[41] The claim that the twin on the spaceship would return younger than his twin on Earth is problematic for physicists as well as for solipsists. From the point of view of each twin, it is the other twin who is moving, so while the twin on Earth may see that his brother is not aging, the twin on the spaceship, looking at Earth, will think that the twin on Earth is aging more slowly. When the twins are reunited, there is no evident reason why the twin on the spaceship would be the one who was younger. At first glance, the twin paradox appears not paradoxical but incorrect. While communications from the twin on the spaceship, received by the twin who remained on Earth, would, on the spaceship's outbound journey, report that the spaceship twin was younger than the Earthbound twin, the compression of the signals caused by the speed of the return journey would rectify the difference. When the earth and the spaceship were reunited, the twins would once again be the same age.

This objection can be resolved, however, if we do not stick too closely to the narrative of the thought experiment. The interest in the twin paradox is not in spaceships but in the behavior of different frames of reference. If we think not of a spaceship but of a traveling frame of reference, the gap in times remains: the space-traveling twin can simply switch from one inertial frame of reference traveling away from the earth to another traveling toward it. If the traveling twin switches frames of reference, the two twins are no longer in equivalent states, and it becomes possible for one of them to experience a different duration.[42]

To understand the twin paradox, then, it becomes vital to allow for not two but three frames of reference: Earth, the outbound spaceship, and the inbound spaceship. This leap of the imagination is nearly impossible for Van. It is easy for him to believe in his own frame of reference, and just possible to believe in Ada's, but he is entirely unable to admit a third: indeed, Van's inability to believe in outside subjectivities drives Lucette to suicide. The closest Van comes to imagining an outside frame of reference is when he posits the "gigantic hand" spanning the distance between stars—a godlike universal frame of reference that renders both the earth and the spaceship measurable within a single system, like Bergson's "single time." Van's "gigantic hand" transforms two frames of reference into one in the same way that his narrative spans the divide between Russia and America: by insisting that the two are in the same place.

Van's sense that the twin paradox is "grotesque" stems not from its apparent internal failures of logic, however, but from the implicit comparison it draws between Van and the members of the Lions Club whose bus is blocking his way. Van does not wish to resemble the interchangeable Lions in their "romp suits"; he considers himself unique. But despite his dislike of the twin paradox, he seems to be participating in it: throughout the novel, Ada takes the role of his twin. Ada is Van's mirror image, and his obsession with her is, as Mason argues, also a "self-obsession."[43] Among their many similarities, Van and Ada have the same birthmark on opposite hands, a phenomenon common among identical twins. Van, moving toward Ada at high speed, should appear (from Ada's point of view) to be aging more slowly; and when they meet in Mont Roux, Van is shocked by how much Ada has aged.

Van refuses to believe that he and Ada may be in separate frames of reference. He cannot contemplate leaving his "twin," and his insistence on the single frame of reference of the "gigantic hand" is also an insistence that he and Ada have not really been apart. But Van's refusal to recognize his resemblance to the Lions causes trouble. The sign in its "vermilion ring" that forbids passing is also an indication that he is operating in a frame of reference shared with other vehicles and people, and his attempts to pass the bus leave him forced to "back out." As we shall see, Van's objections to relativity are similarly undermined throughout "The Texture of Time," revealing the partial and relative nature of his own frame of reference.

Van's Car and the Mechanics of *Ada*

In keeping with his self-centered notion of time, Van's argument in his novella reflects the motions of the car he is driving. Since Van is wholly dependent on his own sensations to articulate his understanding of time, his physical present, driving from the Dolomites to Mont Roux, intrudes on his metaphysics. The "ramp of my argument" is also the ramp down which he backs as he begins his journey, and the "reverse gear" into which he puts his memory coincides with the gear his car.

Van claims that his physical motion over the course of the novella is secondary to the temporal motion he describes along with it. As Van leaves for Mont Roux, he contrasts space and time as rival objects of love: "One can be a lover of Space and its possibilities: take, for example, speed, the smoothness and sword-swish of speed; the aquiline glory of ruling velocity; the joy cry of the curve; and one can be an amateur of Time, an epicure of duration."[44] As Van distinguishes between space and time, however, the contrast is diminished by his invocation of speed, which is expressed in terms of both space (distance traveled) and time (duration of travel). N. Katherine Hayles notes that Van "risks making it impossible to measure Time at all" by removing the "similitude" of time intervals.[45] Nonetheless, time and space reassert themselves throughout the novella, as Van, echoing Bergson, tries and fails to describe time without recourse to spatial metaphors, and as his surroundings influence his thoughts. But while, as Mason argues, "Van's mixture of art and science reflects his inability to maintain clear control over either art or life," *Ada* nonetheless suggests that remembered events can be reclaimed when the time-compressing mixture of art and science is attempted from an outside position.[46]

While Van rejects space as a category, it nonetheless requires his attention. Van's physical location regularly obtrudes into his narrative as a point of comparison for his discussions of time: "It is like rummaging with one hand in the glove compartment for the road map—fishing out Montenegro, the Dolomites, paper money, a telegram—everything except the stretch of chaotic country between Ardez and Somethingsoprano, in the dark, in the rain, while trying to take advantage of a red light in the coal black, with the wipers functioning metronomically, chronometrically: the blind finger of space poking and tearing the texture of time."[47] Van's frame of reference will be familiar to relativists: the red light, which has a set duration, is measured by the tick of the windshield wipers. Van's confusion with the maps suggests that his refusal to account for space puts him at risk of making erroneous measurements. Similarly, in the middle of a long aside about Aurelius Augustinius, Van interrupts himself, saying,

"Lost again. Where was I? Where am I? Mud road. Stopped car,"[48] suggesting that his physical motion is reflected in, and may even determine, the course of his narration: getting lost in one coincides with getting lost in the other. Even Van's most vehement rejections of space contain implicit dependence on it, as when his denunciation of space turns out to be made possible by a pause in the trip: "Space, the impostor, has been already denounced in these notes (which are now being set down during half a day's break in a crucial journey)."[49] Van's rejection of space seems, in fact, to be responsible for his difficulties: his refusal to pay attention to his whereabouts gets him lost. Immediately following his remark about the "phoney" hybrid space-time, he adds, "There are people who can fold a road map. Not this writer."[50] Van is incapable of managing or understanding his physical location.

Van's inability to deal with space may be understood two ways. The first interpretation, which Van intends, is that space is irrelevant to time. His arrival at the Trois Cygnes Hotel in time for his rendezvous with Ada, despite his inability to fold a map, appears to justify this position, as does his ability to transform his present through mnemonic juxtapositions: for example, when Van visits a decrepit brothel, he perceives it as Ada's childhood home, Ardis Hall, and turns a young prostitute into "trembling Adada."[51] Van intends his superpositions of the past onto the present to indicate that time and space function on independent continuums and create the same kind of superimposed spaces as the America-Russia in *Speak, Memory*.

Van's argument is flawed, however, and it seems unlikely that Nabokov (who writes elsewhere, "I loathe Van Veen"[52]) has made it so by accident: no one is more aware than Nabokov that the prostitute Van holds is not Ada. Even Van eventually admits that his juxtaposition of past and present is only in his imagination: "silly pity—a sentiment I rarely experience"[53] prevents him from having sex with the girl, demonstrating that Van is capable in principle of recognizing frames of reference outside his own. The orgy that follows Van's encounter with "trembling Adada" is interrupted by the noise of "A lorry [that] had got stuck in the mud of a forbidden and unfinished road,"[54] echoing Van's stopped car; Van's attempts to regain Ada with the help of prostitutes and memory are evidently going nowhere.

In fact, Van's entire frame of reference in "The Texture of Time" is undercut by a "heckler" who opens the novella by arguing that the future "could hardly be considered nonexistent, since 'it possessed at least one future, I mean, feature, involving such an important idea as that of absolute necessity.'"[55] Van's responds with denial: "Throw him out. Who said

I shall die?" Van argues that "perceptual time," the time of which he is conscious, allows motion backward ("I can put my Past in reverse gear"[56]) but not forward, because time is not perceived, but rather is created by perception. "The Texture of Time" argues that time consists of the past and present, whereas the future—whatever comes after the present—is so speculative as to be nonexistent.

While Van rejects the possibility of a future outside his current experience, Nabokov and the reader know that "With the exception of Mr. and Mrs. Ronald Oranger, a few incidental figures, and some non-American citizens, all the persons mentioned by name in this book are dead." The editor's note, placed before the text, indicates that Van's argument against the inevitability of future death is false; more importantly, it demonstrates that the text itself is a frame of reference different not only from that of the editor and the reader but also, by the time of its publication, from that of the narrator.

Not only is Van's account of time made suspect by the apparatus of the book but it is also directly contradicted by what he tells us about his perceptions during the drive. While Van dislikes the idea that time dilates in relation to velocity, he provides evidence that it does:

> And now I drive into Mont Roux . . . Today is Monday, July 14, 1922, five-thirteen P.M. by my wrist watch, eleven fifty-two by my car's built-in clock, four-ten by all the timepieces in town. The author is in a confused state of exhilaration, exhaustion, expectancy and panic. He has been climbing in the incomparable Balkan mountains. He spent most of May in Dalmatia, and June in the Dolomites, and got letters in both places from Ada telling him of her husband's death (April 23, in Arizona). He started working his way west in a dark-blue Argus.[57]

Van is on Greek time (and a Greek heroic quest, indicated by the brand of his car): his receipt of Ada's letters takes place in the same time zone as Athens. It is, then, reasonable that his watch would be set for one hour later than the time shown on the clocks in Mont Roux. (Montreux, on which Mont Roux is based, is one hour before Athens.) But while the time zone accounts for the difference of an hour, it cannot account for the three minutes—which Van has gained by moving toward Mont Roux at high speed. While the twin in the thought experiment steps off the spaceship younger than his counterpart on earth, Van arrives in Mont Roux three minutes older than his surroundings.

This passage also implies an additional frame of reference beyond Van's, through the place and date of Ada's husband's death: April 23 is Nabokov's birthday. Van's moment of time compression is also a moment whose import he cannot know: the compression of time and space occurs alongside the compression of real and fictional significance. The final frame of reference of the book is not Van's memoir, or even Oranger's editorial viewpoint, but Nabokov and the reader's more distanced perspective. Like Gibreel and Allie in *The Satanic Verses*, Van cannot step outside the fictional frame of reference to see the full significance of his knowledge. Instead, the reader must assimilate the various time frames—the narrative in Mont Roux, the narrator's retrospective voice, and the author's insertion of privileged information—into a unified and interdependent whole.

Terra and Antiterra

The discrepancy between the clocks in Mont Roux and Van's dashboard suggests a means of accounting for the fifty-year time difference between Terra and Antiterra: the planets are moving away from each other. Antiterra, in this reading, appears to be in the same position as the spaceship in the twin paradox.

Van refuses to address how the planets communicate, except to mention "ondulas"[58] or "wavelets"[59] in his novel *Letters from Terra* and his unfinished dissertation.[60] Whether Van believes it or not, however, the behavior of the ondulas follows the rules of relativity. The ondulas "mostly go . . . one way, our way,"[61] like the unidirectional light signals emitted by spaceships in relativists' thought experiments. The principles of relativity also explain why Theresa, the Terran heroine of Van's novel, arrives on Antiterra shrunken: the hero "has to place her on a slide under a powerful microscope in order to make out the tiny, though otherwise perfect, shape of his minikin sweetheart."[62] Theresa shrinks in the manner brought about by near-light-speed motion, a phenomenon Van elsewhere dismisses as someone else's "bad luck." The problem with Van's novel, then, may arise from its failure to separate between the Terran and Antiterran frames of reference—its insufficient exploration of the "Technology Fiction" Van disdains. If Theresa moves away from Terra at the speed of light, she should appear from the Terran perspective to become infinitely small, but upon arrival at Antiterra and ceasing her motion, she should be a normal size. Van's incomplete understanding of relativity and his belief that Terra and Antiterra occupy a single frame of reference impede his understanding of Terra and Theresa, which is why he cannot describe the "mechanicalism"[63] of communication between the planets.

Van's refusal to consider the principles of relativity accounts for the difficulty of determining whether Terra is the ideal world Antiterrans think it is or a distorted vision of our world, as Van's descriptions of its history and geography suggest. Van's antirelativism renders the measurements he makes of Terra meaningless because he cannot account for the apparent discrepancies between the worlds. In other words, Van's mistake is the opposite of the one Gross and Levitt attack in *Higher Superstition*: his insistence on absolute truth leads him to ignore hard evidence for relativism.

Relativity and Transnational Fiction

Nabokov uses special relativity to define the artist as outside observer and to construct artistic worlds in which space and time are malleable. Since, for Nabokov, the passage of time is marked by travel—Russia to Europe, Europe to America, America to Switzerland—the compression of time is also marked by a compression of separate countries into a single place. Nabokov's use of relativity thus becomes a model for any transnational writer who seeks to meld past and present homelands. But the model is a renunciatory one. Since spacetime locations are only compressed when we are traveling away from them, special relativity suggests that the price of unity is distance.

Relativistic time compression in *Ada* marks a significant departure from the idealized Americas in *Lolita* or *Pale Fire*. The ideal America in *Lolita* turns out to be only a preliminary model for an artistic community that transcends geography by standing outside it. Nabokov's contribution to transnational literature is not simply his success as a multilingual writer, nor even his examination of how exiles revise their past and present into fictional realms. Nabokov's major contribution to transnational fiction is his implication that novels can direct readers to see that their real-world surroundings already fuse past and present. His use of physics in the construction of his imaginary worlds is a response to the dilemma faced by transnational novelists: how the incorporeal, idealized, metaphorical "space" of fiction can substitute for the real physical space of the nation or home country. The novels are full of fictional worlds precisely because those worlds urge readers to see that physical space and time are subject to interpretation and revision. Nabokov's compression of space and time through memory skirts the edge of science and suggests the possibility of a literal, physical blending of separate places. This blending is only possible when the viewer—author or reader—stands at a remove from the subject matter, like Shelley in the "cave of Poesy." The third space of literature provides a place from which to move the world.

Nabokov's novels create new places, identities, and communities, but they remain comparatively private, shared worlds of family, loved ones, and committed readers. This small scale is unusual among transnational writers, however, and most novelists who follow Nabokov adapt his techniques to make their communities extend much further. In the next chapters, we shall see how Salman Rushdie's imagined geographies provide the basis for a community of identity at once nationalist and antinationalist, global and rootedly local. The scale of Rushdie's geography is at first much smaller than that found in *Ada*: *Midnight's Children* and *The Moor's Last Sigh* are set in an imagined Bombay, not an imagined planet. *The Ground Beneath Her Feet*, however, expands into alternate worlds with the same deepening layers of fictionality found in Nabokov's. This layered world-fashioning draws the reader into a larger version of Nabokov's community of outsiders, one that this time includes real-world commitment to political change.

CHAPTER 4

COSMOPOLITANISM AND THE SHIV SENA IN *MIDNIGHT'S CHILDREN* AND *THE MOOR'S LAST SIGH*

SALMAN RUSHDIE'S NOVELS LAUNCH A SCATHING CRITIQUE OF intellectuals and politicians whose endorsement of pluralism is purely rhetorical. By emphasizing the incompleteness of Indian cosmopolitanism, Rushdie shows that people who claim to promote unity are actually complicit in creating ethnic strife. Rushdie's examples come from Bombay, but his critique is global: while Rushdie wants a productive, inclusive cosmopolitanism, he shows that his ideal, when only partially achieved, can have serious unintended consequences.

Rushdie links his critique of failed pluralists to an argument against Hindu nationalism, particularly the Bombay-based Shiv Sena Party. As the Hindu nationalist movement grows, his arguments against it in successive novels become more overt, and his visions of a pluralist, secular India set in a magical alternate world become at once more appealing and more apparently impossible. *Midnight's Children* (1981), *The Satanic Verses* (1988), and *The Moor's Last Sigh* (1995) depict ideal Indias that answer and combat the ideal promulgated by Hindu nationalists. In Rushdie's novels, Hindu nationalism provides both a target and a test case for the broader phenomenon of exclusionary nationalism. *Midnight's Children* and *The Moor's Last Sigh* criticize the hypocrisy and selfishness of two competing political groups in India: pluralist intellectuals, who claim to be inclusive but do not include the poor, and Hindu nationalists, who intend to include almost exclusively the Hindu poor but unwittingly embrace Western practices.

Rushdie's novels offer a counterintuitive solution to the problems facing both transnational writers and pluralist states: instead of seeking unity, national groups should embrace their constructed nature and their internal discord. Rushdie's novels undercut the metaphor of the body politic, suggesting that no emblematic individual or heroic figure can speak for all of India. Instead, Rushdie contends that the best microcosm of the country is the city of Bombay, which embodies both the country's multifarious ethnicities and its fundamentally invented nature. The dissolution of the body politic suggests that we should replace major theories of nationalism—Anderson, Hobsbawm, and Herder—with more open-ended and participatory accounts of national identity, best modeled by the polyvocal, reader-centered novel. In Rushdie's nation, hybridity is always preferable to purity, and the characters who come closest to embodying the nation are those who are most successful at conscious self-hybridization. Rushdie examines and rejects Bhabha and Young's models of hybridity, in which the hybrid is either the product of an unconsciously subversive assimilation or the offspring of a racially mixed sexual union. Instead, Rushdie's hybridity is simultaneously local, as varying Indian groups merge in the genealogy and experiences of a single individual, and global, as Western cultural artifacts enter the Indian mainstream. If Bhabha's hybridity centers around varying interpretations of a single book, Rushdie's more resembles the acquisition of a library; it becomes a form of polyphony. This chapter provides an overview of Bombay's history in order to argue that Rushdie's Bombay novels constitute a diagnosis of and prescription for the ills plaguing secular, pluralist India: the country needs a theory of national identity that privileges both hybridity and rooted, local specificity.

Despite the difference in their real-world ambitions, Rushdie uses the same basic techniques as Nabokov, treating fiction as a liminal space between mythologized national histories and physical reality. An array of physical, historical, and fictional Indias hint at an ideal "India" toward which Rushdie urges his readers to work. Rushdie's treatment of Indian national identity in his Bombay novels takes Nabokov's transnational community- and country-building to the next logical step: the transformation of fiction into an active and participatory national space. The layers of reality and fictionality in *Midnight's Children* remind us that nations' self-defining myths are malleable, subject to interpretation and redefinition by each of their members. Indeed, such layered fictions are essential to pluralist nations, which otherwise become exclusive and totalizing. Fiction, for Rushdie, teaches readers to take conscious control of their mythologized national affiliations and to conceive a national unity built of dialogue and disagreement.

* * *

Like Nabokov, Rushdie urges readers and writers of transnational fiction to view themselves as outsiders in any country. Unlike Nabokov, Rushdie argues that cosmopolitan outsiders are uniquely qualified to reclaim national identities from exclusionary nationalist organizations. For Rushdie, the postmodern novel, which demands that readers participate in its plot and outcome, is a training ground for the construction of real-world political groups. Rushdie's radical pluralism underlies his fragmented, antiheroic vision of India in *Midnight's Children* and *The Moor's Last Sigh.*

Real nationalist and cosmopolitan movements serve Rushdie the same way that Renaissance travel narratives and special relativity serve Nabokov: they situate the novels in a discourse rooted in both objective fact and interpretive truth, supporting fiction's truth claims by revealing the constructed nature of nonfictional narratives. But as we shall see, Rushdie's alternatives to nationalism also grow out of the fantastic nature of his fictional worlds, which emphasize the necessity of imagination for community creation. By placing his fantastic stories in recognizable real-world locations, Rushdie demonstrates that national identity, like fiction, is a liminal ground between physical reality (the hills and buildings of a city, the blood ties within a family) and the imagination. Nabokov's fantastic worlds mediate between reality and the imagination; Kingston's show how immigrants mediate between competing epistemologies; Rushdie's worlds suggest that such mediation is normal, an experience his readers already share.

INDIAN COMMUNITIES AND THE PROBLEMS OF PLURALISM

Readers looking to Rushdie's Bombay novels for solutions to India's political problems find the texts discouraging. At the end of *Midnight's Children,* the narrator, Saleem Sinai, predicts that on his thirty-first birthday, he will succumb to the cracks spreading across his body and crumble into pieces amid the crowds of Bombay. In his prediction, he seems to deny that it is possible to unify or represent India:

> Yes, they will trample me underfoot, the numbers marching one two three, four hundred million five hundred six, reducing me to specks of voiceless dust, just as, in all good time, they will trample my son who is not my

son, and his son who will not be his, and his who will not be his, until the thousand and first generation, until a thousand and one midnights have bestowed their terrible gifts and a thousand and one children have died, because it is the privilege and the curse of midnight's children to be both masters and victims of their times, to forsake privacy and be sucked into the annihilating whirlpool of the multitudes, and to be unable to live or die in peace.[1]

In his last words, Saleem rejects almost all the premises that have carried him through the novel. After more than five hundred pages spent acquiring an army of parents and demonstrating his personal responsibility for the course of Indian history, Saleem rejects the possibility of continuous lineage ("my son who is not my son, and his son who will not be his"), portrays the population of India as inhuman "numbers marching," and denies his own agency in the face of the overwhelming numbers ("reducing me to specks of voiceless dust") and any future agency for later generations in the "annihilating whirlpool." Saleem's final picture of India, with which *Midnight's Children* ends, is of a population too vast and faceless to represent.

Timothy Brennan claims that Rushdie's novels reveal their author's pessimism about India's future.[2] But the novels still argue for the possibility of creating and representing viable pluralist communities. The narrators of *Midnight's Children* and *The Moor's Last Sigh* advocate a version of Appiah's "rooted cosmopolitanism": they are attached to identity-defining local cultural practices but perform a "dialogical universalism" that makes their narratives remarkably polyphonous.[3] Even when they celebrate Indian hybridity, however, the books reflect Rushdie's awareness that his cosmopolitan ideal has not been achieved and that the failure of advocates of cosmopolitanism to include the poor render the movement vulnerable to attack and dissolution. Those excluded from the cosmopolitan group may be driven to ever-greater extremes of militant, violent nationalism, and the cosmopolitans themselves may end up exchanging heterogeneity for uniformity. As we shall see, the ending of *Midnight's Children* prefigures not the destruction of India itself but the necessity of relinquishing exclusionary representations wherein one exemplary body stands for the subjective realities of hundreds of millions of people.

Rushdie's critique of partial cosmopolitanism and national representation is part of what critics like Gillian Gane, Harveen Sachdeva Mann, and Revathi Krishnaswamy detect when they suggest that Rushdie's main characters reflect his own flaws.[4] Saladin Chamcha's sense of superiority over his fellow migrants in *The Satanic Verses* and Saleem Sinai's disintegration at the end of *Midnight's Children* are sometimes treated as failures on Rushdie's part: some readers consider the pessimistic ending of *Midnight's Children* a refusal to work out real solutions. Part of the problem may be that Rushdie never espouses any single, recognizable political position. Instead, he shows that his cosmopolitan ideal, when only partially achieved, can be as bad as the goals of his enemies. Nonetheless, pluralism is central to Rushdie's novels, which present a programmatic vision of what kind of country India should be.

Rushdie's treatment of Indian pluralism requires an explanation of the Indian usage of the word "communal." The word is used roughly like the American "ethnic." "Communities" are groups within India that claim to be culturally, linguistically, or religiously distinct. Muslims, Hindus, and Parsis are different communities, even if they live in the same neighborhood. Communal boundaries are not determined only by religion; the language marchers in *Midnight's Children* are coreligionists of different communities. Community membership is determined by birth and upbringing, although religious conversion may entail movement from one to another. The coexistence of and tension between communities in India makes the major Indian cities into ideal case studies for transnational writers, and we will see in Chapter 6 how Rushdie applies lessons of Indian cosmopolitanism to American national identity.

The ties between communal and national identity are complicated in Indian politics by the competing definitions of the term "nation." Because India is a secular state, members of all religious or linguistic communities are in principle equally "Indian," and Indian nationalism need not distinguish between different communities. This version of Indian nationalism is an example of the civic nationalism defined by Eric Hobsbawm, in which the nation is created by the will of individual participants.[5] While it can vary, the civic nation as conceived by its citizens tends to be based on a set of shared principles: in India's case, democracy, secularism, and egalitarianism. Communal identity is (or can be) irrelevant.

If a community develops its own nationalist movement, on the other hand, that movement will probably resemble the ethnic nationalism described by Johann Gottfried Herder and Clifford Geertz, in which national identity is based on a shared language, culture, and possibly blood.[6] Communal nationalist movements need not advocate separation from India but are liable to advocate some degree of self-government. As Jocelyne Couture, Kai Nielsen, and Michel Seymour argue, however, the distinction between civic and ethnic nationalism is not always clear, and nowhere does this difference become more difficult to define than in India, where the Hindu nationalist movement is seeking to redefine the civic nation described above as a nation determined by shared relig⸺[7]

India contains many subdivisions: citizens belong to states, language groups, religions, ethnicities, tribes, castes, and classes, and each marker potentially carries its own sense of communal identity. Each group—the group of Marathi speakers, for example—imagines its own commonality. For India to hold together as a country, these groups, which define themselves against each other, must also imagine a pan-Indian commonality in which the factions add up to a supernation. The act of imagination that the civic nation of India asks of its citizens, then, is large and difficult. For India to be a "nation," individuals must see themselves as part of the same group as people whom they must also, for the sake of their communal loyalties, consider alien. The idea that India is a pluralist nation—one based on shared civic ideals or Naipaul's "continental racial sense," rather than a country containing Marathis, Tamils, Sikhs, and so on—requires a radical departure from millennia of inherited identity categories.[8] Unsurprisingly, then, communal identity in India is often seen as a predictor of civic national loyalties: since Partition in 1947, Indian Muslims have frequently been suspected of supporting Pakistan, for example.

The tensions between communal and cosmopolitan or pan-Indian identities have shaped Bombay since the arrival of the first European colonists. Rushdie's novels, in treating Bombay as a model for India, are a product of and answer to that tension, creating a shared mythology and unearthing a lineage for the cosmopolitan nation. As Neil Ten Kortenaar puts it, "In *Midnight's Children* the nationalist cosmopolitan has invented a protagonist who may best be described as a cosmopolitan nationalist."[9] But Saleem's cosmopolitan nationalism, like India's, is complicated and undercut by its own internal contradictions.

A Brief History of the City of Bombay and the Shiv Sena Party

In *Midnight's Children*, Saleem draws links between his family history and the major political events of his lifetime. Critics have documented his inaccuracies, slips, and obfuscations (and Rushdie explains some of them himself[10]), but the relationship between Saleem's life and India's history is not in question. Because India is so highly fragmented, however, Saleem's version of history must be partial. While much of the story—Independence, war, the Emergency—is nationwide, the details, the ideal of cosmopolitanism, the method of self-invention, and even the villain are all specific to Bombay, and the cosmopolitanism of the novel is a Bombayite cosmopolitanism.

To explain how Rushdie makes Bombay stand in for India, and why the city provides the primary site of his transnational community-building, it is necessary to discuss the city's history of cosmopolitanism and communalism. The 1995 change in the city's name—it is now known as Mumbai—encapsulates the local debate about post-Independence communal identity that Rushdie addresses in his novels. The name "Bombay" was thought by the British to come from the Portuguese *bom bahia*, "good harbor," itself a corruption of the original name of the local goddess, Mumbadevi. While now called Mumbai on maps, the city's name remains a vexed question. Depending on an inhabitant's politics or native language, the name still varies, and a foreigner is liable to corrections in either direction. For some, the name change is a nationalist reclamation of the state from colonial rule, part of Bombay's transformation into an Indian, rather than a British, capital of world trade. For others, the change signals the city's increasing parochialism; for these critics, the new name belongs to the "sons of the soil" movement that has risen to power over the past twenty years. In this clash, Rushdie is on the side of the earlier name; for that reason this chapter uses the name "Bombay."

The change in Bombay's name, the debate about how to handle India's multicultural population and history, and the battle Rushdie fights in his novels stem from two very different Indian nationalisms: the Independence movement, led by Jawaharlal Nehru and the Mahatma Gandhi, and the current Hindu nationalist movement. These two nationalisms fall neatly into the cosmopolitan, civic nationalist and the communalist, ethnic nationalist camps: while Nehru and Gandhi advocated a diverse secular state, Hindu nationalists are hostile toward minority religious groups. Nehru attended Oxford and was in many ways a proponent of Westernization, whereas Hindu nationalists largely reject Western cultural imports, from blue jeans to political theories. The tension between these two nationalisms and the visions on which they are based—a tension Rushdie describes as one of "the paradoxes at the heart of the India-idea"—will inform my entire discussion of Rushdie's work.[11]

Both groups of nationalists treat Bombay as a microcosm of India. Nehru made the city the focus of the first nationwide economic Five-Year Plan and viewed it as a model for growth and urbanization. Contemporary Hindu nationalists consider the reclamation of Mumbai from colonial Bombay a success that bodes well for their projects throughout the country. As those two examples show (and Sujata Patel and Alice Thorner's *Bombay: Metaphor for Modern India* demonstrates), Bombay's position is a contentious one: while for some, Bombay is a metaphor for India in its history as a multiethnic, multireligious society, for others, that history is exactly what the real Mumbai is about to overcome. And for other millions of Indians, Bombay is not a metaphor for India at all, since while the cosmopolitan center contains representatives of the country's languages and religions, it cannot contain the life of the villages, where the majority of India's population resides.

Saleem's mixed parentage reflects Bombay's history. Bombay was founded as a Portuguese trading post and Jesuit settlement in 1534. The area consisted at that time of seven lightly populated islands at the tip of a peninsula running north-south into the Indian Ocean. The settlement came under the British crown as part of the dowry of Catherine of Braganza, who married Charles II in 1662. Over the next few centuries, Bombay grew to prominence as the "Gateway to India," the primary Western port and shipping center on the subcontinent. Populated largely by immigrants and the children of immigrants—British colonists, Parsi merchants, Muslim and Hindu migrants from the countryside—Bombay was cosmopolitan from the beginning, containing a religious and communal mix remarkable even by the high standards of Indian cities. Also remarkable was the comparative ease with which the communities got along: until the riots set off by the Ayodhya mosque controversies in 1992 and the reprisals on each side that have followed, Bombay enjoyed a reputation for tolerance.[12]

In the nineteenth century, neighborhoods consisted largely of a single class and caste. By Independence, however, new suburbs appeared, which were increasingly linked more by class than by religious or linguistic affiliation: as economic divides in the population of the city became sharper, religious and caste divides faded, creating middle-class neighborhoods instead of Gujarati, Marathi, or Muslim neighborhoods.[13] This increased mixing among the city's communities fostered tremendous cultural activity in the 1950s and 1960s: theater and the visual arts thrived. Sujata Patel identifies Bombay's middle class in the 1950s as "not only multilingual but multiethnic."[14] This class formed a cosmopolitanism that, while enabled by the "spoils of colonialism," also provided a ground for resistance to it.[15] Unlike Bhabha's Indian Christians, Bombayites used hybridity as a form of resistance by improving on the originals—for example, strengthening the English, Gujarati, and Marathi theatrical traditions by swapping techniques among them.[16] Rushdie draws on this tradition of cultural mixtures—between Indian populations as well as between colonizer and colonized—for *Midnight's Children*. Saleem's multiple ancestries make him an embodiment of the cultural phenomena at work during his childhood.

Cultural mixtures seem to have belonged mostly to the middle classes, however. Rushdie's critique of Bombay's cosmopolitanism comes from its failure to cross class, rather than communal, lines. Marathi-speaking working-class Bombayites evolved an ethos of cultural purity epitomized by the beliefs of the Shiv Sena Party, the political party that now dominates the city, which Rushdie parodies throughout his novels. The Shiv Sena's rise, which began shortly after the partition of Bombay State, coincided with a major change in the city's culture. The differences appear in many places: the replacement of Bombay's multiethnic live-theater community with Bollywood and Hollywood films; the increasing isolation of the city's upper classes; and the way the upper classes articulate their cosmopolitan identities, not as Bombayites or Mumbaikars but as members of a global community.[17] In each case, cultural mixtures between communities have been largely replaced by either stricter communalism or a more globally oriented, mass-produced artistic production.

The Shiv Sena Party takes its name from the seventeenth-century Marathi warrior-king Shivaji, who organized a Hindu kingdom and fought campaigns against nearby Muslim states; the name "Shiv Sena" means "Shivaji's Army." Sena membership is formed into local groups called *shakas*, each led by a *dada* or "older brother," a term associated with what Gérard Heuzé calls "a culture of the goon, but also the virile and young culture of the street."[18] *Shakas* resemble sports teams in their approach to group activity—a resemblance Rushdie parodies in *The Moor's Last Sigh*. The Sena views Marathis as the "sons of the soil," the native inhabitants of Bombay and Maharashtra. All others, including Gujaratis but particularly South Indians and Muslims, are seen as immigrants and thus not entitled to the same percentage of scarce resources.

Poor Marathi speakers in Bombay have had cause for complaint. The economic growth of the Five-Year Plan did not improve conditions in the slums, where residents lacked access to clean water, latrines, or trash collection. (This discrepancy between rhetoric and reality plays an important role in Rushdie's work.) Marathi speakers were much poorer than Gujarati speakers in Bombay in the early 1950s[19]; since then, the Sena has helped Marathis find jobs and gain access to education. But this success has come in part from unscrupulous behavior: intimidation of and violence against South Indians and Muslims, the inciting of riots, and the murder of vocal opponents.[20]

Particularly important to Rushdie is the Sena's behavior during Indira Gandhi's three-year State of Emergency: the Sena participated in slum clearance programs, and despite a history of antagonism toward the Congress Party, supported Mrs. Gandhi's policies. Beyond the permanence of *shaka* structure and charismatic leadership by Bal Thackeray, however, the Sena has had no very coherent program. The few constants have been Marathi nationalism, anticommunism, and increasing antagonism toward minority groups; Heuzé notes that "they dislike mixture."[21] The group bases much of its appeal on an image of and rhetoric about virility, expressed as intolerance and violence.

The Shiv Sena is a useful enemy for Rushdie, appearing in his work in many guises. The Sena encapsulates many things Rushdie hates: religious fanaticism, intolerance, belief in cultural purity, and violence. The Sena's communal politics, which first appear in *Midnight's Children*, become a dominant theme in *The Moor's Last Sigh* and are the counterweight, the opposing dream, to Rushdie's ideal India.

MIDNIGHT'S CHILDREN AND THE SHIV SENA

Bombay's history appears in translated form in Saleem Sinai's family. Saleem, like Bombay, is founded by the Portuguese: his nurse (who is responsible for the baby swap that gives Saleem his life of privilege and condemns the Sinais' biological child to the slums) is Mary Pereira, an Indian Christian with a Portuguese name. At the end of the novel, Mary Pereira reappears as Mrs. Braganza, namesake of Catherine of Braganza, who brought Bombay under British rule. Mrs. Braganza brings Saleem back to self-awareness through her chutneys, aided by Saleem's interlocutor Padma, a representative of the "pomfret folk" who were the islands' earliest inhabitants.[22] David Birch shows that those chutneys contain both memory and cultural mixtures, and Mary, the first and last of Saleem's adopted mothers, is responsible for some of the most important cultural mix-ups in the book; like the Portuguese, she started the series of recombinations.[23]

Nursed by a Portuguese-named Indian Christian in childhood and by an embodiment of Mumbadevi during his decline, Saleem's body encapsulates the major forces at work in Bombay.[24] Although he is raised by wealthy Muslims, Saleem is the biological child of Vanita, a poor Hindu woman, and the English colonist William Methwold, who claims descent from one of the founders of the city. Saleem is very much the "half-caste offspring of London," as Nirad Chaudhri calls Bombay.[25] His face, with its Pakistan-shaped birthmarks and peninsular nose, may appear to represent all of India, but his parentage is specific to Bombay. John Su, David Lipscomb, Neil Ten Kortenaar, and Fawzia Afzal-Khan discuss how Saleem advocates unity and cooperation among the Midnight Children[26]; this unity closely resembles the form of cosmopolitanism that, Patel argues, is the hallmark of Bombay in the 1950s.[27] *Midnight's Children* is as much a Bombayite as an Indian book, and Saleem's narrative is a plea for the communal cooperation and cosmopolitan fluidity for which Bombay stands.

Because of Indian city dwellers' uneasy balance between civic and ethnic identity, the threat of communal violence is constantly present. Saleem's advent is announced as a call for peace and cooperation addressed to a Muslim mob threatening the Hindu Lifafa Das. (This scene takes place in Delhi; it is telling that his parents leave for Bombay before his birth.) But with Saleem's arrival there comes also a proponent of violence and communalism: Saleem's double, Shiva. The Sena's list of accomplishments should sound familiar to readers of *Midnight's Children*. Shiva, too, is involved in slum clearance, working for the Widow and running the raid that kills Parvati-the-witch. Like the Sena, he profits from the Emergency, while the rest of the Midnight Children are rounded up and sterilized. Shiva's aspect as the Destroyer, the unscrupulous traitor and suspected murderer, resembles the Shiv Sena's vigilantism. And, like the Sena, Shiva is an embodiment of virility—he impregnates dozens of women. The contradictions of Shiva's nature—creator and destroyer, slum child and clearer of slums—make him further resemble the Sena, which is capable of sudden switches in position or of turning against its former allegiances, such as when they ended their campaign against the Congress Party to support the Emergency. It is just as contradictory for the Sena, the sons-of-the-soil movement of the Marathi poor, to arrange slum clearances as it is for Shiva to participate in them. Shiva embodies the Sena's worst aspects: totalitarianism, communalism, inconsistency, and violence. If Saleem embodies the Indian history of pluralism, Shiva embodies India's parallel history of oppression and intolerance.

Shiva and Saleem represent mutually exclusive alternatives—historically, politically, and philosophically—and embody the competing versions of nationalism in the book. But while the enmity between Saleem and Shiva is clear, the location of the moral high ground is not. To young Saleem's musings about the children's "purpose," Shiva responds with nihilistic skepticism: "What thing in the whole sister-sleeping world got *reason*, yara? For what reason you're rich and I'm poor? Where's the reason in starving, man?"[28] Shiva's questions are troubling. Saleem has an explanation for why one is rich and the other poor—that the babies were switched at birth by their nurse, to please her communist lover—but that explanation is doubly flawed: first, because it answers the question on too small a scale, explaining why these particular individuals are rich and poor, without explaining why the disparity exists to begin with; and second, because once the answer is given, the injustice of the situation becomes even greater when the poor child learns that he "should" have been rich. The real answer, as Shiva knows, is that there is no reason in starving, and Saleem's avoidance of this issue leads to the breakup of the Midnight Children's Conference.

Saleem's refusal to acknowledge the complexities of his situation grants power to Shiva. When Saleem will not become Parvati-the-witch's lover (he sees his sister's face superimposed over Parvati's when they try), Parvati turns to Shiva in reaction to his rejection. Saleem's refusal to consummate their relationship suggests his failure to harmonize his disparate elements: he has joined the (impoverished, communist, Hindu) world of the magicians' ghetto, but he cannot shake his allegiance to the (wealthy, capitalist, Muslim) world of his family.

M. Keith Booker argues that the parodic treatment of the communist magicians suggests that Rushdie's sympathies do not lie with the inhabitants of the ghetto.[29] Patrick Colm Hogan, however, responds that while "Rushdie does appear to repudiate communism as a real option for India,"[30] the communist snake-charmer Picture Singh remains, in Saleem's words, "the greatest man I ever met."[31] Saleem's reluctant rejection of communism and his refusal of Parvati's love coincide with his increasing suspicion that none of the political options he knows will work for India. Into this gap steps Shiva, making the paradoxes of Saleem's position clear:

> one morning in May 1974—is it just my cracking memory, or am I right in thinking it was the 18th, perhaps at the very moment at which the deserts of Rajasthan were being shaken by India's first nuclear explosion? . . . —he came to the magicians' slum. Uniformed, gonged-and-pipped, and a Major now . . . even through the modest khaki of his Army pants it was easy to make out the phenomenal twin bulges of his lethal knees . . . India's most decorated war hero, but once he led a gang of apaches in the back-streets of Bombay; once, before he discovered the legitimized violence of war, prostitutes were found throttled in gutters (I know, I know—no proof).[32]

Shiva, always connected with communalism and selfishness, is now also a figure of heroic nationalism: his appearance, simultaneous with India's first nuclear test, marks the country's turn—like Parvati's—away from Saleem's secular, inclusive ideal and toward a militaristic and aggressive definition of "India." His roots among the "gang of apaches" resemble the Sena's gang culture; Shiva is the most successful of *dadas*, leading his gang not only to prominence in the city but to military victory over Pakistan. Shiva, uniformed and "gonged-and-pipped" with medals, is distinguishable from the "gonged-and-pipped" Pakistani General Zulfikar only by his "lethal knees." This difference marks him as Indian, one of the magical Midnight's Children, but his gift has perversely caused him to resemble his military opponent, as both use their power to establish totalitarian regimes.

After his affair with Parvati, Shiva returns to the magicians' ghetto to perform a "civic beautification programme"[33]—destroying the slum and sterilizing its occupants:

> O shiny buttons on a traitor's uniform! . . . why did he do it? Why did he, who had once led anarchistic apaches through the slums of Bombay, become the warlord of tyranny? Why did midnight's child betray the children of midnight, and take me to my fate? For love of violence, and the legitimizing glitter of buttons on uniforms? For the sake of his ancient antipathy towards me? Or—I find this the most plausible—in exchange for immunity from the penalties imposed on the rest of us . . . yes, that must be it; O birthright-denying war hero! O mess-of-pottage-corrupted rival . . .[34]

Shiva betrays the ideals of independence in order to secure his own advantage. But by calling Shiva a traitor, Saleem hides his own past actions: Saleem has exiled Shiva from his telepathic conferences out of fear that Shiva could supplant him, both as leader of the Children and as his parents' son. Shiva's betrayal is of an ideal that Saleem has not let him share. For all Saleem's love of pluralism, he has always been reluctant to acknowledge Shiva's very existence, let alone his claim on Saleem's good fortune. Inherent in Shiva's banishment from the Midnight Children's Conference lies much of the ambivalence of the novel. Unlike Nehru's death and the Indo-Pakistani War, Shiva's success in the military and the Emergency really is Saleem's fault: Saleem has displaced him, first unintentionally (through the baby swap) and then deliberately (in his exile from the Midnight Children's Conference), leaving Shiva with no reason to change his nihilistic position. As Ten Kortenaar notes, Saleem's reference to the mess of pottage demonstrates his own culpability: like the Biblical Jacob tricking Esau, Saleem has stolen Shiva's birthright.[35] Shiva's participation in the suppression of civil rights and the sterilization of the Midnight Children is not a mere rejection of Saleem's ideal but an active betrayal of the entire group, in return for the group's betrayal of him.

Saleem's narrative treatment of Shiva indicates that Saleem still finds Shiva frightening. Saleem is regularly inaccurate in his memoir, but he only lies once. This lie, which he eventually confesses to, is his claim that Shiva has been shot by a former lover. This deviation from the truth Saleem believes in, "memory's truth,"[36] comes from an attempt to reassure himself that his rival is no longer a threat. This lie is a failure for the same reason that it is necessary: Shiva is, in fact, the victor in their struggle. His triumph comes from Saleem's failure, both personally and politically.

In light of his similarities to the Shiv Sena, Shiva becomes not only Saleem's rival but also an embodiment of a rival view of India and Bombay: that of Hindu nationalism, which wants a land as "pure" as Pakistan. Shiva, unlike Saleem, is traditionally heroic: virile, active, a decorated soldier. Hogan describes the difference between Shiva and Saleem as that between the "authoritarian imagination" and the "pluralistic imagination."[37] But the correspondence is not exact because Shiva reveals the flaw in Saleem's pluralism. Shiva threatens Saleem's birthright and reveals Saleem's own "mess-of-pottage corrupted" nature. His existence is also an indictment of Saleem's betrayal of his own ideals: his inclusivity does not extend to Shiva. If Saleem is the embodiment of Bombay's multiethnic past, Shiva embodies the possibility of a nationalist, homogenous future. In Saleem and Shiva, Rushdie provides two models for India to choose between: multiethnic cosmopolitanism and Hindu nationalism. And he suggests that the success of the Hindu nationalists stems directly from the cosmopolitans' failure to live up to their own inclusive ideals.

THE SHIV SENA AND *THE MOOR'S LAST SIGH*

The subtle jabs at the Shiv Sena in *Midnight's Children* become more overt in *The Moor's Last Sigh*. The novel's secondary villain, Raman Fielding, clearly resembles the Sena leader Bal Thackeray—a satire that outraged Sena activists and led to the book's suppression in India. The differences between Fielding and his model point to the nature of Rushdie's criticism, however. Fielding's group is called "Mumbai's Axis," a name Fielding arrives at after several other alternatives: "In his bizarre conception of cricket as a fundamentally communalist game, essentially Hindu but with its Hindu-ness constantly under threat from the country's other, treacherous communities, lay the origins of his political philosophy, and of 'Mumbai's Axis' itself. There was even a moment when Raman Fielding considered naming his new political movement after a great Hindu cricketer—Ranji's Army, Mankad's Martinets—but in the end he went for the goddess—a. k. a. Mumba-Ai, Mumbadevi, Mumbabai—thus uniting regional and religious nationalism in his potent, explosive new group."[38] Fielding's group parodies the Sena by showing the Western roots of its nationalist rhetoric. The name "Mumbai's Axis" is significant both in what it adds and what it omits. By replacing Shivaji, Mumbai becomes the central focus of the movement, lacking the broader Marathi nationalism associated with the warrior king. Changing "Sena," "army," to "Axis" suggests the fascist alliance of World War II. The adoption of cricket as an "essentially Hindu" game parodies Bhabha's postcolonial mimicry, suggesting a naïve colonial adaptation of the colonizer's imported culture, in which the colonized subject's self-conception is redefined in Western terms.

By turning the real Sena's *shaka* system into an "Axis" philosophically based on cricket, Rushdie undercuts the most successful element of the group's structure. Fielding reduces communalist politics to team sports. The Sena leader with his British novelist's name is revealed as an unwitting anglophile, and by combining cricket with Nazism, this postcolonial rejection of the former colonizer turns out to be rooted in a hodgepodge of European cultures. Fielding's obsession with the "Hindu" game of cricket (which distortively echoes Ashis Nandy's argument that the game's "mythic structures" make it profoundly Indian[39]) suggests that Hindu nationalism is arbitrary in its appropriations, claiming alien cultural artifacts as its own and resenting their "theft" by other groups; worse, the Hindu nationalists fail to realize that they themselves are products of a hybrid society, and their "pure" loves may have the mongrel pasts they condemn elsewhere.

While Rushdie's attack on the Shiv Sena is more overt in *The Moor's Last Sigh* than in *Midnight's Children*, it is also more equivocal. Raman Fielding serves as a foil for the more dangerous and ambiguous villain of the piece: the narrator's father, Abraham Zogoiby, whose actions broaden Rushdie's critique of cosmopolitanism by suggesting the problems of globalism.

Rushdie's work contains two kinds of cosmopolitanism, perhaps best distinguished as local and global cosmopolitanisms. Despite his love of cross-cultural combinations, Rushdie retains a deep appreciation of local specificity. The cosmopolitan communities of Rushdie's Bombay novels are all deeply rooted: like the India Saleem telepathically creates in the Midnight Children's Conference, they establish what Hogan calls a "transgeographical, modern localism."[40] The Bombay of *Midnight's Children* and the first half of *The Moor's Last Sigh* is not a global city but an Indian one, and the city's cultural components cannot be duplicated elsewhere. Appiah's "rooted cosmopolitan" engages in dialogue with cultures from around the world, but Rushdie's, at least in his early novels, may not. The Bombay cosmopolitan is at home in many groups, but they are all indigenous to Bombay.

Global cosmopolitanism, on the other hand, appears in Rushdie's later novels as at best a dubious good. This is the cosmopolitanism of the global consumer, the airport boutique. Global cosmopolitanism fosters not eclecticism but homogeneity, replacing indigenous productions with foreign products without reference to the value of either. At its worst, global cosmopolitanism becomes indistinguishable from the "multinational conglomerates" responsible for such disasters as the release of airborne poisons at Bhopal.[41] Rushdie sees global cosmopolitanism as a process of displacement rather than of mixture. The displacement of local culture, rather than that local culture's parochialism, is the real villain of *The Moor's Last Sigh*—and is embodied by a very slippery character indeed.

The book's narrator, Moor, may not be sure whether his father is responsible for his mother Aurora's death and, later, for the destruction of much of the city of Bombay, but the reader is not left much room to doubt: Abraham is implicated in every tragedy in the book, even those apparently brought about by Fielding. Fielding the nationalist and Abraham the businessman are implacable enemies, but each magnifies the results of the other's actions. They share no ideological positions, but their methods and terminology overlap. Abraham, too, presides over an "Axis": the "Zogoiby-Da Gama Axis," which generates his vast fortune. While the two axes are rivals, their similarities make them partners in the destruction of old Bombay—a Bombay Fielding despises because it is too cosmopolitan and Abraham disdains because it is too old-fashioned.

Abraham's destruction of the old city begins with building: he wants to create a new, international Bombay of steel skyscrapers, at the top of which he lives in an Edenic greenhouse garden. Abraham's architectural ambitions resemble those of Shah Jehan, the emperor who built the Taj Mahal. This comparison implies Abraham's dark side: "He showed how easy it would be to persuade those worthy officers whose job it was to monitor and control the number and height of new buildings in the Reclamation that they would be much advantaged were they to lose the gift of sight—'metaphorically, of course, boy—it was only a figure of speech; don't think we wanted to put out anybody's eyes, not like Shah Jehan with that peeping Tom who wanted a sneak preview of the Taj.'"[42] Like the Taj, Abraham's grand constructions grow out of the suffering of others. In Abraham's Bombay, the builders are legally nonexistent, and the inspectors are "blinded" by corruption. As in the real Bombay, much of the actual construction is done by Bengali laborers whose legal existence is denied by the Sena government.[43] Abraham may be in competition with Fielding, but it is only a competition for power; while their ideologies differ, Abraham is also ready to profit from the disenfranchisement of recent migrants. And while Fielding's agenda, however reprehensible, at least includes some affection for the old Bombay, Abraham has no interest in preserving local culture.

If Saleem's vision of Bombay is one of pluralism, and Shiva-Fielding-Thackeray's is of Marathi unity, Abraham's vision is of Bombay the business center: a global metropolis immersed in international trade at the expense of moral or social considerations. Abraham represents a third option for Bombay: neither Saleem's multiethnic center nor Fielding's Marathi capital, but a Bombay in which the elite belong to a global cosmopolitan culture divorced from the city's distinct character, ignoring the source and price of its own prosperity. Abraham demonstrates that cosmopolitanism can go too far, erasing valuable aspects of a culture (buildings, individuals' legal identities) along with communal tensions.

The ideological competition between Fielding and Abraham has real effects in the novel's world: a change in the physical structure of Bombay. The nationalists and cosmopolitans of *The Moor's Last Sigh* and *Midnight's Children* can give physical reality to their ideas in part because of their placement in fiction. The novels emphasize the interaction between identity and physical place by granting the city itself what Saleem calls an "active-metaphorical" role.[44] Bombay interacts with the characters, physically propelling Saleem into the language marchers, or providing the literal cliff edge on which Aurora dances, straddling two worlds. When the "big rich hill" sends Saleem's bicycle "crashing into history," setting off "the first of the language riots," Saleem claims to be "directly responsible for triggering off the violence which ended with the partition of the state of Bombay, as a result of which the city became the capital of Maharashtra."[45] But the responsibility is shared with the hill itself, which, by propelling Saleem, provides the impetus for defining the city's Mahathi identity. The novel, despite its narrator's claims for his own importance, emphasizes that the city and its citizens are mutually constitutive, granting identity-defining agency to both.

The city and the characters in *The Moor's Last Sigh* shape each other even more actively than those of *Midnight's Children*. Abraham directs land-reclamation schemes, and he is responsible for the city's destruction when he provides Sammy Hazaré with explosives for a huge and destructive bombing spree. By acting as both creator and destroyer of Bombay, Abraham outdoes even Shiva's creative-destructive powers. In doing so, he also creates and destroys his son. Moor's magically explosive growth, as Alexandra Schultheis points out, mirrors that of the city itself[46]; his death occurs simultaneously with the destruction of the cosmopolitan city of his youth. Abraham's role in his son's death suggests that Fielding and the thinly disguised Shiv Sena are only distractions from the real threat to Bombay and Indian pluralism: homogenization in the name of global progress. Dangerous as fanaticism and communalism are, they are comparatively harmless without Abraham's complicity.

The bombings in *The Moor's Last Sigh* finish *Midnight's Children* by eliminating the last people and places Saleem cared about: "The mahaguru Khusro perished in the bombings; the pink skyscraper at Breach Candy, where 'Adam Zogoiby' had been raised, was also destroyed."[47] The city Moor flees bears no resemblance to his, or Saleem's, childhood home. The Malabar Hill that propelled Saleem into the language marchers no longer exists. It is as a result of the bombings, not of Fielding's machinations, that Moor rides his airplane to Spain thinking, "It was no longer my Bombay, no longer special, no longer the city of mixed-up, mongrel joy. Something had ended (the world?) and what remained, I didn't know."[48] Roger Clark argues that *Midnight's Children* is based on the loss of an Edenic Kashmir[49]; in *The Moor's Last Sigh*, Bombay, too, becomes a lost Eden, destroyed by global consumerism.

Rushdie's critiques of the Shiv Sena in *The Moor's Last Sigh* outraged Sena activists, who were insulted by Rushdie's parody of Bal Thackeray and considered the accusations of assassination libelous. But they might have been more incensed had they realized that they are not the real enemy in the books. *The Moor's Last Sigh* shows that the dualism of the Saleem-versus-Shiva battle overlooks a more insidious enemy. Rushdie objects to the Sena's goals and methods, but he also uses the Sena's origins to critique his own position. Shiva and the Sena are created by a cosmopolitanism that is only partially inclusive and that thus is responsible for the eventual destruction of Bombay. When inclusivity remains rhetorical rather than real, the result may be one of two terrible extremes: the violent, bigoted communalism of the Shiv Sena or the exploitative internationalism of the Da Gama-Zogoiby Axis. In *Midnight's Children* and *The Moor's Last Sigh* Rushdie shows how his "city of mongrel joy" became a place of violence and of gleaming, faceless skyscrapers, and ruthlessly examines his ideal's failure.

EMBODYING THE NATION: THE PROBLEM WITH CHARISMA

Midnight's Children and *The Moor's Last Sigh* critique nationalist visions of India for their failures of inclusion. But both novels remain committed to finding a substitute for Naipaul's "continental racial sense," the sense of "Indianness" that can unite communities across class, linguistic, and religious lines. Rushdie's critique of the body politic and his rejection of charismatic figures—Saleem, Shiva, Thackeray, Indira Gandhi, or the Mahatma Gandhi himself—reveals a fundamental reformulation of the sources of national identity and argues that the nation requires the broadest possible participation. The puzzling references to Mohandas Gandhi embedded in *Midnight's Children* demand that readers decode the problems inherent in nationalist movements led by charismatic leaders. In the long run, the novel urges us to replace such movements with a radically democratic, participatory, leaderless national sense.

The Shiv Sena is based to a large degree on Bal Thackeray's charisma and persuasive powers. This, like the Sena's intolerance and violence, is disturbing to Rushdie: movements based around charismatic leaders are suspect both because they cannot outlast the leader's lifetime and because they subordinate difference among the group members to obedience to the group's leader. As Jon Thompson demonstrates, Rushdie is wary of notions of heroism, particularly those that depend on schematic, us-versus-them dichotomies.[50] Such dichotomies are rhetorically indispensable to Saleem's competitors, Shiva and the Widow, whose rise to power depend on Saleem's destruction.

Saleem struggles with Indira Gandhi for the right to "be" India. Their competition concentrates the metaphor of the body politic into real individuals: Indira's positioning as "mother India," exemplified by her campaign slogan, "Indira is India, India is Indira," challenges Saleem's claim to embody India himself. As Mujeebuddin Syed points out, this is a battle between Indira's "fascist" tendencies and Saleem's "plural identity," a contest of systems as well as of individuals.[51] Indira wins by imprisoning and castrating Saleem, but his fate is equivocal: John Su demonstrates that the struggle with the Widow is a critique of "the equation of leader and nation" that "removes social agency from individuals," and therefore Saleem's final disintegration is the most optimistic outcome possible, since it undermines the nationalist hero myth, returning agency to individuals.[52]

Indira is not Saleem's only challenger for the position of incarnation of India. The other most obvious incarnation is Mohandas K. Gandhi, who is almost absent from the book: as Brennan notes, "the very staple of a major branch of Indo-English historical fiction . . . is impertinently excised from the narrative outright."[53] Su calls Gandhi's absence "bizarre," but it is inevitable: if Rushdie is to take on the Indian hero myth, Gandhi must be one of his primary targets. If any figure is acknowledged, in India and out, as an embodiment of the country, it is Gandhi. Hogan demonstrates the importance of Gandhi's socialism to Saleem's political thought, and Rushdie cannot but admire Gandhi's ideal of inclusivity. As a heroic figure, however, Gandhi is made suspect by many things, including his skill at theatrical gestures and his inability to speak for elements of India Saleem and Rushdie hold dear, including both Muslims and nonbelievers. Saleem unseats Gandhi from his position as embodiment of India because Saleem wants that position for himself, but Rushdie does it because, in the end, it is a position that no one should occupy.

Hogan gives a compelling account of Rushdie's ideological debt to Gandhi, citing Gandhi's emphasis on localism over centralization, which, as we have seen, Rushdie adapts for his vision of the local cosmopolitan. Hogan argues that Saleem's emphasis on his mistake about the date of Gandhi's assassination suggests that Gandhi really did die at the "wrong" time: "In Rushdie's view, Gandhi should not have died when he did. He should have lived, shaping the nation's future."[54] But Gandhi is so systematically suppressed throughout the novel that more may be at stake than the untimeliness of his death. Instead, through Saleem's rivalry with Gandhi for the position of embodiment of India, Rushdie critiques the notion of heroic figures. National heroes, no matter how inclusive they wish to be, cannot include everyone.

Gandhi's absence from the sections of the book set during the Independence movement is peculiar, particularly those regarding the Convocation of Mian Abdullah, a Muslim political group advocating a secular, unified India. This is precisely the kind of organization that would have joined forces with Gandhi, who opposed Partition and advocated Hindu-Muslim unity.[55] Yet Gandhi is not, as far as Saleem tells us, associated with the Convocation, nor does he appear at all in *Midnight's Children* before his assassination. Much as he did with the very un-Gandhian Shiva, Saleem suppresses his rival's existence. The suppression fails, however, because Saleem takes it too far, first changing the date of Gandhi's death to suit his own narrative necessity, then confusedly correcting his error.

Contemplating his misplaced history, Saleem is disoriented and self-justifying:

> But today, I feel confused . . . Re-reading my work, I have discovered an error in chronology. The assassination of Mahatma Gandhi occurs, in these pages, on the wrong date. But I cannot say, now, what the actual sequence of events might have been; in my India, Gandhi will continue to die at the wrong time.[56]

Saleem's India depends upon a deliberate misstatement of history. Even when the "real" facts can be verified, Saleem cannot use them: he is unable to adapt his memories to objective truth, so he argues that objective truth is irrelevant. The pressure of present chronology (writing his autobiography before he dies) takes precedence over past chronology, and imagined national history supercedes verifiable historical fact. As a result, Gandhi's assassination takes place while Saleem is watching his uncle and aunt's movie, *The Lovers of Kashmir*:

> The serpent can take most unexpected forms; now, in the guise of this ineffectual house-manager, it unleashed its venom. Pia and Nayyar faded and died; and the amplified voice of the bearded man said: "Ladies and gents, your pardon; but there is terrible news." His voice broke—a sob from the Serpent, to lend power to its teeth!—and then continued, "This afternoon, at Birla House in Delhi, our beloved Mahatma was killed. Some madman shot him in the stomach, ladies and gentlemen—our Bapu is gone!"
>
> The audience had begun to scream before he finished; the poison of his words entered their veins—there were grown men rolling in the aisles clutching their bellies, not laughing but crying, *Hai Ram! Hai Ram!*—and women tearing their hair: the city's finest coiffures tumbling around the ears of the poisoned ladies—there were film-stars yelling like fishwives and something terrible to smell in the air—and Hanif whispered, "Get out of here, big sister—if a Muslim did this thing there will be hell to pay."
>
> For every ladder, there is a snake . . . and for forty-eight hours after the abortive end of *The Lovers of Kashmir*, our family remained within the walls of Buckingham Villa ("Put furniture against the doors, whatsitsname!" Reverend Mother ordered. "If there are Hindu servants, let them go home!"); and Amina did not dare to visit the race-track.
>
> But for every snake, there is a ladder: and finally the radio gave us a name. Nathuram Godse. "Thank God," Amina burst out, "It's not a Muslim name!"
>
> And Aadam, upon whom the news of Gandhi's death had placed a new burden of age: "This Godse is nothing to be grateful for!"
>
> Amina, however, was full of the light-headedness of relief, she was rushing dizzily up the long ladder of relief . . . "Why not, after all? By being Godse he has saved our lives!"[57]

Saleem's description of the news of Gandhi's death as an aspect of "the serpent" implies a danger and a loss of innocence on several levels, invoking the serpent of Eden as well as the fatidic serpents of Saleem's Snakes and Ladders. Gandhi's death is India's loss of innocence,[58] demonstrating the internal ruptures in Indian society.

Gandhi's assassination destroys the community of the film's audience. The assassin, Nathuram Godse, was a Hindu nationalist angered by Gandhi's position on Indo-Pakistani relations: Gandhi's final fast was a protest against the communal divisions following an undeclared war in Kashmir. The news of Gandhi's death divides the people in the theater along communal lines: while the Hindus cry "*Hai Ram,*" the Muslims fear there will be "hell to pay." The moment is also a loss of innocence for Saleem, who has never thought of himself as a target for communal violence. As

Kashmir changes from Aadam Aziz's Edenic home to a war zone, the "Lovers of Kashmir" are replaced by assassins, mobs, and victims. Kashmir is lost, both through the border dispute with Pakistan and through its role as a catalyst of Gandhi's assassination.

Gandhi's death alienates the Sinai family from India: they are suddenly Other, barricading themselves indoors. For Saleem, the worst consequence of Gandhi's death may be that it forces the Sinais to think of themselves as Muslims rather than as Bombayites. It is important, then, that Ten Kortenaar demonstrates Saleem's account to be not just placed on the wrong day but misremembered in its substance: Ten Kortenaar, citing Catherine Cundy's account of Rushdie's historical sources, reminds us that news of Gandhi's death "was actually withheld from the public for forty-five *minutes* until it could be confirmed that the assassin was a Hindu . . . In other words, Gandhi's death was not the moment of great fear that Saleem records."[59] Saleem's "mistake" deliberately links the Sinais' communal alienation directly to Gandhi.

The Mahatma is a harder target than Indira, one readers may be unwilling to acknowledge.[60] Ten Kortenaar suggests that Rushdie suppresses Gandhi because he prefers Nehru's secular vision of the state to Gandhi's more mystical one, but the division between the two figures is not so obvious.[61] Stanley Wolpert, to whose *New History of India* Rushdie referred while writing *Midnight's Children*, writes that "for young intellectuals like Jawaharlal Nehru . . . Gandhi was the incarnation of *Bharat Mata* (Mother India), traditional guru and revolutionary hero in one unique person."[62] While David Lipscomb demonstrates that Rushdie's use of Wolpert is highly critical, this description of Gandhi as "incarnation of *Bharat Mata*" is a powerful image, and Saleem must fight it.[63] The decision to separate Nehru from Gandhi entirely is a deliberate divergence from both objective history (the men influenced each other considerably) and from perceived history, the collective myth Saleem often endorses. Nehru is less threatening to Saleem than Gandhi: Nehru's privilege and British education is rather like Baby Saleem's and even more like Rushdie's, and as the "father of his nation," he is another of Saleem's many parents. Gandhi, Nehru's ascetic, Hindu mentor, is less easily adapted to Saleem's purposes. He does not fit into Saleem's picture of India—the India Saleem himself embodies—and thus he is removed almost entirely from the story.

After the assassination, Gandhi makes one final, covert appearance in the book, which Saleem does not recognize and therefore cannot hide. Commander Sabarmati, whom Saleem informs of his wife's infidelity, and who murders her along with her lover, is named after the town in

Gujarat where Gandhi located his headquarters in 1917.[64] The details of the Sabarmati murder case are otherwise very close to those of the real-life Nanavati case, in which an officer's murder of his wife and her lover became a national scandal; Rushdie describes the affair as a contest between the "heroic" and the "rule of law."[65] Saleem tells the Commander about Lila Sabarmati's infidelity because he is outraged by his own mother's clandestine meetings with her first husband, but the resulting legal wranglings also contain a criticism of Gandhi, and a reminder that the "heroic"—the primacy of character—is a poor way to run a country. If we idolize Gandhi for his character, we risk acquitting the murderer Sabarmati-Nanavati for the same reason, and if we depend on charismatic figures for leadership, we may easily end up following Bal Thackeray. In either case, dependence on a charismatic leader results in alienation from the citywide or countrywide community, whether as a result of the leader's exclusionary policies or as a result of fragmentation when he dies. The body politic is a bad model for the state, Rushdie suggests, because the body is mortal.

Hogan points out that the anonymous note to Commander Sabarmati, which Saleem pastes together out of newspaper headlines, includes a reference to "local Gandhian socialism" in the form of Acharya Vinobha Bhave, who "spent ten years persuading landowners to donate plots to the poor"[66]: "When J. P. Narayan announced the dedication of his life to Bhave's work, the headline NARAYAN WALKS IN BHAVE'S WAY gave me *my* much-sought 'WAY.'"[67] Hogan argues that "Bhave's Gandhian work does provide Saleem with his way (not, perhaps, the way he actually manages to follow, but the ideal, the possibility)" and adds that, since the note is "designed to draw [Saleem's] mother away from Qasim the Red, Saleem learns the 'WAY' not of improving the lives of ordinary people but of drawing supporters away from communism."[68] But this reading does not mention the terrible consequences of Saleem's note. Saleem's "WAY" here is not Gandhian pacifism, but the less honorable way of the writer of anonymous letters. The note Bhave and Narayan have indirectly helped him write leads to two murders, a suicide, an incarceration, and the near-breakdown of the rule of law. The way Bhave and Gandhi provide the young Saleem is not the way of pacifism but the myth of the national hero, which will inevitably betray him.

Imaginary and Physical Cities

The cosmopolitan ideal fails, in Rushdie's fiction, because characters refuse to admit that it *is* an ideal rather than a reality. Saleem's exclusion of Shiva from the Midnight Children's Conference reveals that Saleem is not willing to take inclusivity far enough—that he, too, suppresses dissent when it reflects badly on him. Personal concerns trump Saleem's concern for the group, and that selfish exclusion causes his downfall. Until the cosmopolitan group can be fully inclusive, it will be subject to the same charges of self-interested inconsistency as Fielding's Axis, which ludicrously includes Western artifacts in its essentialist account of the nation.

When he critiques individuals embodying India, Rushdie attacks not just particular leaders but the concept of heroism as a whole. *Midnight's Children* is, in the end, a profoundly democratic novel, in which the disintegrating hero is replaced by a crowd. In this, more than in anything else, *Midnight's Children* programmatically represents the world's largest democracy, imagining India as a country that can only be represented by an unheroic multitude. The novel embodies India not in its dubious historical accuracy but in its deliberately tendentious representation—both realist and antirealist—of the primacy of the group over the individual. The battle fought in *Midnight's Children* and *The Moor's Last Sigh* is over the nature of that group: both novels enact the struggle between totalitarian communalism, which dictates homogeneity, and cosmopolitanism, which encourages multifarious individual identities to cooperate.

Rushdie's fictions begin in an imaginary city, the inclusive and cosmopolitan Bombay of his narrators' childhoods. This idealized Bombay is not replaced with a "real" version of the city, despite Rushdie's insistence on the knowability of its physical components and the lives of its inhabitants. Instead, one ideal version of Bombay is replaced with others, until the multiple fictions of the city become so mutually contradictory that the real inhabitants turn against each other and the city as a cohesive community ceases to exist. The blurring of metaphor and reality in both books indicates the immense real-world repercussions of nationalist imaginings of community. The cracks that destroy Saleem and the bombings that destroy Bombay are physical manifestations of the ideological differences that cause the imagined communities of the city and the nation to disintegrate. So powerful is the city dwellers' imaginary community that physical reality is dependent on it: buildings fall and people die when the socially constructed community is lost.

By making Bombay the microcosm of India, Rushdie makes forming a national identity India's greatest problem, eclipsing even Indira Gandhi's "abolish poverty" campaign. Rushdie's first two Bombay novels present local cosmopolitanism, which provides city dwellers with an inclusive group identity, as a delicate balance between two dangerous extremes. Aurora, dancing on the wall above the Ganpati festival, with her husband

Abraham the global businessman on one side and Fielding's nationalist movement on the other, is the icon of this dangerous tightrope walk, and her fatal fall is a warning of the cosmopolitan city's possible fate.

Gandhi's murder reveals why pluralist groups cannot depend on charismatic figureheads, and cosmopolitanism makes emblematic heroes less useful. Instead, the novels aim for a Bakhtinian dialogue not only in fiction but in the construction of the nation. Since telepathy and disintegration are impossible and unappealing ways to distribute responsibility for community building, *Midnight's Children* and *The Moor's Last Sigh* appear to leave readers without a way to reconcile the competing demands of cosmopolitans and communalists. Instead, the novels offer a vision of the absorption of the narrator into the surrounding crowds. This redistribution of the emblematic figure of the nation both denies that a single individual can represent the pluralist whole and magically completes that representation by merging signifier and signified. Saleem's flawed claims to represent India through his ancestry, biography, and telepathy come true at the moment of his death. The knowledge of India's internal diversity we have acquired over the course of the book leads us to see Saleem's unifying presence across "so-many too-many persons" only after—and because—he has crumbled to dust.[69]

When Saleem merges with the population of India, his narrative dialogue between self and other is replaced by a dialogue between a vast number of alternate selves. This discourse constitutes both the logical extension of the polyphonous narrative of the book and the final model of a pluralist India. The competing myths of the nation embodied by Shiva, Fielding, and Abraham can only be reconciled if the nation is redefined as the space of dialogue between rival groups, each of which must recognize its difference from and similarity to its interlocutors. The novel, mimicking the supernation of India with its many ethnic subnations, first provides this space of discourse, then returns the national conversation to the real world with the death of the narrator. Rushdie's pessimism, then, is not necessarily about India's future per se: it is about the possibility of emblematically representing that pluralist supernational future in a single heroic figure.

Physical disintegration is hardly a solution to real political problems. But Rushdie's skepticism of national heroes is not purely political: it is also an artistic critique of the possibility of the one speaking for the many, a rejection of what Bakhtin calls "literature's secondhand, externalizing and finalizing approach to the 'little man.'"[70] If a writer wants to assimilate multiple cultures and viewpoints, individual characters—particularly narrators—are a liability, as no one, not even the psychic

Saleem, can encompass the multifarious identities of a polyglot, polyvocal community.

Saleem is rich, poor, Indian, Pakistani, and so on, but these many identities are not enough to represent India; he must also be constantly displaced by the shifting meaning of his use of "I" in the narrative voice, as he speaks of his experiences in the past and the present. This shifting narrative "I" appears throughout transnational literature: Van's shifts in *Ada*, and the same phenomenon occurs in Isak Dinesen's *Out of Africa* or in Maxine Hong Kingston's *The Woman Warrior*. V. S. Naipaul's "I" in *The Enigma of Arrival* is diffuse, almost impossible to pinpoint to an actual individual. In each case, this shifty "I" arises from the tension between the individual at the moment of action—the Saleem who rides a bike down the hill—and the polyvocal speaker at the moment of narration—the Saleem who writes the text. Rushdie's speaker, however, pushes the boundaries of selfhood far further than others. His fluid "I" extends the narrator's ability to represent a multitude not only because it makes possible self-awareness and self-criticism but also because it renders the individual plural. Saleem's "I" is in constant dialogue both with his many selves and with the "'I.' 'I.' 'And I'" of the other Midnight Children whom he hears over his telepathic "All-India Radio."[71]

As Shiva demonstrates, Saleem falls short of his own ideal of inclusivity, but the novel succeeds where he fails. The fictional world, not the individual narrator, becomes the means of representing the nation. By replacing the body politic with a *novel* politic, Rushdie transfers agency away from the heroic individual—the political leader, the fictional hero, the author himself—and into the hands of the many. Not only is power shared between the polyphonous voices within the novel, but it is finally ceded to the crowd, the readers, who bring experiences not contained in the book into the community. The disintegrating narrator mirrors the process modeled by the books themselves: at the end of the novel, agency is transferred from the individual author or narrator to the group of reader-citizens. When Saleem hands off his story to the next generation, "my son who is not my son," he leaves each reader with the responsibility of assembling a different partial, patchwork, dialogic identity for India. Far from rejecting the notion of lineage, Saleem is expanding it, adopting the novel's audience into his own story in defiance of genetic and ethnic definitions of community and continuity. Rather than urging readers to subscribe to Picture Singh's communism or Raman Fielding's Hindu nationalism, *Midnight's Children* and *The Moor's Last Sigh* draw readers into the contentious unity of "mongrel joy." The multiple solutions to the books' internal problems (Saleem is and is not Jamila's brother, is and is not tied to history) demand a multiplicity of readerly interpretations, ensuring that the nation produced by the novels will be based on shared commitment to pluralism and inclusivity rather than a shared interpretation of a single text. The polyphony of the novel and the fictional community is self-reinforcing, as it becomes part of the polyphonic inner lives of individual readers.

This emphasis on the plurality of readerly interpretations is central to *Midnight's Children* but even more important in *The Satanic Verses* and *The Ground Beneath Her Feet*: like Nabokov, Rushdie grows increasingly invested in multiple-solution puzzles and coexisting truths in his later fiction. In the next chapter, we will see how Rushdie's exploration of participatory group identities shifts from the national to the international scale in *The Satanic Verses*. Rushdie's emphasis on the fantastic tradition in transnational literature continues and enables his expansion of Nabokov's private communities: when Gibreel Farishta criticizes Nabokov in *The Satanic Verses* for writing in "a made-up lingo all his own," he reminds us that the responsibility for rendering the fictional world comprehensible lies with both the reader and the writer of the novel.[72]

Rushdie's fantastic geographies can be read as metaphors for immigrant perceptions of a new country, but they also reveal the consensus nature of truth: in *The Satanic Verses*, even British weather is treated as a social construct. Rushdie's work shows that the territories of postcolonial and postmodern theory are, like the fictional nations of the books, separated largely by theorists' self-conceptions. The novels destabilize these identities in order to empower their interpreters. As readers decode layers of truth, falsehood, and subjectivity, they learn not only that they *can* create their communities, but that they already have. They find not just answers to questions set up by didactic authors, but genuinely new solutions to complex, open-ended problems, akin to the authors' own fictional creations.

In Chapters 2 and 3 we saw that Nabokov transforms traditional geography and history to reveal how outsiders can form communities of shared displacement. Rushdie expands Nabokov's intimate groups to include the millions of India, incorporating competing versions of commonality from Hindu nationalism to Western-dominated globalism into his ever-expanding national family. The next two chapters show how Rushdie expands his account of productive displacements: his celebration of the self-creating migrant artist overturns the postcolonial account of isolated hybrids. In Rushdie's later novels, new nations and communities can only be formed from a state of exile.

CHAPTER 5

AUTHORITY, SELF, AND COMMUNITY IN *THE SATANIC VERSES*

IF *MIDNIGHT'S CHILDREN* CHALLENGES THE IDEA THAT INDIVIDUALS CAN represent a nation, *The Satanic Verses* goes further, destabilizing not only its characters' representations but also the very notion that there is an absolute truth to represent. The status of "fact," of objectively verifiable truth, is assigned in the novel almost entirely to internal, personal experience, while the physical truths central to Nabokov's novels and even *Midnight's Children* become unstable. While Saleem's insistence on "memory's truth" in *Midnight's Children* marks his unreliability, *The Satanic Verses* seems to validate Saleem's position, treating "fact" as provable only through personal experience. Michael Gorra, noting how Saleem asks us to take his autobiography literally, says that *Midnight's Children* is "a world without metaphor."¹ In *The Satanic Verses*, however, proliferating viewpoints render even such subjective literalism difficult because the "incompatible" truths of the novel cannot be reconciled.² It is easy to call this instability prototypically postmodern. More complicated and productive is the problem of how such postmodern privileging of subjective truths helps Rushdie and his readers construct viable real-world communities, rather than leading—as postmodern narratives like Brett Easton Ellis's *American Psycho* (1991) do—to a rejection of meaningful communion and communication.

The Satanic Verses' privileging of individual experience seems incompatible with forging a community; indeed, the primary target of the novel's critiques is Mahound, who seeks to unite his followers. *The Satanic Verses* itself has been infamously divisive. Even setting aside the *fatwa*, the book's portrayal of British Muslims drew fire from critics of postcolonial literature: Feroza Jussawalla, for example, sees Rushdie as a "successful mainstream Westernized immigrant" guilty of orientalizing the community he claims to support and address.[3] The text's emphasis on subjective experience, however, also constitutes a claim about the common subjectivity of humanity. Each person in Rushdie's work is made of multiple internal selves, and community formation in *The Satanic Verses* begins by recognizing the plurality of selves we each contain. While the book attacks communities formed around exclusive, monistic defining principles—Mahound's monotheism, Saladin's Proper London, Hindutva—it simultaneously teaches the reader to make her own internal multiplicity the model for an inclusive multicultural community. *Midnight's Children* fragments the body politic; *The Satanic Verses* replaces it with the psyche politic.

This chapter shows how *The Satanic Verses'* rejection of orthodoxies teaches readers of any background to join the hybrid community modeled by and partially described in the novel. The novel's emphasis on individual experience redefines truth in humanistic terms, not as indeterminate but as partial and nonabsolute. Rushdie's siting of narrative authority in the individual avoids solipsism by emphasizing the fragmented and plural nature of the self: only through the recognition, acceptance, and unification of his alternative selves can the individual achieve happiness.

Groups in the novel are unified through a parallel self-recognition and acceptance achieved through artistic creation. For Rushdie, the role of art is to provide us with both access to and a synthesis of competing, sometimes contradictory truths, unifying diverse groups into hybrid identity categories. As always, however, Rushdie remains suspicious of his own ideals and examines the pitfalls as well as the means of hybrid unification; his discussion of pluralist communities focuses on the process rather than the outcome of multiculturalism.

* * *

The Satanic Verses has become a touchstone in discussions of postcolonial hybridity. Sara Suleri—while arguing for the book's deep-seated allegiance to "Islamic secularism"[4]—describes its "productive absence of cultural cohesion"[5]: the mutability that makes new ideas possible in *The Satanic Verses* is "equally aligned to Western and Eastern aesthetic forms."[6] Many critical evaluations of the novel's intertexts (Antje Rauwerda's discussion of Rushdie's use of Milton and Simona Sawhney's article on poetry and prophecy, for example) show how Rushdie juxtaposes his international source materials in order to contest their authority: the hybridity of the novel constitutes a systematic attack on other texts' pretensions to exclusive knowledge.[7] When Satish Aikant argues that, for Rushdie, "one of the ennobling features of a migrant's position is the resistance it provides him to cultural authoritarianism and its claims to speak the absolute truth,"[8] he points us toward the possibility that no single truth is "absolute" at all but rather that each text Rushdie refers to—the Koran, Defoe's *History of the Devil*, Dickens' *Our Mutual Friend*, Blake's *The Marriage of Heaven and Hell*, Bulgakov's *The Master and Margarita*, Shakespeare's *Othello*, Urdu *ghazals*, or the Bollywood film *Shri 420*—supplies part of a series of coexisting, contradictory truths.[9]

The hybridity of Rushdie's novel extends far beyond the superficial pastiche of boutique multiculturalism, however, in part because culture is only one of the subjects of hybridization. Rushdie attacks purity itself, whether cultural, moral, or genetic. Rushdie writes in "Is Nothing Sacred?" that fiction "tells us there are no answers; or, rather, it tells us that answers are easier to come by, and less reliable, than questions."[10] This idea of a reliable question—privileging not only doubt over faith but also inquiry over knowability—makes *The Satanic Verses* a programmatically empowering text, designed to teach its readers to question even its own internal authority.

The hybridity of *The Satanic Verses* is not simply the "both/and" unification of opposites beloved of postcolonial critics. As Booker argues, "Rushdie's incessant assault on totalitarianism involves attacks on dualistic thinking."[11] The novel blurs the boundaries between established opposites like England and India, self and other, and good and evil: Martine Hennard Dutheil argues that "through [the] problematization of the absolute distinction between God and the Devil, Rushdie is indicting a whole epistemological system based on binary oppositions."[12] But the breakdown of binaries also occurs through the insertion of third and fourth terms into such pairings. If, as Bhabha writes, colonial governments are "two-faced," the characters and plot of *The Satanic Verses* are hydra headed.[13] Although many characters are paired with "opposites" in their own story lines (Saladin Chamcha and Gibreel Farishta; the Imam and Ayesha; Mahound and Bilal), each character has myriad other pairings, doubles, and shadows throughout the book, so that *The Satanic Verses* becomes a web of interconnecting reflections: Gibreel's atheism in Bombay and England resembles Mirza Saeed's in Titlipur; Ayesha of Desh shares a name with one of Mahound's wives, the whore who takes that name, and the leader of the Ayesha Haj; the latter Ayesha shares the prophetic stage with Mahound and the Imam. Each character has some vital element in common with or directly opposed to almost every other character in the novel's proliferating plot threads and chronotopes, establishing a complex pattern of relationships in which simple oppositions only conceal the characters' similarities. *The Satanic Verses* is Rushdie's first rejection of Manicheanism, something he works out more thoroughly in *The Ground Beneath Her Feet*. His rejection of binaries constitutes the basis for a pluralist community in which the dichotomy of self and other is replaced with the recognition that human relationships are not simple dialogues but elaborate polyvocal networks.

This breakdown of binaries extends to the opposition between author and character or author and reader, making *The Satanic Verses* radically antiauthoritarian in literary as well as political terms. The fundamentalist response to the book is largely based on superficial and often inaccurate understandings of its content.[14] But fundamentalists might also be horrified by the book's attack on revealed truth itself. While critics of *The Satanic Verses* debate whether one can separate the text from the scandal it generated (Gayatri Spivak says it is "impossible," then proceeds to try[15]), the *fatwa* and the ongoing discussion of hybridity in the novel are equally responses to the book's central concern: rejecting purity and absolute truth. *The Satanic Verses*' great contributions to the transnational canon are its attack on immutable identity categories and its demonstration that such attacks can have real, devastating results.

UNDERCUTTING TEXTUAL AUTHORITY

The novel's attack on traditional authority figures is clearest in the sections treating Mahound, the name Rushdie gives the prophet Muhammad. Mahound's claims of authority rest on his contact with the divine, and the authenticity of that contact is repeatedly called into question. The primary reason for doubt is the incident of the Satanic Verses: Mahound, in what appears a self-serving gesture to placate the ruler of Jahilia, acknowledges the goddesses Al-Lat, Uzza, and Manat as the "exalted birds."[16] At his next revelation, Mahound rejects the verses, saying that they came from the devil. While Mahound claims that the contradictory verses come from different sources, however, Gibreel Farishta, whose name means "angel Gabriel" and who has taken on the angel's role as the messenger of the revelation, reports that "*it was me both times, baba, me first and second also me.*"[17] Gibreel's source for his "revelation" to Mahound is not God, but Mahound himself, who somehow puts the words he wishes to hear in Gibreel's mouth: Gibreel feels "the power, starting within Mahound, reaching up to *my vocal cords* and the voice comes."[18] Mahound fails to recognize his internal contradictions, instead inventing outside sources to explain his competing motives and desires. Divine revelation in the novel becomes a kind of supernaturally puissant bad faith, in which prophets unwittingly coerce the angel into delivering the message they wish to hear.

The characters' doubts are not enough to undercut divine authority in the novel as a whole, however: after all, they could be wrong. (Kinbote's account of Zembla does not necessarily make New Wye less plausible.) More disturbingly, the narrative as a whole refuses to give us a definite answer on the subject of prophecy. The scenes in which Mahound hears the Satanic Verses and their retraction take place in effect off-camera. We glimpse Mahound in his prophetic trance, working Gibreel's jaw, and are told that Gibreel produces "out of my mouth, up my throat, past my teeth: the Words" but not what those words are. Instead, we are given nothing but Gibreel's sensory experience of unity with Mahound as "the miracle starts in his my our guts."[19] While Gibreel is certain that "God isn't in this picture," that picture remains otherwise unclear. The reader has no privileged access; instead, we learn the words along with the faithful, when Mahound recites them to the ruler of Jahilia. Rushdie denies us the certainty that straightforward narration of the scene could give. Gibreel objects to this uncertainty, asking, "who asks the bloody audience of a 'theological' to solve the bloody plot?"[20] but his protest goes unanswered. Lacking definitive reports even within the text's fictional world, we must come to our own determination of the prophecy's source rather than being allowed to take Mahound, Gibreel, or the narrator's accounts on faith.

By refusing to confirm or deny the divine origin of the Koran, Rushdie's narrator replaces divine with readerly authority: we have nothing to fall back on but ourselves. The difference between these two kinds of authority is that readers may have less faith in their own conclusions than in the directly reported Word of God. The narrative distance from the scenes of revelation renders absolute certainty impossible in the world of the novel. In undermining the Koran, the text also undermines the possibility that *The Satanic Verses* itself could provide an alternative absolute truth about God, an atheist "no" to the Koran's theist "yes."

The nondefinitive narration of the novel is not limited to the revelation. Other supernatural events are similarly told through partial and untrustworthy viewpoints. Gibreel's angelic status is subject to constant questioning and verification. On the one hand, his dreams give us access to the prophet Muhammad, his halo is occasionally "clear to everyone,"[21] and even skeptical Alicja agrees that London experiences a "tropical heat wave"[22] after Gibreel decides to "tropicalize" the city.[23] On the other hand, Gibreel is clearly insane: his belief that he is a colossus is revealed as hallucination when he steps into traffic, and his irrational jealousy makes him vulnerable to Chamcha's anonymous phone calls insinuating that Allie is unfaithful. (The narrator describes those phone calls, too, as "satanic verses," placing Gibreel and Allie's affair in the same dubious position as the revelation.[24]) We cannot choose between these alternatives; instead, we must accept that Gibreel is equally aligned with two truths that he himself considers mutually exclusive—he is both an angel and mad.

The novel's mixture of opposites is complicated by the ways Gibreel's angelhood and lunacy are established. Rushdie's suspicion of "official versions" is well documented. In *Midnight's Children*, the official war news is only good for determining what is *not* true: "in a country where the truth is what it is instructed to be, reality quite literally ceases to exist, so that everything becomes possible except what we are told is the case."[25] In *The Satanic Verses*, this suspicion extends even to the novel's "official" plot. We learn about Gibreel's supernatural abilities through the eyes of third parties, minor characters who have no reason to collude with Gibreel's madness. This means of establishing Gibreel's nature seems more reliable than, for example, taking Gibreel's word for it. But those minor characters' accounts are also subject to doubt. In Gibreel's return to the stage at Earls Court, as in the accounts of Mahound's revelation, the point of view shifts from third-person omniscient to a more limited and retrospective third-person narrative—in this case, the narrative of the "official" and unofficial versions:

> The official version of what followed, and the one accepted by all the news media, was that Gibreel Farishta had been lifted out of the danger area in the same winch-operated chariot in which he'd descended... This version proved resilient enough to survive the "revelation" in the *Voice* that the assistant stage manager in charge of the winch had not, repeat not, set it in motion after it landed;—that, in fact, the chariot remained grounded throughout the riot of the ecstatic film fans;—and that substantial sums of money had been paid to the backstage staff to persuade them to collude in the fabrication of a story which, because totally fictional, was realistic enough for the newspaper-buying public to believe. However, the rumour that Gibreel Farishta had actually levitated away from the Earls Court stage and vanished into the blue under his own steam spread rapidly through the city's Asian population, and was fed by many accounts of the halo that had been seen streaming out from a point just behind his head.[26]

As before, the reader is not given explicit access to the "true" version: instead, we receive conflicting reports about the event, including a "revelation" that may be either news of a miraculous event or a con by a self-serving individual (here, the opportunistic newspaper the *Voice*, a parody of the voice that speaks through Gibreel in the Jahilia sections).

The result in this passage is doubly antiauthoritarian. While the report that stagehands have been bribed suggests that readers should choose the "unofficial" version, the narrative voice refuses to make that choice for us; instead, readers must again determine what the novel's "real" plot is.

The narration of the novel is both antiauthoritarian and manipulative: it claims to leave the conclusion open but nonetheless guides us to a particular choice. While Jaina Sanga argues that the "dialectical process . . . articulates hybridity," here the multiple voices within the novel seem to be the material as well as the expression of the narration's hybridity: it is composed of multiple voices (the "official version," the "*Voice*," and the "Asian community") in collaboration with the reader.[27]

If the "official version" is suspect, however, so is this apparently empowering indeterminacy. We come to distrust the narration not only in its truth claims but also in its intentions: Are we to be thinking for ourselves here or not? How far are we to take our skepticism? Is there a reliable central truth to the novel, and if so, how can we reach it? The episode in which Salman the Persian changes words in the Koran takes this destabilization of textual authority further, undermining not only the Koran but the reliability of texts in general by revealing the vulnerability of the written word.

A text's authority comes from its permanence; once written, words become stable and thus reliable. Salman's alteration of the Koran shows that stability is an illusion: texts are vulnerable to alteration in transcription. Even honest scribes introduce errors, but so-called authoritative texts are particularly vulnerable to malicious alteration as scribes test or modify the words they copy. Here textual evidence itself is revealed as unreliable. It is bad enough that unreliable narrators can introduce inconsistencies into the text or draw on erratic sources. Far more destabilizing is the prospect that extra errors and inconsistencies may be introduced into the text after its composition, rendering the patterns we see accidental instead of intentional: while Kinbote's "flimsy nonsense" gives way to a "web of sense," the text of the Koran presents a deceptive, illusory order.

Salman the Persian's blasphemous revisions contain a straightforward argument against scriptural authority. When Salman tells Bilal that he must avoid confrontation with Mahound because "It's his Word against mine," the implication is that Salman, too, has a capital-W Word, and while his Word cannot compete with Mahound's, it is of equal intrinsic value.[28] Booker notes that "By challenging the authority of that ultimate monologic word, the Word of God, Rushdie (like Bakhtin) emphasizes the inherent dialogic power of words."[29] Naturally, however, the critique goes further. By assigning the story of textual alteration to his own namesake, Rushdie calls his own narrative authority into doubt—while at the same time placing himself squarely within the Koran's history. Doubt, Rushdie suggests, is written into every text, even the Koran itself.

These attacks on textual authority are based on accusations of deliberate mendacity and obfuscation by a narrator, character, or editor who sabotages a text. But even ostensibly honest texts are subject to similar scrutiny and turn out to be similarly untrustworthy. The television camera recording the Brickhall riots, for example, is described as independent and objective. Its limitations appear to make it trustworthy: "less gifted than the human eye, its night vision is limited to what klieg lights will show," so it does not display the city's mass hallucinations.[30] At the same time, however, the camera's "fragility makes it fastidious. A camera requires law, order, the thin blue line. Seeking to preserve itself, it remains behind the shielding wall."[31] The camera's technical limitations prevent it from "observing the shadow-lands," and the instrument that claims to be capable of honest reportage becomes the tool of authoritarian domination. Reportage itself, here, is by definition guilty of censorship: the limitations of any medium demand that important details be omitted. Narratives that claim to report objective truths are in fact more suspect than those that admit their partiality because objective reporting of human experience is impossible.

This multipronged attack on textual authority is part of what Harveen Sachdeva Mann describes as the text's lack of "a pure, originary meaning."[32] But the novel's indeterminacy originates in its consistent antiauthoritarianism and is how it sidesteps the temptation to mirror the monism of the Koran. Sawhney argues that *The Satanic Verses*' equivocal relationship with revelation reveals the paradoxical ambition of the novel: "The hidden desire of literature *is* to be the law itself, even as its work is to transgress the law. Literature cannot conceal its own desire to become revelation, even while its mode of narration mocks its claim to the authority of truth. Perhaps more than anything else, it is this impossible desire that makes literature 'satanic.'"[33] The unstable narrative authority in the novel protects against usurpation: by undercutting monistic truths, the novel avoids providing another "law" to replace Mahound's monotheism. While this rejection of law in favor of pluralistic indeterminacy appears to lead to the anarchic chaos of the Brickhall riots, it can also provide the foundation of a nation-like community based not on widespread similarity between the citizens but on shared attitudes toward difference and assimilation. As we shall see, the novel rejects law as the basis for a community, instead arguing that commonality grows out of the subjective and individual affiliations of personal ambivalence and love.

Indeterminacy and the Narrator

In order for the text to have any meaning at all, it must contain some form of internal "truth," which can only be present if the text as a whole—whether through the reportage of a single narrator or through the combined perspective of multiple characters—contains indisputable facts. (The Emma Bovary test is only applicable if a novel leaves us certain whether or not Emma Bovary is dead.) While an overly authoritative narrator simply replaces one "law" with another, an overly unreliable narrator—or collection of unreliable narrators—will devolve into nonsense. The text cannot undermine narrative authority too far without becoming meaningless because (unlike the real world) fictional texts draw their realities from the claims of their characters. Even while it teaches us to distrust its internal sources, *The Satanic Verses* must also create a series of internally consistent referents and facts, so that it can, as Joel Kuortti argues, create "a universe, a 'reality', perceived as dominated, sustained and created by language."[34] In the process, the novel begins to privilege the internal truth of individual experience—a subject on which everyone has expert knowledge—over the objective truth of authoritative claims about physical and metaphysical facts.

The way subjective experience supplants authoritative fact is perhaps clearest in the persona of the probably-omniscient narrator, a figure even harder to trust than Humbert or Kinbote. The narrator's simultaneous reliability and unreliability is set up in one of his first intrusions in the narrative:

> I know the truth, obviously. I watched the whole thing. As to omnipresence and -potence, I'm making no claims at present, but I can manage this much, I hope. Chamcha willed it and Farishta did what was willed.
> Which was the miracle worker?
> Of what type—angelic, satanic—was Farishta's song?
> Who am I?
> Let's put it this way: who has the best tunes?[35]

The narrator's self-introduction is almost a rejection of reliability: not only does he imply that he is the devil, he refuses to actually tell us anything. We are in the same position vis-à-vis the narrator's identity as we are to the book's revelations: we can tell what conclusion we are being directed toward, but we cannot be sure that our conclusion is correct. Moreover, the speaker's statement that he is "making no claims at present" implies that there is a knowable answer to which we do not have access. This implication demands, once again, that we both trust and distrust the speaker: while he appears to have the answer we are looking for, he will not share it, and his evidence must be treated as potentially misleading.

The narrator's reliability becomes more equivocal the more we know. At first he appears clearly to be the devil. His account of dissent makes his identity seem obvious:

> To will is to disagree; not to submit; to dissent.
> I know; devil talk. Shaitan interrupting Gibreel.
> Me?[36]

By the middle of the book, however, the narrator's identity becomes more slippery. After Gibreel's vision of a balding, sardonic "God" in Allie's apartment, which Sawhney calls "a thinly disguised Salman Rushdie," the narrator begins to fuse with both "God" and a version of Rushdie's authorial persona.[37] While this is not the only time Rushdie walks onstage in one of his books—the narrator of *Shame*, too, is unabashedly Rushdie-like and frankly unreliable—*The Satanic Verses*' divine and authorial intervention in the text is unusual for how little Rushdie is willing to explain:

> I'm saying nothing. Don't ask me to clear things up one way or the other; the time of revelations is long gone. The rules of Creation are pretty clear: you set things up, you make them thus and so, and then you let them roll. Where's the pleasure if you're always intervening to give hints, change the rules, fix the fights? Well, I've been pretty self-controlled up to this point and I don't plan to spoil things now. Don't think I haven't wanted to butt in; I have, plenty of times. And once, it's true, I did. I sat on Alleluia Cone's bed and spoke to the superstar, Gibreel. *Ooparvala or Neechayvala*, he wanted to know, and I didn't enlighten him; I certainly don't intend to blab to this confused Chamcha instead.[38]

The narrator claims, in terms equally applicable to the author or the divine, to have created the characters he describes. He suggests once again that enlightenment is possible, and that there is a definitive answer to Gibreel's question of whether he is *Ooparvala* or *Neechayvala*, God or the devil. But such a revelation would "spoil" the story, a concern more authorial than divine. Revealed truth, direct communication from God, becomes a form of "butting in"; the supernatural narrator's only commandments to his readers instruct us neither to look for more nor to give up hope completely: "don't ask" and "don't think I haven't wanted to." According to this creator, revelation is inferior to solutions individuals work out for themselves—hence, presumably, his refusal to tell us what happens in the novel's pivotal scenes. The narrator's emphasis on Chamcha's name (changed from Salahuddin Chamchawala), which literally means "spoon" but colloquially means "toady" or "suck-up," suggests that an unambiguously authoritative narrator is also guilty of spoon-feeding his readers. If, as Brennan argues, *chamchas* "continue the logic of imperial domination," the narrator's refusal to facilitate Gibreel, Chamcha, or the reader's search for enlightenment is also a refusal to enact a narrative version of that imperial domination.[39]

By removing the distinction between God and the devil, Rushdie also undercuts the nature of authority itself. God's authority over man comes from his role as creator, which is analogous to paternal authority. If, like Saladin's estranged father Changez, the creator turns out to be both generally hands-off and morally suspect when he does interfere, then hierarchies tracing their origins to the divine, whether clerical, governmental, or parental, lack the justification of divine right. The narrator's refusal to interfere, in fact, constitutes an argument for rethinking all familiar power structures. This sounds at first like a recipe for anarchy, but the riot scenes at the end of the book are a clear rejection of anarchic chaos. Instead, as we shall see, authority in the novel arises from precisely the point at which the individual becomes the universal: the characters' few internal certainties provide the grounds for consensus not so much about external facts but about the common plurality of human nature.

The Multiplicity of the Individual

The narrator's multiple personae—God, devil, Rushdie—reflect the multiple selves of the other characters. Booker, too, sees the narrator's unreliability as indicative of the disunity of the self in Rushdie's work. But while Booker argues that "if the very idea of a stable, unified self is revealed by Rushdie to be a fiction, then the Romantic notion of the self as a basis of authority or source of truth must be a fiction as well," the self seems to provide the only access to truth in the novel: a broader understanding of the world begins, in *The Satanic Verses*, with recognizing one's own internal plurality.[40] The variety and complexity of selves varies from character to character: Mirza Saeed consists of a city self and a country self, whereas Chamcha is the "Man of a Thousand Voices and a Voice."[41] But humanity in the novel is synonymous with multiplicity. When Sufyan says that Chamcha must choose between Lucretius and Ovid, continuous versus discontinuous change, he implies that the one impossible option is stasis. The Imam, cocooned in his London apartment, appears inhuman in his absolutism not because it is extreme but because it is unlike all the other characters: even Mahound, with his reversal about the Satanic Verses, changes.

internal pluralisms as sec-

Chamcha has a particularly fragmented interiority. The narrator emphasizes the humanity of multiplicity and moral ambiguity in his descriptions of Chamcha during the riots. He first claims, through Gibreel, that Chamcha is absolutely evil: "the evil is not external to Saladin, but springs from some recess of his own true nature . . . it has been spreading through his selfhood like a cancer, erasing what was good in him . . . and doing so with many deceptive feints and dodges, seeming at times to recede . . . and now, no doubt, it has filled him up."[42] According to Gibreel, evil has a physical presence, analogous to cancer (a dominant image of fatality in the book). This image implies that evil is both fatal and absolute: it is innate, springing from the individual's "true nature," and also alien, "erasing" the healthy parts of the body or spirit. Furthermore, if cancer is analogous to evil, its destructive power is irreversible: a body that has lost organs to cancer cannot regrow them.

Gibreel's understanding of evil is called into question a few pages later, however, when the men meet outside the burning Shaandaar Café. There, "evil Mr Chamcha," who is having a heart attack, runs into the building to try to rescue Mishal, Sufyan, and Hind—a heroic action contradicting Gibreel's notion of evil as cancer, since Chamcha is behaving in a way the absolutist cancer metaphor renders impossible.[43] If Chamcha the Satanic traitor cannot remain a figure of absolute evil, then absolute evil is no more sustainable than Gibreel's tarnished absolute good. The notion of absolute good and evil is undercut not only by their fusion in the narrator but also by the impossibility of representing either in a single human being: since we are all mixed, the novel implies, concepts of the absolute are meaningless because there is nothing to which to apply them. Absolute concepts are less true even than fiction: while fiction recounts possible events, absolutes are impossible even in a fictional world.

Recognizing one's own internal pluralism turns out to be the road to finding a community. On his return to India, following his reconciliation with his father, Chamcha discovers a different model of plural selfhood: "Although he kept it quiet, . . . Saladin felt hourly closer to many old, rejected selves, many alternative Saladins—or rather Salahuddins—which had split off from himself as he made his various life choices, but which had apparently continued to exist, perhaps in the parallel universes of quantum theory."[44] This reunion with rejected selves contrasts both with Gibreel's all-or-nothing understanding of selfhood, in which individuals are simply "good" or "evil," and with Chamcha's discontinuous, "translated" English self.[45] Booker notes that Chamcha's English persona is "hopelessly multiple."[46] Chamcha's reclamation of his Indian past, by contrast, is *optimistically* multiple. Chamcha suggests that we understand selfhood as perpetually *in potentia*. He has hitherto thought of himself in terms of the "chimera with roots" he sees on *Gardners' World*, in which a laburnum and a broom plant are sewn together, "growing vigorously out of a piece of English earth."[47] On his return to India, however, the "incompatible" pieces of his nature turn out to be more multifarious and accessible than this model of hybridity implies.[48] Greater self-knowledge and self-acceptance lead to lesser certainty, as the "real" self is revealed as one of many possible, nondefinitive selves. This uncertainty teaches Chamcha to see himself as part of a group of "alternative Saladins," in which each self recognizes its alternatives. As Chamcha's self-recognition grows, even the binary between yes and no breaks down, and the alternate worlds of "various life choices" become accessible and visible to the "real" Chamcha. When Chamcha stops peeling off the past, alternative presents become available; he loses his single-minded English self and its truncated name but gains a set of varied Indian selves. If the novel places authority in the individual, that authority is nonetheless rooted in a group: subjective authority is both antisolipsistic and antianarchic because it arises from the consensus of a cooperative *internal* community of possible selves.

As he loses his certainties, Chamcha comes to understand nonabsolute truths, particularly the deeply personal truth of love. Rushdie emphasizes love's antiauthoritarian nature in *Imaginary Homelands*: "the devotion of the lover is unlike that of the True Believer in that it is not militant . . . I will . . . accept that your tastes, your loves, are your business and not mine. The True Believer knows no such restraints."[49] Such an avowedly subjective commitment is only possible when Chamcha abandons his absolutist understanding of the self. His recognition of his internal plurality leads to self-awareness; that self-awareness helps him recognize his love for the activist and art critic Zeeny Vakil. By the end of the novel, as he agrees to participate in a protest Zeeny organizes against the Shiv Sena, Chamcha notes with surprise that his personal, subjective experience is drawing him into community action: "*Me, taking part in a CP(M)* [Communist Party (Marxist)] *event. Wonders will never cease; I really must be in love.*"[50] For Chamcha, a local connection between two people translates into participation in a group—one that is dedicated to the formation of intentional communities and also anticommunal in the Indian sense: the CP(M) shares Zeeny and Saleem's vision of India as secular and pluralist. Chamcha's love for Zeeny yokes the personal and the political, extending the unity of the self first to a union of paired selves and then a union of like-minded yet multifarious individuals.

As Michael Wood notes, for Rushdie, "Home can be any place *except* home."[51] But Chamcha, alone among Rushdie's migrant characters, finds his new home in India. This return to the native land follows the erasure of its former authority figure—Chamcha's father—and his replacement not with a new authority but with a voluntary commitment to pluralism. This pluralism is at once locally Indian and internationally connected, as embodied by Zeeny and her CP(M). Chamcha's rerooting in his home soil is made possible by a model of selfhood based on the "take-the-best-and-leave-the-rest" model Zeeny describes as fundamentally Indian—which provides the final link between the self, textual authority, and community.

Artistic Models of Community

Loving Zeeny is a road to community open only to Chamcha. The rest of us must take a less direct route, in which culture, instead of romantic love, is the unifying force. The novel's most overt examinations of community formation take place in the world of Indian art. Zeeny's art history book, Changez Chamchawalla's collection of *Hamza-nama* cloths, Hind Sufyan's pan-Indian cooking, and Gibreel's film career all demonstrate different aspects—and pitfalls—of how art appropriates, fuses, and reframes local productions and international imports into the dialogic zone of the cultural nation. Art constructs an "Indian" identity out of the imported and the regional, creating an imaginary-yet-real intermediate space between the local and the global. This artistic identity differs from nationalist versions of Indian identity, whether the Shiv Sena's or an English xenophobe's, through its fluidity and nonprescriptiveness.

Much as Mahound provides a model of the authoritative author, the Koran shows how authoritative texts create monistic communities. The Koran follows the standard model of both religious and conventional narrative texts: a single author provides a "true" version of events, and the audience can either assent or dissent. As a result, readers agree on the facts: God is One; Emma Bovary swallowed arsenic. The other art forms in the novel—and *The Satanic Verses* itself—take a different approach: rather than asking us to assent to a single truth, these texts contain myriad approaches to describing the world, which may include but not be limited to the audience's own. If literature, as Sawhney argues, seeks to become law, then the literature Rushdie believes in provides a "Rule Book" that, rather than prohibiting certain behaviors, guides readers through the process of "taking the best" from new and unfamiliar cultures.[52]

Zeeny's book on Indian art argues for an Indian "national culture" of artistic appropriation. Her book, on the confining myth of authenticity, that folkloristic straitjacket which she sought to replace by an ethic of historically validated eclecticism, for was not the entire national culture based on the principle of borrowing whatever clothes seemed to fit, Aryan, Mughal, British, take-the-best-and-leave-the-rest?—had created a predictable stink, especially because of its title. She had called it *The Only Good Indian*. "Meaning, is a dead," she told Chamcha when she gave him a copy. "Why should there be a good, right way of being a wog? That's Hindu fundamentalism. Actually, we're all bad Indians. Some worse than others."[53]

For Zeeny, the defining principle of Indian culture is hybridity—a rational, conscious "take-the-best-and-leave-the-rest" ethos in which invaders become, perhaps paradoxically, fodder for the "national" culture. (This is the argument Naipaul dismisses as outdated.) "Bad" Indians *are* good Indians, and vice versa: an Indian who borrows is a "better" Indian than a Hindu fundamentalist. By this definition, the "Indian" is not a stable cultural category but a process of appropriation and adaptation.

Zeeny also argues that difference and sameness are subjective categories, determined by a variety of markers, including racial or national identity, education, attitude, or the range of cultural artifacts she describes in the word "clothes." While Gibreel's song during his transformative fall from the *Bostan* apologizes for his "red Russian hat" and reasserts that "my heart's Indian" despite it, Zeeny considers wearing foreign clothes fundamentally Indian.[54] The "live" Indian community is by this definition both inclusive and selective, basing its boundaries not on geography but on shared eclecticism.

Zeeny articulates the self-aware multiculturalism that is the hallmark of the transnational identity. Her use of the term "clothes" recalls Fish's "boutique multiculturalism," but for Zeeny, the important cultural process is not the wearing of clothes (which are superficial and replaceable) but *selecting* them—trying them on for fit. Zeeny's transnationality, however, remains rootedly "national." Unlike Mahound, who accepts converts from anywhere, Zeeny's India retains racial and genealogical demarcations that delineate the pluralist community's frontiers. Her rooted artistic eclecticism is inseparable from her national politics, and, as Rashmi Varma argues, the human chain she helps the CP(M) form across Bombay enacts the pan-Indian unity we see in the works of art depicted in the novel.[55]

Zeeny's India is only partially a model of the eclectic community Rushdie wants to forge: its inclusivity is limited not only to those who choose to join it but also to those who also have the correct ancestral passport. For Rushdie, on the other hand, the boundaries of the group are not determined by national origin. Instead, the precondition for membership in *The Satanic Verses*' larger community is conscious participation in an exile or diaspora. Indians who do not see themselves as hybrid would not be eligible for membership, whereas British Jews like Allie Cone or Mimi Mamoulian, who practice forms of adaptation similar to Zeeny's prototypically "Indian" one, participate in the book's international hybrid community.

Membership in an ethnic minority is not a necessary or sufficient condition for participation in the transnational community, either. Alicja Cone rejects assimilation and reverts to self-consciously "Jewish" practices after her husband's death, separating herself from her hybrid daughter; Pamela Chamcha, on the other hand, the British "class traitor,"[56] enters voluntary exile by rejecting her own background. While, as Bhabha argues, "the national memory is always the site of the hybridity of histories and the displacement of narratives," individuals who participate in the national memory can elide or embrace the hybrid nature of their affiliation.[57] India does not have a monopoly on self-invention and hybridity; instead, Zeeny's account of Indian art becomes a model for a broader transnational practice rather than a national self-definition.

Another version of Zeeny's eclectic unity, which manages to be both locally Indian and broadly transnational, appears in Changez Chamchawala's *Hamza-nama* cloths. These cloths, drawing on every style of Indian art, "create a many-headed, many-brushed Overartist who, literally, *was* Indian painting."[58] The *Hamza-nama* cloths are what Rushdie describes as a "hotch-potch,"[59] but the result is a coherent, legible whole: "One hand would draw the mosaic floors, a second the figures, a third would paint the Chinese-looking cloudy skies. On the backs of the cloths were the stories that accompanied the scenes. The pictures would be shown like a movie: held up while someone read out the hero's tale. In the *Hamza-nama* you could see the Persian miniature fusing with Kannada and Keralan painting styles, you could see Hindu and Muslim philosophy forming their characteristically late-Mughal synthesis."[60] The "fusing" styles form a "synthesis" that comes to be revered as canonical, creating the kind of stable national identity that transnational art is designed to lead into. Again, as in Zeeny's description of selecting clothes, art is a *process* rather than a product. The "late-Mughal synthesis" is its own style, but its list of components—Chinese, Persian, Kannada, Keralan—exposes its roots within and beyond the boundaries of "India." The end product becomes proof of the vitality of Indian hybridity and, just as importantly, slightly changes the grounds for inclusion in Rushdie's reformulation of Indian identity. In the *Hamza-nama* cloths, the "Indian" and the "transnational" fuse: whereas Zeeny's Indians are locals who adapt foreign imports, here the foreign imports themselves become the new Indian citizens—or at least the Overcitizen's component parts.

The fact that the hero of the cloths may be Mahound's mixture-deploring uncle makes the *Hamza-nama* sequence a particularly pointed victory of hybridity over absolutism. Hamza's transformation into an Indian hero comes through the very process the Hamza of Jahilia most distrusts. In the *Hamza-nama*, Zeeny's eclectic India triumphs over Mahound's monotheism, adapting monistic Islam into the polyphony of Indian art.

Hind Sufyan, the avatar of the "Overartist" of Indian cooking, presents a utopian vision of Indian unity and a warning against privileging unity over pluralism. Hind's cooking forges a single "Indian" identity, a kind of fusion Monica Fludernik describes as moving from a "merely mythic" notion of commonality to a "new identity of geographical ascription," made possible when the diverse Indian community becomes part of a larger non-Indian population.[61] The notion of "Indian" rather than Kashmiri, Hyderabadi, or South Indian cooking is embodied in both the cook and the country:

> she struggled, in her kitchen, towards . . . eclecticism, learning to cook the dosas and uttapams of South India as well as the soft meatballs of Kashmir. Gradually her espousal of the cause of gastronomic pluralism grew into a grand passion, and while secularist Sufyan swallowed the multiple cultures of the subcontinent—"and let us not pretend that Western culture is not present; after these centuries, how could it not also be part of our heritage?"—his wife cooked, and ate in increasing quantities, its food. As she devoured the highly spiced dishes of Hyderabad and the high-faluting yoghurt sauces of Lucknow her body began to alter, because all that food had to find a home somewhere, and she began to resemble the wide rolling land mass itself, the subcontinent without frontiers, because food passes across any boundary you care to mention.[62]

Hind's body, like the *Hamza-nama*, incorporates a wide variety of styles. Living up to her name, she becomes a gustatory "Mother India." When she opens her restaurant, her work is reclassified not as Kashmiri or Hyderabadi but "Indian food"—a category of cuisine that only exists outside India in comparison with other national cooking styles.

This fusion is, as Fludernik suggests, also a loss: in England, Hind's "Indian" identity makes her one of many "women-like-her."[63] Despite its real eclecticism, the "Indian" food is almost the opposite of the *Hamza-nama* cloths: instead of showing us the sources of an evolving art form, the category "Indian food" turns many distinct styles into a single, dialectically opposable national form. True assimilation suppresses pluralism as thoroughly as forced conversion. Rushdie's siting of authority in individuals rather than groups stems from his aversion of such erasures, the cost of which is not only Hind's individuality but also, paradoxically, the hybridized Indian identity she embodies. Since Hind's "India" is defined in contrast with her British surroundings, it is vulnerable to counterdefinition just as immigrants are vulnerable to immigration cops' "power of description."[64] "Indian" food is twice the object of racist attacks in the novel, first when a judge is traumatized into silence after a white British racist spits in his food, and second when the incident is repeated in front of Gibreel and Chamcha. Hind's cooking makes "India" identifiable and consumable both for Indian emigrants and for outsiders. Her synthesis is problematic because, by helping create the category of "Indian," it also enables the kind of binary opposition (India versus England) the novel elsewhere undercuts.

Gibreel's film career enacts another kind of pan-Indian fusion, which is problematic for the opposite reason from Hind's: it remains within the boundaries of the nation, neither drawing on outside sources nor engaging with international interlocutors. Gibreel, like Saleem, makes himself an emblem of India, playing one deity after another, until he becomes an embodiment of the Indian notion of the divine:

> Gibreel had spent the greater part of his unique career incarnating, with absolute conviction, the countless deities of the subcontinent in the popular genre movies known as 'theologicals.' It was part of the magic of his persona that he succeeded in crossing religious boundaries without giving offence. Blue-skinned as Krishna he danced, flute in hand, amongst the beauteous gopis and their udder-heavy cows; with upturned palms, serene, he meditated (as Gautama) upon humanity's suffering beneath a studio-rickety bodhi-tree. On those infrequent occasions when he descended from the heavens he never went too far, playing, for example, both the Grand Mughal and his famously wily minister in the classic *Akbar and Birbal*. For over a decade and a half he had represented, to hundreds of millions of believers in that country in which, to this day, the human population outnumbers the divine by less than three to one, the most acceptable, and instantly recognizable, face of the Supreme. For many of his fans, the boundary separating the performer and his roles had longago ceased to exist.[65]

Gibreel's roles make him a composite of Indian mythology—not only the religious mythologies of Hinduism and Buddhism but also the pan-Indian spiritualism of the emperor Akbar, who created a syncretic religion based on Sufi Islam and elements borrowed from Hindus, Jains, Parsis, Sikhs, and Christians.[66] (Birbal, the "wily minister," was a "not-too-serious" convert to Akbar's Divine Faith from Hinduism; Gibreel's cross-casting puts him on both sides of the divide the Faith was intended to bridge.[67]) Gibreel covers the legendary history of pre-Raj India, with emphasis on its messianic and reforming religious heroes; his face becomes an icon not just for God but for a charismatic religious history of the Subcontinent, akin to the role Saleem attempts to usurp from Gandhi.

Akbar's inclusion in the list elucidates the link between Indian civic and religious unity: Gibreel's embodiment of the Indian supernatural is also an embodiment of Indian national self-conception, a combination through which a secular state can forge a pan-religious commitment among its citizens. By embodying one deity after another, Gibreel unites his viewers in their admiration both of his films and of himself. During his illness, "the whole of India was at Gibreel's bedside" regardless of communal affiliation: "In the mosques and temples of the nation, packed congregations prayed, not only for the life of the dying actor, but . . . for themselves."[68] Gibreel's stardom makes him both an individual and a plurality: he shows how art can command affiliation across ethnic or religious divides.

Unlike Hind's embodiment of the Subcontinent, however, Gibreel's pan-mythological career seems superficial: the bodhi tree is "studio-rickety." Nor does his Bollywood religious history acknowledge the external roots of the figures he portrays: Akbar is descended from Genghis Khan via the Timurid dynasty, which invaded northern India in the sixteenth century. Gibreel passes for authentic—he is the "untranslated man," in contrast with Chamcha's "selected discontinuities"[69]—but to read him as "untranslated" we must not examine his origins or his actions too closely.

When Chamcha returns to Bombay, he enters an India he has never seen before. At the end of the book, "India" has been redefined as Zeeny's hybrid, process-oriented nation, replacing Chamcha's previous conception of the nation as hidebound and paternalistic. His return both narrows and broadens his perspective:

> He stood at the window of his childhood and looked out at the Arabian Sea. The moon was almost full; moonlight, stretching from the rocks of Scandal Point out to the far horizon, created the illusion of a silver pathway, like a parting in the water's shining hair, like a road to miraculous lands. He shook his head; could no longer believe in fairy-tales. Childhood was over, and the view from this window was no more than an old and sentimental echo. To the devil with it! Let the bulldozers come. If the old refused to die, the new could not be born . . .

'Come along,' Zeenat Vakil's voice said . . . 'My place,' Zeeny offered. 'Let's get the hell out of here.'
'I'm coming,' he answered her, and turned away from the view.[70]

Chamcha's view across the Arabian Sea is the same as the view Baby Saleem (and the young Rushdie) grew up with, and as Saleem points out, it faces toward England; by turning "away from the view" and toward Zeeny, Chamcha finally chooses India over England. Turning to Zeeny, however, is very different from turning to the India Chamcha initially fled, embodied by the tyrannical Changez (whose name is another version of Genghis). Chamcha's turn to Zeeny not only replaces England with India but also replaces a Mughal, paternalistic India with the secular pluralist India of the CP(M) and the *Hazma-nama*. When Chamcha says, "Let the bulldozers come," he takes a very different position on the destruction of Bombay from the one in *Midnight's Children* and *The Moor's Last Sigh*. While in the first and third of his Bombay novels Rushdie treats the destruction of old Bombay architecture as the end of a pluralist era, here, in the second, the bulldozers become the harbingers of change, making the pluralism of India possible.

By locating cultural and narrative authority within individuals' subjective consciousness, the novel establishes its one universal truth: that each of us contains a multitude and that pluralist communities are made possible through recognizing our own internal multiplicities. What matters most in *The Satanic Verses* is not the "clothes" we choose but the process of choice: the fundamental cultural value endorsed by Zeeny's book—and Rushdie's—is self-aware participation in the ongoing process of hybridization.

THE COMMUNITY OF READERS

Mann argues that Rushdie's "unequal translations of terms" in *The Satanic Verses* show that he is "targeting an elite, metropolitan readership" distanced from the book's immigrant characters by their Western educations and financial security.[71] The list of Western references is long: Mann cites "Nietzsche, Blake, Joyce, and T. S. Eliot . . . Alice in Wonderland, Red Riding Hood, Snow White, and Punch and Judy."[72] But Rushdie also makes unexplained references—many of them important to the plot—to the Shiv Sena, Bombay's geography, and medieval Islam. Every reader of *The Satanic Verses* is in the same position as Gibreel, the autodidact who has never heard of Nabokov. Most English-speaking readers will find some cultural references familiar: if not Nabokov, then the Koran; if not *Doctor Who*, then *Shri 420*. At the same time, *The Satanic*

Verses' shifts between England, India, and seventh-century Arabia ensure that any reader will encounter something unfamiliar. References that strike one reader as obtrusively obvious—the name Jahilia ("ignorance," used to designate the time before the Revelation), the names of the two main characters, or the many Joyce references—may pass another reader by entirely.[73] *The Satanic Verses* makes readers insiders while reminding them that they are outsiders. The final authority the novel undercuts is our own: we learn that whatever our cultural knowledge, we do not have access to the experiences of those around us. Instead, for mutual understanding, we must turn to sympathy based on the fundamental human experience of forging a coherent self out of fragmented parts.

Locating authority in the self is an especially convenient position for the migrant or exiled writer, since internal authority is perhaps the only portable kind. Rushdie's approach to cultural and narrative authority is not only pluralistic: despite its Indian roots, it is explicitly adapted to the transnational setting. When readers share the experience of privilege and exclusion, they become part of the new diaspora of transnational literati. The novel's art forms—*Hamza-nama* cloths, Hind's cooking, and the text itself—are an education in both self-assembly and community formation not only because the two processes follow the same pattern but also because each makes the other possible.

CHAPTER 6

WHAT ACTUALLY HAPPENS

DEGREES OF REALITY IN *THE GROUND BENEATH HER FEET*

WHILE *THE GROUND BENEATH HER FEET* (1999) OPENS WITH a nostalgic description of the 1950s Bombay pluralism central to *Midnight's Children*, *The Satanic Verses*, and *The Moor's Last Sigh*, it is in the end an American novel, doing for America what *Midnight's Children* does for India. In what Anshuman Mondal describes as "a profound ideological shift," *The Ground Beneath Her Feet* is centered not in Bombay but in New York, and rock music, the dominant art form of the book, is treated as both a global and a specifically American phenomenon.[1] Rushdie himself describes it as "my first American novel."[2] Like his Indian novels, however, *The Ground Beneath Her Feet* makes the pluralist city stand in for the nation, suggesting that pluralism is essential to American identity and treating New York-style multiculturalism as the next iteration in Rushdie's ongoing examination of rooted cosmopolitanisms.

When Rushdie pulls this trick with Bombay, critics approve, perhaps because the city's pluralism is so locally rooted. When he performs the same sleight of hand with New York, however, critics accuse Rushdie of making Abraham Zogoiby's mistake of replacing the local with a faceless globalism. Rushdie's New York is less deeply rooted than his Bombay; in *Fury* (2001), too, the city's eclecticism lacks the accrued history we see in the Bombay novels. Reviewers found *The Ground Beneath Her Feet* messy and self-indulgent. But the appearance of chaos is deceptive because chaos is, for Rushdie, the necessary precondition of novelty and creation. *The Ground Beneath Her Feet* finds in overabundance, discontinuity, and disorientation the basis of a community of displaced persons and provides Rushdie's most thorough account of how novels can transform readers' personal and political affiliations.

The book's appearance of chaos arises from the complexity of Rushdie's alternate worlds. In *The Ground Beneath Her Feet*, Rushdie examines, endorses, and rejects dozens of approaches to world-creation. Some of the novel's alternate realities are familiar: unreliable narrators present erroneous versions of events; nostalgic accounts of childhood give idealized visions of the real world. The alternate realities of art and mythology suggest another, equally familiar idealism, in which art provides an alternate world containing absolute, unambiguous value—Kinbote's "special reality."[3] In contrast to these subjectively constructed interpretive "worlds," the novel itself is set in a literal other world, a planet on which historical events vary from those on our own. To complicate matters further, the novel's world collides with and destroys a second alternate world: the one inhabited by Maria, a world hopper who appears to Ormus and Rai.[4] These objectively "real" alternate worlds are systematically contrasted with the subjectively alternate worlds of childhood or art and also with the "worlds" of differing cultures and continents. The novel differentiates between types of otherworlds, suggesting a multitiered system of alterity that recognizes the existence of some alternate realities while treating others as fantastic or paranoid.

What makes *The Ground Beneath Her Feet* unusual is the shifting epistemologies of the "real" world of the novel itself. While *Midnight's Children* is clearly a fairy tale from its beginning, and *Ada* immediately indicates the alterity of Antiterra, *The Ground Beneath Her Feet* jumps from one narrative framework to another. The novel opens as a straightforward account of fictional events in the recognizable real world; shifts with Ormus's visions of Gayomart to a ghost story set in that otherwise real world; and then reveals, almost a hundred pages in, that the apparently familiar supernatural-in-the-real-world narrative is actually set in a world differing from our own in its day-to-day as well as its supernatural reality. As we saw in Chapter 1, each of these types of fiction—realist, supernatural, alternate world—makes a different set of imaginative demands on its readers. By moving between types of fictional worlds, *The Ground Beneath Her Feet* forces readers to revise, reconstruct, and take conscious control of the text's fictional worlds. While Rushdie's earlier novels asked us to read through a sense of cognitive dissonance to see how two cultures might be synthesized, *The Ground Beneath Her Feet* asks us to concentrate on that sense of cognitive dissonance for its own sake, foregrounding our simultaneously distanced and participatory roles in reading.

The multiplicity of worlds in *The Ground Beneath Her Feet* appears to render truth in the novel unstable, and certainly many of the narratives turn out to be suspect. But underneath the appearance of chaos is order:

as Viktoria Tchernichova demonstrates, the novel is organized around the central chapter, "Membrane," and the novel's eighteen chapters reflect the eighteen *parvas* of the *Mahabharata*.[5] While not all literal events in *The Ground Beneath Her Feet* are subject to the Emma Bovary test (we don't know exactly how Vina and Ormus die), the novel retains a central and absolute truth: the human and individual power of love, which creates worlds and endows them with meaning. Love provides the core reality beneath the novel's shifting epistemologies. Love is private—"your tastes, your loves, are your business and not mine."[6] But it is made accessible and thus a viable basis for a shared understanding of the world, by art, which mediates between the personal and the public, the outsider and the insider, and the competing systems by which characters interpret and construct their worlds.

REVISITING BOMBAY AND THE EMBODIED NATION

The Ground Beneath Her Feet revisits Rushdie's experiments with building national and transnational communities in *Midnight's Children* and *The Satanic Verses*: indeed, the later novel makes explicit the implicit experimentations in the earlier ones. As in *Midnight's Children*, several characters position themselves as embodiments of Bombay. These claims for representation are instantly revealed as flawed in their accuracy and ideology. Saleem's main rival for embodiment of Bombay in *The Ground Beneath Her Feet* is the hero's anglophile father: "Sir Darius Xerxes Cama, honoured with a baronetcy for services to the Indian Bar, liked to say with a great laugh that he, too, was a great metropolitan creation of the British, and proud of it. 'When you write this city's history, Merchant,' he roared one night over a club-house dinner of mulligatawny and pomfret, 'you might just find it's my biography you've penned.'"[7] Sir Darius's embodiment of Bombay is very different from Saleem's. While Saleem's multiracial, multireligious background is systematically inclusive, representing a pluralist India, Sir Darius's Bombay is a "metropolitan" colonial creation, distinct from the rest of the country. He tells Methwold, "Bombay isn't India. The British built her and the Parsis gave her her character. Let them have their independence elsewhere if they must, but leave us our Bombay under beneficent Parsi-British rule."[8] While Sir Darius sees himself as an embodiment of his city, the city he defines is almost the opposite of Saleem's. Sir Darius's Bombay is undermined by his own history of fraud—his legal credentials are forged—but his claim to represent the city nonetheless challenges Saleem's treatment of Bombay as the locus of pluralist nationalism, corroborating Rushdie's critique of individuals seeking to embody the pluralist state. The narrator, Rai, is also unwittingly in dialogue with Saleem: speaking of his parents' love for the city, Rai says, "Bombay was my rival."[9] Like Saleem and Sir Darius, Rai treats the city as an individual, but for Rai, that individuality is in competition with its inhabitants, and Rai must leave town to make good. *The Ground Beneath Her Feet* suggests that even Bombay's pluralism is limited and limiting when the city is viewed as a corporate whole.

The Ground Beneath Her Feet revisits the Bombay we see built and destroyed in *Midnight's Children* and *The Moor's Last Sigh*, but while the visit is deeply nostalgic, it is also a decisive farewell to the city and to the notion that an individual can stand in for a plurality. Like *The Moor's Last Sigh*, *The Ground Beneath Her Feet* chronicles the destruction of Bombay in which, once again, the narrator's loved ones are complicit. But while *The Moor's Last Sigh* ends on loss, *The Ground Beneath Her Feet*, like *The Satanic Verses*, takes readers through the next step: the creation of a community of shared displacement to replace the community of geographical affiliation.

Here, too, *The Ground Beneath Her Feet* revisits territory Rushdie covers in an earlier novel, making explicit the role of the outsider implied throughout *The Satanic Verses*. *The Ground Beneath Her Feet* turns *The Satanic Verses*' account of exile into a statement of the human condition:

> For a long while I have believed—this is perhaps my version of Sir Darius Xerxes Cama's belief in a fourth function of *outsideness*—that in every generation there are a few souls, call them lucky or cursed, who are simply *born not belonging* . . . without strong affiliation to family or location or nation or race; that there may even be millions, billions of such souls, as many non-belongers as belongers, perhaps; that, in sum, the phenomenon may be as "natural" a manifestation of human nature as its opposite, but one that has been mostly frustrated, throughout human history, by lack of opportunity.[10]

"Not belonging" becomes an identity marker as meaningful as "belonging." In *The Ground Beneath Her Feet*, nonbelonging, expressed through the new art form rock 'n' roll, becomes the dominant form of identity, shared worldwide by the people who throng to stadiums to hear Vina and Ormus's band, VTO, and later to mourn Vina's death. The peculiarity in Rushdie's account of outsideness is his suggestion that *everyone*—not only the exile or the migrant—is at some point an outsider. While Rai treats nonbelonging as a permanent exile, as we shall see, the novel transforms it into an alternative form of community affiliation, to which everyone has access.

Outsideness is directly related to fictionality and alterity. The world of *The Ground Beneath Her Feet* gradually separates from and partially returns to our reality, its alterity waxing and waning with Vina's advent and death. Like many of Rushdie's books, *The Ground Beneath Her Feet* is about the interplay of history and the personal for both characters and readers. The alternate-world setting makes the reader the most outside of outsiders, the necessary observer who sees the big picture and both defines and inhabits the boundaries of community. The novel's return to a familiar reality, as Rai moves from one anchoring love to another, also shows that the outsider—artist, reader, exile, and unrequited lover—becomes an insider through nothing more than a shift of the frame.

OUTSIDERS AND *VNENAKHODIMOST*

Sir Darius is the first to suggest the importance of outsideness. During his mythological research with William Methwold, Sir Darius decides that Dumézil's three functions "aren't enough"; they omit "outsideness . . . all that which is beyond the pale, above the fray, beneath notice."[11] Sir Darius argues that the fourth function is to observe and understand: "The only people who see the whole picture . . . are the ones who step out of the frame."[12] Throughout *The Ground Beneath Her Feet*, each character is somehow distanced from events. But while each can be characterized as "outside" (Sir Darius is an Indian anglophile, Ormus is an artist, Vina is a migrant and of mixed race, Rai is the "outside man" in Vina and Ormus's marriage, etc.), each character is also a direct participant in the action of the book (Sir Darius brains Virus with a cricket ball; Ormus and Vina become stars; Rai becomes Vina's lover). The story's frame repeatedly shifts, and with it the centrality or outsideness of each character.

The outsider-insider dichotomy is a symbiotic relationship, as the outsider observes and defines the boundaries of the story, determining who and what constitute the inside. In *The Satanic Verses*, the outsider is defined purely by his or her otherness, as when Hind becomes an example of "women-like-her." In *The Ground Beneath Her Feet*, by contrast, outsiders both demarcate and participate, empowered to interpret and act by the shifting narrative frame. The outsider is at once artist and audience, and his readings of the world endow events with meaning. The outsider's role is, in fact, precisely what Homi Bhabha says the hybrid is *not*: "a third term that resolves the tension between two cultures."[13]

Rai's photography suggests how outsiders enable stories: without the photographer to place the frame, there is no picture. But as Rai unwittingly demonstrates, no one connected to a story can be entirely outside it: the true outsiders of *The Ground Beneath Her Feet* are not Rai or Virus, or even Rushdie, but the readers, who see the novel's layers of fictionality.

By fulfilling the fourth function of observing and understanding, readers become essential—not part of the world but part of its meaning.

Ormus takes a term for outsideness from Bakhtin, linking the concept directly to textual, rather than social, ways the outsider transforms chaos into order: "There's this Russian word, he says. *Vnenakhodimost.* Outsideness."[14] While Ormus uses "*vnenakhodimost*" to speak of outsideness within one's world, like that of artists or exiles, Bakhtin also uses the term to discuss the role of the reader. Bakhtin argues that only by recognizing and embracing one's own otherness can one understand and enter into dialogue with the other, whether face to face or reader to text. Much as Rushdie treats the juxtaposition of incommensurable ideas as "how newness enters the world,"[15] Bakhtin treats dialogue between individuals who acknowledge their own otherness as the path to revelations: "each side realizes the 'potentials' of the other in a way neither could have foreseen."[16] Outsideness, for Bakhtin, underlies the work of the reader: it is necessary both for correct superficial understandings of a novel (the novel is not about you) and for correct fundamental understandings of the novel (the novel's meaning depends on dialogue, which requires that the reader and the novel be nonidentical).

We see the centrality of Bakhtinian dialogue in the book during Ormus' first encounter with She:

> Talk radio's over, she says, Dialogue's dead.
> This is stunning information. In five words the neo-Kantian, Bakhtinian definition of human nature—that we change each other constantly through dialogue, through intersubjectivity, the creative interplay of our several incompletenesses—is laid to rest. The essentially Apollonian universe of communication shrivels beneath the contemptuous force of She's Dionysiac post-verbalism.[17]

Bakhtin argues that dialogue creates a "truth" that cannot be reached through "monologue." This "truth" resembles Rushdie's hybrid "newness": it is expressed through dialogue by at least two consciousnesses, whereas monologic truth is merely a series of propositions. Bakhtin argues that modern novels are essentially heteroglossic, depending on a plurality of voices to present truths that no single voice can provide on its own.[18] She's "post-verbalism" rejects not only speech but also Bakhtin's notion of truth itself, which demands linguistic and dialogic expression. But while Bakhtinian dialogue is central to the book, Ormus seeks to bring order to what he and Bakhtin describe as the "carnival" of heteroglossia: he wants to combine Bakhtin's disparate voices into a fused whole rather than leaving them in polyvocal confusion.

Ormus's use of the word *vnenakhodimost* has two important implications. First, it demonstrates Ormus's understanding of the fictional world he lives in: uniquely among Rushdie's heroes, he seems to recognize that he inhabits the world of a novel and that it is possible to treat that world from the distanced perspective of a reader. Second, the word suggests that Ormus, despite his visions and stardom, can never be a true outsider, since he must remain a character in the novel *The Ground Beneath Her Feet*. No characters can be true "outsiders" in the text: that role is reserved for the reader.

As *Midnight's Children* and *The Ground Beneath Her Feet* show, one person cannot stand in for a pluralist community. The individual who embodies the group, by becoming the consummate group member, obtains the most inside of positions, leaving all other members comparatively excluded, thus undercutting the unifying intent of embodiment. By emphasizing the role of the outsider, Rushdie paradoxically distributes insider status far more evenly than he can through Saleem's system of pluralist representation: everyone has the potential to be an outsider, and the outsider can identify an indefinite number of insiders. Ormus's attempt to fuse competing worlds and worldviews is in direct contrast with Saleem's approach to community formation, in which outsiders who do not fit Saleem's narrative—whether they are Shiva or Gandhi—can be erased entirely. Ormus does what Saleem cannot: he acknowledges that his representations of the world, no matter how diverse and wide ranging, are still partial and challenges his audience to see—and move—the edges of the frame.

FACT, FANTASY, AND COMPETING TWINS

While *The Ground Beneath Her Feet* is full of alternate worlds, not all those worlds are to be taken seriously. Some are fantasies or forgeries, "truths" that everyone knows to be false, like the imaginary worlds in government propaganda or irresponsible reporting:

> We go to bed thinking—just a random example—that Mr. N— M— or Mr. G— A— is a notorious terrorist, and wake up hailing him as the savior of his people. One day the islanders inhabiting a particular cold wet lump of godforsaken rock are vile devil worshippers swigging blood and sacrificing babies, the next day it's as if nothing of the sort ever occurred . . . Men and women recover memories of having been sexually abused as children. Whoosh, no they don't, their parents are reinstated as the most loving and laudable people you could imagine. Genocide occurs; no it doesn't. Nuclear waste contaminates large swathes of entire continents, and we all

learn words like "half-life." But in a flash all the contamination has gone, the sheep aren't ticking, you can happily eat your lamb chops.[19]

These claims are clearly false and indicate not an unstable reality but an unscrupulous news media and an amnesiac public. We have seen such critiques of media "truth" before in Saleem's condemnation of Pakistani war reporting or the varying accounts of Gibreel's disappearance. While the language here is of alternate realities, the truth is that the indeterminacy of newspaper accounts stems from political expedience. The changes in readers' perceptions of the facts suggest how easily readers, not facts, are manipulated by those in authority. In this paragraph, we are in the same position as the psychiatric patients with recovered memories of abuse: facts are rendered unstable not by their vulnerability to interpretation but by our own susceptibility to authoritative statements. Neither Rai nor Rushdie thinks propaganda can change reality: treating changing political winds as changing truth emphasizes how far from mutable truth really is. Suffering happens. Death is absolute, whether or not we call it genocide.

Just as false "alternate realities" mark the limits of truth's malleability, overtly fantastic fictional worlds identify irrationality or escapism. One such fantastic otherworld appears only three pages into the novel, as a reaction to Vina's death:

> a fantasy-fiction wonk hailing from the Castro district of San Francisco and nicknamed <elrond@rivendel.com> explained that Raúl Páramo had been speaking Orcish, the infernal speech devised for the servants of the Dark Lord Sauron by the writer Tolkien: *Ash nazg durbatulûk, ash nazg gimbatul, ash nazg thrakatulûk agh burzum-ishi krimpatul.* After that, rumors of Satanic, or perhaps Sauronic, practices spread unstoppably across the Web. The idea was put about that the mestizo lover . . . had given Vina Apsara a priceless but malignant ring, which had caused the subsequent catastrophe and dragged her down to Hell. But by then Vina was already passing into myth, becoming a vessel into which any moron could pour his stupidities . . . *One ring to rule them all, one ring to find them, one ring to bring them all and in the darkness bind them.* I sat next to Vina Apsara in the helicopter to Tequila, and I saw no ring on her finger, except for the talismanic moonstone she always wore, her link to Ormus Cama, her reminder of his love.[20]

The fictional world of Tolkien is here the domain of the Internet conspiracy theorist, and "myth" appears to be the realm of fan-fiction, a derivative genre providing its practitioners—like <elrond@rivendell.com>—with prefabricated, pseudomystical identities. Rai refutes the conspiracy theory, claiming that Vina's life is governed not by magic but by her love for Ormus: there is nothing supernatural here, he suggests, or if there is, it is the "talismanic" power of love, the opposition of which to death is "the subject" of the book.[21] This critique is not of *The Lord of the Rings* itself, which Vina loves, but of the fan's obsessive attachment to Tolkien's fantasy world.

These parodic, debased fantasies, however, reflect the book's very real otherworlds. These worlds may be malign, like the political otherworlds of propaganda, or mythic, like Tolkien's Middle-earth, but they are also indisputably real. While <elrond@rivendell.com> oversimplifies the connection between the real and the fantastic, he is nonetheless correct, in the metaphysical framework of the novel, that literary and "real" worlds interpenetrate and affect each other, not in a one-way transaction whereby the real world informs the fictional, but in a dialogic relationship wherein fiction and reality are mutually constitutive. Indeed, that mutuality is what differentiates the book's substantive alternate worlds from propagandistic or paranoid alterities.

The novel stages this dialogue between fiction and reality by repeatedly shifting its own fictional framework. At first, *The Ground Beneath Her Feet* appears to be set in the same 1940s and 1950s Bombay as Rushdie's other Bombay novels. Appearances by characters from *Midnight's Children* and *The Moor's Last Sigh* appear to anchor readers who know Rushdie's work in the familiar chronotope of the previous books: Sir Darius becomes friends with William Methwold and Homi Catrack and is insulted by Aurora Zogoiby. Other characters are slight variations on those in earlier novels: Dr. Shaapstecker, who saves Baby Saleem's life in *Midnight's Children*, becomes Snooty Utie Shaapstecker, the nurse who assists at Ormus's birth. These differences between characters in one novel and another are easily overlooked, however, since they are tiny variations in the nature of the fictional world; while fans of a science fiction series might point out such changes as "errors," less purist readers are often willing to allow authors a degree of freedom to modify their own created worlds. Similarly, small changes in historical events—especially those in the novel's implied future rather than its past—appear well within the bounds of standard fictional variations: Rai's passing mention of the collapse of the San Francisco Bay Bridge in an earthquake does not initially appear to indicate that his world's history differs from ours any more than Saleem's does.[22]

It comes as surprise, then, when on page ninety of *The Ground Beneath Her Feet* we receive our first indication that the novel's world is substantially different from our own not only in its supernatural occurrences but also in its quotidian reality. The extent of the world's alterity appears during Vina and Ormus's first meeting at the record store, Rhythm Center, where Ormus hears Jesse Garon Parker sing "Heartbreak Hotel"—a song sung in our world by Elvis Aaron Presley.

Until this moment, readers of *The Ground Beneath Her Feet* have been collaborating in the construction of one kind of possible world: our own world with a small amount of magic thrown in, familiar to us from fairy tales, magical realist texts, and Rushdie's earlier Bombay novels. With the change in the name of the singer of "Heartbreak Hotel," however, we discover that our understanding of the world we have helped create has been flawed. The introduction of Jesse Garon Parker is profoundly disorienting. The world that appeared to have a familiar basis in fairy-tale coherence shifts under our feet, and we are in another kind of possible world for which we do not yet know the rules. The stabilizing world boundaries of literary genre are abruptly permeable; Emma Bovary has run off with an enchanted prince.[23]

The difference between Elvis and Jesse shows the nature of the divergence between our world and the book's. The real Elvis Presley, like the fictional Ormus, had a stillborn identical twin: if he had lived, Elvis' brother would have been named Jesse Garon Presley. Like the competing twins, the alternative worlds within the book are mutually exclusive choices stemming from identical genealogies. The first major difference between our world and the book's indicates both that the origins of the two worlds are the same and that they are in direct competition.

It is a surprise, after the deep-seated antidualism of *The Satanic Verses*, that this novel's repeated question is, "If we are all twins, which twin must die?"[24] The competing twins of *The Ground Beneath Her Feet* contrast with the "alternative Saladins" of *The Satanic Verses*[25] because they are not multiple facets of a single personality: they are mutually exclusive alternatives, selves so different as to be irreconcilable even within a many-worlds or possible-worlds understanding of the self. While the "alternative Saladins" are potential parts of a psychic whole, the alternative twins of *The Ground Beneath Her Feet* do not add up to a single person any more than political about-faces in newspapers amount to a single truth. These incompatible realities are the philosophical opposite of Bakhtinian dialogue: the competing-twin model of alternate worlds renders discursive or dialogic unity impossible. The dead twin is an alternate self so different as to be unassimilable: he is not a way to acknowledge the inherent otherness of the self but a way to externalize it and treat it as an enemy, antimatter to the self's matter.

Nonetheless, the possibility of unifying competing twins into a single consciousness haunts the novel's twin story. Despite the repeated statement that the twins and the worlds are irreconcilable, what separates "real" alternative realities from fake ones like recovered memories is not their plausibility but their flexibility. The false otherworlds of the book present us with simple binary choices. The parents of patients with recovered memories are either abusive or laudable; Tolkien's battle is a clear competition between good and evil. The twinned worlds of *The Ground Beneath Her Feet*, on the other hand, are *both* mutually exclusive *and* fluid, continually influencing each other, just as the dead Gayomart directs Ormus's musically prophetic dreams.

The competing-twin model of alternate worlds draws on both the Parsi Cama family's Zoroastrian mythology and the rhetoric of postcolonial criticism. Fausto Ciomi points out that Ormus's name and his relationship with Gayomart parallel the Parsi deity Ahura Mazda, who competes with his twin brother Ahriman.[26] Ciomi's observation helps explain the Manichean divisions of the book: while the term "Manichean" is frequently used in postcolonial criticism to describe competition between the colonizer and colonized, the term originally refers to the Manichean heresy, a third-century syncretic sect drawing on Christianity and Zoroastrianism. The Manicheans believed in "two principles, eternal and independent of each other, one of which has no goodness and can stop the plans of the other": the Manichean universe contains two rival omnipotent beings, one infinitely good and the other infinitely evil.[27] By invoking the Zoroastrian origins of the Manichean divide—the competition between evil Ahriman and good Ahura Mazda—Rushdie treats a familiar description of postcoloniality as a local, theist, contested account of the origins of good and evil. This association suggests that the book's oppositional structure—its assertion that one twin must die—is potentially flawed. The problem with the Manichean divide, for Rushdie, is its interpretive inflexibility: in a Manichean system, one twin must be good, the other evil, and the kind of moral ambiguity so central to *The Satanic Verses* becomes impossible.

The Ground Beneath Her Feet plays it both ways. The novel pairs the story of Ormus, the surviving twin, with his world, which clashes with and destroys the mysterious twinned world of Maria. But Ormus's synthetic music and the text of the novel itself provide noncompetitive models of how alternative worlds can be combined into a single, unified whole. By resembling Orpheus as well as Ormuzd, Ormus mediates not only between life and death but also between absolutism and relativism, superimposing Bakhtinian dialogue onto Manichean competition.

Authorial Identity and Layers of Fictionality

Elvis's replacement by Jesse Garon Parker is the first of a series of substitutions among the world's artists. As the novel progresses, familiar artists—who have been mentioned by name earlier in the novel—are replaced by their artistic alter egos. Nabokov is one of the first to undergo this transformation. Vina, explaining that she did not have sex with Ormus when she was underage, says, "Bombay's Lolita I was not,"[28] and Rai mentions *Lolita* in a list of Bombayite hypocrisies: "What's the *Kama Sutra*? A Disney comic? Who built the Khajuraho temples? The Japanese? And of course in the 1950s there were no girl tarts in Kamathipura working eighteen hours a day, and child marriages never took place, and the pursuit of the very young by lecherous old humberts—yes, we'd already heard of the new Nabokov shocker—was utterly unknown. (Not.)"[29] Rai's series of counterfactual assertions suggests the alternate world of an unerotic India to demonstrate its impossibility: the colloquial, scathing "(Not.)" at the end asserts the obvious truth of facts the hypocrites deny. The alternate reality of an asexual India is no more plausible than the alternate realities of government propaganda or Mordor.

This passage establishes Nabokov as a "real" writer in the novel's world. His fiction provides a framework and terms for describing real-world actions—Rai's term "humbert" plays with the popular use of "lolita" to describe a sexually alluring young girl—but in this passage, it remains clearly fiction, in contrast with the indisputable truth of sexual hypocrisy.

Nabokov's presence in the novel is unstable, however. Despite appearing as a "real" writer, he is replaced by his own fictional character. After Ormus leaves India, passing through a "rip . . . in the surface of the real,"[30] fiction and reality blend in ways the characters cannot discern. This shift is marked by the novel's punctuation: when the narrative leaves India, the text ceases marking dialogue with quotation marks, suggesting that the accuracy of reported dialogue is in question and that the distinction between narrator and character is beginning to blur. More importantly, Ormus's reading on the *Frederica* demonstrates that the major authors of his world are similar but not identical to the major authors of ours:

> Books by famous American writers, Sal Paradise's odes to wanderlust, Nathan Zuckerman's *Carnovsky*, science fiction by Kilgore Trout, a playscript—*Von Trenck*—by Charlie Citrine, who would go on to write the hit movie *Caldofreddo*. The poetry of John Shade. Also Europeans; Dedalus, Matzerath. The one and only *Don Quixote* by the immortal Pierre Ménard. F. Alexander's *A Clockwork Orange*.

> Here's the year's hit fantasy-thriller, *The Watergate Affair*, in which the future President Nixon (President Nixon! that's how wild a fantasy it is) has to leave office after trying to bug the Democrats' offices, an accusation that's finally proved true, in a wildly implausible twist, when it turns out that Nixon also bugged himself, ha ha ha, the things these guy think of to make us laugh.³¹

Ormus's reading is a compendium of authorial alter egos in twentieth-century literature. In our world, Ormus would be reading Kerouac, Roth, Vonnegut, Bellow, Nabokov, Joyce, Grass, Borges, and Burgess—all writers Rushdie admires. Each is replaced by a character associated, more or less accurately, with his own persona; these are literary Jesse Garon Parkers, artists' twins, born into fiction in one world and reality in another.

Once Ormus passes through the membrane in the sky, Rai's world moves deeper into fictionality than when Rai and Vina were talking about *Lolita*: where before they were reading Nabokov novels, they now share the stage with Nabokov characters. As Rai's world diverges from our own, in an eerie similarity to the government propaganda denying genocide or nuclear accidents, its retrospective reality also seems to change. Nabokov *has* existed in this world, but he no longer does. These differences between worlds do not depend on a single moment of change, the death of one twin or the other, but on gradual movement down divergent historical tracks, in which after-the-fact interpretations and alterations of events really do have the effect Rai parodies in his account of recovered memories. At the same time, real events in our world are transformed into fiction: while authors are replaced by their fictional alter egos, the novel *The Watergate Affair* suggests that we, too, are living a series of "fictional" events. Just as our fiction becomes Rai's world's truth, so our truth becomes their fiction, and each world enacts the possible-world scenarios imagined in the other.

Other such transformations take place. Vina reads Kerouac's *On the Road* on a trip to Kashmir, but Ormus reads work by Kerouac's character Sal Paradise on the *Frederica*. Rai refers to the novel *The Manuscript Found at Saragossa* but cannot make the connection a hundred pages later when "A Polish patriot, Zbigniew Cybulski, has been murdered in a back yard, amid sheets blowing from washing lines."³² Cybulski starred in the book's Polish movie adaptation, *The Saragossa Manuscript* (*Rekopis znaleziony w Saragossie*, 1965). His death in Rai's world echoes another Cybulski film, *Ashes and Diamonds* (*Popiól i diament*, 1958), about the end of World War II, in which a bloodstained sheet resembles the red and white Polish flag. The difference between the two worlds is primarily in the process, rather than the outcome; in our world, Cybulski also died young, at the age of thirty-nine, in a train accident.[33] This change renders Cybulski's death both more politically meaningful in Rai's world—the image of blood on the sheets from *Ashes and Diamonds* is full of elegiac nationalism, lamenting Russia's annexation of Poland—and less legible: the film director's camera is needed to show that Cybulski's blood mimics the Polish flag. While the murder of a patriot has clear meanings even without directorial framing, the full effect is lost without the camera's composition of the shot. Both the artist and the outsider's view are necessary to render life's meaning comprehensible: the director constructs the shot, and the audience sees and interprets it. In this case, Rai's world is more meaningful from the perspective of our world, which sees the fictional framing of the "real" events.

While Ormus reads writers' literary doppelgangers, the world of *The Ground Beneath Her Feet* is not one of simple correspondences: Shade writes poetry, not novels, and Borges is replaced with both Pierre Ménard and Vina's "Chinese genius, the former governor of Yunnan province, Ts'ui Pên."[34] Literary alternate realities are too complicated to map onto the living twin–dead twin divide: the Manichean model does not hold for literature.

Bouncing It Down

Paths fork, but they also recombine, and Rai's world becomes first more and then less unlike our own. The book's dominant metaphor for this dialogic recombination, as well as the antidote it suggests to the Manichean battle between twins, is in Ormus's music. When Ormus "bounces down" different musical tracks, he mirrors the synthesis the book's realities also undergo:

> Bouncing down is what you do when you need to keep tracks free. You mix together two tracks and transfer the mixed sound to a third track. Then you can re-use the first two tracks to record two more parts of the music and you bounce these down to the free fourth track. Now you've got two tracks containing mixes of two tracks each. If you've still got a lot of parts to record, you can bounce these two tracks into one, giving you a single track with four parts on it and three free tracks.
> And so on.
> The problem is that once you've done this you can never separate the tracks again. The mix you make is what you're stuck with. You can't pull the music apart and play with it any more. You're making final, irrevocable decisions as you go. It's a recipe for disaster, unless the person doing it is a genius.[35]

Ormus's genius—despite its origins in his status as the surviving twin—is fundamentally anti-Manichean: it directs the fusion of entirely separate elements. Ormus himself, by implication, gets his genius not from his successful competition with Gayomart but from being the "bounced down" combination of the living and the dead. Mariam Pirbhai, observing how Ormus confronts musical hybridity, notes that "Ormus Cama's challenge is a virtual replication of Sinai's plight in *Midnight's Children*, albeit at the global level."[36] But while Saleem cracks under the strains of millions of Indias, Ormus "bounces down" the entire world. Ormus does for artistic pluralism what characters in the previous novels do for personal identity: he shows how "many selves can be, in song, a single multitude."[37] This musical assimilation does not destroy the individual components—the "many selves" remain *audible* on the combined tracks—but they are no longer *separable*. Each voice becomes a permanent part of the larger dialogue.

While Ormus's fusion of musical tracks is impossible to duplicate, the novel suggests that there are other, less literal ways the rest of us can imitate him. Vina's account of American national identity describes a synthesis similar to Ormus's music, with the important difference that synthesis requires no "genius." According to Vina, America is composed of distinct, unassimilated ethnic types: an American can be "a Bombay singer singing the Bombay bop or a voodoo cab driver with zombies on the brain or a bomber from Montana or an Islamist beardo from Queens . . . slave owners' sons from Yoknapatawpha, or those sad sacks on the daytime confession shows."[38] The precondition for joining the group called "American" is not cultural or even, surprisingly, geographical. Instead, "You get to be an American just by wanting," Vina says. "Not belonging, that's an old American tradition, see?, that's the American way."[39]

Vina's America takes Ormus's fusion of diverse elements a step further, redefining even outsideness as a form of assimilation. For Vina, potential Americans are like the tracks on Ormus's mixer: once they bounce themselves down into the American nation, they change not their own identities but the larger category of "kinds of American it's possible to be." Vina's America follows neither the melting-pot nor the "tossed salad" model of assimilation, in which ingredients either lose their individuality or remain unmodified; instead, it offers an intermediate version—the pizza-topping model?—in which individuals both retain their character and are bonded to other elements around them. Rushdie's "ideological shift" to New York is flagged as a way of expanding and altering his own identity while also retaining its distinctiveness. An American, says Vina, can still be a "Bombay singer," though once he becomes American, he will never really return to Bombay.

The book's worlds enact a synthesis similar to those Ormus performs in his music and Vina identifies in America. The collision of unlike objects may risk "disaster," the dissolution we see in both the catastrophic earthquakes and the book's chaotic structure, but can also lead to "irrevocable" fusion. The book's Manichean counterforces—Gayomart and Ormus, Jesse and Elvis, Sikh nationalist and Westernized music mogul, and so on—become assimilated into the whole, and the conflict between the alternatives is transformed into harmonic dissonance. Ormus's combinatorial art is the only possible answer to Manichaeism, as it is only by assimilation rather than refusal that the oppositional mindset can really be countered.

The novel shows how to assimilate alterities most clearly in Rai's accounts of political events. Just as the novel's artistic alterity becomes visible when Ormus meets Vina, politics in Rai's world deviate from those in our world when Vina leaves Bombay. Unlike its artistic alterity, however, which is flagged by Ormus's incredulity at Jesse Garon Parker's "theft" of his songs, the political alterity of Rai's world is introduced in terms that initially appear to be purely personal. Ormus senses that something is wrong as soon as Vina leaves, but Rai mistakes his disorientation for lovesickness: "'This isn't how things should be . . . Everything's off the rails. Sometimes a little off, sometimes a lot. But things should be different. Just . . . different.' . . . As if he had access to some other plane of existence, some parallel, 'right' universe, and had sensed that our time had somehow been put out of joint. Such was his vehemence that I found myself believing him, believing, for example, in the possibility of that other life in which Vina had never left and we were making our lives together, all three of us, ascending together to the stars."[40] Rai understands Ormus's longing as personal yearning for an "other life in which Vina had never left." He responds with his own anti-idealistic credo: "The world is what it is."[41] But while Rai's pessimism seems reasonable, it becomes jarring in light of the first major change in the book's political reality, which immediately follows Ormus's musings on the wrongness of "things": the problem is greater than Rai realizes, and Rai's repeated assertion that he concentrates personally and professionally on "What Actually Happens"[42] is made absurd by context. Ormus's big musical break comes "The day after the President of the United States had that narrow escape in Dallas, Texas, [as] we were all becoming familiar with the names of the would-be assassins, Oswald, whose rifle jammed, and Steel, who was overpowered on some kind of grassy knoll by a genuine hero, a middle-aged amateur cameraman called Zapruder, who saw the killer's gun and hit him over the head with an 8 mm ciné camera... Ormus Cama... [was] informed that among the audience for his late-night set would be... [the record mogul] Mr. Yul Singh himself."[43] Rai cannot recognize the wrongness he reports. He can regret the world's failure to conform to his personal wishes, and yearn, as he imagines Ormus does, for "that other life in which Vina had never left," but he has no grounds from which to see that his single sentence linking the failed Kennedy assassination to Ormus's rise to stardom unites his world's political and artistic alterities. Rai, through the conjunction of these revelations, unwittingly tells us that his world's alterities are mutually supporting and that Vina's arrival in and departure from Bombay are part of the same alterity that produces Ormus's career and the apparently unrelated political events of her era. Despite his repeated assurances that he is an outsider both in Vina and Ormus's relationship and in his own world, Rai reveals his own insider status—and thus his inability to understand the meaning of the events he reports.

The links between artistic and political alterities, and the role of artists and outsiders in defining reality's boundaries, are emphasized by Zapruder's camera. Photography, an art form that at least appears to represent objective reality, here shows that art and political action can construct truths far more meaningful than newspaper propaganda. Zapruder, using his camera as a bludgeon instead of a recording device, is transformed from author to "hero," from Nabokov to John Shade, suggesting that historical narratives, like novels, contain layers of fictionality that individuals can cross. As the artist becomes more directly powerful in his world, and Zapruder's camera becomes a weapon, the image and the narrative surrounding that image become both more effective and less subject to interpretation. The failure of the Kennedy assassination, through the transformation of the cameraman from observer to actor, renders the assassination attempt legible. Instead of providing fuel for conspiracy theories, Zapruder's repurposed camera really does what our world's cameras can only claim to do: it shows an unambiguous truth. The artist has a choice between framing the world or acting in it, and while framing the world may make it legible, acting in the world appears to make it *knowable*. The measurement of truth on which Rai depends, the camera, is subject to manipulation (as when Rai takes credit for film he has taken from the boot of a murdered photographer), but it is also capable—in a most unphotographic manner—of revealing layers of reality not visible to the naked eye.

Despite Zapruder's heroism, however, Kennedy will still be shot, and once again the personal, artistic, and political alterities of Rai's world are inextricable from each other—although their relationship remains inscrutable to Rai himself. Vina loses a gig

> when she casually referred to her stuffed-shirt audience as "dead Kennedys." The United States, still at war both with itself and in Indochina, had been plunged into deep mourning by the freak double killing of President Bobby Kennedy and his elder brother and predecessor, ex-President Jack, both slain by a single bullet fired by a delusional Palestinian gunman. This was the so-called magic bullet which bounced around the lobby of the Ambassador Hotel, L.A., whining like a demented hornet, and ended up scoring an appalling double hit . . . hundreds of thousands of Americans reported sledgehammer migraine headaches and violent dizzy spells, and people stood dazed on street corners murmuring "It shouldn't be this way[.]" Vina was probably lucky that her gibe only lost her a job.[44]

Rai's world again appears more legible than ours: while the assassination still produces the term "magic bullet," there is no doubt that it was the work of a single gunman, and the bullet's behavior is a "freak" accident rather than evidence of conspiracy. The political-artistic world of the novel, even as it becomes more familiar, is easier for its inhabitants to parse. While Rai cannot understand the full resonance of his world's events—he misses Vina's unwitting reference to the Dead Kennedys, a punk band formed in 1978—he lives in a world where ballistic and narrative trajectories follow paths that, while "appalling," are rational and comprehensible.

We have seen how ignorance of their location in fiction dooms Allie and Gibreel in *The Satanic Verses*. Here, the implication is that we are all placed in some world's fictional narrative—and all more or less unable to read the narratives we live in. What sets Rai's world apart is not its coincidences and narrative contrivances, which, as Nixon's tapes demonstrate, occur in our own world, too; instead, the distinctive feature of Rai's world is that its population half-recognizes its own fictionality. The mourners across America almost intuit their placement in a fictional universe and transform the visionary outsider position into a common human experience.

After Vina and Ormus die, the differences between the book's world and our world become both more superficial and less clearly literal. When Rai lists the "frontier earthquakes," it is difficult to read the list as reportage instead of metaphor:

> These frontier earthquakes are the wonder of the age, aren't they? Did you see that fault that just ripped out the whole iron curtain? . . . And after the Chinese opened fire in Tiananmen, did you see the rift open up along *the*

entire length of the Great Wall of China? So now there's nothing in China (but there's a big new airport in Japan) that can be seen from the surface of the moon, that'll teach 'em, right? Right.

Oh, man, the things these quakes are throwing up. Poets for presidents, the end of apartheid, the Nazi gold buried for fifty years deep in Swiss bank accounts, Arnold Schwarzenegger, the *Titanic*, and we guess communism just got buried in the rubble there somewhere. And those Ceaușescus? *So not missed*.[45]

The list of earthquakes and their ramifications is an ironic summary of the history of the 1990s. With the exception of the reference to the Great Wall of China, every name and event is perfectly familiar. The destruction of the wall, too, can be read as indicating that China's separation from the West is fading: in this reading, the earthquakes become a metaphor for globalization and seem merely a poetic statement of fact. As in Rai's early accounts of government propaganda, it is not possible (as it was during the middle portions of the novel) to take his counterfactual histories at face value—even if they are literally true.

The unambiguous differences between Rai's world and ours fade after Vina's death and the destruction of Maria's world. In the end, when Rai and his new lover Mira (whose name, as Judith Leggatt points out, combines Vina's and Maria's and echoes the word "mirror")[46] are eating their breakfast muffins, the difference between Rai's world and ours is so small as to be meaningless: the television's broadcast of an old performance by Ormus and Vina reminds us that Rai's world is still fiction but does not constitute a substantial ontological schism.

Postmodern Frames and Assimilating the Fantastic

The ending of *The Ground Beneath Her Feet* suggests that fantastic glimpses of alternate worlds must eventually be abandoned in favor of simple perceptual reality—albeit a reality whose meaning those fantastic alternatives have helped to construct, much as transnational boundary crossing can construct identities for its practitioners. In a narrative move that both assimilates fantastic fiction into the "real" world and marks the necessity of forsaking the fantastic in favor of everyday life, Rai's farewell to Vina and Ormus and embrace of Mira and her daughter Tara mirrors the ending of *The Lord of the Rings*. Years after the end of the war with Mordor, the heroes Frodo, Gandalf, and Elrond abandon Middle-earth, leaving faithful, ordinary Sam Gamgee to return to his wife and family. Sam accompanies Frodo to the ship that will take him away, watches its departure, and mournfully returns home:

> And he went on, and there was yellow light, and fire within; and the evening meal was ready, and he was expected. And Rose drew him in, and set him in his chair, and put little Elanor upon his lap.
>
> He drew a deep breath. 'Well, I'm back,' he said.[47]

In Tolkien's world, the war and its trauma are only over when the heroic figures have gone. Sam is only "back" from the war once his comrades in arms have departed. His return to Rose and Elanor parallels Rai's new domestic arrangement with Mira and Tara. Significantly, Rai pays particular attention to the ending of *The Lord of the Rings* when he mentions Vina's affection for the books: "You could see why she liked *The Lord of the Rings*. This offered the end of a world too, but, unusually, it was a sort of happy ending."[48] Mira, by contrast, hates fantasy novels, and Rai's love for her removes him from the realm of the fantastic and anchors him in a stable reality: on the last page of the novel, he says, "What remains is ordinary human life."[49]

Randy Boyagoda argues that the book "rejects the 'other-worldly' and constant movement as desirable ends in and of themselves."[50] The novel ends with postmythological, comfortable normality. This "normality," however, can only be achieved through the process of artistic and metaphysical recombination that underlies not only Ormus's music and Vina's America but also Rai's narrative; "ordinary human life" is made by "bouncing down" the fantastic into the quotidian.

The novel's meaning arises out of dialogues between the "outside" and "inside": Rai's life and the lives of the lovers he watches; would-be rock stars in India and successful rock stars in America; and the world of the reader and the world of the novel. The theme of outsideness accounts for the novel's asymmetrical structure: the final chapter takes place outside the epic narrative of VTO. The band's career cannot be understood without the juxtaposed scene of Rai's life with Mira. Only by providing a double context—the story of Vina's life, framed by the story of Vina's death, followed by the story of Rai's new beginning—can Rai find a ground outside the story on which to stand—a place in which he can, for the first time, step outside the frame.

Klaus Stierstorfer argues that "Rai's private solution . . . creating his own, local reality and piece of ground to stand on in the midst of the continued ragings of chaos" constitutes a rejection of postmodernism's "playfulness and apparent lack of ethical commitment," the "flip side" of which is "violence and barbarism."[51] But it is not simply Rai and his local reality that have shifted away from Ormus and Vina's melodrama: the whole planet, with Ormus's death, enters a post-postmodern moral and ontological framework, returning to an "ordinary" world familiar both to the characters and to the readers. Rushdie's engagement with postmodernism rejects indeterminacy as a means to unite competing twins because indeterminacy, too, is a matter of framing. Much as Rushdie dismisses Manichean postcolonialism as overdeterministic, he treats postmodern indeterminacy as too superficial to achieve a meaningful fusion of unlike others.

The colliding literary worlds of *The Ground Beneath Her Feet* both destabilize reality and assert the existence of a fundamental core truth: like Ormus's mixed tracks, the novel makes a final, unified whole out of apparently unstable and incompatible elements. The novel's contradictory geographies and levels of reality are constantly foregrounded, with the result that the novel expands McHale's "zone" to include, at least *in potentia*, the world we inhabit as well as the fictional one. The novel's fictive history and geography induces the head-spinning sense of disorientation McHale discusses as much in the characters as in the readers. But while the narrative appropriates the terms and images of postmodern uncertainty, it also undercuts them by providing stabilizing contexts for the destabilizing confusions of postmodern indeterminacy. Yul Singh, for example, turns out to be one of the bidders at an auction for "the memorabilia of some defunct immigrant cabal, used to go around writing DEATH on people's walls. Don't Ever Antagonize The Horn. They had a trumpet logo."[52] Yul's presence at the auction demystifies Pynchon's *The Crying of Lot 49*, in which the question of whether or not the Tristero "cabal" exists is left permanently unanswered. By placing Yul at the auction, Rushdie suggests that such indeterminacy is possible only if the fictional world is entirely contained in the text. While readers of *The Crying of Lot 49* are left without a resolution to the novel's quest, its heroine, Oedipa, will get an answer if she continues existing after the last page. Pynchon's novel is ambiguous because it ends immediately before the auction begins. In the fictional world Oedipa shares with Yul, however, the frame is removed, and questions become answerable. Narrative framing is the origin of ambiguity.

The alternate reality of *The Ground Beneath Her Feet*, unlike that of *The Crying of Lot 49*, is both continually in flux and ultimately knowable. Despite the problems with Rai's assertion that "the world is what it is," the novel's insistence on the verifiability of reality is not naïve or uncomplicated. In *The Ground Beneath Her Feet*, individual facts may not remain objectively true, but there is such a thing as objective truth: the real world continues even if it is not verified by observers. Death is death, love is love. The narratives surrounding those core truths, and the interpretations to which such narratives lead, are all that is subject to change.

The novel's placement in America also teaches us to recognize and value the coexistence of individualism and group identity, belonging and not belonging. *The Ground Beneath Her Feet* invites us into a community of readership not only of the novel but also of the world: it teaches us to frame and reframe our surroundings, looking for the fictional constructions both of propaganda or paranoia and of historical or personal narrative. The goal of shifting our frames is not to debunk fantasies but to gain control over them. As we acknowledge the frames through which we view our world, we recognize the extent to which our framings are partial and see that there are aspects of our realities that cannot be fully understood from within.

The novel's shifting alterities demand that readers participate in the creation and recognition of their own outsideness, their roles in determining the bounds of the "real." Through their participation in the dialogic creation of the novel's world, readers are led to reject Manichean binarisms. *The Ground Beneath Her Feet* becomes an entry point into alterity not only through the access it grants to Rai's world but also through the process of displacement and re-placement to which it subjects its readers. If reality is constantly shifting, the book suggests, we shift with it, and we, too, are all outsiders. The community the novel models is not a national or cultural community in the traditional sense, but Rushdie's "community of displaced persons," in which shared displacement, disorientation, and assimilation become the grounds for both sympathy and realism. In this community, the self is neither primary nor subsumed into the larger whole, and a relativistic reading of other people's narratives is humanized by the primacy of the personal, absolute truths of love and of mortality.

CONCLUSION

INCEST, MONSTERS, AND THE "INTERNATIONAL FRATERNITY"

OVER THE LAST FIVE CHAPTERS, WE HAVE SEEN HOW Nabokov and Rushdie renegotiate the line between physical and imaginative truths: the hard truths of geography, physics, and genetics on one side, and the constructed truths of nation, memory, identity, and family on the other. Nabokov works through the tensions between physical geography and the abstract sense of community, emphasizing the dangers of hybridity in *Lolita* and *Pale Fire*, and in *Ada* suggesting the peculiar solution of collapsing spacetime through artistic distance. Rushdie transforms Nabokov's outsider artist into an activist who literally changes the world. The interplay between physical and constructed truths in these novels is complex: they are frequently mutually supporting, but when they come into competition, the results can be a deep disorientation comparable to the most preposterous geographies of postmodern fiction. For Nabokov and Rushdie, physical truths do not always trump constructed truths, and the novels provide a space in which to stage, examine, and reframe what happens when the two are in conflict. These writers exemplify the transnational movement and inspire those who come after them, just as James Joyce, Isak Dinesen, Ernest Hemingway, James Baldwin, and other transnational writers of the first half of the twentieth century inform Nabokov and Rushdie's work. The growing canon of transnational literature provides an alternative and a supplement to national literary traditions, offering deeply rooted affiliations to the exile, the expatriate, and the wanderer: in addition to the canons of their home countries, these writers see themselves as part of a long and established tradition of boundary crossing.

As we have seen, transnational fiction consistently uses metaphors that put the abstract in physical terms—what Saleem would call the "active-metaphorical." These metaphors are at once the underpinnings and the epitome of the novels' shared projects: they mediate between small, physically defined things (individual people or places) and large, abstractly defined things (communities or nations). By treating the community as primarily an abstract concept, transnational fiction separates communal affiliations (whether they are familial or political) from geography; instead, the novel itself does the work of a nation-state by making the physical and the abstract overlap. Transnational fiction grew alongside and within postmodern fiction over the course of the twentieth century, and transnational writers draw on the postmodern emphasis on reading as a performative act in their mediation between physical and abstract truths. But while Thomas Pynchon may emphasize the constructed nature of reality in order to make his readers doubt their own perceptions, transnational fiction is essentially empowering, teaching readers to become editors of their own worlds.

Fiction provides a testing ground in which to determine how far readers and writers can privilege constructed and contextual truths without devolving into empty fantasy, postmodern surreality, or nonsense. Fictional spaces let readers and writers step away from real-world obstacles to community formation, not by solving the problems of identity politics and global injustice, but by treating them as, at least for the duration of the novel, less important than the fundamental commonality among boundary-crossing intellectuals.

As we have seen, the emphasis Nabokov and Rushdie place on constructed over physical truth is intended to bring readers into a sense of community and shared responsibility with the characters, authors, and other readers of the novels. But for the community to be viable outside the novels—for readers to retain that affiliation after they have finished reading—the novels must make their abstract claims of community a meaningful part of the real world. Transnational writers deal with the problem of importing fictional constructions into reality in their treatment of monstrous bodies, through which they acknowledge the difficulty of blending fiction with reality and dramatize the interdependence of fact and interpretation. Nabokov, Rushdie, and others use monstrosity as a marker of failed negotiations between the physical and the abstract. Their monsters also indirectly suggest what a successful mediation would look like. When we have examined how monsters demonstrate the ways that the physical and the imaginary are mutually constitutive, we will turn to Michael Chabon's adaptation of the transnational fantastic, which shows how conscious, voluntary affiliations with a fictionally based community can rescue the hybrid from the danger of monstrosity.

Incest, Monsters, and the Limits of Community

Fictionally fashioned communities differ from geographically determined ones in part because of the flexibility of their boundaries. Novelists seeking to create a community independent of geographic constraints—a community based on intellectual likeness, rather than shared lineage or cultural practices—must determine what degree of likeness is necessary for community membership. As it examines the temptations of inclusivity and exclusivity, transnational fiction repeatedly turns to narratives of incest and monstrosity, which inscribe in the body the dangers and attractions both of groups that demand extreme fidelity and of groups that seek to attract membership so diverse as to risk incompatibility.

Edward Said argues that modernist narratives often privilege affiliation (voluntary, critical commitment to a group) over filiation (extending the group through biological reproduction), replacing the "natural forms of authority" like "obedience, fear, love, respect, and instinctual conflict" with "transpersonal forms" like "guild consciousness, consensus, collegiality, professional respect, class, and the hegemony of a dominant culture."[1] For Said, affiliation has the potential to build a more democratic group, "less a hierarchy than a community,"[2] but it also risks its own kind of sterility and provinciality: "affiliation then becomes in effect a literal form of *re-presentation*, by which what is ours is good."[3] The hybrid monsters of transnational fiction combine these two approaches to community formation, finding a way to retain family bonds and the inherent optimism of biological reproduction while simultaneously making community membership earned and voluntary rather than biologically determined.

Incest and monstrosity provide transnational writers with ways of exploring an essential problem of their work: how to transform an abstract idea into a physical reality. The idea of incest straddles the boundary between physical and social identity: kinship is both objectively real and socially constructed, and the sometimes bizarre and thrown-together families of transnational fiction provide a way of testing how far we can choose to see others as like ourselves. Mary Louise Pratt notes a version of this phenomenon in Juana Manuela Gorriti's story "He Who Does Evil Should Expect No Good," in which incest "allegorize[s] the transcultural relationships between creoles and Europe on the one hand and between creoles and indigenous Americans on the other."[4] In the context of transnationally constructed families, the prohibition against incest can be used as the (parodic) basis for a prohibition on monoculturalism: transnational incest narratives suggest that the only way to avoid a hint of incest is to seek out sexual partners as unlike ourselves as possible.

By contrast, the monstrous bodies of transnational fiction provide an allegory of failed hybridity, not only between cultures, but also between fact and interpretation: the monster is the product of a mismatch, in which absolute and constructed truths are in conflict rather than in harmony. Monsters play a multifaceted role in transnational fiction, staging the dilemma of the migrant, who appears monstrous in his new surroundings; embodying the migrant's anxieties about adaptation; demonstrating the risks of cultural fusion; and, when the monsters are the product of incestuous unions, providing an argument against cultural purity as inbred and ultimately sterile.

Monsters warn against both failed hybridity and monoculturalism in part because of the double meaning of the word "monstrosity." First, there is physical monstrosity, which is a deformity or grotesque shape, sometimes consisting of the fusion of incongruous elements and sometimes of a skewed version of the human form—a failure of the offspring to resemble its parents, produced, Marie-Hélène Huet argues, by the parental imagination's power to distort the child's physical body.[5] Second, there is moral monstrosity, which is cruelty or amorality so horrible as to seem inhuman. For transnational writers, these two forms of monstrosity meet in the physical and moral outcomes of failed transnational encounters when representatives of different cultures produce both literal and metaphorical offspring.

It is striking how many transnational novels deal with incest and monstrosity and how frequently incest becomes both a trope for the self-absorption of a narrator and a test of the absorption of an outsider into a biological family. Similarly, monstrosity and anxieties surrounding fertility—particularly deformed, stillborn, or aborted fetuses—are everywhere in transnational fiction. Failures of fertility are generally linked to failed past attempts at making a real place for an imaginary community: stillborn children indicate their parents' inability to achieve a sustainable identity, and novels' monstrous protagonists, like Saladin Chamcha (whose chromosomes leave him sterile and lucky not to be a "deformed freak")[6], are perpetually out of place. But the monstrous offspring of failed syntheses are only half the picture. Hybridizing writers use incest narratives to counterbalance the possibility that their texts will be monstrous by showing that the true source of monstrosity lies not in difference but in sameness.

As we have seen, hybridity is a biological notion, and intellectual and cultural fusions have long been subject to sometimes perversely biologized scrutiny. We see variations on the monstrosity of the hybrid colonist (Kurtz in Conrad's *Heart of Darkness*) or the colonized subject (the absurdly Anglophile Hurree Chunder Mookerjee in Rudyard Kipling's *Kim* [1901]) throughout the British colonial oeuvre, and the theme recurs in postcolonial texts like *The Satanic Verses* and *The God of Small Things* (1997). In the twentieth century, this intersection of incest and hybridity appears in texts as varied as Faulkner's *Absalom, Absalom!* (1936) and Marion Zimmer Bradley's *The Mists of Avalon* (1982)—both of which, while written by authors with uncomplicated national identities, deal with the difficulty of uniting individuals from different races and cultures. *Lolita* and *Midnight's Children* provide useful paradigms for a discussion of the relationship between incest and monstrosity in transnational novels, and the ramifications of this argument will extend to much of transnational and postmodern fiction. As we shall see, the true risk of monstrosity in these novels lies not in physical deformity—which is consistently treated as the subjective product of interpretation—but in the moral monstrosities that arise from overemphasizing unlikeness rather than likeness: failed sympathy, failed synthesis, and failed communication. For these novels, the juxtaposition of physical and moral monstrosity both marks the boundary between objective and subjective truth and reveals the abstract truths of sympathy and human commonality as the least subject to interpretation.

Umberto Eco's Monstrous Fusions

The treatment of monstrosity in Umberto Eco's novels offers a clear exposition of both the challenges and the payoff of transnational world-fashioning, in part because Eco makes his theoretical framework so explicit. Eco provides a useful example not only because his novels directly discuss the problem of reconciling physical and abstract identity categories but also because he demonstrates how varied the writers interested in that problem can be. Eco is neither exiled nor a citizen of a postcolonial nation; instead, his transnationalism stems from his interest in a shared European culture and in the possibility of enfolding Middle Eastern and North African epistemologies into European Christianity. His use of the same techniques of fantastic world-fashioning as Nabokov and Rushdie suggests the extent to which those techniques pervade recent boundary-crossing literature: far from being limited to exiled or migrant communities, transnational imaginary worlds appear whenever writers seek to unify groups that have hitherto viewed themselves as distinct.

Eco's fantastic worlds are frequently populated by hybrid monsters, who provide points of contrast and means of access to his novels' idealized synthetic worlds. Eco's protagonists generally seek not only the solution to a mystery but also a way to bring together conflicting kinds of cultural knowledge. His characters are particularly fond of using geographical schemas to synthesize apparently contradictory ideas. The pinnacle of these syntheses is the library in *The Name of the Rose* (1980), which is "truly laid out and arranged according to the image of the terraqueous orb"[7]: the floor plan of the library is a map of the world, which William and Adso explore "as if we were exploring a mysterious continent or a terra incognita."[8] The librarians' classification of texts by their author's country of origin disguises and confuses the truths the books contain: "among monsters and falsehoods they have also placed works of science from which Christians have much to learn."[9] Geographical boundaries impede the synthesis of different branches of knowledge, and the library's destruction is also a tragic end to the quest to arrive at an inclusive understanding of human experience.

Along with the library, however, the novel offers a second vision of partial synthesis: the monstrous Salvatore, a "creature" whose "face bore a resemblance to those monsters I had just seen on the [church's] capitals."[10] Salvatore's resemblance to the "hairy and hoofed hybrids" Adso sees carved on the church's portal places his hybridity in the realm of the monstrous and artificial, thereby also placing in doubt the library's potential to synthesize diverse forms of knowledge.[11] This human-animal speaks in a language that is unidentifiable but paradoxically comprehensible:

> Nor, for that matter, could I call Salvatore's speech a language, because in every human language there are rules and every term signifies ad placitum a thing, according to a law that does not change, for man cannot call the dog once dog and once cat . . . And yet, one way or another, I did understand what Salvatore meant, and so did the others. Proof that he spoke not one, but all languages, none correctly, taking words sometimes from one and sometimes from another. I also noticed afterward that he might refer to something first in Latin and later in Provençal, and I realized that he was not so much inventing his own sentences as using the disiecta membra of other sentences, heard some time in the past, according to the present situation and the things he wanted to say, as if he could speak of a food, for instance, only with the words of the people among whom he had eaten that food, and express his joy only with sentences that he had heard uttered by joyful people the day when he had similarly experienced joy.[12]

Salvatore's language is not a synthesis but a pastiche. He takes Adso's notion of "consensus" as the basis of verbal meaning too far: for Salvatore, concepts are too distinctly linked both to context and to previous usage for words to have fluid meanings. The result of his overdefinition of words is that rather than learning a language, Salvatore speaks in an accretion of unconnected lexicons, in which each word apparently has only a single meaning, and his attempts at flexibility devolve into nonsense. Like the librarians, Salvatore overcompartmentalizes his knowledge, and the result is a peculiar mixture of pan-European fluency and Babelish incomprehension.

Salvatore, in other words, reveals the book's intellectual stakes: if we do not seek a coherent synthesis of human knowledge, we risk becoming the monstrous keepers of "disiecta membra." Salvatore's "hybrid" body is a physical analogue for his speech in the "language of primeval confusion."[13] Unsynthesized knowledge is unproductive, incomprehensible, and animalistic. Monstrosity arises for Eco not from attempted synthesis but from excessive compartmentalization: hybridity is not dangerous when it really does combine disparate elements, but rather when elements retain their original meanings unmodified. If we can achieve synthesis, we regain hope for both physical and spiritual salvation: as William says, "The people of God cannot be changed until the outcasts are restored to its body."[14] Overemphasis on the contextual or geographical origins of knowledge and on the differences between individuals blinds us to nuance; cultural fusion, on the other hand, is both healing and humanizing.

* * *

Baudolino (2000) reframes Eco's interest in the relationship between geography and knowledge by suggesting that the legitimizing fictions of nationalism can become literal truths. Like Rushdie and Nabokov, Eco starts by examining hybrid individuals but moves on to describe the formation of a hybrid community.

Baudolino also describes a pan-European compendium of knowledge, in which the quest for synthesis has very physical real-world stakes. In *Baudolino*, this compendium takes the form of a letter ostensibly written by Prester John to the Emperor Frederick Barbarossa, recognizing him as a fellow Christian monarch and legitimizing the Holy Roman Empire. The letter is the work of a multilingual, multicultural alliance, including the Italian Baudolino, the Jewish Rabbi Solomon, the Irish-Provençal-Arab Abdul, and a man from Cologne known as the Poet (although he writes no poetry). This coalition fails to help Barbarossa but succeeds in uncovering the actual existence of the country they have invented for the purposes of their letter. That country turns out to be populated by the monsters of medieval European travelers' tales, like skiapods (monsters with a single large foot) and blemmyae (creatures with no heads, with faces in their torsos). The travelers' depiction of this country in their letter is at once highly accurate and incomplete: all the parts they have predicted are there, but they have not imagined its full complexity. While one conspiracist "kept murmuring in wonderment," "Just as was written in the books," the imaginary-turned-real country of Pndapetzim takes on an independent reality of its own outside its creation in text.[15] By the end of the novel, Pndapetzim has superseded the real Holy Roman Empire, even though the travelers initially thought they were creating Pndapetzim for the Empire's benefit.

Early in the novel, Abdul justifies the attempt to describe Prester John's kingdom by claiming that "You don't have to be in a place in order to know everything about it . . . Otherwise sailors would be more learned than theologians."[16] Abdul privileges abstract over concrete knowledge, and his claim appears to be supported by the accuracy of the forgers' predictions: they do indeed know a great deal about the place without having actually been there. As in *The Ground Beneath Her Feet*, outsiders here appear to have a better view: theologians (and forgers) can assemble information from diverse sources into an overarching understanding of things they have never seen. Abdul suggests that this knowledge is superior to that of "sailors," who have experience of many places but lack synthetic understanding of the worlds they have glimpsed.

The claim that outside knowledge of a place can surpass local knowledge is undercut, however, by the first inhabitant of Pndapetzim the travelers meet: a skiapod named Gavagai. W. V. O. Quine makes up the word "gavagai" in *Word and Object* (1960) to illustrate the impossibility of perfect translation: if we do not share a language with the native who shouts "Gavagai!" when he sees a rabbit, we can never be certain either of the word's precise meaning or what prompted the native to shout it, even if we can (eventually) predict the circumstances in which the word is used.[17] Gavagai the skiapod reminds us that, as outsiders in Pndapetzim, we cannot attain local knowledge, calling into question not only the observations of the narrators but also our own readerly ability to understand what we are told. We discover that we are in the same position as Salvatore: Baudolino and the reader alike are linguistic outsiders in the country, assembling an understanding of Pndapetzim from a patchwork of discrete experiences rather than a contextually based consensus. Our factual knowledge—the local observations we share with Abdul's sailors, or our predictions of when the native will shout "gavagai"—may be accurate, but our interpretation of nuance is suspect. Gavagai's name, in other words, contradicts Abdul, suggesting that his "theologians" cannot understand the true meanings of the facts they assemble.

Gavagai, like Salvatore, reminds us that linguistic meaning is contextual, and, as we shall see, he takes us further, reminding us that our knowledge of physical facts is also contextually determined. As a result, our initial reading of the physically alien inhabitants of Pndapetzim as monstrous must be reexamined. Our assumption that their lack of heads or legs makes them monsters is the result of our imported interpretations rather than our local knowledge. The Pndapetzimites' bodies demonstrate an important challenge of transnational fiction: readers must learn to recognize how far their understanding of the physical world rests on interpretation.

The idea of monstrosity itself is one of the most important differences in interpretation between the travelers and the locals. While Baudolino and his friends see the skiapods and blemmyae as monsters, defined by their physical deformity, the Pndapetzimites overlook physical difference in favor of philosophical difference. Baudolino and his friends find this refusal to recognize physical difference bizarre:

"Why I different you?"
"Oh, for God's sake," the Poet said. "To begin with, you have only one leg! We and the blemmyae have two!"
"Also you and blemmyae if you raise one leg, you have only one."
"But you don't have another one to lower!"
"Why should I lower leg I don't has? Do you lower third leg you don't has?"
Boidi intervened, conciliatory: "Listen, Gavagai, you must agree that the blemmy has no head."
"What? Has no head? Has eyes, nose, mouth, speaks, eats. How possible if has no head?"
"But haven't you noticed that he has no neck, and above the neck that round thing that you also have on your neck and he doesn't?"
"What means noticed?"
"Seen. Realized that. You know that."
"Maybe you say he not entirely same as me; my mother couldn't mistake him for me. But you too not the same as this friend because he has mark on cheek and you no. And your friend different from that other one black like one Magi, and him different from that other with black beard like rabbi."[18]

The Pndapetzimites appear to lack the category of physical otherness entirely. Where the travelers see the differences between groups as demarcating race or even species, Gavagai sees physical distinctions as minor and mutable. According to Gavagai, a two-legged creature could resemble a skiapod simply by raising a leg. Gavagai's reading of the differences between individuals renders European racial categories trivial: blackness and Jewishness become the minor marks distinguishing one person from another, the reasons that "my mother couldn't mistake him for me." For Gavagai, physical difference is outweighed by ideological or philosophical difference, and according to him, the terms "blemmyae" or "skiapods" indicate not racial but religious groups: the skiapods and blemmyae do not get along because "Blemmyae think wrong . . . They Christians who make mistake. They *phantasistoi*."[19] Baudolino realizes that "the various races existing in this province give no importance to bodily differences, to color or shape, as we do, when even if we see a dwarf we consider him a horror of nature. But instead, like many of our learned men, for that matter, they attach great importance to the difference of ideas about Christ, or the Most Holy Trinity, of which we have heard so much talk in Paris. It is their way of thinking. We must try to understand this; otherwise we'll be forever lost in endless arguments."[20] Pndapetzim is a place in which the idea of physical monstrosity is entirely absent—or is present only when an individual's body has been damaged or diseased, as in the case of the leprous deacon in charge of the city. Physical monstrosity, in *Baudolino*, becomes a distraction from or misinterpretation of more substantive affiliational, ideological differences and is only a threat insofar as it indicates the disunity of the group. (Those substantive differences, importantly, arise from varying interpretations of the relationship between the physical and the abstract: the disagreement between the skiapods and the blemmyae is about the physicality of Christ's incarnation.)

Nonetheless, the physical differences between the monsters are immutable, and Gavagai's insistence on their fundamental physical likeness suggests that Pndapetzim is actually in peril: the city's residents do not understand their own limitations, and the combination of those limitations with their ideological differences brings about their defeat in the final battle against the invading White Huns. In this fight the skiapods, blemmyae, and so on are defeated because their commanders overlook their unique attributes in placing them on the battlefield. The travelers' belief that the Pndapetzimites are monsters is the product of their preconceptions about the physical grounds of difference, and this understanding is flawed. But so is the skiapods' and blemmyae's interpretation of difference as purely intellectual. Treating either physical or intellectual difference—purely filiative or purely affiliative properties—as the sole demarcation of identity groups is equally useless. The inhabitants of Pndapetzim demonstrate the dangers of overlooking physical absolutes as clearly as the dangers of communal fragmentation.

Eco's imaginary worlds are unabashedly Borgesian: the worlds within his novels are directly brought into being by the conscious invention of his characters. The library in *The Name of the Rose*, like that in "The Library of Babel," is a miniature world, built to contain the books that create and define its meaning. The invention and discovery of Pndapetzim in *Baudolino* owes much to "Tlön, Uqbar, Orbus Tertius." But where Borges is interested in world-creation within the text, Eco roots his imaginary worlds in meticulous real-world detail—not of physical locations but of epistemologies and metaphysics. His discourses on medieval heresies in *The Name of the Rose* and *Baudolino* suggest the purpose of his imagined worlds: Eco wants to delineate the truths that Western Europe has constructed for itself as a cultural whole. While he identifies his characters by nation, Eco uses the novels to explore not only the way heresies distinguish his characters but also how the central shared text around which the heresies are spun—the Bible—provides a common ground between them. That commonality produces a shared space that can be grotesque (Salvatore's body), elevated (the library), or both (the burning library, Pndapetzim), but, in the end, the novels' monsters reveal both the possibility of transcending difference in a community and the catastrophic results of failed synthesis.

Eco's monsters define the stakes of the transnational monster story not only for its characters but also for its texts, authors, and readers. Monsters in transnational literature warn against overclassification, against finalizing or totalizing judgments, and against overprivileging either physical or abstract truths. By calling absolute classifications into question, monstrosity provides a place for the objective and the subjective, the filiative and affiliative to meet, and reveals both what truths are negotiable and what interpretive biases individuals bring to their interactions. At the same time, the monsters remind us of the necessity of finding a clear real-world basis for our claims of community: if we insist on the primacy of abstract truths over physical ones, we risk destruction along with the citizens of Pndapetzim.

These texts have their limitations, however. *Baudolino* is rather schematic—more thought experiment than novel—in its account of the psychology of the diverse community: Gavagai's position is a parodic one and not something on which we can base an attempt to find real-world mutuality across physical and cultural differences. Eco sets out the underlying problem—that an overcompartmentalized view of the world leads us to see difference without recognizing sameness—and suggests the philosophic underpinnings of a solution—that meaning is constructed through consensus and thus can be adapted to privilege unity over division through a shared emphasis on a central text. But it is hard to use his suggestions to advocate any real-world action or sense of affiliation precisely because of the directness with which he sets them out: Eco does not appear very interested in examining how we, like Baudolino, can find a place where the text and the physical world overlap.

Perhaps more importantly, Eco's novels are vulnerable to the kind of accusations of elitism and impracticality most frequently leveled at cosmopolitan thinkers. Gavagai's refusal to see physical differences between skiapods and blemmyae might uncharitably be characterized as the kind of half-baked relativism Stanley Fish attacks in "Boutique Multiculturalism": a reductive understanding of shared humanity that, despite its claims to privilege diversity, asserts the speaker's own superiority. Eco is interested in problems that are most pressing to someone in a position of privilege: the nuances of self-definition are only important after more urgent concerns (escaping the Nazis, ejecting a colonial power) have been resolved. Cosmopolitan writers often write from positions of privilege, and narratives of imaginative assimilation are not helpful in dealing with the problems faced by poorer migrants—as Appadurai's critics emphasize, you may consider yourself a citizen of the world, but border guards still demand your passport. Eco's hybrid project is a long way from the hybrid literature of the postcolony, not only because its sources are perhaps less varied, but also because its stakes are lower: Eco wants to redefine our understanding of a dominant identity category, rather than to carve out a new literary and political territory.

To argue that Eco shares the primary concerns of many postcolonial writers would appear divorced from political realities. Eco's cultural fusions are all located, one way or another, among elite groups with no need to resist the impositions of a hegemonic culture as they look for their common ground. (On the contrary, Baudolino's letters from Prester John are forged with the idea of legitimizing the Holy Roman Empire.) But the power struggles postcolonial writers and critics examine—the position of the postcolonial subject on the periphery of empire, the subordination of self in the face of larger group demands, the continual redefinition of identity—distinctly resemble Eco's concerns. More interestingly, while the real-world problems that these writers address are quite different, the basic techniques of world-building and of mediation between the concrete and the abstract that they adopt are profoundly similar. If, as Peter Jackson, Philip Crang, and Claire Dwyer argue, "increasing numbers of people participate in transnational space, *irrespective of their own migrant histories or 'ethnic' identities*," the result must be that the politics of that space will become more varied.[21] It is useful to look at these varying transnationals together because their similarities reveal how transformative fictional accounts of community can be: the use of novels to fashion transnational worlds is not a postcolonial or an exilic but a global phenomenon.

When Aijaz Ahmad critiques Rushdie for writing about South Asian migrants from a position of privilege he identifies a real problem in the novel's political agenda.[22] At the same time, however, his critique indirectly suggests the breadth of the novel's hybridizing ambition. The fact that we can make the same critique of Eco and Rushdie (that their fantastic fictions set them at a distance from political realities) seems telling because it reveals not so much a unity of purpose as a unity of technique, a shared understanding of the role of fiction in the creation of community and also of the limitations to which fictionally created communities are subject.

Eco's work provides us with a theoretical framework for the transnational monster story and suggests the criticisms to which that story is vulnerable. *Lolita* resolves at least the first problem of Eco's work—its schematic approach to subjective and objective truth. It also complicates (without definitively resolving) the problem of the transnational novel's political purpose. As we shall see in the final discussion of Michael Chabon, Nabokov's novels and those of his followers both address and avoid addressing the necessity of real-world spaces for fictional communities to inhabit.

LOLITA'S "CESSPOOLFUL OF ROTTING MONSTERS"

Just as Eco's monsters critique failed syntheses and explore the benefits of synthetic interpretation, Nabokov and Rushdie's monsters initially seem to critique fusion but ultimately suggest that cultural purity is a form of intellectual incest. Incestuous monsters in *Lolita* and *Midnight's Children* demonstrate the risks both of hybridity and of cultural purity and help us distinguish subjective and objective truths.

Humbert frequently describes himself as a moral "monster": he speaks of "a cesspoolful of rotting monsters behind his slow boyish smile"[23] and describes "the sensualist in me" as "a great and depraved monster."[24] It is this metaphorical, moral sense of the word monstrosity that most readers associate with the book.[25] But as Kellie Dawson points out, Humbert's self-description is also physically monstrous in its mixture of human and animal parts:[26] Humbert calls himself "Humbert the Wounded Spider,"[27] or writes of "my awkward, aching, timid claws."[28] Humbert's moral and physical monstrosities overlap in his apology to Lolita: "I was a pentapod monster, but I loved you."[29] Humbert's "central forelimb,"[30] his penis, becomes a monstrous deformity through its disproportionate power to propel its owner into amoral acts. The text of *Lolita* challenges us to disentangle this physical and moral monstrosity, but Humbert tries to blur the line between the two, slipping from one form of monstrosity to another as he redefines himself, his history, and his victim. Humbert's monstrosity, like Salvatore's, comes from his inability to synthesize: not, in this case, a linguistic failure but a failure of perspective and sympathy in which we are constantly seeing parts of the story but never, if Humbert has his way, the whole.

Humbert's attitude toward Lolita is morally monstrous because the two of them are too different—he is an adult, she a child; his remembered beloved Annabel is a consenting European equal, whereas Lo is a non-consenting American victim. But Humbert initially insists that he and Lo are engaged in a different kind of monstrous relationship: rather than being too different, Humbert claims, they are too similar. By marrying Lolita's mother, Humbert has become, legally, her father, a relationship Lo emphasizes when they share a room at the Enchanted Hunters:

"Two people sharing a room, inevitably enter into a kind—how shall I say—a kind—"
"The word is incest," said Lo.[31]

Humbert revels in the incestuous nature of his relationship with Lo as he dreams of "a litter of Lolitas"[32]: "with patience and luck I might have her produce eventually a nymphet with my blood in her exquisite veins, a Lolita the Second, who would be eight or nine around 1960, when I would still be *dans la force de l'âge*; indeed, the telescopy of my mind, or un-mind, was strong enough to distinguish in the remoteness of time a *vieillard encore vert*—or was it green rot?—bizarre, tender, salivating Dr. Humbert, practicing on supremely lovely Lolita the Third the art of being a granddad."[33] Humbert's relationship with Lolita both is and is not incestuous: there is no consanguinity, but Humbert increasingly refers to himself as Lolita's father, especially when he wishes to assert his adult authority and invoke a legitimate ground for his love for her. Humbert uses his paternal status to emphasize what they have both familially and culturally in common: when Lo complains, "Speak English," Humbert replies, "I am your father, I am speaking English, and I love you."[34] The "parody of incest"[35] Humbert constructs offers him a negative image of his relationship with Annabel: while young Humbert and Annabel are similar by virtue of their multifarious, hybrid European identities, Humbert and Lolita, if they have anything in common, are united by a family relationship that precludes sexual relations.

George Steiner writes that "incest is a trope through which Nabokov dramatizes his abiding devotion to Russian."[36] Humbert and his "salad of racial genes"[37] embody Nabokov's difficult position as a writer of what Steiner calls "macaronic" texts, and his artificially incestuous relationship with Lolita is a response to and an exacerbation of his rootlessness. If we follow Steiner's lead, incest actually becomes a means of denying monstrosity—Humbert is not a poorly patched-together hybrid because he is the father of a normal American girl—while reinforcing it. As we have seen, Humbert's moral monstrosity stems in part from his yearning for this kind of coherent identity, which in turn is a product of his physical monstrosity, his partial hybridization. When Humbert attempts to legitimize his love for Lolita by replacing an exogamous with an incestuous rape, he becomes triply monstrous: not only a moral monster as both a father and an unrelated rapist, but also a monster in his ambiguity as he flickers between his two self-conceptions.

Lolita provides a model for how the physical and moral definitions of monstrosity interpenetrate in transnational fiction. Monstrosity both marks and crosses the line between postmodern subjectivity and absolute truth: while the unsettling nature of racial or cultural mixture arises from the preconceptions of the beholder, hybrid figures who attempt to negotiate the subjective bounds of morality and identity risk objectively monstrous actions. As in Eco, an ambitious attempt at an erudite, polyglot, pan-European synthesis produces a monstrous hybrid, whose presence alerts us to a problem of interpretation—a mismatch between objective and subjective, between physical and emotional fact. Both writers' monsters show us the danger of incomplete fusion not only of physical parts but also of concepts: Salvatore's language and Humbert's self-image are monstrous because they are made out of "disiecta membra," in which each piece remains unconnected to the other components.[38] Humbert, looking with Lolita at dismembered mannequins in a shop window, finds them "a rather good symbol of something or other"[39]; they are what he has made of Lo and himself.

Monstrosity and Biology in *Midnight's Children*

The undertones of racial mixture inherent in Humbert's self-description are more overt in Rushdie's *Midnight's Children*, which, as part of its wide-ranging discussion of monstrosity and hybridity, draws on the long-standing colonial association of monstrosity with miscegenation. Saleem considers whether his mixed racial and communal identity make him monstrous but ultimately rejects the idea not on physical but on imaginative grounds.

Saleem implies that his physical deformities may be monstrous: he has horn-like bumps on his temples, a grotesquely large nose, and birthmarks the shape of the East and West Wings of Pakistan on his forehead. His psychic powers also mark him as monstrous in his exceptionality. But Saleem explicitly addresses the possibility that he is a monster only when he confesses his true parentage to Padma. Padma first uses the word: "'All the time,' Padma wails angrily, 'you tricked me. Your mother, you called her; your father, your grandfather, your aunts. What thing are you that you don't even care to tell the truth about who your parents were? You don't care that your mother died giving you life? That your father is maybe still alive somewhere, penniless, poor? You are a monster or what?'"[40] Padma's charge of monstrosity comes from the link she sees between the physical and the moral: she is shocked by Saleem's indifference toward his biological parents. Parenthood, to Padma, confers obligations on the child, and Saleem's rejection of those obligations strikes her as morally monstrous—as does Saleem's betrayal of his audience, since he has misled her into thinking that the Sinais are his biological parents. Saleem's monstrosity is in his willingness to betray trust, both of his listener and of his family.

Saleem responds that the physical basis of monstrosity is meaningless. In defending himself against Padma's charge, he dismisses the notion of biologically grounded moral imperatives and argues that while children have a responsibility to their parents, it does not spring from a physical cause: "No: I'm no monster. Nor have I been guilty of trickery. I provided clues . . . but there's something more important than that. It's this: when we eventually discovered the crime of Mary Pereira, we all found out that it *made no difference!* I was still their son: they remained my parents. In a kind of collective failure of imagination, we learned that we simply could not think our way out of our pasts."[41] Saleem agrees that it is monstrous not to love one's mother but not that motherhood is determined biologically. Echoing Anderson, Saleem bases the family's group identity on imagination—or, interestingly, on "collective failure of imagination": rather than imagining likeness, as Anderson's conationals do, Saleem's family *fails* to imagine *un*likeness. Saleem becomes truly monstrous when he rejects his imaginatively determined family after falling in love with his sister Jamila. Saleem's love for Jamila is, like Humbert's for Lolita, at once incestuous and exogamous: the two have been raised as siblings, but they are not genetically related—Jamila is the Sinais' biological daughter.

The question of whether Saleem's love for Jamila constitutes incest is complicated by his own pluralist version of Indian national identity. Saleem describes himself as hybrid throughout the novel. His psychic powers have made him into "All-India Radio," the meeting ground for the Midnight Children, drawn from every group on the subcontinent. Jamila, by contrast, blossoms when the family moves to Pakistan, the

"Land of the Pure," severing Saleem's pan-Indian psychic connection. She becomes a famous singer, serenading the Pakistani army from behind a pristine white burka. In her purity, her patriotism, and her paradoxically decorporealized embodiment of Pakistan, Jamila is Saleem's opposite, and his fascination with her is a fascination with a purity he cannot achieve. It is also the greatest transgression available to him: throughout the book, "sister-sleeping" is the primary expletive. Like Humbert, Saleem is drawn to a girl who is entirely unlike him, and with whom he shares no blood, but who is still sexually off limits because of the nonbiological truths of family relationships. This definition of incest defines identity—and the monstrosity that arises from transgressing identity's boundaries—as a moral, rather than biological, fact.

The narrators of *Lolita* and *Midnight's Children* render the notion of monstrosity unstable. Each suggests several readings of his situation by which he can be construed as a monster (physical deformity, hodgepodge identity, incestuous desire), but these monstrosities are incompatible. We can accuse Saleem of incest, or we can accuse him of monstrous ingratitude to his real parents, but not of both at once. In the case of Humbert, the collection of seemingly incompatible monstrosities (incestuous desire for his daughter and abduction of an unrelated child) adds up to an indictment of Humbert's self-delusion, demonstrating that, as we saw in Chapter 2, his true monstrosity lies in his solipsism; in Saleem's case, incest is monstrous because, in order to justify his desire, Saleem privileges the physical truth over the moral one. In both cases, the narrator becomes a monster when he seeks to replace the abstract truth of family relationships with the physical truth of biological difference.

Monstrosity, in other words, occurs when we privilege hard fact over abstract truth—when we make the same mistake as the travelers in *Baudolino*, who cannot see a unity among skiapods and blemmyae. The monsters of transnational fiction suggest that we need not worry whether it is possible for constructed truths to survive outside the novel; on the contrary, we should be concerned about what will happen if we do not acknowledge that they are already at work in the real world.

KINSHIP AND PRECONCEPTIONS

To return to Bakhtin's term, monsters demonstrate the importance of unfinalizability both in the novel and in conceptions of identity: the term "monster" is problematic precisely because it is a finalizing judgment. Monsters are both the product of and the impetus behind the ongoing processes of culture, in which the physical and the abstract are brought into conflict.

Both moral and physical monstrosity, in other words, are the result of processes of interpretation: both arise from a failure to recognize similarity between the self and the other. But whereas in physical monstrosity, that failure is on the part of the person who identifies the monster, in moral monstrosity, that failure is on the part of the monster himself. The task of the hybrid community is to provide a place in which interpretation leads not to identifying hybridity as monstrous (and thus sterile, nonproductive, and alien) but to the recognition of kinship in difference.

Monstrous hybrids and their mirror images, the monstrous offspring of incest, illustrate the transnational concern with the intersection of physical and affiliational identity. The monsters of transnational fiction embody the anxieties associated with the splicing together of different cultures. Incest and miscegenation—the unions of the too similar and the too different—are consistently contrasted and overlaid in texts dealing with cultural collisions and cultural fusion, from Arundhati Roy's tale of the choice between "Inbreeding or Divorce"[42] faced by a pair of twins with a "single Siamese soul"[43] to William Faulkner's story of black versus white and north versus south conflict in *Absalom, Absalom!* The competing constructions of kinship and difference in Faulkner lead to appalling disjunctions as characters are forced to define themselves by single aspects of their multifarious identities. The novel's defining moment is when Bon rejects Henry's offer of kinship:

—You are my brother.
—No I'm not. I'm the nigger that's going to sleep with your sister.[44]

For Faulkner, miscegenation produces monsters not in the physical offspring of the interracial union but in the actions to which his characters are driven by their absolutist understanding of race.

The hybrid bodies of transnational fiction frequently become subject to a scrutiny that reveals the origins of their monstrosity not in genetic flaws or physical deformity but in the context in which the hybrid body is examined. The mixed-race characters in Faulkner are physically monstrous only to the extent that their beholders find them alien. At the same time, however, their humanity is undercut by the ways in which their bodies are construed by onlookers in positions of interpretive and political power. While monstrosity is not an absolute truth, it is a real condition arising from a mismatch between physical and abstract realities, and that mismatch causes real damage to the individual so construed.

By locating the intersection of the subjective and the objective in the body, transnational writers make the stakes of identity and affiliation immediate and urgent, with long-term physical consequences. They also set the stage for the novels' larger experiments in intentional community-building by showing how imaginative and physical truths are mutually constitutive—and thus inseparable.

"INTERNATIONAL FRATERNITY": THE PAYOFFS OF TRANSNATIONAL FICTION

Complex as monsters are, they cannot provide the solution to transnational writers' problems of allegiance and affiliation; instead, they only dramatize failed responses. Even asserting that monstrosity is in the eye of the beholder does nothing to alter the beholder's vision. Instead, hybrid monsters show us the fate that transnational fiction must avoid: a physicality so unfamiliar or implausible as to jar us out of the illusion of reality that novels are meant to create.

Transnational fiction redraws both the boundaries and the requirements of community to circumvent the problems of belonging raised by hybrid monsters. We have seen the preliminary stages of this reconfiguration in Nabokov's work, in which community becomes interchangeable, for good or ill, with family; Rushdie expands Nabokov's definition of community to those who are like us by virtue of the experience of displacement. As this reconception of the boundaries of community continues in twenty-first-century fiction, transnational writers are increasingly looking for ways to respond to accusations that their fictional worlds are elitist or politically naïve. Michael Chabon's 2007 novel *The Yiddish Policemen's Union* renegotiates once again the tension between the practicalities of citizenship and the identity-defining nature of nations, providing our final example of how—and how much—the underpinnings of community can be redefined away from geography and genetics in favor of an explicitly fictional and linguistic self-conception.

Chabon's work examines the same tensions as the hybrid monster story, but rather than leaving us, as Eco and Rushdie do, with an intransigent monstrous body as a metaphor for failed assimilation, Chabon suggests a nonfinalizing understanding of community as predicated upon processes rather than absolutes. Chabon's novel suggests the solution to the problem of the hybrid monster: a recognition that identities are always subject to revision and expansion.

Michael Chabon is part of a new generation of American and British writers (others include Jeffrey Eugenides, Myla Goldberg, and Zadie Smith) who take transnational writers as models and, in the process, revise or reinvent the concerns of earlier transnational texts. These writers identify a canon of transnationality, both in the lists they give of their influences and in their covert references. They root their cosmopolitanism in the exiled and expatriate writers of the twentieth century, who provide a precedent and a lineage for the growing transnational community.

Like Nabokov, Chabon makes puzzle solving the key not only to his fiction but also to his community. Like Rushdie, he rejects the possibility that a single heroic figure can stand for and unify a diverse population; for both writers, heroism is fatally flawed by its emphasis on a single perspective. Chabon, too, demonstrates the problems of heroism, and the alterity of the world in which he explores it, through failed or monstrous births: his heroes also have flawed chromosomes and dead twins. Unlike Rushdie, however, Chabon rejects the nation-state as an end in itself, treating the urgent practical problems of passports and settlement rights as nuisances that arise out of the more important central problem of defining the boundaries and purpose of a community. Instead, Chabon returns to the family as the basic unit of identity but reframes family not as a genetic but as an affiliational group, one whose boundaries are determined by shared thought processes rather than blood—an exogamous family that outsiders can join. We see the source and the payoff of making the family resemble a community of readership when Chabon borrows one of Nabokov's chess problems to demonstrate how fiction can transform national identity into something malleable, personal, and voluntary.

Like Eco, Chabon is transnational not by biography but by disposition: he was born in Maryland, raised in Pittsburgh, and now lives in California—all in the United States. Nonetheless, Chabon considers himself a member of the transnational community in the tradition of Nabokov: "I write from the place I live: in exile," he says, in the first line of an essay titled, like Rushdie's first book of essays, "Imaginary Homelands."[45] In a speech he made at the Nabokov Museum in 2000, drawing on an American tradition that reaches through Henry James back at least to Melville, Chabon says of American writers, "Our literature has always been an exile's literature."[46] In *The Yiddish Policemen's Union*, as in *The Amazing Adventures of Kavalier and Clay* (2000), Chabon identifies himself as doubly exiled: he is not only an American novelist but also a member of the Jewish diaspora.

Chabon's identifications with transnationalism explain why his work draws so explicitly on Nabokov's. In the acknowledgments to *The Yiddish Policemen's Union*, Chabon cites the source of a chess problem that provides the book's essential clue: it "was devised by Reb Vladimir Nabokov and is presented in his *Speak, Memory*."[47] While affiliating Nabokov with Jews is not without precedent (his wife was Jewish, and the Nabokovs escaped from Europe in 1940 on a ship for Jewish refugees, with half their fare forgiven in memory of Nabokov's father's work against pogroms),

Chabon's use of the honorific "Reb" is startling, all the more so because he applies it to no one else in the acknowledgments. The Yiddish honorific makes Nabokov part of the novel's Jewish tradition, a member of the "Yiddish policemen's union" of the title. Chabon's appropriation of Nabokov's chess problem affiliates his antinationalist, non-Messianic Jewish identity not with the history of Zionism but with the history of transnational fiction. As this enlistment of Nabokov suggests, Chabon's "Jewishness" is a fluid category, based not on religious practice or even ethnicity but on a set of shared characteristics, including, but not limited to, linguistic play, passionate intellectual or ideological commitments, and political vulnerability. Using Nabokov's participatory world-creation as his starting point and this fluid understanding of Jewishness as his testing ground, Chabon argues in favor of a personal, portable form of national identity based on shared language, curiosity, and family love.

Chabon shows us Nabokov's reasons for embedding puzzles in his art: when Nabokov asks readers to solve a puzzle (the location of Zembla's crown jewels, the date of Lolita's death, or how white can mate in two moves), he increases readers' involvement in and responsibility for the fictional worlds of the novels. Readers become participants in the novels' action and join Nabokov in his project of cultural synthesis and reclamation. If monsters show us how transnational world-fashioning can go wrong, puzzles embedded in the novels show how it can go right.

Don Barton Johnson and Janet Gezari note that chess problems (as opposed to chess games) encapsulate Nabokov's theory of art.[48] In *Speak, Memory*, Nabokov writes, "It should be understood that competition in chess problems is not really between White and Black, but between the composer and the solver (just as in a first-rate work of fiction the real clash is not between the characters but between the author and the world)."[49] In *Strong Opinions* (1973), Nabokov revises this statement: "I believe I said 'between the author and the reader,' not 'the world,' which would be a meaningless formula . . . a good reader is bound to make fierce efforts when wrestling with a difficult author, but those efforts can be most rewarding when the bright dust has settled."[50] In the introduction to *Poems and Problems* (1970), Nabokov writes that the composer of chess problems must have "the same virtues that characterize all worthwhile art: originality, invention, conciseness, harmony, complexity, and splendid insincerity."[51] In each case, readers take an active role in "solving" the novel; the problem-writer's insincerity must be seen through in order to be splendid. After solving the problem, the solver is akin to "the finder" who "cannot unsee" the ship's smokestack peeking through the chimneys in the game of "Find What The Sailor

Has Hidden" at the end of *Speak, Memory*: a piece of the pattern of life is permanently revealed.[52]

Chabon borrows Nabokov's chess problem to show how artistic puzzles can reframe national identity. The problem is a node at which three vital themes in transnational writing meet: political realities, the power of art to transcend geography, and the danger that such transcendence may be sterile. Chabon's use of Nabokov's chess problem constitutes both an acknowledgment of the physical danger faced by the stateless and a critical evaluation of utopian and artistic ways to avert it.

* * *

The Yiddish Policemen's Union is a story about competing notions of Jewish identity—Zionist, assimilationist, cosmopolitan, exilic—and the approaches to nationality on which those notions are based. The novel is set in an alternate world in which a temporary Jewish state, the Sitka Federal District, has been established along the southern coast of Alaska following World War II.[53] When the novel opens, the district is about to revert to the governance of the United States, and the Jews of the district will reenter a stateless legal limbo. The outlook for the residents is bleak: there is no state of Israel, and other countries are reluctant to admit Jews.

The novel's hero is a policeman named Landsman, a name that in Yiddish means "fellow national" or "fellow Jew." Landsman is warily attracted to one of the novel's competing forms of Jewish nationalism: the secular nationalism represented by his uncle Hertz Shemets, a former U.S. Central Intelligence Agency operative who has campaigned for decades to have the Sitka District granted permanent status. Landsman loves his gritty hometown, but sees no way to preserve Sitka's Jewish community; instead, as the novel progresses, he abandons any form of nationalism in favor of a dangerously vulnerable individualism: "My homeland is in my hat," he says.[54] The language associated in the novel with both Hertz Shemets's nationalism and Landsman's secular individualism is Yiddish, which is spoken throughout the district. When Chabon gives Nabokov the honorific "Reb" in the acknowledgments, he associates Nabokov with this movement.

Landsman is also allied with a broader humanistic transnationalism. He lives in the Hotel Zamenhof, named after Ludovic Zamenhof, the inventor of Esperanto. Zamenhof, a Jew from Bialystok, Poland, got the idea for Esperanto from his belief that tensions among Poles, Belarusians, and Jews in Bialystok could be resolved if the three groups spoke a common language. Esperanto was intended to promote "Homaranismo" or humanitarianism,⁵⁵ a Kantian philosophy rejecting nations as an ethical category in favor of the "purely human."⁵⁶ Landsman and Chabon are both drawn to this ideal, but as Eco's Salvatore suggests, synthetic languages are hard to create and even harder to sustain; Zamenhof's idealism is no match for the competing groups in Sitka. The ideal of the "purely human" appears to have been too large an order for Sitka to meet. The Hotel Zamenhof is a flophouse, the Esperanto signs in the hallways "long gone,"⁵⁷ and the residents are misfits and junkies. Zamenhof, Esperanto, and Homaranismo are identified from the start with failed idealism. Similarly, the Jewish secular nationalism associated with Yiddish is in deep decline. At the beginning of the novel, Landsman is isolated and in despair, an alcoholic, recently divorced after the failure of his wife's pregnancy: the fetus was aborted after DNA testing revealed a flaw in its chromosomes, and the viability of Landsman's secular humanist ideal is implicitly called into question along with the viability of the baby. In parallel with Landsman's failures, the nationalist Hertz Shemets has been disgraced and removed from any position of power.

The other form of Jewish nationalism in the novel is Zionism, a movement Chabon assigns to Orthodox Jews, particularly the Verbover rebbe, the head of both a sect and a crime family. These two forms of nationalism meet in the novel's murder mystery. Landsman is investigating the murder of one of the junkies staying at the Hotel Zamenhof. The dead man turns out to be Mendel Shpilman, the son of the Verbover rebbe. The encounters between the two schools of nationalism embodied by secular and Orthodox Jews start at the Sitka chess club, and their contest, which drives the mystery, is itself staged as a chess game, with Landsman playing a grimy white against the Orthodox "black hats."

Chess provides a series of thematic and literal clues to the mystery of *The Yiddish Policemen's Union*. It stages the contest between different notions of Jewish identity as a zero-sum game; it provides a vital clue that identifies Mendel Shpilman's killer; it suggests the thematic reason for Shpilman's death; and, when we examine the passages in *Speak, Memory* from which Chabon took his key problem, it also reveals Chabon's attempt to transform the zero-sum game of nationalist politics into an inclusive artistic dialogue, in which winning and losing are replaced by a shared construction of community.

The chess problem Chabon takes from "Reb Vladimir Nabokov's" *Speak, Memory* is connected in Nabokov's memoir with competing national identities and traditions. Nabokov introduces the problem with an overview of chess problem styles:

the Anglo-American one that combines accurate construction with dazzling thematic patterns, and refuses to be bound by any conventional rules; the rugged splendor of the Teutonic school; the highly finished but unpleasantly slick and insipid products of the Czech style with its strict adherence to certain artificial conditions; the old Russian end-game studies, which attain the sparkling summits of the art, and the mechanical Soviet problem of the so-called "task" type . . . Deceit, to the point of diabolism, and originality, verging upon the grotesque, were my notions of strategy; and although in matters of construction I tried to conform, whenever possible, to classical rules . . . I was always ready to sacrifice purity of form to the exigencies of fantastic content, causing form to bulge and burst like a sponge-bag containing a small furious devil.[58]

Nabokov implicitly raises the question of what "school" his own work belongs to. The "dazzling thematic patterns" of the Anglo-American model sound like Nabokov's writing, except that Nabokov tries "to conform, whenever possible, to classical rules," which the Anglo-American "refuses." Like the composers of the "old Russian" style, Nabokov is interested in "end-game studies," but that description lacks the playful spark of "diabolism." His description of chess schools encapsulates a classic Nabokovian move: he contrasts several national identities, Anglo-American, Teutonic, Czech, old Russian, and Soviet, and then, rather than choose among them, moves away from the geographical terminology he has just established in favor of the supernatural: "diabolism . . . verging upon the grotesque."

This switch of terms from the physical and political to the supernatural is mirrored by the chess problem Nabokov then describes. The problem has three possible "thetic," "antithetic," and synthetic approaches, only one of which will lead to a solution.[59] The "thetic" solution is an obvious move, the promotion of the pawn at B7 to queen, which the solver will know to avoid. Instead, the

> very expert solver . . . would start by falling for an illusory pattern of play based on a fashionable avant-garde theme . . . Having passed through this "antithetic" inferno the by now ultrasophisticated solver would reach the simple key move (bishop to C2) as somebody on a wild goose chase might go from Albany to New York by way of Vancouver, Eurasia and the Azores. The pleasant experience of the roundabout route (strange landscapes, gongs, tigers, exotic customs, the thrice-repeated circuit of a newly married couple around the sacred fire of an earthen brazier) would amply reward him for the misery of deceit, and after that, his arrival at the simple key move would provide him with a synthesis of poignant artistic delight.[60]

Chess is again first linked to and then removed from geography: the direct route from Albany to New York is the wrong answer, and the indirect route, via Eurasia and the Azores, allows "synthesis." The image of a Hindu wedding suggests that the chess solver is assimilating the "exotic customs" he passes. The reference to Hinduism is repeated on the same page in Nabokov's own chess set, in which "the top of the king's rook and the brow of the king's knight still showed a small crimson crown painted upon them, recalling the round mark on a happy Hindu's forehead."[61] The Hindu imagery suggests that the chess problem teaches us to transcend time and geography: the "ultrasophisticated" solver has access to the history of the game (which is Indian in origin) and experiences a mystical union analogous to the Hindu marriage. As in Nabokov's history of the national schools of chess, rational geography is rejected in favor of synthetic geography, and the chess set, the physical manifestation of the world of art, encapsulates the globe. Chess problems illustrate two opposite ways of understanding national identity: the black and white, self-versus-other zero-sum game on the board itself and the history of chess as a whole, which transcends and encompasses an indefinite number of times, places, and languages. Chess problems, which Nabokov refers to in *Poems and Problems* as "extravagantly sterile," turn out to provide both a synthesis of global conflicts and a means of resolution.[62]

Nabokov describes his chess problem as transcending geography, but when he composes it, geography and politics are pressing concerns:

> The season was May—mid-May, 1940. The day before, after months of soliciting and cursing, the emetic of a bribe had been administered to the right rat at the right office and had resulted finally in a *visa de sortie* which, in its turn, conditioned the permission to cross the Atlantic. All of a sudden, I felt that with the completion of my chess problem a whole period of my life had come to a satisfactory close. Everything around was very quiet; faintly dimpled, as it were, by the quality of my relief. Sleeping in the next room were you and our child. The lamp on my table was bonneted with blue sugarloaf paper (an amusing military precaution) and the resulting light lent a lunar tinge to the voluted air heavy with tobacco smoke. The headline of a newspaper drooping from the seat of a chair spoke of Hitler's striking at the Low Countries.[63]

Far from being independent of geopolitics, the solution to the problem arrives because geographic concerns are at once so urgent and so recently resolved. This moment of peace and transcendence is framed by very real political threats that chess cannot answer. The moment of the problem's composition is also the moment of transition between danger in Europe and safety in America, and Johnson points out that the thetic, antithetic, and synthetic solutions encapsulate the Russian, European, and American portions of Nabokov's life, respectively.[64]

The sudden appearance of a date—mid-May, 1940—recasts Nabokov's brief recap of national schools of chess problems: Nabokov describes his problems as leaning toward the Anglo-American just as he is on the verge of entering America.[65] The problem's geographical limbo seems all the more significant when we note that, as Boyd points out, Nabokov's dating is inaccurate: the chess problem was really composed on November 19, 1939.[66] Chess in *Speak, Memory* encapsulates both the pressure of political realities—the Nabokovs are fleeing for their lives—and the possibility of transforming those realities into a transcendent art form. Chess does not solve political problems; instead, it offers a way to make them philosophically meaningful.

In *The Yiddish Policemen's Union*, Landsman finds the chess problem, the "before" picture, on a chessboard in the dead Shpilman's room. He sees the first "after" picture, the "thetic" solution that the "very expert solver" falls for, on a board belonging to Shpilman's killer: uncle Hertz Shemets, the secular nationalist. (Landsman has another semifamilial connection to Mendel, as well. Like Ormus Cama in *The Ground Beneath Her Feet*, Mendel had a stillborn twin brother, a fact suggesting both the fragile alterity of his world and his link to Landsman's unborn child.) Landsman solves the problem at the same moment that he solves the mystery because the problem illustrates the motive for the killing:

> "White is all set up to promote his pawn, see. And he wants to promote it to a knight. That's called underpromotion, because usually, you want to get yourself a queen. With a knight here, he has three different ways to mate, he thinks. But that's a mistake, because it leaves Black—that was Mendel—with a way to drag the game out. If you're White, you have to ignore the obvious thing. Just make a dull move with the bishop, here at c2. You don't even notice it at first. But after you make it, every move Black has leads directly to a mate. He can't move without finishing himself. He has no good moves . . . They call that *Zugzwang* . . . 'Forced to move.' It means Black would be better off if he could just pass."[67]

The death of Mendel Shpilman is not murder after all but a form of suimate: he has asked Shemets to kill him so he cannot be used as a pawn of the "black hat" Zionists. He persuades Shemets by showing him the chess problem: "He said if I solved it, then I would understand how he felt," Shemets explains.[68] Mendel's solution to the *zugzwang*, like Luzhin's in *The Defense*, is to remove himself from the board.

Mendel's self-sacrifice is both necessary and tragic because Mendel is the Tzaddik Ha-Dor, the individual who appears once in each generation with the capacity to become the Messiah. This status is linked to his wizardry at chess, both as an analogy for his superiority over his partners and his own ambivalence toward his capabilities. His choice of Hertz as his killer indicates his respect for the book's strongest representative of secular nationalism and reveals the parallels between the two nationalist movements: while each group bills itself as dedicated to saving the Jews, both are prepared to sacrifice the Tzaddik Ha-Dor to acquire a Jewish homeland.

Chabon uses Nabokov's chess problem to reveal both the supernatural stakes of the game and the necessity of changing from competitive to cooperative play. Mendel Shpilman's name reaffirms the connection between national identity, chess, and art: "Shpilman" means both "game man" and "story man," and his relationship with chess mirrors the novel's rejection of nationalist narratives.[69] Mendel's death, which removes him from the nationalist framework, is the final step in his transformation from chess *player* to chess *problem writer*: at the end of the novel, he has left the zero-sum game of chess entirely, treating the game as a form of dialogue.

Mendel's suimate redefines the players' roles, replacing heroic competition with collaborative insight. By dying, Mendel may be delaying the coming of the Messiah, but he is also refusing to grant the appearance of Messianic endorsement to any nationalist group. As his residence in the Hotel Zamenhof suggests, Mendel's final move in the *zugzwang* is the culmination of a quest for an alternative to both Zionism and secular nationalism. Given that both Mendel and the hotel are on their last legs, however, it is clear that his search has so far failed.

The Messianic vision of the novel is one of transnational synthesis—some time in the future. Meanwhile, the solution is, like Nabokov's, one of family love in exile. But the family is demarcated not by genetics but by the "union" of puzzle solving. Much as Nabokov ends his European exile with a brief address to Véra, "you and our child" asleep in the next room, Chabon ends the novel with Landsman's reunion with his wife, who is also a policewoman: "Landsman has no home, no future, no fate but Bina. The land that he and she were promised was bounded by the fringes of their wedding canopy, by the dog-eared corners of their cards of membership in an international fraternity whose members carry their patrimony in a tote bag, their world on the tip of the tongue."[70] For both Chabon and Nabokov, geography turns out to be a metaphor for a real but nonphysical home made up of family love, language, and puzzle solving: the "international fraternity" of chess and of policemen, who seek intellectual solutions to physical problems. For Chabon, however, this family is created by choice rather than by genealogy; while a biological child may come from Landsman's reunion with Bina, the novel's happy ending comes from his reentry into the "union" of consciously created family affiliations between adults.

The chess problem is only one way that Nabokov's work balances between geopolitical concerns (e.g., war, exile, dictatorships) and supernatural or artistic syntheses in which such problems are rendered trivial. While Nabokov's work almost always ends with some transcendent access to an otherworld, the threat of physical violence against the exile or the dissident—*Invitation to a Beheading*'s executioners, *Bend Sinister*'s torturers, *Pale Fire*'s assassin Gradus—is never far away. This balance between the imminent political threat and the transcendent escape attracts later transnational writers. Chabon's use of Nabokov illustrates the fluid and voluntary nature of national identity for both writers and the degree to which that identity is independent of things like passports. Chabon and Nabokov replace traditional, geographical nationalism with a transnational understanding of group identity, an identity that depends not on national borders but on love, language, and a passion for puzzle solving. For Chabon, this group identity is explicitly rooted in transnational fiction—not only his own but also that of his predecessors, the "international fraternity" of novelists.

The Yiddish Policemen's Union represents a departure from Chabon's approach to artistic world-fashioning in his novel *The Amazing Adventures of Kavalier and Clay*. Like Mendel, Chabon has changed in his understanding of both the boundaries and the purpose of artistic communities. Where *The Yiddish Policemen's Union* suggests the possibility of making fictional worlds (first Jewish Sitka, then the artificial world of the chess problem, and finally the fragile shelter of family love under the wedding canopy) into the basis of shared identity, the fictional worlds of *Kavalier and Clay* are deliberately nonproductive. *Kavalier and Clay* celebrates art as escapism. The main characters, two Jewish comic book artists named Joe Kavalier and Sam Clay, create a superhero called the Escapist. Comic books, the novel's dominant art form, are lauded in the book for the escape from reality they provide, offering Joe a fantasy world in which he can sock Adolph Hitler on the jaw or rescue his family from Nazi-occupied Prague. In the terms of the novel's plot and its moral development, "escapism"—a word used to condemn how fantastic literature avoids real-world responsibilities—is recast as a means of regaining one's sanity in the face of the unthinkable. After the destruction of Czech Jewry, Joe's only option is to transmute his agony into the "escapism" of art: first through the propagandistic comics he draws in 1940 and 1941, and later, in the 1950s, in his redemptive comic book *The Golem*.

But while *Kavalier and Clay* treats comics both as a form of personal redemption and as the common ground between many of its characters, Chabon stops short of suggesting that comics can provide an otherwise absent community or suggest alternative models for self-definition. Instead, comics in *Kavalier and Clay* serve the double purpose of escapist wish fulfillment (hitting Hitler, rescuing the threatened children of Europe) and of illustrating the longings their readers already share (the comics instantly appeal to the "remarkably bloodthirsty children of America"[71]). Art in *Kavalier and Clay* reveals and redeems but offers no new political alternatives. *The Yiddish Policemen's Union*, on the other hand, suggests the possibility of reframing and reconstructing both the artistic subject and the identity of the artist and audience. Chabon cites Nabokov as one of his lifelong artistic models, but Nabokov's cameo in *The Yiddish Policemen's Union* and his absence from *Kavalier and Clay* suggest how far Chabon's attitude toward transnational world-fashioning has progressed between the two novels: his fiction moves from elegiac to active. Writing of the inception of *The Yiddish Policemen's Union*, Chabon says, "the idea began to assemble itself: I would build myself a home in my imagination as my wife and I were making a home in the world."[72] In the later novel, the imagination ceases to be the realm of escape and becomes instead the realm of "real life": a creative, creating, stable yet changeable and productive world.

The shift in Chabon's treatment of the fantastic exemplifies the larger trend in transnational fiction: transnational writers are increasingly using their novels to create a political allegiance that is both identity defining and contingent, both aware of and apart from geographical and racial boundaries. Passports and citizenship are and will remain vital components of daily life; we are not in the postnational world described by Arjun Appadurai. A world without meaningful borders seems, if anything, more fantastic than the alternate worlds of fiction. Nonetheless, Appadurai's description of the "plurality of imagined worlds" implied by global migrancy takes on new meaning in light of the direction of contemporary transnational fiction.[73] And if, as Appadurai says, "the imagination, especially when collective, can become the fuel for action," the alternate worlds of transnational fiction may provide the underpinnings for future real-world change.[74]

* * *

Transnational fiction is full of stories about monsters because they provide such a useful means of examining the central problems of fictionally fashioned hybrid communities. Monsters embody the anxieties of hybridity, the risk that fusion will turn out to be mere pastiche and the danger that the hybrid individual will be sterile, disfigured, or outcast; their bodies provide a meeting ground for objective and subjective truth; they demonstrate the practical difficulty of importing fictional constructions into the real world; and, at the same time, they uphold the importance of constructed truths, reminding us that love is at least as real as genetics. Transnational fiction's rejection of the category of physical monstrosity comes from its awareness of the moral monstrosity of solipsism. The deepest problem transnationals face in these novels is not incomplete fusion of unlike parts but an inability—either in the protagonists or in others—to recognize likeness across difference and to see that hybrids of differing cultures are already producing vibrant new shoots. Van Veen's lifelong yearning for the twelve-year-old Ada and Raman Fielding's passion for the "Hindu" game of cricket are similarly misguided, these novels suggest, because they ignore the processes of change and assimilation their beloveds have undergone—the same transformation Naipaul laments in *The Enigma of Arrival*. Both men become morally monstrous in their attempts to stop the clock.

The solution transnational writers suggest to the problems monsters embody is to decouple identity from physicality. Transnational fiction reminds us that the metaphor of the body politic is a limiting and sometimes ludicrous way to understand communities. Instead, these novels suggest that, rather than seeing communal identity in physical (and thus static) terms, we should understand community membership as a process, something to be continually affirmed, renewed, and recreated as our understandings of our own affiliations and our likeness to those around us shift. Chabon's treatment of puzzle solving as central to the "Yiddish" identity makes a particularly telling example as it transforms Jewishness—a racial and ethnic category that for millennia has been understood by Jews and non-Jews alike as biological—into an approach to knowledge that can be learned and shared by almost anyone and that not everyone ethnically "Jewish" may possess.

THE ETHICS OF TRANSNATIONAL READERSHIPS

This study provides a model for further exploration of how transnational writers constitute a cohesive community, with common goals and values. While it would be impossible to assemble an exhaustive list of the writers whom it would be useful to examine on these terms, we can trace a history and even a canon of transnationalism through the shared references of recent practitioners. Membership in the transnational community is determined not by a writer's biographical status but by his or her chosen and constructed affiliations. Writers like Kazuo Ishiguro, Michael Ondaatje, Zadie Smith, Jhumpa Lahiri, Jeffrey Eugenides, Sara Suleri, or William Faulkner, who examine the boundaries of community and find them to be misplaced, may be productively considered as transnational writers, whether or not the communities they examine require passports to visit.

Recognizing writers as members of the transnational community helps us understand the ambition of their work. The transnational syntheses in postcolonial or exilic novels remind us that the critical fields through which we approach them are our own constructions: these fields provide a means of delineating areas of critical expertise, but they are not the full contexts of the novels. Nonetheless, some familiar fields are good places to look for further examples of transnational fiction. Postcolonial fiction is full of transnational writers, as Rushdie implies when he argues that much of the best Indian fiction since Partition has been written in English, comparing nonresident Indian writers to "wanderers"[75] like "Henry James, James Joyce, Samuel Beckett, Ernest Hemingway, Gertrude Stein, Mavis Gallant, James Baldwin, Graham Greene, Gabriel García Marquez, Mario Vargas Llosa, Jorge Luis Borges, Vladimir Nabokov, [and] Muriel Spark."[76] Similarly, as Chabon suggests, many American writers view the American experience as inherently transnational and, like Nabokov, treat America as one of the most overtly invented of nations. (Willa Cather, who deals with the formation of immigrant communities and their transformation of the American landscape, seems a particularly appropriate subject for this kind of inquiry.) Finally, contemporary fiction abounds with texts influenced by fifty years of postmodern self-scrutiny and a rising awareness of globalization: Nicole Krauss's *The History of Love* (2005) and Geraldine Brooks's *People of the Book* (2008) exemplify an increasing trend toward transnational community building in popular literature. Global mobility and postmodern experimentation have created a new genre: the book that relocates and redefines the meaning of home.

* * *

Throughout this book, we have seen how transnational fiction teaches readers to take conscious control of the kind of interpretive process Bhabha identifies as the origin of hybridity. Textual ambiguity, which Bhabha reads as accidentally empowering, becomes the means of a deliberate transfer of power from writer to reader. As they examine the evidence to determine the meaning and, in some cases, the outcome of the text, readers are guided through a process of synthesis designed not only to help them find ways of making the text's competing cultures and epistemologies overlap but also to draw them into a version of the Kantian ideal of cosmopolitan humanity. At the same time, unlike the Kantian cosmopolitan, readers are reminded of their own positionality: the ambiguous transnational text is deeply rooted in several spaces at once, with the result that it shows us how limited our perspectives are.

These limitations are not permanent or absolute, however, and transnational texts show us how to pick up new cultural references and assumptions: the ideal reader of the transnational text, as we have seen, is the rereader who has learned to recognize that text's many source materials. The polyvocal nature of transnational discourse emphasizes that identity is a process, not a stable product, subject to reaffirmation and reconstruction, during which an individual's attributes and affiliations can be reinterpreted as the grounds of similarity to or difference from the people she encounters. The goal of transnational fiction is to teach readers to see awareness of that process, rather than simple ethnic or national affiliations, as a key part of their own identities.

This emphasis on process over product is central to the novels' epistemologies, their world-creation, their theories of art, and their construction of authorship. The transnational use of fantastic, science-fictional, and alternate-historical worlds teaches readers to recognize how subjective their own interpretations of the world are, to negotiate between constructed and absolute fact, and to take authorial control of their own constructions of reality. Perhaps more daringly still, the transnational fantastic reframes that authorial control as participatory rather than authoritarian, transforming both readership and group membership into active, powerful positions. The world of the text teaches us not only to negotiate the real world but also to recreate it, both within our own polyphonic inner lives and in our understanding of what we have in common with the people around us. Just as Zeeny defines the "good Indian" not by what clothes he chooses but by the fact of choice, transnational fiction asks its members to conceive of their community based not on the location of their roots but on a shared willingness to reach beyond them. At the same time, transnational fiction rejects postmodern subjectivism, instead treating the constructed truths of identity as part of a continuum of variously malleable physical and imaginative facts. The fantastic transnational novel teaches mediation—between one country and another, between fact and interpretation, and between absolutism and relativism. It teaches us, in other words, to see the world in terms of Bakhtinian dialogue rather than Manichean competition. The cultural fusions in transnational fictions are both the goal and the medium, the end and the means. Art—whether a novel, a miniature painting, or the Zemblan crown jewels scattered through the American landscape—does not provide an idealized finished product but demonstrates that the process of interpretation, definition, selection, and placement continues for as long as there are people to practice it.

Transnational fiction makes the stakes of readers' participation in world-creation very high because we are all more or less constrained by the narratives in which we find ourselves. Just as ignorance of her location in fiction renders Allie helpless to protect herself in *The Satanic Verses*, so we may be doomed to follow our own national or ideological narratives if we do not recognize them. Perhaps more oddly, however, the transnational fantastic suggests that by recognizing the narratives we inhabit, we gain the power to change not just their outcome but their genre: the constructed nature of both national identity and narrative convention means that each requires our conscious or unconscious assent to gain power over our lives. While Emma Bovary is doomed by reading too may romantic novels, readers of transnational fiction learn to navigate levels and kinds of fictionality. Transnational fiction, by treating the boundaries between reality and the imagination as analogous to those between countries, makes it possible to jump between genres and epistemologies in precisely the way Emma cannot. These fantastic worlds are far from escapist; they are, instead, the testing ground for real affiliations and practices, the places where we learn through our shared experiences to recognize our common humanity and thus gain control of our self-perceptions. Transnational fiction asks us to see the framing devices that surround us—and to step outside the frame, becoming the photographer as well as the doomed woman in the photograph.

* * *

The roots that individuals and texts sink into national cultures are real and nourishing, and to read transnational literature as separate from its countries of origin would be to miss much of each text's richness and depth. By looking at novels as participants in both national and transnational canons, however, we can see the growth of a common lineage, a community that treats the process of displacement and synthesis as something substantial and valuable in itself. The global humanity of the cosmopolitan is not found in artifacts or in the items we borrow from new cultures we encounter; it is, instead, in the willingness to recognize that we must continually reevaluate our demarcations of commonality and difference. Transnational literature teaches us the ethical necessity of recognizing ourselves in strangers, and strangers in ourselves.

Notes

Introduction

1. Brian McHale, *Postmodernist Fiction* (New York: Routledge, 1987).
2. Homi Bhabha, *The Location of Culture* (New York: Routledge, 1994), 103.
3. Ibid., 112.
4. Ibid., 110.
5. Ibid., 102.
6. Ibid., 115.
7. Sara Suleri, *The Rhetoric of English India* (Chicago, IL: University of Chicago Press, 1992), 3.
8. Salman Rushdie, *Imaginary Homelands: Essays and Criticism 1981–1991* (London: Granta, 1991), 394.
9. Robert J. C. Young, *Colonial Desire: Hybridity in Theory, Culture and Race* (New York: Routledge, 1995).
10. See Mary Louise Pratt, *Imperial Eyes: Travel Writing and Transculturation* (New York: Routledge, 1992), 90–102.
11. Revathi Krishnaswamy, "Mythologies of Migrancy: Postcolonialism, Postmodernism and the Politics of (Dis)location," *ARIEL* 26, no. 1 (1995): 125.
12. Immanuel Kant, *Political Writings*, ed. Hans Reiss (Cambridge: Cambridge University Press, 1991), 51.
13. Martha C. Nussbaum, *For Love of Country: Debating the Limits of Patriotism* (Boston: Beacon, 1996), 4.
14. Jonathan Rée, "The Experience of Nationality," in *Cosmopolitics: Thinking and Feeling beyond the Nation*, ed. Pheng Cheah and Bruce Robbins (Minneapolis, MN: University of Minnesota Press, 1998), 79.
15. Stanley Fish, "Boutique Multiculturalism or, Why Liberals Are Incapable of Thinking About Hate Speech," *Critical Inquiry* 23, no. 2 (1997): 378.
16. Ibid., 379.
17. Kwame Anthony Appiah, "Cosmopolitan Patriots," in *Cosmopolitics: Thinking and Feeling beyond the Nation*, ed. Pheng Cheah and Bruce Robbins (Minneapolis, MN: University of Minnesota Press, 1998), 91.
18. Homi Bhabha, "Unsatisfied Notes on Vernacular Cosmopolitanism," in *Text and Narration*, ed. Peter C. Pfeiffer and Laura García-Moreno (Columbia, SC: Camden House, 1996).
19. Kwame Anthony Appiah, "Cosmopolitan Reading," in *Cosmopolitan Geographies: New Locations in Literature and Culture*, ed. Vinay Dharwadker (New York: Routledge, 2001), 208.

20. Rob Wilson and Wimal Dissanayake discuss how "transnational corporations like Sony and Coca-Cola" seek to obscure this difference by claiming "global localization: crossing borders and segmenting markets via flexible production" (4–5). Rob Wilson and Wimal Dissanayake, ed., *Global/Local: Cultural Production and the Transnational Imaginary* (Durham, NC: Duke University Press, 1996).
21. Appiah, "Cosmopolitan Reading," 223.
22. Arjun Appadurai, *Modernity at Large: Cultural Dimensions of Globalization* (Minneapolis, MN: University of Minnesota Press, 1996).
23. Nina Glick Schiller, "The Situation of Transnational Studies," *Identities* 4 (1997), 159.
24. Appadurai, *Modernity at Large*, 5.
25. Ibid., 7.
26. Ibid., 12–13.
27. Benedict Anderson, *Imagined Communities: Reflections on the Origin and Spread of Nationalism* (New York: Verso, 1991), 6.
28. Kachig Tölölyan notes that while "For all too many theorists of diaspora . . . the project of re-articulating the nation-state seems also to require the option of dis-articulating it," diasporas properly understood "act in consistently organized ways to develop an agenda for self-representation in the political or cultural realm, either in the hostland or across national boundaries." Kachig Tölölyan, "Rethinking Diaspora(s): Stateless Power in the Transnational Moment," *Diaspora* 5, no. 1 (1996): 16–17.
29. Anderson, *Imagined Communities*, 10.
30. Michael Peter Smith, *Transnational Urbanism: Locating Globalization* (Oxford: Blackwell, 2001), 3.
31. Brenda S. A. Yeoh et al., *Approaching Transnationalisms: Studies on Transnational Societies, Multicultural Contacts, and Imaginings of Home*, ed. Brenda S. A. Yeoh, Michael W. Charney, and Tong Chee Kiong (Boston: Kluwer Academic Publishers, 2003), 2.
32. James Clifford, *The Predicament of Culture: Twentieth-Century Ethnography, Literature, and Art* (Cambridge, MA: Harvard University Press, 1988), 17.
33. Pheng Cheah, "Given Culture: Rethinking Cosmopolitical Freedom in Transnationalism," in *Cosmopolitics: Thinking and Feeling beyond the Nation*, ed. Pheng Cheah and Bruce Robbins (Minneapolis, MN: University of Minnesota Press, 1998), 302.
34. Lina Basch, Nina Glick Schiller, and Cristina Szaton Blanc, ed., *Nations Unbound: Transnational Projects, Postcolonial Predicaments and Deterritorialized Nation-States* (Basle, Switzerland: Gordon and Breach, 1994), 8.
35. Gayatri Chakravorty Spivak, *A Critique of Postcolonial Reason: Toward a History of the Vanishing Present* (Cambridge, MA: Harvard University Press, 1999), 355.
36. Nirmala Lakshman, "A Columbus of the Near-At-Hand," in *Salman Rushdie Interviews*, ed. Pradyumna S. Chauhan (Westport, CT: Greenwood, 2001), 283.
37. Derek Walcott, *Selected Poems*, ed. Edward Baugh (New York: Farrar, Straus, and Giroux, 2007), 6.
38. Pratt, *Imperial Eyes*, 4.

Chapter 1

1. Clifford, *The Predicament of Culture*, 276.
2. See Wolfgang Iser, *The Implied Reader* (Baltimore, MD: Johns Hopkins University Press, 1974).
3. Wolfgang Iser, *The Act of Reading: A Theory of Aesthetic Response* (Baltimore, MD: Johns Hopkins University Press, 1978). For a critique of Iser, see Steven Mailloux, *Interpretive Conventions: The Reader in the Study of American Fiction* (Ithaca, NY: Cornell University Press, 1982), 43–56.
4. Anderson, *Imagined Communities*, 26.
5. Peter Jackson, Philip Crang, and Claire Dwyer, *Transnational Spaces* (New York: Routledge, 2004), 3. Italics in original.
6. Ursula K. LeGuin, *The Left Hand of Darkness* (New York: Ace, 1976), v.
7. Mikhail Bakhtin, *The Dialogic Imagination*, ed. Michael Holquist, trans. Caryl Emerson and Michael Holquist (Austin, TX: University of Austin Press, 1981), 61.
8. Michel Foucault, *The Order of Things: An Archeology of the Human Sciences* (New York: Pantheon, 1970), xviii.
9. McHale, *Postmodernist*, 45.
10. Ibid.
11. Jhumpa Lahiri, *Interpreter of Maladies* (New York: Houghton Mifflin, 1999), 82; Vladimir Nabokov, *The Annotated Lolita*, ed. Alfred Appel, Jr. (New York: Vintage, 1991), 129.
12. Lubomír Doležel, *Heterocosmica: Fiction and Possible Worlds* (Baltimore, MD: The Johns Hopkins University Press, 2000), 23.
13. Ibid., 3.
14. Woody Allen, *Side Effects* (New York: Random House, 1980), 67.
15. V. S. Naipaul, *India: A Wounded Civilization* (New York: Vintage, 2003), 112.
16. Ibid., 132.
17. Ibid., 160.
18. V. S. Naipaul, *The Enigma of Arrival* (New York: Penguin, 1987), 318.
19. Maxine Hong Kingston, *The Woman Warrior: Memoirs of a Girlhood Among Ghosts* (New York: Vintage, 1989), 19.
20. Ibid., 159.
21. Isak Dinesen, *Out of Africa and Shadows on the Grass* (New York: Vintage, 1989), 134–35.
22. For similar fusions in Dinesen's fiction, see Rachel Trousdale, "Self-Invention in Isak Dinesen's 'The Flood at Norderney,'" *Scandinavian Studies* 74, no. 2 (2002).
23. Dinesen, *Out of Africa*, 49.
24. Ibid., 264.
25. See Judith Lee, "The Mask of Form in *Out of Africa*," in *Isak Dinesen: Critical Views*, ed. Olga Anastasia Pelensky (Athens, OH: Ohio University Press, 1993), 267–82; Judith Thurman, *Isak Dinesen: The Life of a Storyteller* (New York:

Picador, 1982), 165–66 and Olga Anastasia Pelensky, *Isak Dinesen: The Life and Imagination of a Seducer* (Athens, OH: Ohio University Press, 1991), 86–87.
26. Dinesen's account of life in British East Africa has provoked criticism. One of the best readings is in Abdul R. JanMohammed's *Manichean Aesthetics: The Politics of Literature in Colonial Africa* (Amherst, MA: The University of Massachusetts Press, 1983).
27. See John Clement Ball, *Imagining London: Postcolonial Fiction and the Transnational Metropolis* (Toronto: University of Toronto Press, 2004); Robert Alter, *Imagined Cities: Urban Experience and the Language of the Novel* (New Haven, CT: Yale University Press, 2005); and Burton Pike, *The Image of the City in Modern Literature* (Princeton, NJ: Princeton University Press, 1981).
28. John Burt Foster, *Nabokov's Art of Memory and European Modernism* (Princeton, NJ: Princeton University Press, 1993).
29. Vladimir Nabokov, *Strong Opinions* (New York: Vintage, 1990), 43.
30. Vladimir Nabokov, *Bend Sinister* (New York: Vintage, 1990), xiii.
31. Nabokov, *Strong Opinions*, 3.
32. Rushdie, *Imaginary Homelands*, 38.
33. Salman Rushdie, "The Birth Pangs of *Midnight's Children*," *The Times (London)*, April 1, 2006.
34. Patrick Colm Hogan, "*Midnight's Children*: Kashmir and the Politics of Identity," *Twentieth Century Literature* 47 (2001).
35. Mujeebuddin Syed, "*Midnight's Children* and Its Indian Con-Texts," *Journal of Commonwealth Literature* 29, no. 2 (1994).
36. Andrew S. Teverson, "Fairy Tale Politics: Free Speech and Multiculturalism in *Haroun and the Sea of Stories*," *Twentieth Century Literature* 47, no. 4 (2001). For Rushdie's use of medieval Islam, see Feroza Jussawalla, "Rushdie's *Dastan-e-Dilruba: The Satanic Verses* as Rushdie's Love Letter to Islam" in *Critical Essays on Salman Rushdie*, ed. M. Keith Booker (New York: G. K. Hall, 1999).
37. Berad-Peter Lange, "Dislocations: Migrancy in Nabokov and Rushdie," *Anglia: Zeitschrift für Englische Philologie* 117, no. 3 (1999).
38. Salman Rushdie, *The Satanic Verses* (Dover, DE: The Consortium, 1988), 311.
39. Ibid., 441.

Chapter 2

1. Nabokov, *The Annotated Lolita*, 312.
2. *Pnin* (1957) belongs in this discussion, although I am not addressing it for reasons of space. While not set in an overtly alternate world, *Pnin* juxtaposes and combines the American and Russian landscapes.
3. Don Barton Johnson, *Worlds in Regression: Some Novels of Vladimir Nabokov* (Ann Arbor, MI: Ardis, 1985), 79; Susan Elizabeth Sweeney, "'By some sleight of *land*': How Nabokov Rewrote America," in *The Cambridge Companion to Vladimir Nabokov*, ed. Julian W. Connolly (New York: Cambridge University Press, 2005), 66.

4. Johnson, *Worlds in Regression;* and Vladimir Alexandrov, *Nabokov's Otherworld* (Princeton, NJ: Princeton University Press, 1991).
5. Nabokov, *The Annotated Lolita*, 317.
6. Ibid., 9.
7. Ibid., 11.
8. Ibid., 10.
9. Ibid., 27.
10. Ibid., 17.
11. Ibid., 10.
12. Ibid., 13.
13. Ibid., 12.
14. Ibid., 36–37.
15. See David Castronovo, "Humbert's America," *New England Review* 23, no. 2 (2002) for Humbert's descriptions of American vapidity.
16. Nabokov, *The Annotated Lolita*, 17.
17. Ibid., 37–38.
18. Ibid., 39.
19. Ibid., 149; brackets in original.
20. Ibid., 167.
21. Michael Wood, *The Magician's Doubts: Nabokov and the Risks of Fiction* (Princeton, NJ: Princeton University Press, 1994), 121.
22. Nabokov, *The Annotated Lolita*, 168.
23. Ibid., 145.
24. Priscilla Meyer, *Find What the Sailor Has Hidden* (Middletown, CT: Wesleyan University Press, 1988), 13.
25. Nabokov, *The Annotated Lolita*, 145.
26. Ibid., 277.
27. Christina Tekiner, "Time in *Lolita*," *Modern Fiction Studies* 25 (1979). See also Alexander Dolinin, "Nabokov's Time Doubling: From *The Gift* to *Lolita*," *Nabokov Studies* 2 (1995).
28. Pratt, *Imperial Eyes*, 201.
29. Nabokov, *The Annotated Lolita*, 307–8.
30. Ibid., 129.
31. Ibid., 125.
32. Susan Elizabeth Sweeney, "Executing Sentences in *Lolita* and the Law," *Punishment, Politics, and Culture* 30 (2003).
33. Much critical energy has gone into debating the (fictional) authorship of *Pale Fire*. Some critics, starting with Andrew Field, *Nabokov: His Life and Art* (Boston: Little, Brown and Co., 1967), believe Shade invented Kinbote and is the "real" author of the apparatus criticus; others believe Kinbote invented Shade and wrote "Pale Fire" himself; most critics—myself included—take the poem and commentary as the work of two authors, unified by Nabokov's direction. Brian Boyd has been a major participant in the discussion. In "Shape and Shade in *Pale Fire*," *Nabokov Studies* 4 (1998), Boyd argues that Kinbote wrote the commentary with help from Shade's shade, visible in the text as Gradus. More

recently, in *Nabokov's* Pale Fire: *The Magic of Artistic Discovery* (Princeton, NJ: Princeton University Press, 1999), Boyd has the dead Hazel ghostwrite both poem and commentary. For a summary of the debate, see Boyd, *Magic*, 114–15.
34. See Boyd, quoting Nabokov's diary, *Vladimir Nabokov: The American Years*, (Princeton, NJ: Princeton University Press, 1991), confirming Johnson's reading in *Worlds in Regression*, 69–70. The first explication of this multilayered novel is in Mary McCarthy's "A Bolt from the Blue," in *The Writing on the Wall*, (New York: Harcourt, Brace and World, 1962).
35. Wood, *The Magician's Doubts*, 179.
36. See Ronald E. Peterson, "Zemblan: Nabokov's Phony Scandinavian Language," *Vladimir Nabokov Research Newsletter* 12 (1984); and John R. Krueger, "Nabokov's Zemblan," *Linguistics* 31 (1967). For a more thorough discussion of Zemblan's roots, see Meyer, *Find What the Sailor Has Hidden*, 87–98.
37. Vladimir Nabokov, *Pale Fire* (New York: G. P. Putnam's Sons, 1962), 214.
38. Ibid., 238.
39. Ibid., 289.
40. Ibid., 62.
41. Ibid., 138.
42. Ibid., 143.
43. Ibid., 143–44.
44. Ibid., 296.
45. Ibid., 52.
46. Ibid., 115.
47. Ibid., 62.
48. Percy Bysshe Shelley, *Poetry and Prose*, ed. Donald H. Reiman and Sharon B. Powers (New York: Norton, 1977), 89–93.
49. Ibid., 478–506.
50. Nabokov, *Pale Fire*, 150.
51. Monica Manolescu, "'Verbal Adventures in the Inky Jungle': Marco Polo and John Mandeville in Vladimir Nabokov's *The Gift*," *Cycnos* 24, no. 1 (2007). Meyer also notes Mandeville's presence in *Pale Fire* in *Find What the Sailor Has Hidden*, 178–79.
52. Sir John Mandeville, *The Travels of Sir John Mandeville: The Version of the Cotton Manuscript in Modern Spelling* (London: Macmillan, 1923), 134.
53. Nabokov, *The Annotated Lolita*, 176.
54. Nabokov, *Pale Fire*, 73.
55. Ibid., 169.
56. Ibid., 315.
57. Ibid., 276.
58. Ibid., 41.
59. See Nabokov, *Strong Opinions*, 92.
60. Meyer, *Find What the Sailor Has Hidden*, 75, 51.
61. Nabokov, *Pale Fire*, 291.
62. Ibid., 247.

63. James F. English, "Modernist Joke-Work: *Pale Fire* and the Mock Transcendence of Mockery," *Contemporary Literature* 33, no. 1 (1992), 77, 85–6.
64. Nabokov confirms this in an interview with Alfred Appel, Jr. Nabokov, *Strong Opinions*, 74.
65. Nabokov, *Pale Fire*, 300–301.
66. Wood, *The Magician's Doubts*, 203–4.
67. William Shakespeare, *The Riverside Shakespeare*. Edited by G. Blakemore Evans and J. J. M. Tobin. (New York: Houghton Mifflin, 1996), *As You Like It* II.vii.174.
68. Vladimir Nabokov, *Ada, or Ardor* (New York: Vintage, 1990), 587.
69. Nabokov, *The Annotated Lolita*, 309.
70. Nabokov, *Ada*, 17–18.
71. Brian Boyd, *Nabokov's Ada: The Place of Consciousness* (Ann Arbor, MI: Ardis, 1985), 14.
72. Nabokov, *Ada*, 580.
73. Ibid., 582.
74. Ibid., 35.
75. Robert Alter, "*Ada*, or the Perils of Paradise," in *Vladimir Nabokov: His Life, His Work, His World: A Tribute*, ed. Peter Quennell (London: Weidenfeld & Nicolson, 1979); and Douglas Fowler, *Reading Nabokov* (Ithaca, NY: Cornell University Press, 1974).
76. Fowler, *Reading Nabokov*, 182.
77. Nabokov, *Ada*, 300.
78. Ibid., 17.
79. Ibid., 437.
80. Magnus Magnusson and Hermann Palsson, trans., *The Vinland Sagas: The Norse Discovery of America. Grænlendinga Saga and Eirik's Saga* (Baltimore, MD: Penguin Books, 1965).
81. Nabokov, *Ada*, 588.
82. Brian Boyd, "Annotations to *Ada* Part 1 Chapter 1," *The Nabokovian* 30 (1993), 22.
83. Manolescu, "'Verbal Adventures in the Inky Jungle,'" 119.
84. Bobbie Ann Mason, *Nabokov's Garden: A Guide to* Ada (Ann Arbor, MI: Ardis, 1969), 70.
85. Nicolò Zeno, *The Voyages of the Venetian Brothers, Nicolò and Antonio Zeno, to the Northern Seas, in the XIVth Century, Comprising the Latest Known Accounts of the Lost Colony of Greenland; and of the Northmen in America Before Columbus*, ed. and trans. Richard Henry Major (New York: Burt Franklin, 1964), 19–20.
86. Ibid., 23.
87. Ibid.
88. Ida Sedgwick Proper, *Monhegan, the Cradle of New England* (Portland, ME: The Southworth Press, 1930), 25–33.
89. The use of dubiously accurate travel narratives to legitimize the colonization of America is as old as colonization itself: Charlotte Artese shows that, in the 1570s, John Dee cites legends of Prince Madoc and King Arthur as evidence

that America is a lost British territory. Charlotte Artese, "King Arthur in America: Making Space in History for *The Faerie Queene* and John Dee's *Brytanici Imperii Limites*," *Journal of Medieval and Early Modern Studies* 33, no. 1 (2003).
90. Nabokov, *Pale Fire*, 98.
91. For more on unreliable narrators in *Ada*, see Charles Nicol, "Ada or Disorder," in *Nabokov's Fifth Arc: Nabokov and Others on His Life's Work*, ed. J. E. Rivers and Charles Nicol (Austin, TX: University of Texas Press, 1982), 230–41.
92. Zeno, *The Voyages of the Venetian Brothers*, 34–35.
93. See Wood, *The Magician's Doubts*, 104.
94. Manolescu, "'Verbal Adventures in the Inky Jungle,'" 119–20.
95. Zeno, *The Voyages of the Venetian Brothers*, xxi.
96. Ibid., 19n.
97. Nabokov, *Ada*, 494.
98. Ibid., 437.
99. Ibid., 341.
100. N. Katherine Hayles says, "Van does not edit," arguing that he does not omit episodes that reflect badly on him. He does obfuscate this incident, however, and the blurrings of memory in the book are not all accidental. N. Katherine Hayles, "Making a Virtue of Necessity: Pattern and Freedom in Nabokov's *Ada*," *Contemporary Literature* 23 (1982), 46.
101. Nabokov, *Ada*, 341.
102. Ellen Pifer, *Nabokov and the Novel* (Cambridge, MA: Harvard University Press, 1980), 153. Michael Seidel argues that the ambiguities of Antiterra come from the fact that love must be both heaven and hell. "Stereoscope: Nabokov's *Ada* and *Pale Fire*," in *Vladimir Nabokov*, ed. Harold Bloom (New York: Chelsea House, 1987).
103. Boyd, *Nabokov's Ada*, 210.

Chapter 3

1. Carl Freedman, *Critical Theory and Science Fiction* (Hanover, NH: Wesleyan University Press, 2000), 15.
2. A few critics treat *Ada* as "soft" science fiction. See David Field, "Fluid Worlds: Lem's *Solaris* and Nabokov's *Ada*," *Science Fiction Studies* 13 (1986); and Roy Arthur Swanson, "Nabokov's *Ada* as Science Fiction," *Science Fiction Studies* 2, no. 1 (1975).
3. Rachel Trousdale, "Faragod Bless Them: *Anna Karenin* and Electricity in *Ada*," *Nabokov Studies* 7 (2003).
4. Johnson, *Worlds in Regression*, 117; Annapaola Cancogni, *The Mirage in the Mirror: Nabokov's* Ada *and Its French Pre-Texts* (New York: Garland, 1985).
5. See Penny McCarthy, "Nabokov's *Ada* and Sidney's *Arcadia*," *Modern Language Review* 99, no. 1 (2004); Alter, "Perils of Paradise"; and Rachel Trousdale, "Incest and Intertext: *Mansfield Park* in *Ada*," *The Nabokovian* 61 (2008).
6. Pifer, *Nabokov and the Novel*, 147.
7. Boyd, *Nabokov's* Pale Fire, 4.

8. See Kurt Johnson and Steve Coates, *Nabokov's Blues: The Scientific Odyssey of a Literary Genius* (New York: McGraw-Hill, 2001).
9. See Gene Barabtarlo, "Vanessa Atalanta and Raisa Orlova," *The Nabokovian* 13 (1984); and Dieter E. Zimmer, *A Guide to Nabokov's Butterflies and Moths* (Berlin: D. E. Zimmer, 2003).
10. Stephen Blackwell, "The Poetics of Science in, and around, Nabokov's *Gift*," *Russian Review* 62 (2003): 246.
11. Vladimir Nabokov, *Speak, Memory* (New York: G. P. Putnam's Sons, 1966), 137.
12. Nabokov, *Speak, Memory*, 138–39; John Burt Foster discusses the unification of America and Russia in this passage in *Nabokov's Art of Memory*, 185–86.
13. Nabokov, *Speak, Memory*, 136.
14. Ibid., 138.
15. Ibid., 139.
16. Nabokov, *Pale Fire*, 129–30.
17. Blackwell, "The Poetics of Science," 254–55. Robert Grossmith suggests that Nabokov seeks to refute relativity because he finds it aesthetically displeasing. "Shaking the Kaleidoscope: Physics and Metaphysics in Nabokov's *Bend Sinister*," *Russian Literature Triquarterly* 24 (1991).
18. Julie M. Johnson, "The Theory of Relativity and Modern Literature: An Overview and *The Sound and the Fury*," *Journal of Modern Literature* 10 (1983): 219.
19. Paul R. Gross and Norman Levitt, *Higher Superstition: The Academic Left and Its Quarrels with Science* (Baltimore, MD: Johns Hopkins University Press, 1994), 78.
20. Wai Chee Dimock, "Nonbiological Clock: Literary History against Newtonian Mechanics," *South Atlantic Quarterly* 102 (2003): 154.
21. Teri Reynolds, "Spacetime and Imagetext," *The Germanic Review* 73 (1998): 161.
22. Vladimir Nabokov, "Texture of Time." Holograph notes (undated). The main note in brackets is in the original. The Berg Collection of English and American Literature, The New York Public Library, Astor, Lenox and Tilden Foundations. Card "The Present 8." Space-time appears in *Pale Fire*, too: Martin Gardner quoted a line of Shade's in *The Ambidextrous Universe*, provoking Nabokov then to recycle the line in *Ada* and attribute it to "John Shade, a modern poet, as quoted by an invented philosopher ('Martin Gardiner') in *The Ambidextrous Universe*, page 165" (542). See Johnson, *Worlds in Regression*, 170.
23. Nabokov, *Strong Opinions*, 116.
24. See Albert Einstein, *Relativity*, trans. Robert W. Lawson (Amherst, NY: Prometheus Books, 1995). Nabokov would have had access to Einstein's work for the lay reader. He also took extensive notes on G. J. Whitrow, *The Natural Philosophy of Time* (New York, NY: Harper, 1963).
25. Nabokov, *Speak, Memory*, 218.
26. Ibid.
27. Ibid., 139.
28. Salman Rushdie, *Midnight's Children* (New York: Penguin, 1981), 253.
29. Nabokov, *Ada*, 541.
30. Ibid., 548.

31. Nabokov, Berg collection. Card "Relativity 4." Brackets in original.
32. Leona Toker, "Nabokov and Bergson on Duration and Reflexivity," in *Nabokov's World, Volume One: The Shape of Nabokov's World*, ed. Jane Grayson, Arnold McMillin, and Priscilla Meyer (London: Palgrave, 2002); Foster, *Nabokov's Art of Memory*, 86.
33. Henri Bergson, *Duration and Simultaneity, With Reference to Einstein's Theory*, trans. Leon Jacobson (New York: Bobbs-Merrill, 1965), 38.
34. Ibid., 79.
35. Ibid., 113.
36. Ibid., 44.
37. Nabokov, *Ada*, 536.
38. Johnson, "The Theory of Relativity and Modern Literature," 219.
39. Nabokov, Berg collection. Card "The Past 22."
40. Nabokov, *Ada*, 543–44.
41. Bergson discusses the twin paradox at length in *Duration and Simultaneity* for the same reason: a perceptual account of time demands that both the twin on Earth and the twin on the spaceship be accurate in their self-perception.
42. See the standard college text: Edwin F. Taylor and John Archibald Wheeler, *Spacetime Physics* (San Francisco, CA: W. H. Freeman and Co., 1963).
43. Mason, *Nabokov's Garden*, 18.
44. Nabokov, *Ada*, 537.
45. Hayles, "Making a Virtue of Neccesity," 36.
46. Mason, *Nabokov's Garden*, 70.
47. Nabokov, *Ada*, 537.
48. Ibid.
49. Ibid., 540.
50. Ibid., 543.
51. Ibid., 354.
52. Nabokov, *Strong Opinions*, 120.
53. Nabokov, *Ada*, 354.
54. Ibid.
55. Ibid., 535.
56. Ibid., 536.
57. Ibid., 551.
58. Ibid., 182.
59. Ibid., 342.
60. Ibid., 342.
61. Ibid., 341.
62. Ibid., 340.
63. Ibid., 342.

CHAPTER 4

1. Rushdie, *Midnight's Children*, 552.
2. Timothy Brennan, *Salman Rushdie and the Third World: Myths of the Nation* (New York: St Martin's, 1989), 165–66. John Su and John Clement Ball acknowledge pessimistic aspects of Rushdie's work but find hope in his characters' catastrophes. See John Su, "Epic of Failure: Disappointment as Utopian Fantasy in *Midnight's Children*," *Twentieth Century Literature* 47 (2002); and John Clement Ball, "Pessoptimism: Satire and the Menippean Grotesque in Rushdie's *Midnight's Children*," *English Studies in Canada* 24, no. 1 (1998).
3. Appiah, "Cosmopolitan Reading," 208.
4. Gillian Gane, "Migrancy, the Cosmopolitan Intellectual, and the Global City in *The Satanic Verses*," *Modern Fiction Studies* 48 (2002), Harveen Sachdeva Mann, "'Being Borne across': Translation and Salman Rushdie's *The Satanic Verses*," *Criticism* 37, no. 2 (1995); Krishnaswamy, "Mythologies of Migrancy."
5. E. J. Hobsbawm, *Nations and Nationalism Since 1870* (Cambridge: Cambridge University Press, 1990).
6. Johann Gottfried Herder, *Outlines of a Philosophy of the History of Man* (London: J. Johnson, 1800); Clifford Geertz, ed., *Old Societies and New States: The Quest for Modernity in Asia and Africa* (New York: Free Press, 1963).
7. Jocelyne Couture, Kai Nielsen, and Michel Seymour, ed., *Rethinking Nationalism* (Calgary, Canada: University of Calgary Press, 1996).
8. Naipaul, *India*, 160.
9. Neil Ten Kortenaar, *Self, Nation, Text in Salman Rushdie's* Midnight's Children (Montreal: McGill-Queen's University Press, 2004), 7.
10. Rushdie, *Imaginary Homelands*, 22–25. See also Ronny Noor, "Misrepresentation of History in Salman Rushdie's *Midnight's Children*," *Notes on Contemporary Literature* 26 (1996).
11. Rushdie, *Imaginary Homelands*, 41–46.
12. Sujata Patel and Alice Thorner, ed., *Bombay: Metaphor for Modern India* (Bombay: Oxford University Press, 1996), ix.
13. Sujata Patel, personal interview, Pune, India, June 9, 2003.
14. Ibid.
15. Ibid.
16. Shanta Gokhale, "Rich Theatre, Poor Theatre," in *Bombay: Mosaic of Modern Culture*, ed. Sujata Patel and Alice Thorner (Bombay: Oxford University Press, 1995), 209.
17. Patel, interview.
18. Gérard Heuzé, "Cultural Populism: The Appeal of the Shiv Sena," in *Bombay: Metaphor for Modern India*, ed. Sujata Patel and Alice Thorner (Bombay: Oxford University Press, 1996), 225.
19. D. K. Lakdawala, *Work, Wages and Well-Being in an Indian Metropolis* (Bombay: Bombay University Press, 1963); Vaibhav Purandare, *The Sena Story* (Bombay: Business Publications, 1999).

20. The murder of communist M. L. A. Krishna Desai on June 5, 1970, for example. Purandare, *The Sena Story*, 141.
21. Heuzé, "Cultural Populism," 236.
22. Rushdie, *Midnight's Children*, 106.
23. David Birch, "Postmodernist Chutneys," *Textual Practice* 5 (1991).
24. Rushdie's allegiances show in this encapsulation of the city's communities. By collapsing the Hindu community into one woman, he homogenizes a very diverse population.
25. Nirad Chaudhri, *A Passage to England* (New York: St. Martin's, 1959), 64. As Ten Kortenaar points out, it is not clear how Saleem knows that Methwold is his father. Neil Ten Kortenaar, "*Midnight's Children* and the Allegory of History," *ARIEL* 26 (1995): 52.
26. Ten Kortenaar, "*Midnight's Children* and the Allegory of History"; Su, "Epic of Failure"; David Lipscomb, "Caught in a Strange Middle Ground: Contesting History in Salman Rushdie's *Midnight's Children*," *Diaspora: A Journal of Transnational Studies* 2 (1991); Fawzia Afzal-Khan, "Myth De-Bunked: Genre and Ideology in Rushdie's *Midnight's Children* and *Shame*," *Journal of Indian Writing in English* 14 (1986).
27. See Sujata Patel, "Bombay and Mumbai: Identities, Politics, and Populism," in *Bombay and Mumbai: The City in Transition*, ed. Sujata Patel and Jim Masselos (New Delhi: Oxford University Press, 2003).
28. Rushdie, *Midnight's Children*, 263.
29. M. Keith Booker, "*Midnight's Children*, History, and Complexity: Reading Rushdie After the Cold War," in *Critical Essays on Salman Rushdie*, ed. M. Keith Booker (New York: Hall, 1999).
30. Hogan, "*Midnight's Children*," 512.
31. Rushdie, *Midnight's Children*, 474.
32. Ibid., 486.
33. Ibid., 511.
34. Ibid., 513.
35. Neil Ten Kortenaar, "Salman Rushdie's Magical Realism and the Return of the Inescapable Romance," *University of Toronto Quarterly: A Canadian Journal of the Humanities* 71 (2002). Ten Kortenaar returns to this argument in *Self, Nation, Text* 197–98.
36. Rushdie, *Midnight's Children*, 253.
37. Hogan, "*Midnight's Children*," 513.
38. Salman Rushdie, *The Moor's Last Sigh* (New York: Pantheon, 1995), 231.
39. Ashis Nandy, *The Tao of Cricket: On Games of Destiny and the Destiny of Games* (New York: Viking, 1989), viii.
40. Hogan, "*Midnight's Children*," 524.
41. Salman Rushdie, *The Ground Beneath Her Feet* (New York: Henry Holt, 1999), 511.
42. Rushdie, *The Moor's Last Sigh*, 186.
43. See Sharada Dwivedi and Rahul Mehrotra, *Bombay: The Cities Within* (Bombay: Eminence Designs Pvt. Ltd., 1995), 314–16.

44. Rushdie, *Midnight's Children*, 286.
45. Ibid., 228–29.
46. Alexandra W. Schultheis, "Postcolonial Lack and Aesthetic Promise in *The Moor's Last Sigh*," *Twentieth Century Literature* 47 (2001).
47. Rushdie, *Midnight's Children*, 374.
48. Ibid., 376.
49. Roger Y. Clark, *Stranger Gods: Salman Rushdie's Other Worlds* (Montreal: McGill-Queen's University Press, 2001), 63. See also Hogan, "*Midnight's Children*."
50. Jon Thompson, "Superman and Salman Rushdie: *Midnight's Children* and the Disillusionment of History," *Journal of Commonwealth and Postcolonial Studies* 3 (1995).
51. Mujeebuddin Syed, "*Midnight's Children* and Its Indian Con-Texts," 103.
52. Su, "Epic of Failure," 552–53.
53. Brennan, *Salman Rushdie and the Third World*, 84.
54. Hogan, "*Midnight's Children*," 515.
55. See Stanley Wolpert, *A New History of India: Fifth Edition* (Oxford: Oxford University Press, 1997), 309.
56. Rushdie, *Midnight's Children*, 197–98.
57. Ibid., 168–69.
58. Nehru described it as "the loss of India's soul." Wolpert, *A New History of India*, 355.
59. Ten Kortenaar, *Self, Nation, Text*, 235–36; Catherine Cundy, *Salman Rushdie* (Manchester: Manchester University Press, 1996).
60. D. C. R. A. Goonetilleke, for example, says that "only Gandhi measures up" as a hero in *Midnight's Children*. D. C. R. A. Goonetilleke, *Salman Rushdie* (New York: St. Martin's, 1998), 32.
61. Ten Kortenaar, *Self, Nation, Text*, 46.
62. Wolpert, *A New History of India*, 303.
63. Lipscomb, "Caught in a Strange Middle Ground," 166. Neil Ten Kortenaar suggests that Rushdie's use of Wolpert is meant to "encourage a self-reflexiveness in the reader to match the reflexiveness which is required from Saleem in his attempt to make his history comprehensible" (Ten Kortenaar, "*Midnight's Children* and the Allegory of History," 56).
64. Wolpert, *A New History of India*, 295.
65. Jean-Pierrre Durix, "Salman Rushdie," in *Conversations with Salman Rushdie*, ed. Michael Reder (Jackson, MS: University of Mississippi Press, 2000), 11.
66. Hogan, "*Midnight's Children*," 521.
67. Rushdie, *Midnight's Children*, 312.
68. Hogan, "*Midnight's Children*," 534.
69. Rushdie, *Midnight's Children*, 552.
70. Mikhail Bakhtin, *Problems of Dostoevsky's Poetics*, ed. and trans. Caryl Emerson (Minneapolis, MN: University of Minnesota Press, 1984), 58.
71. Rushdie, *Midnight's Children*, 200.
72. Rushdie, *The Satanic Verses*, 441.

CHAPTER 5

1. Michael Gorra, *After Empire: Scott, Naipaul, Rushdie* (Chicago, IL: University of Chicago Press, 1997), 118.
2. Rushdie, *The Satanic Verses*, 406.
3. Feroza Jussawalla, "Resurrecting the Prophet: The Case of Salman, the Otherwise," *Public Culture* 2, no. 1 (1989): 113.
4. Suleri, *The Rhetoric of English India*, 189.
5. Ibid., 198.
6. Ibid., 193.
7. Antje M. Rauwerda, "'Angelicdevilish' Combinations: Milton's Satan and Salman Rushdie's *The Satanic Verses*," *Journal of Postcolonial Writing* 41 (2005); Simona Sawhney, "Satanic Choices: Poetry and Prophecy in Rushdie's Novel," *Twentieth-Century Literature* 45, no. 3 (1999).
8. Satish C. Aikant, "Salman Rushdie's *Midnight's Children*: The Middle Ground of Diaspora," in *Interrogating Post-Colonialism: Theory, Text and Context*, ed. Harish Trivedi and Meenakshi Mukherjee (Rashtrapati Nivas, Shimal: Indian Institute of Advanced Study, 1996): 214.
9. See Martine Hennard Dutheil, "The Epigraph to *The Satanic Verses*: Defoe's Devil and Rushdie's Migrant," *Southern Review* 30 (1997), and "Rushdie's Affiliation with Dickens," *Dickens Studies Annual* 27 (1998); David Suter, "Of the Devil's Party: The Marriage of Heaven and Hell in *Satanic Verses*," *South Asian Review* 16, no. 13 (1992); Neil Cornwell, "Masters of the Satanic: Mikhail Bulgakov, Salman Rushdie and Umberto Eco," in *Bulgakov: The Novelist-Playwright*, ed. Lesley Milne (Luxembourg: Harwood, 1995); Arnold McMillin, "*The Satanic Verses* and *Master i Margarita*," in *Bulgakov: The Novelist-Playwright*, ed. Lesley Milne (Luxembourg: Harwood, 1995); Radha Balasubramanian, "The Similarities Between Mikhail Bulgakov's *The Master and Margarita* and Salman Rushdie's *The Satanic Verses*," *International Fiction Review* 22, no. 1–2 (1995). Suleri discusses Rushdie's thematization of the *ghazal* in *The Rhetoric of English India*, 193. For *Shri 420*, see Rashmi Varma, "Provinicalizing the Global City: From Bombay to Mumbai," *Social Text* 22, no. 4 (2004). Ania Loomba and Jonathan Greenberg have both written on *Othello* in *The Moor's Last Sigh*. The prominent *Othello* subtext in *The Satanic Verses* has, as far as I know, yet to be explored. Ania Loomba, "'Local-Manufacture Made-in-India Othello Fellows': Issues of Race, Hybridity and Location in Post-Colonial Shakespeares," in *Post-Colonial Shakespeares*, ed. Ania Loomba and Martin Orkin (London: Routledge, 1998); Jonathan Greenberg, "'The Base Indian' or 'The Base Judean'?: *Othello* and the Metaphor of the Palimpsest in Salman Rushdie's *The Moor's Last Sigh*," *Modern Language Studies* 29, no. 2 (1999).
10. Rushdie, *Imaginary Homelands*, 423.
11. M. Keith Booker, *Techniques of Subversion in Modern Literature: Transgression, Abjection, and the Carnivalesque* (Gainesville, FL: University Press of Florida, 1991), 51.
12. Dutheil, "The Epigraph to *The Satanic* Verses," 67.

13. Bhabha, *The Location of Culture*, 97.
14. Allegations include that Rushdie maligns Abraham (the narrator does call him a "bastard" for abandoning Hagar [95]); that he says Muhammad's wives were prostitutes (they live "chastely in . . . the harem quarters" [381]); that Rushdie says Muhammad visited prostitutes (he does not); and so on. Lisa Appignianesi and Sara Maitland provide a good picture of reactions to the novel: Lisa Appignianesi and Sara Maitland, ed., *The Rushdie File* (London: Fourth Estate, 1989). See also Anouar Abdallah, ed., *For Rushdie: Essays by Arab and Muslim Writers in Defense of Free Speech*, trans. Kevin Anderson and Kenneth Whitehead (New York: George Braziller, 1994). Some critics read the Muslim and Western responses as examples of clashing cross-cultural aesthetics, making *The Satanic Verses* a counterexample of artistic synthesis. See Pnina Werbner, "Allegories of Sacred Imperfection: Magic, Hermeneutics, and Passion in *The Satanic Verses*," *Current Anthropology: A World Journal of the Human Sciences* 37 (1996).
15. Gayatri Chakravorty Spivak, *Outside in the Teaching Machine* (New York: Routledge, 1993), 217.
16. Rushdie, *The Satanic Verses*, 114.
17. Ibid., 123.
18. Ibid., 112, italics in original.
19. Ibid.
20. Ibid., 108.
21. Ibid., 141.
22. Ibid., 356.
23. Ibid., 354.
24. Ibid., 445.
25. Rushdie, *Midnight's Children*, 389.
26. Rushdie, *The Satanic Verses*, 352.
27. Jaina C. Sanga, *Salman Rushdie's Postcolonial Metaphors: Migration, Translation, Hybridity, Blasphemy and Globalization* (Westport, CT: Greenwood, 2001), 85.
28. Rushdie, *The Satanic Verses*, 367.
29. Booker, *Techniques of Subversion in Modern Literature*, 63.
30. Rushdie, *The Satanic Verses*, 454.
31. Ibid., 454–55.
32. Mann, "'Being Borne Across,'" 281.
33. Sawhney, "Satanic Choices," 272.
34. Joel Kuortti, "'Nomsense': Salman Rushdie's *The Satanic Verses*," *Textual Practice* 13, no. 1 (1999): 137.
35. Rushdie, *The Satanic Verses*, 10.
36. Ibid., 93.
37. Sawhney, "Satanic Choices," 271.
38. Rushdie, *The Satanic Verses*, 408–9.
39. Brennan, *Salman Rushdie and the Third World*, 89.
40. Booker, *Techniques of Subversion in Modern Literature*, 57.
41. Rushdie, *The Satanic Verses*, 60.
42. Ibid., 463.

43. Ibid., 466.
44. Ibid., 523.
45. Ibid., 427.
46. Booker, *Techniques of Subversion in Modern Literature*, 55.
47. Rushdie, *The Satanic Verses*, 406.
48. Ibid.
49. Rushdie, *Imaginary Homelands*, 416.
50. Rushdie, *The Satanic Verses*, 538.
51. Michael Wood, "Enigmas and Homelands," in *On Modern British Fiction*, ed. Zachary Leader (Oxford: Oxford University Press, 2002), 84.
52. Rushdie, *The Satanic Verses*, 385.
53. Ibid., 52.
54. Ibid., 5.
55. Varma, "Provinicalizing the Global City," 77–78.
56. Rushdie, *The Satanic Verses*, 399.
57. Homi Bhabha, "DissemiNation," in Homi Bhabha, ed., *Nation and Narration* (New York: Routledge, 1990): 319.
58. Rushdie, *The Satanic Verses*, 70.
59. Rushdie, *Imaginary Homelands*, 395.
60. Rushdie, *The Satanic Verses*, 70.
61. Monika Fludernik, "The Diasporic Imaginary: Postcolonial Reconfigurations in the Context of Multiculturalism," in *Diaspora and Multiculturalism: Common Traditions and New Developments*, ed. Monika Fludernik (New York: Rodopi, 2003), xx.
62. Rushdie, *The Satanic Verses*, 245–46.
63. Ibid., 250.
64. Ibid., 168.
65. Ibid., 16–17.
66. Rushdie returns to the subject of the Emperor Akbar in *The Enchantress of Florence*. Salman Rushdie, *The Enchantress of Florence* (New York: Random House, 2008).
67. Aziz Ahmad, *Studies in Islamic Culture in the Indian Environment* (New Delhi: Oxford University Press, 1964), 180.
68. Rushdie, *The Satanic Verses*, 28–29.
69. Ibid., 427.
70. Ibid., 547.
71. Mann, "'Being Borne Across,'" 290.
72. Ibid.
73. See M. Keith Booker, "*Finnegans Wake* and *The Satanic Verses*: Two Modern Myths of the Fall," *Critique* 32, no. 3 (1991); Jean Kane, "Embodied Panic: Revisiting Modernist 'Religion' in the Controversies over *Ulysses* and *The Satanic Verses*," *Textual Practice* 20, no. 3 (2006); and Susan Cannon Harris, "Invasive Procedures: Imperial Medicine and Population Control in *Ulysses* and *The Satanic Verses*," *James Joyce Quarterly* 35, no. 2–3 (1998).

CHAPTER 6

1. Anshuman A. Mondal, "*The Ground Beneath Her Feet* and *Fury*: The Reinvention of Location," in *The Cambridge Companion to Salman Rushdie*, ed. Abdulrazak Gurnah (Cambridge: Cambridge University Press, 2007), 169.
2. Peter Kadzis, "Rushdie Rocks: Interview with Salman Rushdie," *The Boston Phoenix*, May 10, 1999, 28-31.
3. Elena Rossi argues that Rushdie's "ironic lowering" of myth replaces gods with art; Elena Rossi, "'Against an amnesiac culture': Greek and Latin Mythology in *The Ground Beneath Her Feet*," in *The Great Work of Making Real: Salman Rushdie's* The Ground Beneath Her Feet, ed. Elsa Linguanti and Viktoria Tchernichova (Pisa: Edizioni ETS, 2003). Shaul Bassi treats Orpheus as a colonial agent; Shaul Bassi, "Orpheus's Other Voyage: Myth, Music, and Globalisation," in *The Great Work of Making Real: Salman Rushdie's* The Ground Beneath Her Feet, ed. Elsa Linguanti and Viktoria Tchernichova (Pisa: Edizioni ETS, 2003). See also Alessandro Monti, "A Hoarding of Goats and Rumours of Mermaids: Puzzling out Myth in *The Ground Beneath Her Feet*," in *The Great Work of Making Real: Salman Rushdie's* The Ground Beneath Her Feet, ed. Elsa Linguanti and Viktoria Tchernichova (Pisa: Edizioni ETS, 2003); Sylvia Albertazzi, "'Why do we care about singers?' Music in *The Ground Beneath Her Feet*," in *The Great Work of Making Real: Salman Rushdie's* The Ground Beneath Her Feet, ed. Elsa Linguanti and Viktoria Tchernichova (Pisa: Edizioni ETS, 2003).
4. Elsa Linguanti argues that Maria represents Ormus's abandoned possibilities and the destruction of her world condemns the violence of our own. Elsa Linguanti, "Different Whatnesses," in *The Great Work of Making Real: Salman Rushdie's* The Ground Beneath Her Feet, ed. Elsa Linguanti and Viktoria Tchernichova (Pisa: Edizioni ETS, 2003).
5. Viktoria Tchernichova, "'The solutions to the problems of art are always technical': Some Observations on Textual Topologies," in *The Great Work of Making Real: Salman Rushdie's* The Ground Beneath Her Feet, ed. Elsa Linguanti and Viktoria Tchernichova (Pisa: Edizioni ETS, 2003), 167.
6. Rushdie, *Imaginary Homelands*, 416.
7. Rushdie, *The Ground Beneath Her Feet*, 31.
8. Ibid., 49.
9. Ibid., 79.
10. Ibid., 72–73.
11. Ibid., 42.
12. Ibid., 43.
13. Bhabha, *Location of Culture*, 113.
14. Rushdie, *The Ground Beneath Her Feet*, 350.
15. Rushdie, *Imaginary Homelands*, 394.
16. Gary Saul Morson and Caryl Emerson, "Bakhtin," in *The Johns Hopkins Guide to Literary Theory and Criticism*, ed. Michael Groden and Martin Kreiswirth (Baltimore: Johns Hopkins University Press, 1994), 67.
17. Rushdie, *The Ground Beneath Her Feet*, 284.

18. See Bakhtin, *The Dialogic Imagination*, 259–422.
19. Rushdie, *The Ground Beneath Her Feet*, 352.
20. Ibid., 6.
21. Ibid., 202.
22. Ibid., 10.
23. See Doležel, *Heterocosmica*, 20.
24. Rushdie, *The Ground Beneath Her Feet*, 389.
25. Ibid., 523.
26. Fausto Ciomi, "Wor(l)d-shifts, Functions, Dialogue in *The Ground Beneath Her Feet*: More Skirmishes in the War of Meanings," in *The Great Work of Making Real: Salman Rushdie's* The Ground Beneath Her Feet, ed. Elsa Linguanti and Viktoria Tchernichova (Pisa: Edizioni ETS, 2003), 220.
27. Pierre Bayle, *Historical and Critical Dictionary*, trans. Richard H. Popkin and Craig Bush (Indianapolis, IN: Bobbs-Merrill, 1965), 145.
28. Rushdie, *The Ground Beneath Her Feet*, 101.
29. Ibid., 112.
30. Ibid., 268.
31. Ibid., 280.
32. Ibid., 293.
33. Roger Manvell and Lewis Jacobs, *The International Encyclopedia of Film* (New York: Bonanza, 1975), 150.
34. Rushdie, *The Ground Beneath Her Feet*, 351.
35. Ibid., 300–301.
36. Mariam Pirbhai, "The Paradox of Globalization as an 'Untotalizable Totality' in Salman Rushdie's *The Ground Beneath Her Feet*," *The International Fiction Review* 28 (2001).
37. Rushdie, *The Ground Beneath Her Feet*, 299.
38. Ibid., 331.
39. Ibid.
40. Ibid., 184.
41. Ibid. As Tchernichova argues, Rai's literalism opposes Ormus's asceticism: the alternative to renunciation is to "acknowledge the world as it is, with all its horrors, and thus acquire a Dionysian or tragic vision of life." Viktoria Tchernichova, "'The outsideness of what we're inside': Double Vision as Künstlerästhetik in *The Ground Beneath Her Feet*," in *The Great Work of Making Real: Salman Rushdie's* The Ground Beneath Her Feet, ed. Elsa Linguanti and Viktoria Tchernichova (Pisa: Edizioni ETS, 2003), 84. See also Carmen Concilio, "'Worthy of the world': The Narrator/Photographer in Salman Rushdie's *The Ground Beneath Her Feet*," in *The Great Work of Making Real: Salman Rushdie's* The Ground Beneath Her Feet, ed. Elsa Linguanti and Viktoria Tchernichova (Pisa: Edizioni ETS, 2003).
42. Rushdie, *The Ground Beneath Her Feet*, 14.
43. Ibid., 185.
44. Ibid., 225–26.
45. Ibid., 501.

46. Judith Leggatt, "Other Worlds, Other Selves: Science Fiction in Salman Rushdie's *The Ground Beneath Her Feet*," *ARIEL* 33, no. 1 (2002): 123.
47. J. R. R. Tolkien, *The Return of the King* (New York: Ballantine Books, 1972), 385.
48. Rushdie, *The Ground Beneath Her Feet*, 415.
49. Ibid., 575.
50. Randy Boyagoda, "'Three Kings of Disorient': A Globalized Search for Home in *The Ground Beneath Her Feet*," *South Asian Review* 24, no. 1 (2003): 131.
51. Klaus Stierstorfer, "Wobbly Grounds: Postmodernism's Precarious Footholds in Novels by Malcolm Bradbury, David Parker, Salman Rushdie, Graham Swift," in *Beyond Postmodernism: Reassessments in Literature, Theory, and Culture*, ed. Klaus Stiersorfer (New York: Walter de Gruyter, 2003), 220.
52. Rushdie, *The Ground Beneath Her Feet*, 401.

CONCLUSION

1. Edward W. Said, *The World, the Text, and the Critic* (Cambridge: Harvard University Press, 1983), 20.
2. Ibid., 19.
3. Ibid., 21.
4. Pratt, *Imperial Eyes*, 194.
5. Marie-Hélène Huet, *Monstrous Imagination* (Cambridge: Harvard University Press, 1993).
6. Rushdie, *The Satanic Verses*, 50.
7. Umberto Eco, *The Name of the Rose*, trans. William Weaver (New York: Warner, 1984), 385.
8. Ibid., 386.
9. Ibid., 379.
10. Ibid., 46.
11. Ibid., 48.
12. Ibid., 47–48.
13. Ibid., 47.
14. Ibid., 237.
15. Umberto Eco, *Baudolino*, trans. William Weaver (New York: Harcourt, 2000), 373.
16. Ibid., 77.
17. W. V. O. Quine, *Word and Object* (Cambridge: MIT University Press, 1960), 29–40.
18. Eco, *Baudolino*, 366–67.
19. Ibid., 368.
20. Ibid., 369.
21. Jackson, Crang, and Dwyer, *Transnational Spaces*, 2; italics in original.
22. Aijaz Ahmad, *In Theory: Classes, Nations, Literatures* (London: Verso, 1992), 156. In response, see Shaijla Sharma, "Salman Rushdie: The Ambivalence of Migrancy," *Twentieth Century Literature* 47, no. 4 (2001).

23. Nabokov, *The Annotated Lolita*, 44.
24. Ibid., 124.
25. See Frederick Whiting, "'The Strange Particularity of the Lover's Preference': Pedophilia, Pornography, and the Anatomy of Monstrosity in *Lolita*," *American Literature* 70, no. 4 (1998).
26. Kellie Dawson, "Rare and Unfamiliar Things: Vladimir Nabokov's 'Monsters,'" *Nabokovian* 9 (2005).
27. Nabokov, *The Annotated Lolita*, 54.
28. Ibid., 56.
29. Nabokov, *The Annotated Lolita*, 284.
30. Ibid., 216.
31. Ibid., 119.
32. Ibid., 300.
33. Ibid., 174.
34. Ibid., 150.
35. Ibid., 287.
36. George Steiner, *Extraterritorial: Papers on Literature and the Language Revolution* (New York: Atheneum, 1976), 8.
37. Nabokov, *The Annotated Lolita*, 9.
38. Eco, *Name of the Rose*, 48.
39. Nabokov, *The Annotated Lolita*, 218.
40. Rushdie, *Midnight's Children*, 136.
41. Ibid., 136–37.
42. Arundhati Roy, *The God of Small Things* (New York: Harper Perennial, 1998), 59.
43. Ibid., 40.
44. William Faulkner, *Absalom, Absalom!* (New York: Vintage, 1991), 286.
45. Michael Chabon, *Maps and Legends: Reading and Writing Along the Borderlands* (San Francisco: McSweeney's, 2008), 169.
46. Michael Chabon, "Our Nabokov." *Nabokovia*, June 1, 2000, http://community.livejournal.com/nabokovia/64269.html, accessed June 10, 2007. The American writer's exilic position also allows him to reframe the country from which he is exiled. As Rob Kroes puts it, "it is for Americans rather than Europeans to conceive of Europe as a whole, and to transcend Europe's patterns of cultural particularism." Rob Kroes, *Straddling Borders: The American Resonance in Transnational Identities* (Amsterdam: Vrije Universiteit Press, 2004), 12.
47. Michael Chabon, *The Yiddish Policemen's Union* (New York: HarperCollins 2007), 414.
48. Johnson, *Worlds in Regression*, 86–87; Janet Gezari, "Chess and Chess Problems," *The Garland Companion to Vladimir Nabokov*, ed. Vladimir Alexandrov (New York: Garland, 1995).
49. Nabokov, *Speak, Memory*, 290.
50. Nabokov, *Strong Opinions*, 183.
51. Vladimir Nabokov, *Poems and Problems* (New York: McGraw-Hill, 1970), 15.
52. Nabokov, *Speak, Memory*, 310.

53. The premise is drawn from life: the real-world U.S. Department of the Interior proposed in 1939 that German and Austrian Jews be resettled into southern Alaska as part of a development program.
54. Chabon, *The Yiddish Policemen's Union*, 368.
55. Edmond Privat, *The Life of Zamenhof*, trans. Ralph Eliott (London: George Allen and Unwin, Ltd., 1931), 65.
56. Ibid., 18.
57. Chabon, *The Yiddish Policemen's Union*, 3.
58. Nabokov, *Speak, Memory*, 227.
59. See Chris Ackerley, "*Pale Fire*: Three Notes Towards a Thetic Solution," *Nabokov Studies* 2 (1995).
60. Nabokov, *Speak, Memory*, 228–29.
61. Ibid., 229.
62. Nabokov, *Poems and Problems*, 15.
63. Nabokov, *Speak, Memory*, 229.
64. Johnson, *Worlds in Regression*, 79.
65. His underpromotion of his pawn may also mirror his knight's move to America, where he is unknown as a novelist. See Priscilla Meyer, "Anglophonia and Optimysticism: *Sebastian Knight*'s Bookshelves," *Russian Literature and the West: A Tribute for David M. Bethea*, ed. Alexander Dolinin, Lazar Fleishman, and Leonid Livak (Stanford: Stanford University Press, 2008).
66. Brian Boyd, *Vladimir Nabokov: The Russian Years* (Princeton: Princeton University Press, 1990), 514.
67. Chabon, *The Yiddish Policemen's Union*, 400–401.
68. Ibid., 404.
69. Chabon chose Mendel's name thinking of a Yiddish listserv called Mendele, whose participants treat Ashkenaz—"the lands of northern European Jewry," which are both "an actual geographical region" and "a culture and a state of mind"—as a physically existing place for which one might need a Yiddish-language phrasebook. Chabon, *Maps and Legends*, 187.
70. Chabon, *The Yiddish Policemen's Union*, 411.
71. Michael Chabon, *The Amazing Adventures of Kavalier and Clay* (New York: Picador, 2000), 174.
72. Chabon, *Maps and Legends*, 190.
73. Appadurai, *Modernity at Large*, 5.
74. Ibid., 7.
75. Salman Rushdie, *Step Across This Line* (New York: Random House, 2002), 146.
76. Ibid., 151.

Bibliography

Abdallah, Anouar, ed. *For Rushdie: Essays by Arab and Muslim Writers in Defense of Free Speech*. Translated by Kevin Anderson and Kenneth Whitehead. New York: George Braziller, 1994.
Ackerley, Chris. "*Pale Fire*: Three Notes Towards a Thetic Solution." *Nabokov Studies* 2 (1995): 87–103.
Afzal-Khan, Fawzia. "Myth De-Bunked: Genre and Ideology in Rushdie's *Midnight's Children* and *Shame*." *Journal of Indian Writing in English* 14 (1986): 49–60.
Ahmad, Aijaz, *In Theory: Classes, Nations, Literatures*. London: Verso, 1992.
Ahmad, Aziz. *Studies in Islamic Culture in the Indian Environment*. New Delhi: Oxford University Press, 1964.
Aikant, Satish C. "Salman Rushdie's *Midnight's Children*: The Middle Ground of Diaspora." In *Interrogating Post-Colonialism: Theory, Text and Context*, edited by Harish Trivedi and Meenakshi Mukherjee, 213–20. Rashtrapati Nivas, Shimal: Indian Institute of Advanced Study, 1996.
Albertazzi, Sylvia. "'Why do we care about singers?' Music in *The Ground Beneath Her Feet*." In *The Great Work of Making Real: Salman Rushdie's* The Ground Beneath Her Feet, edited by Elsa Linguanti and Viktoria Tchernichova, 91–97. Pisa: Edizioni ETS, 2003.
Alexandrov, Vladimir. *Nabokov's Otherworld*. Princeton, NJ: Princeton University Press, 1991.
Allen, Woody. *Side Effects*. New York: Random House, 1980.
Alter, Robert. "*Ada*, or the Perils of Paradise." In *Vladimir Nabokov: His Life, His Work, His World: A Tribute*, edited by Peter Quennell, 103–18. London: Weidenfeld & Nicolson, 1979.
———. *Imagined Cities: Urban Experience and the Language of the Novel*. New Haven, CT: Yale University Press, 2005.
Anderson, Benedict. *Imagined Communities: Reflections on the Origin and Spread of Nationalism*. New York: Verso, 1991.
Appadurai, Arjun. *Modernity at Large: Cultural Dimensions of Globalization*. Minneapolis, MN: University of Minnesota Press, 1996.
Appiah, Kwame Anthony. "Cosmopolitan Patriots." In *Cosmopolitics: Thinking and Feeling beyond the Nation*, edited by Pheng Cheah, Bruce Robbins, 91–114. Minneapolis, MN: University of Minnesota Press, 1998.
———. "Cosmopolitan Reading." In *Cosmopolitan Geographies: New Locations in Literature and Culture*, edited by Vinay Dharwadker, 197–227. New York: Routledge, 2001.

BIBLIOGRAPHY

Appignianesi, Lisa, and Sara Maitland, ed. *The Rushdie File*. London: Fourth Estate, 1989.

Artese, Charlotte. "King Arthur in America: Making Space in History for *The Faerie Queene* and John Dee's *Brytanici Imperii Limites*." *Journal of Medieval and Early Modern Studies* 33, no. 1 (2003): 125–41.

Bakhtin, Mikhail. *The Dialogic Imagination*. Edited by Michael Holquist. Translated by Caryl Emerson and Michael Holquist. Austin, TX: University of Texas Press, 1981.

———. *Problems of Dostoevsky's Poetics*. Edited and translated by Caryl Emerson. Minneapolis, MN: University of Minnesota Press, 1984.

Balasubramanian, Radha. "The Similarities Between Mikhail Bulgakov's *The Master and Margarita* and Salman Rushdie's *The Satanic Verses*." *International Fiction Review* 22, no. 1–2 (1995): 37–46.

Ball, John Clement. *Imagining London: Postcolonial Fiction and the Transnational Metropolis*. Toronto: University of Toronto Press, 2004.

———. "Pessoptimism: Satire and the Menippean Grotesque in Rushdie's *Midnight's Children*." *English Studies* in Canada 24, no. 1 (1998): 61–81.

Barabtarlo, Gene. "Vanessa Atalanta and Raisa Orlova." *The Nabokovian* 13 (1984): 27–28.

Basch, Lina, Nina Glick Schiller, and Cristina Szaton Blanc, ed. *Nations Unbound: Transnational Projects, Postcolonial Predicaments and Deterritorialized Nation-States*. Basle, Switzerland: Gordon and Breach, 1994.

Bassi, Shaul. "Orpheus's Other Voyage: Myth, Music, and Globalisation." In *The Great Work of Making Real: Salman Rushdie's* The Ground Beneath Her Feet, edited by Elsa Linguanti and Viktoria Tchernichova, 99–114. Pisa: Edizioni ETS, 2003.

Bayle, Pierre. *Historical and Critical Dictionary*. Translated by Richard H. Popkin and Craig Bush. Indianapolis, IN: Bobbs-Merrill, 1965.

Bergson, Henri. *Duration and Simultaneity, With Reference to Einstein's Theory*. Translated by Leon Jacobson. New York: Bobbs-Merrill, 1965.

Bhabha, Homi. *The Location of Culture*. New York: Routledge, 1994.

———. "DissemiNation." In *Nation and Narration*, edited by Homi Bhabha, 219–322. New York: Routledge, 1990.

———. "Unsatisfied Notes on Vernacular Cosmopolitanism." In *Text and Narration*, edited by Peter C. Pfeiffer and Laura Garcìa-Moreno, 191–207. Columbia, SC: Camden House, 1996.

Birch, David. "Postmodernist Chutneys." *Textual Practice* 5 (1991): 1–7.

Blackwell, Stephen. "The Poetics of Science in, and around, Nabokov's *Gift*." *Russian Review* 62 (2003): 243–61.

Booker, M. Keith. "*Finnegans Wake* and *The Satanic Verses*: Two Modern Myths of the Fall." *Critique* 32, no. 3 (1991): 190–207.

———. "*Midnight's Children*, History, and Complexity: Reading Rushdie After the Cold War." In Critical Essays on Salman Rushdie, edited by M. Keith Booker, 283–313. New York: Hall, 1999.

———. *Techniques of Subversion in Modern Literature: Transgression, Abjection, and the Carnivalesque*. Gainesville, FL: University Press of Florida, 1991.

Boyagoda, Randy. "'Three Kings of Disorient': A Globalized Search for Home in *The Ground Beneath Her Feet*." *South Asian Review* 24, no. 1 (2003): 130–43.

Boyd, Brian. "Annotations to *Ada* Part 1 Chapter 1." *The Nabokovian* 30 (1993): 9–48.

———. *Nabokov's Ada: The Place of Consciousness*. Ann Arbor, MI: Ardis, 1985.

———. *Nabokov's Pale Fire: The Magic of Artistic Discovery*. Princeton, NJ: Princeton University Press, 1999.

———. "Shape and Shade in *Pale Fire*." *Nabokov Studies* 4 (1998): 173–224.

———. *Vladimir Nabokov: The American Years*. Princeton, NJ: Princeton University Press, 1991.

———. *Vladimir Nabokov: The Russian Years*. Princeton, NJ: Princeton University Press, 1990.

Brennan, Timothy. *Salman Rushdie and the Third World: Myths of the Nation*. New York: St. Martin's, 1989.

Cancogni, Annapaola. *The Mirage in the Mirror: Nabokov's Ada and Its French Pre-Texts*. New York: Garland, 1985.

Castronovo, David. "Humbert's America." *New England Review* 23, no. 2 (2002): 33–41.

Chabon, Michael. *The Amazing Adventures of Kavalier and Clay*. New York: Picador, 2000.

———. *Maps and Legends: Reading and Writing Along the Borderlands*. San Francisco: McSweeney's, 2008.

———. "Our Nabokov." *Nabokovia*, June 1, 2000, http://community.livejournal.com/nabokovia/64269.html, accessed June 10, 2007.

———. *The Yiddish Policemen's Union*. New York: HarperCollins, 2007.

Chaudhri, Nirad. *A Passage to England*. New York: St. Martin's, 1959.

Cheah, Pheng. "Given Culture: Rethinking Cosmopolitical Freedom in Transnationalism." In *Cosmopolitics: Thinking and Feeling beyond the Nation*, edited by Pheng Cheah and Bruce Robbins, 290–328. Minneapolis, MN: University of Minnesota Press, 1998.

Cheah, Pheng, and Bruce Robbins, ed. *Cosmopolitics: Thinking and Feeling beyond the Nation*. Minneapolis, MN: University of Minnesota Press, 1998.

Ciomi, Fausto. "Wor(l)d-shifts, Functions, Dialogue in *The Ground Beneath Her Feet*: More Skirmishes in the War of Meanings." In *The Great Work of Making Real: Salman Rushdie's* The Ground Beneath Her Feet, edited by Elsa Linguanti and Viktoria Tchernichova, 213–51. Pisa: Edizioni ETS, 2003.

Clark, Roger Y. *Stranger Gods: Salman Rushdie's Other Worlds*. Montreal: McGill-Queen's University Press, 2001.

Clifford, James. *The Predicament of Culture: Twentieth-Century Ethnography, Literature, and Art*. Cambridge, MA: Harvard University Press, 1988.

Concilio, Carmen. "'Worthy of the world': The Narrator/Photographer in Salman Rushdie's *The Ground Beneath Her Feet*." In *The Great Work of Making Real:*

Salman Rushdie's The Ground Beneath Her Feet, edited by Elsa Linguanti and Viktoria Tchernichova, 117–27. Pisa: Edizioni ETS, 2003.

Conrad, Joseph. *Heart of Darkness and Other Tales*. New York: Oxford University Press, 2003.

———. *Nostromo*. New York: Penguin, 2007.

Cornwell, Neil. "Masters of the Satanic: Mikhail Bulgakov, Salman Rushdie and Umberto Eco." In *Bulgakov: The Novelist-Playwright*, edited by Lesley Milne, 225–31. Luxembourg: Harwood, 1995.

Couture, Jocelyne, Kai Nielsen, and Michel Seymour, ed. *Rethinking Nationalism*. Calgary, Canada: University of Calgary Press, 1996.

Cundy, Catherine. *Salman Rushdie*. Manchester: Manchester University Press, 1996.

Dawson, Kellie. "Rare and Unfamiliar Things: Vladimir Nabokov's 'Monsters.'" *Nabokovian* 9 (2005): 114–31.

Dimock, Wai Chee. "Nonbiological Clock: Literary History against Newtonian Mechanics." *South Atlantic Quarterly* 102 (2003): 153–77.

Dinesen, Isak. *Out of Africa and Shadows on the Grass*. New York: Vintage, 1989.

Doležel, Lubomír. *Heterocosmica: Fiction and Possible Worlds*. Baltimore, MD: The Johns Hopkins University Press, 2000.

Dolinin, Alexander. "Nabokov's Time Doubling: From *The Gift* to *Lolita*." *Nabokov Studies* 2 (1995): 3–40.

Durix, Jean-Pierrre. "Salman Rushdie." In *Conversations with Salman Rushdie*, edited by Michael Reder, 8–16. Jackson, MS: University of Mississippi Press, 2000.

Dutheil, Martine Hennard. "The Epigraph to *The Satanic Verses*: Defoe's Devil and Rushdie's Migrant." *Southern Review* 30 (1997): 51–69.

———. "Rushdie's Affiliation with Dickens." *Dickens Studies Annual* 27 (1998): 209–26.

Dwivedi, Sharada, and Rahul Mehrotra. *Bombay: The Cities Within*. Bombay: Eminence Designs Pvt. Ltd., 1995.

Eco, Umberto. *Baudolino*. Translated by William Weaver. New York: Harcourt, 2000.

———. *The Name of the Rose*. Translated by William Weaver. New York: Warner, 1984.

Einstein, Albert. *Relativity*. Translated by Robert W. Lawson. Amherst, NY: Prometheus Books, 1995.

English, James F. "Modernist Joke-Work: *Pale Fire* and the Mock Transcendence of Mockery." *Contemporary Literature* 33, no. 1 (1992): 74–90.

Faulkner, William. *Absalom, Absalom!* New York: Vintage, 1991.

Field, Andrew. *Nabokov: His Life and Art*. Boston: Little, Brown and Co., 1967.

Field, David. "Fluid Worlds: Lem's *Solaris* and Nabokov's *Ada*." *Science Fiction Studies* 13 (1986): 329–44.

Fish, Stanley. "Boutique Multiculturalism or, Why Liberals Are Incapable of Thinking About Hate Speech." *Critical Inquiry* 23, no. 2 (1997): 378–95.

Fludernik, Monika. "The Diasporic Imaginary: Postcolonial Reconfigurations in the Context of Multiculturalism." In *Diaspora and Multiculturalism: Common Traditions and New Developments*, edited by Monika Fludernik, xi–xxxviii. New York: Rodopi, 2003.

Fowler, Douglas. *Reading Nabokov*. Ithaca, NY: Cornell University Press, 1974.
Freedman, Carl. *Critical Theory and Science Fiction*. Hanover, NH: Wesleyan University Press, 2000.
Foster, John Burt. *Nabokov's Art of Memory and European Modernism*. Princeton, NJ: Princeton University Press, 1993.
Foucault, Michel. *The Order of Things: An Archeology of the Human Sciences*. New York: Pantheon, 1970.
Gane, Gillian. "Migrancy, the Cosmopolitan Intellectual, and the Global City in *The Satanic Verses*." *Modern Fiction Studies* 48 (2002): 18–49.
Geertz, Clifford, ed. *Old Societies and New States: The Quest for Modernity in Asia and Africa*. New York: Free Press, 1963.
Gezari, Janet. "Chess and Chess Problems." In *The Garland Companion to Vladimir Nabokov*, edited by Vladimir Alexandrov, 44–54. New York: Garland, 1995.
Gokhale, Shanta. "Rich Theatre, Poor Theatre." In *Bombay: Mosaic of Modern Culture*, edited by Sujata Patel and Alice Thorner, 194–209. Bombay: Oxford University Press, 1995.
Goonetilleke, D. C. R. A. *Salman Rushdie*. New York: St. Martin's, 1998.
Gorra, Michael. *After Empire: Scott, Naipaul, Rushdie*. Chicago, IL: University of Chicago Press, 1997.
Greenberg, Jonathan. "'The Base Indian' or 'The Base Judean'?: *Othello* and the Metaphor of the Palimpsest in Salman Rushdie's *The Moor's Last Sigh*." *Modern Language Studies* 29, no. 2 (1999): 93–107.
Gross, Paul R., and Norman Levitt. *Higher Superstition: The Academic Left and Its Quarrels with Science*. Baltimore, MD: Johns Hopkins University Press, 1994.
Grossmith, Robert. "Shaking the Kaleidoscope: Physics and Metaphysics in Nabokov's *Bend Sinister*." *Russian Literature Triquarterly* 24 (1991): 151–61.
Harris, Susan Cannon. "Invasive Procedures: Imperial Medicine and Population Control in *Ulysses* and *The Satanic Verses*." *James Joyce Quarterly* 35, no. 2–3 (1998): 373–99.
Hayles, N. Katherine. "Making a Virtue of Necessity: Pattern and Freedom in Nabokov's *Ada*." *Contemporary Literature* 23 (1982): 32–51.
Herder, Johann Gottfried. *Outlines of a Philosophy of the History of Man*. London: J. Johnson, 1800.
Heuzé, Gérard. "Cultural Populism: The Appeal of the Shiv Sena." In *Bombay: Metaphor for Modern India*, edited by Sujata Patel and Alice Thorner, 213–47. Bombay: Oxford University Press, 1996.
Hobsbawm, Eric J. *Nations and Nationalism Since 1870*. Cambridge: Cambridge University Press, 1990.
Hogan, Patrick Colm. "*Midnight's Children*: Kashmir and the Politics of Identity." *Twentieth Century Literature* 47 (2001): 510–44.
Huet, Marie-Hélène. *Monstrous Imagination*. Cambridge, MA: Harvard University Press, 1993.
Iser, Wolfgang. *The Act of Reading: A Theory of Aesthetic Response*. Baltimore, MD: Johns Hopkins University Press, 1978.
———. *The Implied Reader*. Baltimore, MD: Johns Hopkins University Press, 1974.

Jackson, Peter, Philip Crang, and Claire Dwyer, ed. *Transnational Spaces*. New York: Routledge, 2004.

JanMohammed, Abdul R. *Manichean Aesthetics: The Politics of Literature in Colonial Africa*. Amherst, MA: The University of Massachusetts Press, 1983.

Johnson, Don Barton. *Worlds in Regression: Some Novels of Vladimir Nabokov*. Ann Arbor, MI: Ardis, 1985.

Johnson, Julie M. "The Theory of Relativity and Modern Literature: An Overview and *The Sound and the Fury*." *Journal of Modern Literature* 10 (1983): 217–30.

Johnson, Kurt, and Steve Coates, *Nabokov's Blues: The Scientific Odyssey of a Literary Genius*. New York: McGraw-Hill, 2001.

Jussawalla, Feroza. "Resurrecting the Prophet: The Case of Salman, the Otherwise." *Public Culture* 2, no. 1 (1989): 106–17.

———. "Rushdie's *Dastan-e-Dilruba*: *The Satanic Verses* as Rushdie's Love Letter to Islam." In *Critical Essays on Salman Rushdie*, edited by M. Keith Booker, 78–106. New York: G. K. Hall, 1999.

Kadzis, Peter. "Rushdie Rocks: Interview with Salman Rushdie." *The Boston Phoenix*, May 10, 1999, 28–31.

Kane, Jean. "Embodied Panic: Revisiting Modernist "Religion" in the Controversies over *Ulysses* and *The Satanic Verses*." *Textual Practice* 20, no. 3 (2006): 419–40.

Kant, Immanuel. *Political Writings*. Edited by Hans Reiss. Translated by H. B. Nisbet. Cambridge: Cambridge University Press, 1991.

Kingston, Maxine Hong. *The Woman Warrior: Memoirs of a Girlhood Among Ghosts*. New York: Vintage, 1989.

Kroes, Rob. *Straddling Borders: The American Resonance in Transnational Identities*. Amsterdam: Vrije Universiteit Press, 2004.

Krueger, John R. "Nabokov's Zemblan." *Linguistics* 31 (1967): 44–49.

Krishnaswamy, Revathi. "Mythologies of Migrancy: Postcolonialism, Postmodernism and the Politics of (Dis)location." *ARIEL* 26, no. 1 (1995): 125–46.

Kuortti, Joel. "'Nomsense': Salman Rushdie's *The Satanic Verses*." *Textual Practice* 13, no. 1 (1999): 137–46.

Lahiri, Jhumpa. *Interpreter of Maladies*. New York: Houghton Mifflin, 1999.

Lakdawala, D. K. *Work, Wages and Well-Being in an Indian Metropolis*. Bombay: Bombay University Press, 1963.

Lakshman, Nirmala. "A Columbus of the Near-At-Hand." In *Salman Rushdie Interviews*, edited by Pradyumna S. Chauhan, 279–90. Westport, CT: Greenwood, 2001.

Lange, Berad-Peter. "Dislocations: Migrancy in Nabokov and Rushdie." *Anglia: Zeitschrift für Englische Philologie* 117, no. 3 (1999): 395–411.

Lee, Judith. "The Mask of Form in *Out of Africa*." In *Isak Dinesen: Critical Views*, edited by Olga Anastasia Pelensky, 267–82. Athens, OH: Ohio University Press, 1993.

Leggatt, Judith. "Other Worlds, Other Selves: Science Fiction in Salman Rushdie's *The Ground Beneath Her Feet*." *ARIEL* 33, no.1 (2002): 105–25.

LeGuin, Ursula K. *The Left Hand of Darkness*. New York: Ace, 1976.

Linguanti, Elsa. "Different Whatnesses." In *The Great Work of Making Real: Salman Rushdie's* The Ground Beneath Her Feet, edited by Elsa Linguanti and Viktoria Tchernichova, 151–63. Pisa: Edizioni ETS, 2003.

Lipscomb, David. "Caught in a Strange Middle Ground: Contesting History in Salman Rushdie's *Midnight's Children.*" *Diaspora: A Journal of Transnational Studies* 2 (1991): 163–89.

Loomba, Ania. "'Local-Manufacture Made-in-India Othello Fellows': Issues of Race, Hybridity and Location in Post-Colonial Shakespeares." In *Post-Colonial Shakespeares*, edited by Ania Loomba and Martin Orkin, 143–63. London: Routledge, 1998.

Magnusson, Magnus and Hermann Palsson, trans. *The Vinland Sagas: The Norse Discovery of America. Grænlendinga Saga and Eirik's Saga.* Baltimore, MD: Penguin Books, 1965.

Mailloux, Steven. *Interpretive Conventions: The Reader in the Study of American Fiction.* Ithaca, NY: Cornell University Press, 1982.

Mandeville, Sir John. *The Travels of Sir John Mandeville: The Version of the Cotton Manuscript in Modern Spelling.* London: Macmillan, 1923.

Mann, Harveen Sachdeva. "'Being Borne Across': Translation and Salman Rushdie's *The Satanic Verses.*" *Criticism* 37, no. 2 (1995): 281–308.

Manolescu, Monica. "'Verbal Adventures in the Inky Jungle': Marco Polo and John Mandeville in Vladimir Nabokov's *The Gift.*" *Cycnos* 24, no. 1 (2007): 119–29.

Manvell, Roger, and Lewis Jacobs. *The International Encyclopedia of Film.* New York: Bonanza, 1975.

Mason, Bobbie Ann. *Nabokov's Garden: A Guide to* Ada. Ann Arbor, MI: Ardis, 1969.

McCarthy, Mary. *The Writing on the Wall.* New York: Harcourt, Brace and World, 1962.

McCarthy, Penny. "Nabokov's *Ada* and Sidney's *Arcadia.*" *Modern Language Review* 99, no. 1 (2004): 17–31.

McHale, Brian. *Postmodernist Fiction.* New York: Routledge, 1987.

McMillin, Arnold. "*The Satanic Verses* and *Master i Margarita.*" In *Bulgakov: The Novelist-Playwright*, edited by Lesley Milne, 232–43. Luxembourg: Harwood, 1995.

Meyer, Priscilla. "Anglophonia and Optimysticism: *Sebastian Knight*'s Bookshelves." In *Russian Literature and the West: A Tribute for David M. Bethea*, edited by Alexander Dolinin, Lazar Fleishman, and Leonid Livak, 212–26. Stanford: Stanford University Press, 2008.

———. *Find What the Sailor Has Hidden.* Middletown, CT: Wesleyan University Press, 1988.

Mondal, Anshuman A. "*The Ground Beneath Her Feet* and *Fury*: The Reinvention of Location." In *The Cambridge Companion to Salman Rushdie*, edited by Abdulrazak Gurnah, 169–83. Cambridge: Cambridge University Press, 2007.

Monti, Alessandro. "A Hoarding of Goats and Rumours of Mermaids: Puzzling out Myth in *The Ground Beneath Her Feet.*" In *The Great Work of Making Real: Salman Rushdie's* The Ground Beneath Her Feet, edited by Elsa Linguanti and Viktoria Tchernichova, 43–53. Pisa: Edizioni ETS, 2003.

Morson, Gary Saul, and Caryl Emerson. "Bakhtin." In *The Johns Hopkins Guide to Literary Theory and Criticism*, edited by Michael Groden and Martin Kreiswirth, 63–68. Baltimore, MD: The Johns Hopkins University Press, 1994.

Nabokov, Vladimir. *Ada, or Ardor*. New York: Vintage, 1990.

———. *The Annotated Lolita*. Edited by Alfred Appel, Jr. New York: Vintage, 1991.

———. *Bend Sinister*. New York: Vintage, 1990.

———. *The Gift* Translated by Michael Scammell and Vladimir Nabokov. New York: Vintage, 1991.

———. *Pale Fire*. New York: G. P. Putnam's Sons, 1962.

———. *Poems and Problems*. New York: McGraw-Hill, 1970.

———. *Speak, Memory*. New York: G. P. Putnam's Sons, 1966.

———. *Strong Opinions*. New York: Vintage, 1990.

———. "Texture of Time." Holograph notes (undated). The Berg Collection of English and American Literature, The New York Public Library, Astor, Lenox and Tilden Foundations.

Naipaul, V. S. *The Enigma of Arrival*. New York: Penguin, 1987.

———. *India: A Wounded Civilization*. New York: Vintage, 2003.

Nandy, Ashis. *The Tao of Cricket: On Games of Destiny and the Destiny of Games*. New York: Viking, 1989.

Nicol, Charles. "Ada or Disorder." In *Nabokov's Fifth Arc: Nabokov and Others on His Life's Work*, edited by J. E. Rivers and Charles Nicol, 230–41. Austin, TX: University of Texas Press, 1982.

Noor, Ronny. "Misrepresentation of History in Salman Rushdie's *Midnight's Children*." *Notes on Contemporary Literature* 26 (1996): 7–8.

Nussbaum, Martha C. *For Love of Country: Debating the Limits of Patriotism*. Boston: Beacon, 1996.

Patel, Sujata. Personal interview, Pune, India, June 9, 2003.

———. "Bombay and Mumbai: Identities, Politics, and Populism." In *Bombay and Mumbai: The City in Transition*, edited by Sujata Patel and Jim Masselos, 3–30. New Delhi: Oxford University Press, 2003.

Patel, Sujata, and Alice Thorner, ed. *Bombay: Metaphor for Modern India*. Bombay: Oxford University Press, 1996.

Pelensky, Olga Anastasia. *Isak Dinesen: The Life and Imagination of a Seducer*. Athens, OH: Ohio University Press, 1991.

Peterson, Ronald E. "Zemblan: Nabokov's Phony Scandinavian Language." *Vladimir Nabokov Research Newsletter* 12 (1984): 29–37.

Pifer, Ellen. *Nabokov and the Novel*. Cambridge, MA: Harvard University Press, 1980.

Pike, Burton. *The Image of the City in Modern Literature*. Princeton, NJ: Princeton University Press 1981.

Pirbhai, Mariam. "The Paradox of Globalization as an 'Untotalizable Totality' in Salman Rushdie's *The Ground Beneath Her Feet*." *The International Fiction Review* 28 (2001): 54–66.

Pratt, Mary Louise. *Imperial Eyes: Travel Writing and Transculturation*. New York: Routledge, 1992.

Privat, Edmond. *The Life of Zamenhof.* Translated by Ralph Eliott. London: George Allen and Unwin, 1931.
Proper, Ida Sedgwick. *Monhegan, the Cradle of New England.* Portland, ME: The Southworth Press, 1930.
Purandare, Vaibhav. *The Sena Story.* Bombay: Business Publications, 1999.
Quine, W. V. O. *Word and Object.* Cambridge, MA: MIT University Press, 1960.
Rauwerda, Antje M. "'Angelicdevilish' Combinations: Milton's Satan and Salman Rushdie's *The Satanic Verses.*" *Journal of Postcolonial Writing* 41 (2005): 94–107.
Rée, Jonathan. "The Experience of Nationality." In *Cosmopolitics: Thinking and Feeling beyond the Nation*, edited by Pheng Cheah and Bruce Robbins, 77–90. Minneapolis, MN: University of Minnesota Press, 1998.
Reynolds, Teri. "Spacetime and Imagetext." *The Germanic Review* 73 (1998): 161–74.
Rossi, Elena. "'Against an amnesiac culture': Greek and Latin Mythology in *The Ground Beneath Her Feet.*" In *The Great Work of Making Real: Salman Rushdie's* The Ground Beneath Her Feet, edited by Elsa Linguanti and Viktoria Tchernichova, 23–41. Pisa: Edizioni ETS, 2003.
Roy, Arundhati. *The God of Small Things.* New York: Harper Perennial, 1998.
Rushdie, Salman. "The Birth Pangs of *Midnight's Children.*" *The Times* (London) April 1, 2006.
———. *The Enchantress of Florence.* New York: Random House, 2008.
———. *The Ground Beneath Her Feet.* New York: Henry Holt, 1999.
———. *Imaginary Homelands: Essays and Criticism 1981–1991.* London: Granta, 1991.
———. *Midnight's Children.* New York: Penguin, 1981.
———. *The Moor's Last Sigh.* New York: Pantheon, 1995.
———. *The Satanic Verses.* Dover, DE: The Consortium, 1988.
———. *Step Across This Line.* New York: Random House, 2002.
Said, Edward W. *The World, the Text, and the Critic.* Cambridge, MA: Harvard University Press, 1983.
Sanga, Jaina C. *Salman Rushdie's Postcolonial Metaphors: Migration, Translation, Hybridity, Blasphemy and Globalization.* Westport, CT: Greenwood, 2001.
Sawhney, Simona. "Satanic Choices: Poetry and Prophecy in Rushdie's Novel." *Twentieth Century Literature* 45, no. 3 (1999): 253–77.
Schultheis, Alexandra W. "Postcolonial Lack and Aesthetic Promise in *The Moor's Last Sigh.*" *Twentieth Century Literature* 47 (2001): 569–96.
Schiller, Nina Glick. "The Situation of Transnational Studies." *Identities* 4 (1997): 155–66.
Seidel, Michael. "Stereoscope: Nabokov's *Ada* and *Pale Fire.*" In *Vladimir Nabokov*, edited by Harold Bloom, 235–57. New York: Chelsea House, 1987.
Shakespeare, William. *The Riverside Shakespeare.* Edited by G. Blakemore Evans and J. J. M. Tobin. New York: Houghton Mifflin, 1996.
Sharma, Shaijla. "Salman Rushdie: The Ambivalence of Migrancy." *Twentieth Century Literature* 47, no. 4 (2001): 596–618.
Shelley, Percy Bysshe. *Poetry and Prose.* Edited by Donald H. Reiman and Sharon B. Powers. New York: Norton, 1977.
Smith, Michael Peter. *Transnational Urbanism: Locating Globalization.* Oxford: Blackwell, 2001.

Smith, Zadie. *On Beauty*. New York: Penguin, 2005.
Spivak, Gayatri Chakravorty. *A Critique of Postcolonial Reason: Toward a History of the Vanishing Present*. Cambridge, MA: Harvard University Press, 1999.
———. *Outside in the Teaching Machine*. New York: Routledge, 1993.
Steiner, George. *Extraterritorial: Papers on Literature and the Language Revolution*. New York: Atheneum, 1976.
Stierstorfer, Klaus. "Wobbly Grounds: Postmodernism's Precarious Footholds in Novels by Malcolm Bradbury, David Parker, Salman Rushdie, Graham Swift." In *Beyond Postmodernism: Reassessments in Literature, Theory, and Culture*, edited by Klaus Stierstorfer, 213–34. New York: Walter de Gruyter, 2003.
Su, John. "Epic of Failure: Disappointment as Utopian Fantasy in *Midnight's Children*." *Twentieth Century Literature* 47 (2002): 545–68.
Suleri, Sara. *The Rhetoric of English India*. Chicago, IL: University of Chicago Press, 1992.
Suter, David. "Of the Devil's Party: The Marriage of Heaven and Hell in *Satanic Verses*." *South Asian Review* 16, no. 13 (1992): 63–77.
Swanson, Roy Arthur. "Nabokov's *Ada* as Science Fiction." *Science Fiction Studies* 2, no. 1 (1975): 76–88.
Sweeney, Susan Elizabeth. "'By some sleight of *land*': How Nabokov Rewrote America." In *The Cambridge Companion to Vladimir Nabokov*, edited by Julian W. Connolly, 65–84. New York: Cambridge University Press, 2005.
———. "Executing Sentences in *Lolita* and the Law." *Punishment, Politics, and Culture* 30 (2003): 185–209.
Syed, Mujeebuddin. "*Midnight's Children* and Its Indian Con-Texts." *Journal of Commonwealth Literature* 29, no. 2 (1994): 95–108.
Taylor, Edwin F., and John Archibald Wheeler. *Spacetime Physics*. San Francisco: W. H. Freeman and Co., 1963.
Tchernichova, Viktoria. "'The outsideness of what we're inside': Double Vision as Künstlerästhetik in *The Ground Beneath Her Feet*." In *The Great Work of Making Real: Salman Rushdie's* The Ground Beneath Her Feet, edited by Elsa Linguanti and Viktoria Tchernichova, 69–90. Pisa: Edizioni ETS, 2003.
———. "'The solutions to the problems of art are always technical': Some Observations on Textual Topologies." In *The Great Work of Making Real: Salman Rushdie's* The Ground Beneath Her Feet, edited by Elsa Linguanti and Viktoria Tchernichova, 165–83. Pisa: Edizioni ETS, 2003.
Tekiner, Christina. "Time in *Lolita*." *Modern Fiction Studies* 25 (1979): 463–69.
Ten Kortenaar, Neil. "*Midnight's Children* and the Allegory of History." *ARIEL* 26 (1995): 41–62.
———. "Salman Rushdie's Magical Realism and the Return of the Inescapable Romance." *University of Toronto Quarterly: A Canadian Journal of the Humanities* 71 (2002): 765–85.
———. *Self, Nation, Text in Salman Rushdie's* Midnight's Children. Montreal: McGill-Queen's University Press, 2004.
Teverson, Andrew S. "Fairy Tale Politics: Free Speech and Multiculturalism in *Haroun and the Sea of Stories*." *Twentieth Century Literature* 47, no. 4 (2001): 444–66.

Thompson, Jon. "Superman and Salman Rushdie: *Midnight's Children* and the Disillusionment of History." *Journal of Commonwealth and Postcolonial Studies* 3 (1995): 1–23.
Thurman, Judith. *Isak Dinesen: The Life of a Storyteller.* New York: Picador, 1982.
Toker, Leona. "Nabokov and Bergson on Duration and Reflexivity." In *Nabokov's World, Volume One: The Shape of Nabokov's World*, edited by Jane Grayson, Arnold McMillin, and Priscilla Meyer, 132–39. London: Palgrave, 2002.
Tolkien, J. R. R. *The Return of the King.* New York: Ballantine Books, 1972.
Tölölyan, Kachig. "Rethinking Diaspora(s): Stateless Power in the Transnational Moment." *Diaspora* 5, no. 1 (1996): 3–36.
Trousdale, Rachel. "Faragod Bless Them: *Anna Karenin* and Electricity in *Ada*." *Nabokov Studies* 7 (2003): 119–28.
———. "Incest and Intertext: *Mansfield Park* in *Ada*." *The Nabokovian* 61 (2008): 48–52.
———. "Self-Invention in Isak Dinesen's 'The Flood at Norderney.'" *Scandinavian Studies* 74, no. 2 (2002): 205–22.
Varma, Rashmi. "Provinicalizing the Global City: From Bombay to Mumbai." *Social Text* 22, no. 4 (2004): 65–89.
Walcott, Derek. *Selected Poems.* Edited by Edward Baugh. New York: Farrar, Straus, and Giroux, 2007.
Werbner, Pnina. "Allegories of Sacred Imperfection: Magic, Hermeneutics, and Passion in *The Satanic Verses*." *Current Anthropology: A World Journal of the Human Sciences* 37 (1996): 55–86.
Whiting, Frederick. "'The Strange Particularity of the Lover's Preference': Pedophilia, Pornography, and the Anatomy of Monstrosity in *Lolita*." *American Literature* 70, no. 4 (1998): 833–62.
Whitrow, G. J. *The Natural Philosophy of Time.* New York, NY: Harper, 1963.
Wilson, Rob, and Wimal Dissanayake, ed. *Global/Local: Cultural Production and the Transnational Imaginary.* Durham, NC: Duke University Press, 1996.
Wolpert, Stanley. *A New History of India: Fifth Edition.* Oxford: Oxford University Press, 1997.
Wood, Michael. "Enigmas and Homelands." In *On Modern British Fiction*, edited by Zachary Leader, 77–92. Oxford: Oxford University Press, 2002.
———. *The Magician's Doubts: Nabokov and the Risks of Fiction.* Princeton, NJ: Princeton University Press, 1994.
Yeoh, Brenda S. A., Michael W. Charney, and Tong Chee Kiong, ed. *Approaching Transnationalisms: Studies on Transnational Societies, Multicultural Contacts, and Imaginings of Home.* Boston: Kluwer Academic Publishers, 2003.
Young, Robert J. C. *Colonial Desire: Hybridity in Theory, Culture and Race.* New York: Routledge, 1995.
Zeno, Nicolò. *The Voyages of the Venetian Brothers, Nicolò and Antonio Zeno, to the Northern Seas, in the XIVth Century, Comprising the Latest Known Accounts of the Lost Colony of Greenland; and of the Northmen in America Before Columbus.* Translated and edited by Richard Henry Major. New York: Burt Franklin, 1964.
Zimmer, Dieter E. *A Guide to Nabokov's Butterflies and Moths.* Berlin: D. E. Zimmer, 2003.

Index

absolutism, 89, 119, 121–23, 129–31, 135, 151, 173, 180, 194
Akbar, Emperor, 136–37, 212
Albee, Edward, 32
Alexandrov, Vladimir, 38
Alter, Robert, 29, 60
alternate history. *See* worlds, fictional
Alvarez, Julia, 30
America, 37–47, 52–55, 59–62, 63–64, 66, 67–69, 71, 74–75, 89, 141, 155–56, 176, 186, 188
    alternate, 25, 35, 58, 59–62, 66
    belonging in, 25, 41, 54, 155–56, 162, 182
    colonization of, 54, 60, 61–63, 165, 203–4
    as destination of exile, 31, 33, 62, 155–56, 182, 188, 217
    fusion in, 37–41, 46, 52–55, 56, 59–61, 69, 71, 74–75, 84, 86, 141, 155–56, 200, 205
    history of, 57, 59–60, 61–64, 156–58
    idealized, 43, 45, 68, 71, 89
    incompatible with home country, 25, 38, 45, 156
    as invented country, 19, 35, 38, 155–56, 193
    literature of, 40, 76, 141, 152–53, 181–82, 191, 193, 216
    national identity in, 41, 68, 95, 141, 155–56, 186, 193, 216
    natural world of, 42–46, 52–55, 57, 68, 71, 74–75
    pre-Columbian settlement of, 60, 61–62, 63–64, 66

    "real," 42–43, 45, 46, 66
    See also Europe and Europeans; landscape; Russia, synthesized with other places
Anderson, Benedict, 11–12, 16, 92, 178
Antiterra, 19, 58, 59–64, 66–69, 72, 73–74, 80, 88, 142, 204
Appadurai, Arjun, 10, 11–12, 174, 191
Appiah, Kwame Anthony, 8–10, 13, 94, 105
Apsara, Vina, 143, 144–45, 148–49, 150, 152, 153–54, 155–60
    on America, 155–56
Ashes and Diamonds, 153
Austen, Jane, 73
authorial power, 15–16, 56–57, 68, 71, 77, 80, 116–17, 122–23, 128–29, 132, 157
    authorial alter egos, 128, 152–53, 154

Bakhtin, Mikhail, 10, 17–18, 115, 125, 146, 150, 151, 179, 194
Baldwin, James, 163, 193
Beckett, Samuel, 193
Bellow, Saul, 153
Bergson, Henri, 81–82, 84, 85, 206
Bhabha, Homi, 3–5, 7, 8, 10, 12, 13, 22, 92, 105, 121, 134, 145, 193
binaries, 5–6, 76, 109, 121–22, 129, 131, 136, 145, 150–51, 156, 162
Blackwell, Stephen, 74, 76–77
Blake, William, 121, 138
body politic, 92, 108–9, 113, 116, 120, 192
Bollywood, 35, 99, 121, 132, 136–37

INDEX

Bombay, 9, 32, 90, 91–93, 96–101, 104–8, 112, 114, 133, 137–38, 141, 143–44, 149, 152, 155–56, 157
  corruption in, 106, 152
  as cosmopolitan center, 96–99, 105, 107, 114–15, 141
  destruction of, 106–7, 108, 114, 138, 144
  history of, 92, 96–100
  as metaphor for India, 92, 96–98, 104, 114–15, 133, 143
  name of, 97, 104
Booker, M. Keith, 102, 121, 125, 129, 130
Booker Prize, 32
Borges, Jorge Luis, 153, 154, 172–73, 193
Boyd, Brian, 59, 62, 67, 74, 188, 201–2
Bradley, Marion Zimmer, 167
Brennan, Timothy, 94, 109, 129
Brooks, Geraldine, 193
Bulgakov, Mikhail, 121
Burgess, Anthony, 153
butterflies, 52–53, 69, 74–75, 79
Byron, George Gordon, Lord, 73

Calvino, Italo, 18
Cama, Gayomart, 142, 151, 155, 156
Cama, Ormus, 142, 143, 144, 145–57, 158–61, 188, 213, 214
  synthesis through art by, 154–55, 160
Cama, Sir Darius Xerxes, 143–45, 149
Cather, Willa, 193
censorship, 32, 67, 126. *See also* "Rushdie affair," the
Chabon, Michael, 25, 38, 73, 164, 181–85, 189–92, 193, 117
  Amazing Adventures of Kavalier and Clay, The, 182, 190–91
  life, 182, 191
  use of Nabokov, 182–84, 190–91
  Yiddish Policemen's Union, The, 181, 182–85, 188–91

Chamcha, Saladin, 34–35, 94, 121, 124, 127, 128–32, 136, 137–38, 166
  "evil Mr Chamcha," 124, 130
  and pluralist identity, 130–32, 137–38
Chandra, Vikram, 16, 21, 29
charismatic leaders, 99, 108–10, 113, 137
Chateaubriand, François-René, 43, 45, 73
Chaudhri, Nirad, 100
chess, 34, 182–90
Clifford, James, 12, 15
clocks, 82–83, 85, 87–88
colonies, 3–5, 6, 22–23, 26, 28–29, 61, 63, 97–98, 105, 121, 129, 143, 165, 167, 213. *See also* postcolonial theory
communalism, 95–101, 102, 104–5, 107–8, 111–12, 114, 115, 131, 137, 164, 172, 177
communism, 33, 60, 100, 101, 102, 113, 159, 208
communities. *See* nations and nationalism; transnationalism
  alienation from, 24, 96, 111–12, 113, 180
  forming, 1–2, 5–6, 9–10, 15–17, 19, 28, 89–90, 94, 120, 132–34, 136, 144–45, 162, 165, 181–82
  ideal and idealized, 7, 28–29, 55, 60, 67–68, 71, 90, 91, 113–14, 116–17, 167, 184–85, 194–95
  imagined, 11–12, 22, 89–90, 114, 166–67, 177–78
  intentional, 2, 16, 131, 164, 181
  nation-like, 12, 15, 28, 90, 126, 198
  of outsiders, 2, 13, 17, 89–90, 141, 144–45, 162
  and space, 6, 13–14, 16, 22, 26–27, 28–29, 48, 57, 89, 92, 164, 174–75
Cone, Allie, 34, 35, 88, 124, 128, 134, 158, 195

Conrad, Joseph, 14, 17, 21, 22–23, 24, 27, 75, 166
cosmopolitanism, 7–10, 27, 39, 91–101, 105–8, 114–15, 194
  "boutique," 8, 13, 41, 121, 133, 174
  and fiction, 9–10, 29, 89–90, 132, 181–82
  global vs. local, 8–9, 105–6, 110, 114–15, 132, 198
  Kantian, 7–8, 185, 194
  limits of, 7–8, 91, 94–95, 98–100, 104–6, 108, 113–14
  "rooted," 8–10, 12–14, 90, 92, 94–95, 105, 133, 141, 163, 181–82, 190, 194
  urban vs. rural in, 9
cricket, 104–5, 145, 192
crown jewels, 53, 183, 195
Cybulski, Zbigniew, 153–54

Darkbloom, Vivian, 33, 61
Davenport, Guy, 18–19
devil, 35, 51, 121, 122, 127–29, 137, 186
dialogue, 16, 93, 115–16, 125, 132, 146, 150–51, 154–56, 189, 194
  in cosmopolitanism, 8–10, 12, 19, 94, 105, 132–33, 185
  dialogic novels, 17–18, 20–21, 68, 92, 94, 115, 132, 146, 149, 162
diaspora, 11, 13, 134, 139, 182, 198
Díaz, Junot, 21
Dickens, Charles, 121
Dinesen, Isak, 6, 7, 17, 21, 22, 25, 26–29, 30, 80, 116, 163, 199, 200
displacement, shared, 1–2, 13, 16–17, 30, 31, 106, 116–17, 126, 133–34, 139, 141–42, 144, 158, 162, 163–64, 181–82, 189–90, 194–95
Doležel, Lubomír, 19, 72

Eco, Umberto, 167–75, 177, 181, 182, 185
  Baudolino, 169–74, 179
  Name of the Rose, The, 168–69, 173

Eddas, 47, 64
Eden, 43, 62, 68, 106, 108, 111–12
Einstein, Albert, 76, 77–78, 79, 80–81, 82, 205. *See also* special relativity
Eliot, T. S., 138
Ellis, Brett Easton, 119
embodiment of national and transnational spaces, 6–7, 14, 40–41, 44, 56, 92, 94, 98, 100–101, 104, 108–12, 114–16, 120, 132, 135–38, 143, 147, 153–54, 166, 179, 185, 192. *See also* heroism; metaphors: and literalism
Emergency, the, 23, 32, 96, 99, 101, 103
"Emma Bovary test," the, 19–20, 127, 132, 143, 150, 195
epistemologies, 2, 17, 19, 26, 54, 55, 57, 93, 121, 143, 167, 173, 194, 195
Estotiland, 59–64, 66
Eugenides, Jeffrey, 181, 193
Europe and Europeans, 26–28, 33, 37–46, 49, 52, 54, 61, 63, 66, 67–68, 171, 173, 176, 189, 191, 216, 217
  art and culture of, 31, 34, 39, 40–41, 47, 52, 63, 71, 105, 152, 167, 169, 173
  colonization by, 3, 6, 26–27, 61, 66, 96, 98, 105, 143, 165,
  ideas about America of, 43, 45, 54–55, 67–68
exile, 2, 15, 24, 54–56, 60, 74, 112, 117, 131, 134, 144, 182, 189, 216
experience, individual, 119–20, 127, 129, 138–39, 143, 170

family, 26, 30, 59, 89, 159–60, 163, 166, 181–83, 189–90
  allegiance to and of, 7, 102, 112, 144, 178–79
  boundaries of, 59, 117, 166, 178, 182
  history, 65–66, 82, 96, 100
  See also incest

Farishta, Gibreel, 34–35, 88, 117, 121, 122–24, 128–29, 130, 132, 133, 136–37, 138, 148, 158
and Nabokov, 34–35, 117, 138
fatwa. See "Rushdie affair," the
Faulkner, William, 167, 180, 193
fictionality, 17–22, 34, 47–48, 71, 90, 123–24, 130, 142, 144–46 148–50, 152–54, 157–59, 161–62
bridging reality and fiction, 54, 56–57, 58, 63, 66, 71, 88, 107, 152–54, 157, 160, 164, 169–70, 195
and metafiction, 20–21, 34–35, 53–54, 152–54, 158–61
See also memoir; poetry and truth; truth, constructed vs. objective; worlds, fictional
Fielding, Raman, 104–8, 114, 115, 116, 192
Fish, Stanley, 8, 13, 41, 133, 174
Flaubert, Gustave, 20, 43
forgery, 51–52, 64, 66, 143, 147, 169–70, 174
Foster, John Burt, 31, 81, 205
Foucault, Michel, 18
frames of reference, 34, 71, 74, 78, 84, 86–88, 145, 147, 160–62, 195. *See also* relativity; twins: twin paradox
France, 20, 47, 72
Freedman, Carl, 72
future, 55–56, 67, 81–82, 86–87, 93–94, 104, 115, 149, 189

Gallant, Mavis, 193
Gandhi, Indira, 32, 99, 108, 109, 114
as the Widow, 101, 109
Gandhi, Mohandas K., 23–24, 97, 108–13, 115, 137, 147, 209
Geertz, Clifford, 95
geography, 18–19, 26, 37, 39, 54–55, 59, 74–75, 89–90, 135, 144, 161, 163, 168, 181, 217
and imaginative truth, 25–26, 28, 48–50, 100, 165
and synthesis, 55, 74, 135–36, 168–69, 184, 187

globalism and globalization, 5, 9, 10, 99, 105–8, 115, 117, 141, 159, 164, 191, 193, 198,
God and gods, 16, 29, 35, 48, 56, 80, 84, 97, 104, 120, 121, 122–23, 125, 126, 127–29, 132, 135, 136–37, 151, 172, 213. *See also* authorial power
Goldberg, Myla, 181
Gradus, Jakob, 46, 190, 201
Greene, Graham, 193
Gross, Paul, and Norman Levitt, 77, 89

Hamza-nama cloths, 132, 134–35, 139
Hayles, N. Katherine, 85, 204
Haze, Charlotte, 40–42, 65, 68
Hemingway, Ernest, 163, 193
Herder, Johann Gottfried, 92, 95
heroism, 92–93, 102–4, 109–10, 112–16, 130, 134–35, 144, 156–57, 159–60, 182, 189–90, 209
Hinduism, 33, 104–5, 112, 134, 136–37, 187, 192, 208. *See also* nations and nationalism: Hindu
history, 15, 27, 57–59, 63, 67–68, 72, 107, 110, 112, 137, 145, 149, 159, 161, 187, 209
Hobsbawm, Eric, 92, 95
Hogan, Patrick Colm, 32–33, 102, 104, 105, 109–10, 113
houses, 26, 29, 40–42
Huet, Marie-Hélène, 166
Humbert, Humbert, 37, 39–46, 47, 48, 52, 54, 58, 68, 75, 175–77, 178, 179, 201
in *The Ground Beneath Her Feet*, 152
identity of, 18–19, 39–40, 176–77
monstrosity of, 175–77
and narrative reliability, 39, 44, 45, 57, 65, 67, 68, 127, 179
See also solipsism
hybridity, 2–8, 10, 12, 22, 29, 40–41, 46–47, 66, 68, 92, 120–22, 125, 131, 133–35, 138, 145, 155, 165–69, 180, 192
and ambiguity, 4–5, 193–94

and art, 40–41, 42, 53, 55–56, 76, 79–80, 98, 132–37, 154–57, 163, 188, 190–91, 195
biology and, 6, 41, 92, 164, 165–67, 178–79
failures of, 22–25, 94, 103, 166–69
See also Bakhtin, Mikhail; Bhabha, Homi

imagination, 2–3, 11, 23–25, 37, 48, 51–52, 93, 104
limits of, 44–46, 56, 84, 174
and the physical, 38, 45–46, 48, 50–52, 54, 89, 93, 114, 132, 163, 166, 178, 181
incest, 6, 73, 84, 102, 165–67, 175–77, 178–80
incompatible realities, 1, 13, 18–20, 22, 23, 25, 27, 42, 52, 131, 150, 156–57, 161, 179
India, 3–5, 11, 16, 23–24, 91–105, 108, 109–12, 114–17, 130–39, 141, 152, 178–79, 187, 193
communities in, 11, 95–100, 132–33
embodiments and representations of, 93–94, 98, 101, 109–10, 114–16, 135–37, 209
history of, 23, 32, 96–99, 103, 110–13
ideal, 92–93, 100, 114, 132
pluralism in, 23–24, 91, 95, 105, 108, 132–36, 138, 143,
synthesis in, 3–5, 23–24, 132–37
See also Bombay; nations and nationalism
Iser, Wolfgang, 15
Ishiguro, Kazuo, 21, 25, 193
Islam, 33, 120, 135, 137, 148, 165, 200

James, Henry, 182, 193
JanMohammed, Abdul R., 200
Johnson, Don Barton, 38, 73, 183, 188, 202
Johnson, Julie M., 77, 82

Joyce, James, 31, 138–39, 153, 163, 193
Jussawalla, Feroza, 119–20, 200

Kant, Immanuel. *See* cosmopolitanism
Kashmir, 108, 111–12, 135, 153
Kerouac, Jack, 153
Kinbote, Charles, 31, 34–35, 46–49, 51–57, 58, 64, 201
and America, 37, 46, 52–54
and art, 76, 142,
and narrative reliability, 37, 55, 64, 67, 123, 125, 127
Kingston, Maxine Hong, 7, 21, 25–26, 27, 34, 93, 116
Koran, the, 121, 123, 125–26, 132, 138
Krauss, Nicole, 193
"Kreutzer Sonata," 40–41
Krishnaswamy, Revathi, 7, 94
"Kugelmass Episode, The," 20–21

Lahiri, Jhumpa, 18, 25, 193
landscape, 37, 69, 74–75
of America, 41–46, 52–55, 57, 193, 195, 200
of Europe, 39, 41–43, 49
and Lolita's body, 41–42, 43–44
resistant, 42–43
synthetic, 37, 38, 44, 53–55, 66, 74–75, 195
Landsman, Meyer, 184–85, 188–90
language, 10, 11, 15, 25–27, 33, 35, 60–61, 127
creole, hybrid, invented, 26–27, 35, 73, 168–69, 177, 185, 187
Esperanto, 184–85
and fantastic worlds, 18, 25, 35, 152
French, 39, 40, 57, 60–61, 73
Indian languages, 3–4, 95, 96–97, 98, 99–100, 107
and knowledge, 26, 170–71
mixing and switching, 26, 40, 41, 73–74
and nation, 11, 95, 107, 183, 189–90

language (*continued*)
  Russian, 31, 33, 46–47, 57, 59–61, 75, 146, 176–77
  Swahili, 26–27, 28
  Yiddish, 183, 184–85, 192, 217
  Zemblan, 34–35, 46–47, 202
law, 10, 45, 113, 126, 127, 143, 176
LeGuin, Ursula K., 17
Leigh, Annabel, 31, 39–40, 41–42, 68, 176
Lipscomb, David, 100, 112
Llosa, Mario Vargas, 193
love, 39–41, 43, 55, 85, 126, 131–32, 143, 148–49, 156, 160, 162, 175–77, 178, 183, 189–90, 192, 204

madness, 25–26, 34, 46, 48, 53, 55, 57, 64, 123–24, 126
Mahabharata, 143
Mahound, 119–20, 121, 122–23, 124, 125–26, 129, 132, 133, 135
Mailloux, Steven, 199
Major, Richard Henry, 65–66
Mandeville, Sir John, 51–52, 55, 58, 68, 202
Manichaeism, 5, 122, 151, 154–56, 161, 162, 194
Mann, Harveen Sachdeva, 94, 126, 138
Manolescu, Monica, 51, 62, 65
Manuscript Found at Saragossa, The, 153
many-worlds theory, 72, 130, 150.
  See also special relativity; worlds, fictional: alternate
maps, 49, 59, 65, 85–86, 168
Marquez, Gabriel García, 193
Marvell, Andrew, 73
Mason, Bobbie Ann, 63, 84, 85
"Maunder's Praise of His Strowling Mort," 43
Maupassant, Guy de, 73
McHale, Brian, 2, 18–19, 20, 21, 25, 75, 161, 163
Melville, Herman, 182

memoir, 22, 25–29, 62, 81
  fictional, 44, 58, 62, 66, 88, 103
  See also Dinesen, Isak; Kinston, Maxine Hong; Nabokov Vladimir: *Speak, Memory*
"memory's truth," 80, 103, 110, 119
metafiction. *See* fictionality
metaphors
  and literalism, 25, 42, 49–53, 58, 71–72, 73, 74–75, 77–78, 89, 107, 114, 117, 119, 158–59, 163–64, 175, 188–90
  restrictive, 6, 10, 85, 92, 109, 130, 192
Methwold, William, 100, 143, 145, 149, 208
Meyer, Priscilla, 43, 53, 202, 217
Milton, John, 62, 120
miscegenation, 6, 10, 92, 167, 177, 180
monsters and monstrosity, 14, 52, 164, 165–69, 171–73, 175–81, 182, 183, 192

Nabokov, Véra, 31, 38, 187, 189
Nabokov, Vladimir, 21, 30–35, 37–69, 71–90, 93, 163, 164, 175–77, 181, 182–84, 185–90
  Ada, or Ardor, 21, 33, 37, 38, 57–64, 65–68, 71–73, 76–77, 78–90, 116, 142, 163, 192, 204, 205; blurb for, 61–62; composition of, 58, 66, 87; editor's note to, 87; interruptions in, 58, 61, 66, 82, 85–86; notes for, 78–79, 82; Van's transportation in, 57, 81, 83–84, 85–88
  appearance in own work, 33, 55–56, 75, 80, 87
  Bend Sinister, 31, 190
  Defense, The, 34, 35
  fusion of Europe and America by, 37–46, 54–55, 66, 187–88, 205
  Gift, The, 31, 39, 62, 65, 76
  Invitation to a Beheading, 31, 190
  life of, 31–32, 182, 187–88

Lolita, 19, 31, 37–38, 39–46, 56, 57, 58, 67–68, 71, 89, 152, 153, 163, 167, 175–77, 178, 179, 183;
Europe and America in, 39–46
mountains in, 42, 44–45, 48–51, 53, 57, 74–75, 83, 87
"otherworld theme" in, 31–32, 38, 80, 186, 190
Pale Fire, 31, 34–35, 37, 38, 39, 46–57, 58, 64, 68, 71, 72, 76–77, 89, 163, 190, 201–2, 205; authorship of, 46, 201–2; Kinbote's notes, 46, 49, 53; "Mountain View," 49–50; "Pale Fire," 46, 48, 50–51, 201–2; "special reality" in, 76–77, 142
Pnin, 200
Poems and Problems, 183, 187
and politics, 31, 32–33, 67
and puzzles, 39, 44, 58, 117, 182–83, 189
Real Life of Sebastian Knight, The, 31, 74, 217
Speak, Memory, 38, 59, 69, 74–75, 79, 80, 86, 182, 183–84, 185–86, 188
Strong Opinions, 31, 53, 79, 86, 183, 203
"Texture of Time, The" 79, 80–88, 205
and transnational writers, 30–31, 38, 68, 73, 89–90, 163–64, 167, 175, 182, 190–91
See also chess
Naipaul, V. S., 14, 17, 22, 23–24, 27, 75
Enigma of Arrival, The, 6, 24, 116, 192
and India, 11, 23–24, 96, 108, 133
Nanavati case, 113
narrators, 37–38, 39, 57, 62, 71, 87–88, 94, 123–29, 152, 166, 179, 204
and authority, 87–88, 115–16, 123, 125–26, 152
and construction of fictional world, 15, 25, 37–38, 57, 71, 87, 115–16

reliability, 25, 33, 64, 67, 68, 73, 107, 125–26, 127–29, 130, 142, 157, 166, 170, 204
See also Humbert, Humbert; Kinbote, Charles; Shade, John; "shifting 'I'"; Sinai, Saleem; Veen, Van; worlds, fictional; *see also under* Rushdie, Salman: *Satanic Verses*
nations and nationalism, 1–2, 7–8, 10, 11–13, 15–17, 22–24, 37–38, 90, 91–97, 101–2, 108–10, 114–17, 132–37, 182, 183, 184–87, 189, 195
alternatives to, 2, 13, 93, 132–33, 163–64, 186–87, 189–90
civic vs. ethnic, 95–97, 101, 104, 116–17
and fiction, 2, 15–17, 22–24, 31, 59, 89–90, 92–93, 107, 110, 132–33, 137, 169–70, 182, 184
and geography, 10, 18, 107, 133
Hindu, 91, 95, 97, 99, 104–5, 111–12, 116, 117, 120, 133, 192
in India, 23–24, 95, 97–98, 108, 112, 132–38
See also body politic; cosmopolitanism; embodiment of national and transnational spaces; Gandhi, Mohandas K.; Shiv Sena
Nehru, Jawaharlal, 97, 103, 112, 209
Newtonian mechanics, 77, 79
nymphets, 39, 42, 43, 176

Ondaatje, Michael, 7, 16, 21, 22, 25, 29, 193
Oranger, Ronald and Violet, 58, 62, 66, 87, 88
outsiders, 12, 15, 30, 71, 75, 77, 78, 80–81, 89–90, 93, 117, 136, 139, 143, 144–47, 154, 155, 157–58, 160, 162, 163, 166, 170, 182

Pakistan, 32, 96, 100, 102–3, 104, 111–12, 148, 178–79
Parker, Jesse Garon, 150, 152, 153, 156

Parsis, 95, 98, 137, 143, 151
Parvati-the-witch, 101, 102–3
Patel, Sujata, 97, 98, 100
photography and video, 126, 145, 153–54, 157, 195
physics. *See* Newtonian mechanics; science; special relativity
Pifer, Ellen, 67, 73
Plato, 52
pluralism, 16, 24, 91–96, 101, 103–4, 108, 115–17, 120, 126, 130–33, 135–36, 138, 143–44, 155, 178
of the self, 120, 129–31, 137–38, 139, 150, 155, 162, 180, 194
Pndapetzim, 169–73
Poe, Edgar Allan, 40, 42, 48
poetry and truth, 47–48, 50–51, 55, 57, 58, 80, 120, 123–24, 169. *See also* Shelley, Percy Bysshe
postcolonial theory, 2–6, 13, 105, 117, 119, 120–21, 135–36, 151, 161, 174–75, 193
postmodernism, 2, 16, 17–21, 31, 33, 71–72, 73, 77, 93, 117, 119, 160–61, 163–64, 167, 177, 193, 194. *See also* fictionality; worlds, fictional
postnational world, 10, 11, 174, 191
Pratt, Mary Louise, 14, 44, 165
Presley, Elvis. *See* Parker, Jesse Garon
process
in culture and identity, 3, 4, 9, 11, 12–13, 106, 120, 132–34, 137–38, 139, 160, 162, 179–80, 181–82, 193–95
in reading and writing, 15, 30, 37–38, 62, 79–80, 116, 139, 160, 193–94
propaganda, 66–67, 147–49, 152, 153, 157, 159, 162, 191
prostitutes, 32, 67, 86, 102, 211
purity, 31, 92, 99, 100, 104, 105, 121, 122, 166, 175, 179

puzzles, 16, 34, 39, 58, 116–17, 182–83, 189–90, 192. *See also* chess; crown jewels
Pynchon, Thomas, 17, 18, 31, 71–72, 161, 164

Quine, W. V. O., 170

Rai, 142, 143–45, 148, 149, 152–54, 156–60, 161, 162, 214
as insider, 145, 157
reliability, 145, 153–54, 156
readers
distance from text of, 62, 71, 78, 88, 142, 146, 162, 194, 209
education of, 5, 9–10, 30, 57, 75, 89–90, 120–21, 139, 186, 194
incomprehension by, 4, 35, 139, 150, 170–71
of Nabokov, 33–35, 37, 38–39, 56–57, 68, 71
privileged, 34, 56–57, 123, 139
responsibility of and participation by, 16–17, 18–21, 27, 39, 45, 56–57, 58–59, 88–90, 93, 116–17, 123, 142, 146–47, 162, 164, 195
and writers, 15–17, 55, 73–74, 116–17, 122, 139, 148, 149, 183, 193–94
See also worlds, fictional: consensus and consistency of
realism, 17, 71, 72, 73, 114, 124, 150
reality, shifting, 153–54, 160–61
relativity. *See* special relativity
rock 'n' roll, 1, 141, 144, 150, 151, 154–55, 160
Roy, Arundhati, 167, 180
Rushdie, Salman, 5, 13, 16, 21, 30–35, 57, 80, 91–95, 96, 98, 100–17, 119–39, 141–62, 163–64, 175, 177–79, 181, 182, 193
appearance in own work, 126, 128–29
"Birth Pangs of *Midnight's Children*, The" 32

comparison with Nabokov, 32–34, 92–93, 117, 119, 181
cosmopolitan ideal of, 91–95, 100, 120, 133–34, 138–39
Enchantress of Florence, The, 212
Fury, 141
Grimus, 32
Ground Beneath Her Feet, The, 21, 34, 57, 90, 117, 122, 141–62, 170, 188; as American novel, 141, 155–56; artists in, 145, 146, 152–57; ending of, 159–60; levels of reality in, 141–43, 149–54; *Midnight's Children* and, 143–44, 149; quotation marks in, 152
Haroun and the Sea of Stories, 32
Imaginary Homelands, 5, 32, 96, 97, 121, 131, 134, 143, 146
life, 32–33, 138 (*see also* "Rushdie affair," the)
Midnight's Children, 21, 32, 57, 80, 90, 91–96, 98, 100–104, 105, 107, 108–17, 119, 124, 141, 142, 143–44, 147, 149, 155, 167, 175, 177–79; ending of, 16, 93–95, 109, 114–15; Gandhi in, 109–13, 115, 137, 147
Moor's Last Sigh, The, 90, 91, 93, 94, 99, 100, 104–08, 114, 115, 116–17, 138, 141, 144, 149, 210; *Midnight's Children* and, 108, 149
and "official versions," 124–25, 148
Satanic Verses, The, 29, 32, 34–35, 88, 91, 94, 117, 119–39, 141, 143–44, 145, 150–51, 158, 167, 195, 210, 211; atheism and theism in, 121, 122–23, 125–29; narrator of, 34, 123, 124–25, 127–29, 130
Shame, 32, 128
Step Across This Line, 193
and transnational writers, 21, 25, 31, 122, 163–64, 193
use of Nabokov by, 31, 34–35, 92, 138, 152–53, 163, 193

"Rushdie affair," the, 32, 119–20, 122, 211
Russia, 31, 48–49, 55, 133, 154, 176, 186
  incompatible with other places, 38, 61
  synthesized with other places, 37–39, 40–41, 46–47, 56, 59–61, 72, 74–75, 84, 86, 188, 200, 205
  See also Soviet Union

Sabarmati, Commander, 112–13
Saeed, Mirza, 121, 129
Said, Edward, 3, 15, 165
Salman the Persian, 125–26
"satanic verses," 122–23, 124
Sawhney, Simona, 120, 126, 128, 132
Schiller, Nina Glick, 10, 12–13
science, 63, 71, 72–74, 76–85, 88–90. *See also* butterflies; Newtonian mechanics; space-time; special relativity
science fiction, 17, 72, 77, 82, 88, 152, 194
self-invention, 2, 22, 35, 46, 54, 56, 92, 116, 117, 129–32, 133–34, 139, 150, 174, 175–77, 181, 191
Shade, John, 31, 46–53, 54–55, 67, 76, 152, 154, 201, 205
  death of, 39, 46
  lack of ambition in poetry, 51
  "Mountain View," 49–50
  and Nabokov, 157
Shakespeare, William, 47, 53–56, 59–60, 121, 210
Shakespeare alley, 53–55
Shelley, Percy Bysshe, 50–51, 52–53, 55, 58, 59, 62, 71, 89
"shifting 'I,'" 65–66, 116
Shiva, 101–4, 107–9, 110, 113, 115, 116, 147
Shiv Sena, 91, 97, 99–100, 101, 102, 104–5, 106, 107–8, 109, 131–32, 138, 208

Shpilman, Mendel, 185, 188–89, 190, 217
Shri 420, 121, 133, 138, 210
Sinai, Saleem, 16, 93–94, 96, 98, 100–104, 105, 107–17, 119, 131, 136, 137, 138, 143–44, 147, 148, 149, 155, 163–64, 177–79, 208, 209
 and Bombay, 100
 death of (*see under* Rushdie, Salman: *Midnight's Children*)
 reliability of, 96, 103–4, 110, 111–12, 115, 119
Sitka Federal District, 184–85, 190, 217
Smith, Zadie, 16, 25, 29–30, 73, 181, 193
solipsism, 22, 27, 41, 43–45, 68, 73–74, 75, 81–82, 83–84, 120, 131, 166–67, 176, 179, 192
Soviet Union, 31, 33, 59–60, 67, 186
space-time, 75, 78–79, 80–81, 85–86, 163, 205
special relativity, 71, 72, 75, 76–90, 93, 205
 art, fiction, and, 77–81, 85, 89–90
 fundamentals of, 77, 79–80
 Nabokov's case against, 79, 80
 simultaneity in, 79–80, 82–83
 See also space-time; twins: twin paradox; *see also under* Nabokov, Vladimir: *Pale Fire*
Spivak, Gayatri, 13, 122
Steiner, George, 176–77
sterility, 6, 22, 23, 74, 101, 103, 165–67, 169, 180, 182, 184, 185, 187, 188, 192
Stoppard, Tom, 71–72
Stowe, Harriet Beecher, 16
Su, John, 100, 109, 207
Sufyan, Hind, 130, 132, 135–36, 137, 139, 145
suicide, 34, 46, 53, 55–56, 66, 84, 113
suimate, 188–89
Suleri, Sara, 5, 120, 193, 210
supernatural, 25–28, 31–32, 33, 49, 51, 58, 72, 74, 115–16, 122–25, 127–29, 136–37, 142, 148–49, 151, 160, 172, 178–79, 186, 189–90. *See also* devil; God and gods; Nabokov, Vladimir: "otherworld theme" in
Sweeney, Susan Elizabeth, 38, 45
synthesis. *See* hybridity
synthetic knowledge, 167–71, 173

Ten Kortenaar, Neil, 96, 100, 103, 112, 208, 209
Terra, 59, 60, 67, 88–89
Thackeray, Bal, 99, 104, 107, 108–9, 113
time, 60, 77–88, 187
 and displacement, 24, 39, 81, 87–88
 perceptual, 81–82, 87, 206
 scientific measurement of, 78, 79, 81, 83–84, 85,
 synthesis of, 41–42, 71, 74–75, 78, 80–82, 86, 87–88, 89, 187
 See also clocks; future; space-time
Toker, Leona, 81, 82
Tolkien, J. R. R., 20, 148–49, 151, 152, 159–60
transnational fiction, 1–3, 6–7, 9–10, 13–14, 15–19, 21–22, 27, 29–30, 57, 72–73, 77–78, 89–90, 93, 133–35, 163–67, 181–83, 191–92
 and the transnational canon, 31, 117, 122, 134–35, 163–64, 181–83, 191, 193, 195
transnationalism, 12–13, 16, 54, 133, 143, 159, 174–75, 180, 182–85, 190
 and postmodernism, 18–19, 21, 22
 as process, 13, 19, 37, 154–56, 190, 192, 194
 See also cosmopolitanism
travel narratives, 37–38, 44, 48, 51–52, 54, 57, 58, 59, 62–63, 66, 89, 93, 169–70, 203–4. *See also* Mandeville, Sir John; Pratt, Mary Louise; Zeno brothers

truth, constructed vs. objective, 15, 37–38, 46, 58–59, 62, 73, 89, 93, 117, 119, 121, 126, 138, 142–43, 146, 148, 157, 159–62, 163–64, 166–67, 173, 177, 179, 192, 194–95
  revealed and prophetic, 3–4, 120–24, 126–29, 151
  See also "memory's truth"; poetry and truth
twins, 84, 150–51, 153, 154–55, 161, 180, 182, 188
  twin paradox, 82–84, 87, 88, 206
  See also binaries; Manichaeism; special relativity

unfinalizability, 17–18, 20, 179–80
utopia, 38, 43, 57, 68, 72, 135, 184

Vakil, Zeeny, 131, 132–35, 137–38, 194
van Gogh, Vincent, 40–41
Veen, Ada, 58, 59, 60, 61, 66, 68, 84, 86, 87, 192
Veen, Van, 57–63, 64, 66–68, 72, 80–89, 116, 192, 204
  death of, 58, 86–87
  and *Letters from Terra*, 67, 88
  "Mascodagama" act, 63
  reliability, 37, 58, 64, 84, 85–88, 204
  See also memoir: fictional; special relativity
Vinland, 61–62, 63–64
vnenakhodimost, 146–47. *See also* Bakhtin, Mikhail

Walcott, Derek, 13
Wood, Michael, 42, 46, 56, 132
world-fashioning, 2–3, 24, 27, 30, 37, 39, 45–46, 55, 57–58, 62, 68–69, 71, 73, 76, 89–90, 142, 167, 173–75, 183–84, 190–91, 194–95

worlds, fictional
  alternate, 2–3, 14, 16, 21, 25–28, 30, 58, 61–64, 71–73, 142, 145, 147–54, 156–62, 184, 188
  bridging physical and imaginary, 46–53, 58, 78, 89–90, 114, 149–57, 169–70, 173–75
  consensus and consistency of, 15–16, 19, 25–26, 57, 67, 115–17, 123–26, 127, 149–50, 161–62, 168–69
  contradictory, 18, 20, 25–26, 46, 124, 130–31, 142, 147–48, 149–51, 153, 156–57
  fantastic, 17–18, 20, 35, 73, 93, 117, 142, 147–50, 159–60, 172–73, 190–91, 194–95
  imagined, and the nation, 11–12, 15–16, 44–45, 90, 116–17, 169–70, 172–75, 182–83, 189–91
  possible, 18–20, 22, 56, 63, 68–69, 72–73, 75, 124, 130–31, 150–51, 153
  and the real, 19, 21, 67, 68–69, 71, 90, 119, 122, 131, 142, 149, 152–54, 158, 160–61, 173, 179, 190–91, 194–95
  See also fictionality; incompatible realities; many-worlds theory; world-fashioning

Young, Robert J. C., 3, 6, 92

Zamenhof, Ludovic, 184–85, 189
Zapruder, Abraham, 157
Zembla, 31, 35, 46–49, 51–53, 55–57, 67, 76, 183, 195
  and fictionality, 47, 52, 123
Zeno brothers, 58, 62–67, 68
Zionism, 183, 184, 185, 188–89
Zogoiby, Abraham, 105, 106–8, 114–15, 141
Zogoiby, Aurora, 106, 107, 114–15, 149

CPI Antony Rowe
Chippenham, UK
2016-12-27 19:36